IF YOU HAD

A FAMILY

Barbara Wilson

Seal Press

For Tere

Seal Press
3131 Western Avenue, Suite 410
Seattle, Washington 98121
email: sealprss@scn.org

Book design by Stacy M. Lewis
Cover design by Clare Conrad
Cover photograph by Patricia Ridenour

Acknowledgments: The chapter "In Celebration and Remembrance" was first published in *Feminist Studies*. "Still Life" first appeared in *Close Calls: New Lesbian Fiction*, edited by Susan Fox Rogers, New York: St. Martin's Press, 1996.

Printed in the United States of America
First printing, October 1996
1 3 5 7 9 10 8 6 4 2

Library of Congress Cataloging-in-Publication Data
Wilson, Barbara, 1950–
If you had a family: a novel / by Barbara Wilson.
ISBN 1-878067-83-4. ISBN 1-878067-82-6 (pbk.)
1. Lesbians—Fiction. 2. Mothers and daughters—Fiction. I. Title.
PS3573.I45678I36   1996   813'.54—dc20   96-23019

Distributed to the trade by Publishers Group West
In Canada: Publishers Group West Canada, Toronto, Canada
In Europe and the U.K.: Airlift Book Company, London, England

CONTENTS

PART ONE

APRICOTS

COLOR CAME FIRST, before things, before words, and more than any other color: yellow. Yellow was pale and bright, butter and fire. It was Cory's first memory—sun on the grass, wet beads of light pearling down a blade, impossible to catch. Yellow was apricots golden and unreachable up in a dark green tree; it was a flash of Monarch butterflies through the purple-blue jacaranda; it was the melting softness of a yellow rose petal curled in her grasping palm, the soap-smelling cotton folds of her mother's yellow sundress clutched in her hand. Yellow was her duck and her pajamas and the satin on the edge of the coverlet she chewed on as she fell into her afternoon nap.

Yellow was the color of her room. Baby Kevin's room was blue and cool and melancholy at sunset when the dust motes danced in a single ray. But Cory's room was yellow and it blazed in the morning. The sun came through the cafe curtains with their tiny gold-brown print of either dogs or sunglasses, depending on how she looked. The sun fell on the yellow blanket and the white sheets of her maple bed with the four short posts, each topped with a whole carved pineapple. Morning light was like a kiss, inviting her into the day. She could stay there in bed singing songs to herself.

She could jump up in her pajamas, fly on her scatter rug across the shiny wood floor, Aladdin arriving at the closet doors. At night bears lived in the closet, but during the day it was where her clothes hung, where Ginger had her kittens in a cardboard box with a worn dishtowel inside.

Yellow was the color of the fingerpaint squooshing through her fingers when she made a circle sun in the deep blue sky. It was the color of the thick crayon she held hard in her fingers. All day she could draw these pictures. "This is our house and here's you, Mama, and here's a flower."

The house was the center of the known world and all good things were contained within its two perpendicular walls and under its triangle roof.

"Here's you in the kitchen, Mama. Here's the pot and the stove."

"What am I cooking?"

"TOMATO SOUP! It's red, red, red!"

"What's that little bundle?"

"It's Kevin, he's asleep before he's a butterfly."

"And is that you on the roof?"

"Yes, I'm up so high I can see everything and everybody."

"Well, be careful. Is Daddy in your picture?"

"He's at work. I'll make a picture of him. Here he is standing up front, and here's the students and here's the desks."

"What are those things up in the air?"

"Those are numbers. Daddy is teaching them numbers."

Cory drew pictures of everything. Her hand was connected to her eye and she needed to record everything she saw. It was as necessary as breathing.

First came the house, then the people in it. Daddy with a pipe, Mama with a book, little stick brother and Cory with straight blonde hair and green eyes. Sometimes there was a cat or a stuffed animal. Outside the house was nature. Waves and sky. The sun and moon and stars. Some flowers with three petals and a yellow heart. Trees with straight trunks, two parallel lines with thick black crayon. Trees were easier to draw if you made it summertime; then you just put a curly circle of green on top.

But trees change in autumn, even in California, and soon Cory was recording that. The leaves crispy as thin toast on the ground, a blaze of yellow and orange. The rake with its wiry metal fingers scraped the leaves into piles, piles that called to be jumped into with a loud, satisfying crunch. Sometimes the dry Santa Ana winds blew through her pictures and carried the leaves far away.

It was her mother, Polly, who taught Cory to love the apricot tree best of all the trees, from the spring when it blossomed angel-wing white to the autumn when the heart-shaped leaves folded in on themselves and turned into golden paper flutes. The tree shaded the redwood picnic table where Cory made her pictures, and in summer the scent of the ripening fruit made the air thick with sweetness. Cory drew and Polly read and Kevin slept or staggered around on his baby legs just as Cory had once done.

Once, when Cory was four or five, a big ripe apricot fell in Polly's lap as she read. Polly split it in two and gave half to Cory. Polly, smelling the fruit up close, pressed it over her nose and mouth as if it were an oxygen mask. Cory did the same. Then Polly, with a dreamy look, rubbed the fruit first up and down her face and then in a circular motion, like she was applying cold cream. "Oh, I can't get enough of this smell," Polly said, and threw her head back and laughed. "Oh, I can't get enough of this smell," Cory said after her and rubbed her half in circles on her cheeks and forehead. The apricot juices ran down her face like honey liquid and the warmth of the fruit dissolved into the heat of her skin.

"Oh this fruit is divine," said Polly.

"Oh this fruit is divine," said Cory.

"Oh I am the happiest I have ever been," said Polly.

"Oh I am the happiest I have ever been," repeated Cory.

"Or will be."

"Or will be."

Polly's smile was as wide as the sky. A golden glaze of sticky fruit was drying all over her freckled skin. "Oh my God, if my mother could see me now."

Cory lay back and sucked contentedly on the tart skin with shreds of sweetness still clinging to it. " . . . If my mother could see me now," she remembered to say.

The apricot had been the first tree Polly Winter planted that summer she and West moved into a house of their own, six months into Polly's pregnancy, four years after World War II was over.

West laughed and asked her why apricot, he was partial to tart apples, winesaps and pippins—or why not oranges or grapefruit since then they could have freshly squeezed juice for breakfast? He didn't think he'd ever had an apricot from a tree, he said, only the dried ones that looked like preserved ears, and the thought somewhat put him off.

But to Polly, apricots were the fruit of heaven, she had thought so since the first time she was served two halves, smooth-humped islands in a syrup of ambrosial nectar. Mildred Clark had brought them out after a lunch of salad and chicken croquettes two years ago to welcome Polly to Long Beach and the Church of Christ, Scientist. The shallow bowl that held the home-canned apricots had been cobalt blue, the whole dessert like a jewel setting: topaz in amber liqueur set in sapphire that caught the light.

"Apricots," said her new friend Mildred Clark, only a few years older but already with a distinctive white streak in the black hair that waved above her forehead. "I put them up myself every year, from the tree out back," and out the dining room window, as it was spring, Polly glimpsed a flowering mass of white, a cloud floating in this California paradise, with a brick patio underneath where the flowers fell like tiny angel wings and with no sound at all.

"I've read that the apple in the Garden of Eden was really the apricot," said Joan Perkins. Joan was very tan, with thick ash

blonde hair and muscular arms. She had played tennis profession-
ally once, but now, like Mildred, was married to a Christian Scientist who was doing well in real estate. "Apples didn't grow in
that desert climate."

"Really!" said Mildred Clark. "Well, I do find them a tempta-
tion."

So did Polly. Polly wanted apricots.

It was the place and the time in her life where everything
would flourish in abundance. God had said so, in the Psalms she
had read as a child and still read: "The Lord is my Shepherd, I
shall not want."

God loved gardens, Polly wanted to believe, and not just the
productive kind, where potatoes cuddled in the moist brown
earth, or where stalks of Brussels sprouts thrust up their bitter
heads, but gardens for glory, gardens for joy. Gardens so abundant
with fruits and flowers that you needed only to step out your door
to gather them by the basketful.

In Polly's mother's garden in Michigan there had been only
vegetables. During the Depression her mother had dug up half the
back yard to plant root crops of potatoes, turnips, parsnips, carrots. She'd kept rabbits and a few chickens, and it was Polly's job
to hunt for the still warm eggs every morning. Too many hot
summer days had Polly spent hoeing and weeding and watering
that garden, while her mother sat in the cool parlor studying her
Christian Science Lesson for the week, and praying that Stephen,
eight years younger than Polly, would settle down.

Her mother's garden was not for pleasure but for laboring in.
Only for a few days each year, after the harvest when the huge pots
boiled on the old farmhouse stove, could you find the beauty in
your work, when through the almost unbearable steam you
glimpsed the glass jars like diamonds full of brilliant carrots and
ruby-red tomato sauce. Long into the winter Polly's family would
be eating those canned vegetables and they would never taste as
good as they looked—they'd be salty and mushy—but for those

late August and September afternoons, there would be beauty sitting in rows along the counters and window sills, and glowing dimly in boxes in the pantry, their dates (Summer, 1931, 1932, 1933) telling the thrifty story of the Depression and Polly's youth.

Polly's mother was pastel and gray, a pale coral cameo at the neck of her cotton dress, a freshly ironed apron, and shoes like white blocks that stop a vehicle from moving. In her youth, she'd been thin as a string bean, she said, a farm girl who'd once jumped on a team of runaway horses and reined them in. But those stories were from long ago and had been told to Polly in her childhood. Now, every year, Polly's mother grew more solid and slow. There had never been any lightness to her, nothing like the airy joy that Polly felt inside herself when words came into her mind, words like aqua or strawberry, or when something—a bouquet of full-blown roses behind the florist's window perhaps, the starry sky at night—became meaningful, became *more*. When she could almost hear God speaking to her, not to admonish or to instruct or punish, but to say, *Live, Polly, live while you can. Live as much as possible.*

"Why on earth would you want to go across the country to California?" her mother had said. "We spent hard-earned money to send you to college, and now you have a good little teaching job in the next town. We need you here. Your brother needs you nearby. What about when we get old?"

"It's just for a while, Mother," Polly said. "Just to see a little of the world. I'm twenty-seven, Mother."

Her father had come to the train station with her and had stood on the platform trying to think what to say. He had been the one, always, to say, "Cora, let Polly go to college. Let Polly go to California. Let Polly go." Finally he gave her a matched morocco-bound set of *Science and Health* and the Bible and said, "You'll be happier away from here. God bless you, Polly."

God did bless her. Here in California life was abundant and no one could ever go hungry. All year round there were fruits and vegetables; all year round flowers bloomed and bees made honey. "We came unto the land wither thou sentest us and surely it flowest with milk and honey: and this is the fruit of it," Polly read in the Bible as the train came across the country to the city she'd read about in a magazine, a booming city with a port and beaches and thousands of opportunities. California was like Israel, a desert that could bloom, dry barren earth that with water could become a garden, a million gardens.

Her friend Mildred Clark, telling her about the congregation, said Connie was a sweet child, but unreliable. Connie had been born into the church, just like Polly and Mildred, but it didn't sit the same. She didn't take up responsible duties, Mildred confided, she taught Sunday School, but only to the youngest. Connie was the one who wanted Polly to go down to the Majestic Ballroom at the Pike that summer night. She'd met a man, Sal Sabicca, there the previous week, wanted to see him again. "He's everything my mother would hate," said Connie. "He's Italian, he's from New Yawk, he's in the dry-cleaning business, he's not a Scientist—he's Roman Catholic!"

"Roman Catholic," gasped Polly. Mrs. Eddy, their church's founder, despised the sinister rituals of Roman Catholicism.

"He never goes to church," said Connie, who had shrieked with laughter when Polly said she was from Michigan ("Me too! Aren't you so *glad* to be *here* instead of *there*?")

Connie put make-up on Polly's freckled face, dark red lipstick she said would bring out Polly's Loretta Young look. Connie was five years younger than twenty-seven-year-old Polly. Yellow-haired and plump, she'd come out during the war to work in the Douglas factory, and then when the men returned, she took a job in Rose's Bakery decorating cakes. "Well, it's almost the same as welding." She helped Polly buy a swirly maroon rayon dress with a V-neck and big shoulders and said, "You're on your own!"

Polly was watching Connie jitterbug with Sal when she heard him ask her to dance. West Winter, his name was, and the first thing he said about himself was that he was an orphan.

That night waltzing under the glittering ceiling of the Majestic Ballroom (he was handsome, but heavy-set, with glasses, a cleft chin, a serious man who liked a joke), and later walking out on the Rainbow pier, sailors and their girls all around, Sal and Connie a discreet distance away, kissing hard, the waves lapping salt and cold on the pilings, West told her how he had placed his faith in his intelligence and love of hard work, how he had gotten a scholarship to a teachers' college in Illinois.

"I always was a bit of a loner," West said, taking out a pipe. "It's that I lost my parents before I can remember. But if you don't have a family you can do things you couldn't otherwise. No one holds you back, no one says you can't do it. I majored in history, classical history, minored in business. I thought that after the war I'd be going back to Wisconsin to be a history professor, but then I met a man who said they needed teachers at the Business and Technical Division of Long Beach City College, and could I teach anything besides history? Well, business, I said. Fine, he said, we'll put you in charge of the accounting classes. Of course I said yes—I needed a job—and here I am. I guess History," and he smiled into her eyes, "is a thing of the past."

They looked back from the pier towards the dazzling lights of the Pike with its skeeter games and sideshows, its tattoo parlors and hot dog and cotton candy stands, towards the skyline of Long Beach, art deco and bold and exciting, to the sky itself.

West slipped his arm around Polly. "California is the future," he said. "For everyone who came here during the war and isn't going back again. Thousands and hundreds of thousands are staying and more are coming. My classes are full of vets and young people and they'll be full for years to come."

Polly leaned her head back. She heard her father's voice telling her about the stars, those warm summer nights in Michigan long ago. "There's Hercules up there," she said. "The Lyre, the Serpent, the Scorpion, Hercules. He sounds like you, searching for the golden apples."

"He found them, as I recall," said West. "In the garden of the Hesperides, the place they say was the original garden of Eden."

"Did he ever take a bite?" asked Polly.

"He couldn't, poor fellow," said West and kissed her full on the lips. "They were part of his Twelve Labors."

"What a shame," said Polly. "I'm sure they tasted delicious."

Connie said, "He's a dreamboat, Polly, with that cleft chin and those blue eyes. And I adore men with pipes. It's not really like smoking."

Her mother wrote her, "How can you trust a fellow you met at a dance? Who are his people? How can you marry a man who doesn't go to church, didn't you learn anything when you were growing up? You've changed since you went out to California, Polly, your voice is different, your hair flies around in your photos, don't you ever comb it? And your clothes, all those big plaids, those high heels, that loud costume jewelry. You said you'd be coming back after a year or two, and now you want to get married, you're going to stay there, well, don't blame me if it doesn't work out with this strange fellow no one knows."

Mildred Clark said, "He's not a Scientist? Oh dear. Does your mother know? Well, at least he's not a Roman Catholic."

For Connie was going to be married in St. Paul's, and Mildred could not forgive her.

The home that Polly and West moved into was in a suburban tract that Mildred Clark's husband had built on the edge of Long Beach. There were hundreds of tracts like these, spreading over a landscape where there had only been scrub oak and mesquite and then bean fields. Polly's neighbors, also buying in with V.A. loans and no down payment, were planting box hedges and hollies and junipers and sometimes maple trees to remind them of the midwest and eastern states they'd come from. A few people put in spiky yuccas and round bristling cacti whose spines would impale their innocent children later on, but most went for grass, lots of it, and things they'd heard "did well" in California. Some neighbors thought avocados were appropriate and darkened their views with the heavy-leafed tree outside their windows. Everything that people planted was too much, and more than one neighbor struggled to control ivy and artistic bamboo stands that had gotten the better of them. Yolanda next door had uninspiring coffeeberry shrubs around the house itself, but all the rest, front and back, was a lawn that she and her husband Bernie maintained with mowings early, too early, Saturday mornings. On the other side Dolores and Wayne Curtis never bothered with a lawn at all in the back; they stuck in one palm tree and that was it besides a clothesline and a doghouse and piles of car parts. In the front Wayne Curtis worked on his old jalopies on an especially wide concrete driveway.

But Polly, when she planted, did not mean to stint herself in any way. The words she loved best in gardening books were *verdant, rampant, sprawling,* were descriptions beneath color photographs that predicted *spectacular bloom, breathtaking display.* All her flowers would be bright, the colors she had loved her whole life and had never had enough of till she moved to California. On one wall of the garage she staked violet bougainvillea, and on the other magenta. In time these plants would form a wall of rich, tropical color up one side and down the other. In the front yard she outlined the bottom of the house with fragrant oleanders in red and white, and put two hibiscus, with their sweet nectar centers, near the porch. The porch itself she draped with a trumpet vine, and on the other side she placed a scarlet bottle brush. It grew ten feet high and four feet wide and was the first thing you saw when you looked out the front window. It was like fireworks bursting. On the shadow side of the house she put in a waxy-leafed pink camellia.

By the side gate that led to the back yard she planted an acacia tree, with loose, feathery foliage that would partially shade, but not obscure the house, and in the back yard she chose the same kinds of trees, trees that wouldn't hang heavy in the sky and close it off from view, but that would seem to float, plumy as smoke—a mimosa in yellow, a jacaranda blue-violet in the spring. In her borders she had Easter lilies and irises and tulips in the spring, and dahlias and marigolds and zinnias in late summer and fall. But it was roses that she planted in earnest and that perfumed the yard and the house most of the year long.

Yes, roses, and not just a bush or two sickly by the side of the house that gave off a faint persistent scent on those humid summer nights in Michigan. Polly put in a whole garden of roses—trailing roses all along the fence and glorious, heavenly hybrid teas and floribundas, bushes bursting with fat, red-winged golden petals or bright yellow and orange buds that turned pink and then a cherry red. Her hybrid teas were all delicious, from the spicy smell of Chrysler Imperial to the fruity scent of Helen Traubel. Polly especially loved Sutter's Gold, an egg-yolk yellow with salmon-red shadings on the outside, and Tiffany, whose deep pink long pointed buds opened into large, perfectly formed silvery pink blooms touched with maize yellow at the base.

What Polly wanted, what she tried to create, in spite of leaf rot and aphids and mistakes in pruning and overwatering, was a rose garden like heaven, where Spirit would be manifested daily in a blaze of color and fragrance, and where the stern abstract metaphysics of Mrs. Eddy would give way to life's real message, the blindingly beautiful and simple one, which is that God wants us to be happy.

♦

Other children on the block had grandparents in their daily lives. Old people with white hair who told stories and gave piggyback rides. Bobby and Jimmy Palmer's grandparents came over every Sunday. Cory saw them getting out of their big Chevrolet with tins of cookies and sheets of chocolate cake. And the Rays next door had a grandfather living right there, who only spoke Spanish and carved birds and animals out of balsa wood.

Cory knew that her father had nobody to be a grandparent for her, but she had always expected that one day the two black and white photos in the double brass frames on her mother's walnut dresser would come to visit from Michigan. Now that would never happen. Grandpa Cooper was in bed and Polly said he couldn't get up anymore, not even with a cane, and not even with everyone's prayers.

"Can't we go there instead?" asked Cory. "Just to see him?"

"I want to see him too," said Polly. "We'll go this summer when your daddy's finished teaching. I should have gone back long before. Seven years is a long time. I don't know why I didn't. Mother was always asking."

Cory stared at the photos. "He has a nice face," she said.

"My father is nice," said Polly. "He always liked simple things, like fishing and stargazing. He worked in a bank before the Depression but afterwards he got a job in a hardware store. That was enough for him. My mother always thought he could have done better for himself and for us, but I think he liked being a hardware clerk better than a bank clerk. I don't know. Except for a few times, when he took me on a walk or to watch the stars, we never talked much. He helped me in a quiet way, just his being there, between me and my mother. But since I left home I've never heard much from him."

"It's always Grandma on the phone," said Cory.

"Yes," said Polly, smiling. "Checking up on me."

Cory nodded. It seemed reasonable to her. "Mostly she writes you letters though."

"And she sends you and Kevin things," Polly reminded her.

"Kevin gets toys. I get dresses," said Cory. "Frilly *dresses*."

Polly laughed. "I would have given anything for those dresses when I was growing up."

"Didn't your grandmother give you anything?"

"They were too poor for presents. They were farmers. They had a farm in Albion, Michigan. They were Seventh-day Adventists, very very strict. If Grandma Warren caught me doing something I shouldn't be doing, she paddled me good. I can say this for my mother, she never hit me. She used to say she'd been beat within an inch of her life when she was growing up and she'd vowed not to do that to her own children, no matter what they did. She used to say it was because she was so wild and headstrong."

"Like that time she burned down the barn because she was playing fire chief."

"That's right," said Polly. "She was just going to burn a little section of the outhouse, and she had her younger brothers and sisters organized with buckets to put it out. It was just going to be practice, in case there ever really was a fire. But it was a hot dry day with a wind blowing, and within five minutes, a spark had gone from the outhouse to the barn. All the other children ran away screaming, but my mother went into the flames and let the two cows out. She was burned on her back and most of her hair was singed off, but she saved the cows. Afterwards my grandfather said, 'She's the bravest girl I ever saw,' but he practically beat her to death anyway."

"That's what I'd do," said Cory. "Save the cows."

"You take after her in some ways," said Polly. "So does my brother Steve. I'm afraid I'm not that brave. I would have run away and hid."

They didn't drive back to Michigan that summer, the summer Cory was five. Instead, Polly took the train to her father's funeral.

When she came back after two weeks, Grandma Cooper was with her.

"Where's the vegetable garden?" was the first thing Cora said when she saw the back yard.

"We have all the vegetables we could need, all year round, Mother, in the supermarkets."

"That's a waste of money, when you can grow your own."

"Not in California, Mother. By the time you count in the seeds, the fertilizer, the labor, every carrot would cost you twice as much as in the store."

"Labor!" Cora snorted. "And what about the labor of taking care of all these flowers? I never saw anything like this flower circus you have in the back yard. Everything red and purple and yellow and loud and showy. It hurts my eyes to look at it, it comes at me every time I turn around."

The bougainvillea poured its lush purple and magenta waterfall over the garage; the roses blazed with glory up and down the redwood fence and thickly in their bed. The fall flowers gorged the borders, many-petaled yellow chrysanthemums with violently orange marigolds parading around their edges; big-headed zinnias, tile red and velvet purple; and the glory of the garden, dahlias bursting like rockets, peachy-gold, red and white, perfectly shaped, staked high against the side of the house.

Grandma Cooper liked shade and order and obedience and low voices and severe clothing and curtains closed during the day so the hot sun didn't fade the rug and furniture. Now that she was in her sixties, a widow, her skin was soft and wrinkled like crumpled silk, but her back was still rigid and her mouth very tight.

She stayed in Kevin's room, while Kevin slept in Cory's. The days took on a severity. Every morning she rose at five and read the Bible and Mrs. Eddy and prayed. By seven, when the rest of the Winters got up, Cora had made breakfast: hearty pancakes and eggs. "A man can't go to work on an empty stomach," she told

West, who didn't dare to bring out the Frosted Flakes he loved to share with Cory.

At dinner there were pot roasts gray as the gravy that accompanied them, or chicken fried or stewed and piles of potatoes and bowls of canned vegetables. No matter how hot the day, Cora baked. Apple pies and Boston cream pies and chocolate cakes, not Betty Crocker cakes but real ones.

At first West complimented Cora. "Haven't had such good, substantial meals since I lived with the Kiesewalters on their farm outside Madison." And he told them stories of the older couple who'd fostered him a few years. "I had to work *hard*," said West, "but my God, did Mrs. Kiesewalter cook. Rye bread and apple sausages, potatoes every day, fried cracklings, a big crock of sauerkraut and every Thursday she took a few ladles from it and boiled spareribs. And could she make desserts. Cherry tortes and apple pies and cheesecakes. That's when I first began to put on weight," he said. "Imagine, a skinny little orphan boy sitting at a trestle table with them and their farm hands, five meals a day!"

"You see," said Cora to her daughter. "You've been starving him, I can tell. Married seven years and can't make a cake that doesn't come from a box, it's a disgrace. I can tell you, your father wouldn't have put up with it. A woman has her duties, same as a man. You don't let a man come home from a hard day's work to frozen food and store-bought desserts. What I want to know is what you do with your time, Polly. My suspicion is that time that should be going into taking care of your family properly is going into that gardening nonsense of yours, that flower circus out there."

"We don't live on a farm," said Polly and it was all she could think to say.

"I raised you right," said Cora. "And you've thrown it all away. Forgotten everything."

But Polly defended her mother against West when, after a few weeks, he began to ask how long Cora might be staying.

"I told her she can stay as long as she wants," Polly said.

"Of course she can," said West, and looked unhappy. "I just meant, well, it's different having her here."

"She just has her ways of doing things, that's all," Polly said. "She's done them that way all her life, she's not going to stop now."

"But she's in our house, Polly. We have our own ways of doing things."

"You don't understand," said Polly. "You never had a mother and, anyway, you're a man. The mother's ways *are* the ways of doing things. Especially now, just after she's lost my father."

"All I see is how she orders you around, " he said. "And how you're at the church every spare minute."

"Mildred thinks it's wonderful that Mother is such a Scientist," Polly said with a wry smile. "She was worried I was slipping."

But West wasn't in a mood to joke. "I'll never interfere with your beliefs," he said. "As long as you don't take them to an extreme."

Mildred Clark came often while Cora was visiting. She arrived looking prosperous with matching calf-leather pumps and a handbag with a loud brass snap. The distinguished white wave dipped over her forehead and her jewelry was always gold and discreet.

Under the apricot tree a silent Polly poured Sanka and served butter cookies with apricot filling to Mildred and her mother, and to Connie, whom she'd persuaded to stop by, please, just for a minute. Mildred took one cookie, and after a bite, set it aside. She began to tell a story of how her daughter Linda, almost twelve, had recently been healed.

"It was a lovely Demonstration of the Truth," said Mildred. "My daughter Linda woke up with her forehead all hot, and with a feeling of stiffness everywhere, and for an instant, because of course you've heard of what they call infantile paralysis, I was afraid. I called our practitioner immediately and she came right over. We sat by Linda's side all day and prayed, but there was no change. Mrs. Grant went home to sleep, but I stayed up all night, and about four in the morning I woke up from what had been a bad dream, and I realized it was *all* a bad dream, this dream of sickness. I woke Linda up out of her doze and told her she'd been dreaming too. 'Yes, Mother,' she said, and smiled, and then she fell asleep again. In the morning she said, 'I had such a bad dream last night, but now I'm all right again! I'm going to get up.' She got up, and said, 'Do you know what, Mother, the stiffness is all gone!'"

It was a hot afternoon in late September, almost October. The wind was getting up, the dry Santa Ana that felt as if someone had just opened the oven door and turned the fan on. Everything withered in this heat; the grass turned brown, the rose petals curled, the leaves blew off the trees before their seasons.

"I remember when Polly was lying there as a baby, just like that, apparently hot and stiff," Cora said. "Diphtheria, they wanted to call it. I had just joined the Church a year or so before on the basis of a friend's healing, and hadn't yet worked a Demonstration myself. Mr. Cooper was petrified. It was in the early days of our marriage and he didn't know my strong will. He begged me to call a doctor. I refused. I picked Polly up in my arms and said to her—very fiercely Mr. Cooper told me later—'You *will* be healed.' And afterwards he was converted, too."

Polly remembered none of this, but it was a story she'd heard all her life. Her first healing, the one that had saved her life.

"I hear they will be trying to force children to have shots with that new Salk vaccine," said Cora. "We must stand firm. No childhood immunizations, not the DPT, not polio. I know that Polly would never allow little Cora and Kevin to be inoculated."

"Well, I had my kids immunized against everything," said Connie, crossing her arms firmly over her fourth pregnancy. "Sal wouldn't hear of skipping it. You know I come to church regularly, but a father has a say in things."

"*My* husband followed my lead in everything to do with the children," Cora said, pursing her lips, and adjusting her glasses to stare at Connie, far too fat for pedal-pushers, in a big sleeveless shirt, her bleached-blonde hair haphazard in a ponytail. "Just as Polly's does."

Mildred smiled complacently. She didn't need to speak, Polly knew. *Her* husband was the First Reader now and everyone said he enunciated so beautifully. Like Mildred he'd been raised in a Christian Scientist family, a wealthy Republican one back East that had put up the money for his real estate business, a man who exuded the radiant complacency of success, whose positive attitude impressed everyone he came in contact with.

Connie rolled her eyes at Polly, who abruptly got up and spilled the coffee.

"Childrearing changes from generation to generation," said Cora, ignoring her daughter. "I myself was raised in the old-fashioned way. Children should be seen, not heard, and must never talk back. I was whipped nearly every week of my life." Seeing that Mildred looked slightly taken aback, Cora said, "I never touched my own children, of course. With Science, it's not necessary."

"No," said Mildred. "As Mrs. Eddy writes, 'Children are the spiritual thoughts and representatives of Life, Truth and Love.'"

"But it *is* best to be firm from the beginning," said Cora, casting a glance at Cory, who was splashing loudly with Kevin and with Connie's harum-scarum children in the wading pool, and shouting, "No, *I'm* going to be the pirate queen!"

"I agree," said Mildred. "Children so easily get the wrong ideas. They watch everything you do, you know. They pick up things without you even noticing."

Cory tried to get her grandmother to tell her stories of burning down the barn and reining in runaway horses, but Grandma either wouldn't tell them or turned these exciting tales into something improving. "I learned how right my mother was after I became a mother myself," she said. "I learned how a child can break a mother's heart. I learned you have to be firm."

Grandma took Cory on her lap, "My little namesake," she said and sighed. "You're a little handful, that's what you are, like your uncle."

Grandma Cooper smelled of cotton and lavender. She looked soft but when you got close you felt the hard bones under her clothes. Cory wriggled politely. "Want to see my pictures, Grandma?"

"It's nice you like to paint," Cora said. "Your uncle had a gift for it too. But the important thing is to study hard. That's what I always told your mother, and your mother went to college. I never went to college. I worked on the farm until I married your Grandpa. Everyone said how lucky I was, marrying a bank teller who lived in town. Then the Depression came. I can tell you that my years on the farm came in handy then, yes indeed. Your mother never wanted to work in the vegetable garden, but I made her. You should tear up this rose bed, Polly, and plant vegetables. Roses are too much work. The only useful thing in this yard is the apricot tree. If you like apricots, which I never have."

The summer flowers were gone and the leaves of the apricot tree had fallen by the time Cora left with her big suitcase and her satchel in November, three pies on the counter and a freezer full of bread. She'd stayed two weeks longer than she'd planned and would have stayed through Thanksgiving and Christmas except that Uncle Steve suddenly got divorced and needed to come back home for a while.

"I don't know how I raised such useless children," she said with satisfaction. "A girl who can't cook or clean properly, a boy who's in one scrape after the next. I can see that I'm going to be coming back and forth from Michigan to California to look after the two of you. It's just lucky you have someone like Mildred Clark as a friend, Polly. Though I'd like it if you saw a little less of that Connie Sabicca."

The day after Grandma left, Cory and her mother went out to the back yard. Polly took her clippers and a short ladder. She'd decided it was time to prune the apricot tree.

Polly knew that in the spring the apricot would bloom again, and that the fruits would form as the blossoms fell to the ground, hard green knobs that would grow bigger and softer, soft as mush, pulp blanketing the ground. She saw the seasons stretch out before her, not as they had done in the last seven years that she'd been in California, with a glow of joy and possibility about them, but with a kind of blank inevitability. Under her mother's eye the garden she had created would dry up and wither, she'd spend her time in church and not on her knees in the roses.

There was nowhere to hide. Once her father had stood between her and her mother, but he was gone. Polly was in the Garden of Eden with the apple in her hand, caught in the act. What had been lush and colorful and joyous was now revealed as vanity, excess and display. Her mother had entered the garden like an avenging angel, the arm of God, the missionary of Mrs. Eddy, and in a stern fiery voice had made her see her nakedness and shame.

But how could she say no to her mother? She couldn't, anymore than she could stop seeing Mildred Clark. West didn't understand, but a mother was with you all your life. History was not in the past, it was always in the present, much as the future was always out of reach. If a mother loved you, told you she loved you enough to save your life, how could you ever say no and turn your back? All you could do was try, try very hard and so no one noticed and blamed you, to keep a little distance, a little space, a little room.

With the heavy clippers Polly began to prune. What was essential in pruning was to cut back any branches that crossed each other, especially if the branches touched. For when the winter winds came, the branches would rub against each other and wear away the bark. And the bark was the tree's protection, its covering, its skin. Where the bark was worn away, disease could enter. A tree needed its bark like a woman needed her skin. If a tree had no bark, if a woman had no skin, she had no protection, no protection at all. Lushness did not serve a tree if it led to branches crossing. With her heavy pruning shears Polly cut back as much as she could, and Cory took away the branches and piled them by the garage.

A FIRMAMENT IN THE MIDST
OF THE WATERS

"I'VE HEARD," SAID Sharie Palmer conversationally, "that one of the ways that kids get polio is from swimming pools."

Sharie Palmer lived down the block from the Winters on Wildwood Avenue. The three other women sitting around the redwood picnic table in Polly's back yard, eating the coffee cake she'd painstakingly reproduced from one of her mother's recipes, were all Christian Scientist friends of Polly's. Though Connie Sabicca was not *quite . . .* , as Mildred Clark said, never finishing the sentence.

All of them looked across the lawn to the crowded wading pool where six children splashed, Polly's two, three of Connie's and Sharie's youngest. It was May and very warm. Connie, in a Hawaiian muumuu, her feet in rubber thongs, rocked her new baby Sal Jr. in the stroller. She said, "It's a shame, when rumors get started and something children enjoy so much. . . . " She stopped and began eating her second slice of coffee cake, nervously aware of Mildred's stern glance. Although Mildred had two children, she hadn't gained an ounce over the years. She always looked so elegant and today was no exception. She had on a slim gray dress and a tangerine scarf; her white-streaked black hair had been newly done in a French twist.

"Well, even though it might be only a rumor," Sharie said, "I'm keeping them out of public pools this summer. Until those Salk tests are finished and *everybody's* been immunized, there's still a danger."

Sharie was the one woman in the neighborhood that Polly was even slightly friends with. Yolanda next door had given up on Polly years ago, after fruitless attempts to share McCall's patterns and ideas for extending meatloaf. On the other side Dolores Curtis, the night nurse, slept most of the day and didn't have much to say to anyone. Sharie might be too chatty, but she was fun-loving, and sometimes she and Polly went grocery shopping together, because only Sharie had a car every day. She wore her dark hair in a bouffant and looked so young it was hard to believe she had one son in third grade, and a four year old in the wading pool.

Mildred and Joan Perkins, both of whom had older children, well-off husbands and a secure place in the world, looked at each other. Joan, tan and muscular, in a tasteful black-and-white-polka-dot sundress, said to Sharie, "There was a case just last year in our church of a beautiful healing from polio. Mildred's daughter Linda woke up feverish and hot, with a feeling of stiffness everywhere. Mildred and the practitioner prayed all day and Mildred stayed up all night and in the morning Linda got up and went to school as if nothing had happened."

"It was probably just the flu," said Sharie.

"No it was not the flu," said Mildred in her lovely, reasonable voice. "It was, not to give a medical diagnosis, a fairly clear-cut case of infantile paralysis."

"But if you thought it might be polio, you should have taken your daughter straight to the hospital!" said Sharie.

Connie looked as if she'd like to say something, to explain, but instead she only pushed little Peter back and forth.

"But why would we do that?" Mildred said, clearly superior. "We knew that there was no reason to worry, no reason at all. Not with Christian Science on our side."

Sharie glanced at Polly, who changed the subject. "Cory has always loved the water. I used to call her a water baby, after that book I read as a child. I can't imagine keeping her out of the water."

"Oh Joe is just the same way," said Connie, "the two of them, when Polly and I take them to Alamitos Bay, you cannot, I repeat, cannot persuade them to leave the water before they're practically water-logged."

The conversation rolled on, for Mildred and Joan were nothing if not well-bred. But Polly kept looking at Cory and Kevin, who were now leading the other kids in running through the sprinkler this hot afternoon. She remembered how she used to bathe Cory in the little bassinet that Connie gave her as a shower gift. How its shape curled around her baby like an aqua skin.

Once, only for a second, she left the bassinet to find a towel—she would never know how the baby had the strength!—and Cory flipped herself out of the hammock and lay on the end of the table, curious, eyes open, moving her arms and legs as if she were swimming.

Polly's mother would have shouted at her, but West had only laughed when she told him.

"She has no fear, that one."

"I'll have to be more careful. But I don't want to hold her back either."

Polly looked at her clean-limbed children tearing swiftly around the yard, waterdrops sparkling on their brown smooth skin. She'd seen the photographs of children in braces, she'd seen the photos of children in iron lungs. They were scattered all through the magazines she read, *Look* and *Life* and *McCalls* and even *House and Garden*, along with articles that she knew she should skip, but couldn't avoid, with headlines that shouted "What Parents Should Know About Polio," and "Precautions Against Polio for the Summer of 1955." Who could avoid the many newspaper articles about Jonas Salk and his new vaccine, that if it worked, would be given to millions of children this fall? She had never put her faith in medicine, still, how would she stand it if anything happened to her children?

"Look, Mama, look!" Cory shouted to the group under the apricot tree, as she and Kevin hopped back and forth over the rainbow fireworks of the sprinkler, like Jack Be Nimble, Jack Be Quick, Jack Jumped Over the Candlestick. When it wasn't a liquid flame the sprinkler head was a flat metal face spotted with holes. It attached to the hose and Polly used it for watering the grass, because they didn't have a sprinkler system yet. They had other ways of watering, too. A whirligig that made a steady sput-sput as it spun around, and a thin, silky hose that released arcs of water.

Hoses were not just for watering, though, but for fun. Cory liked to put the hose up under her chin and feel the force of it burbling around her ears. She liked to put the hose inside her bathing suit with the elastic legs and watch it make a balloon of her belly. "I'm having a water baby," she would cry, and then slap her stomach and laugh as water spurted out the top and down her thighs. Kevin liked to make holes in the ground around the roses with the hose. The earth spurted up and the hose drove deeper and deeper. Then the hose got stuck when the dirt dried up around it. He had done this two or three times and the last time had gotten in big trouble. Their father had to saw off the hoses, leaving secret green tunnels in the ground.

"Look, Mama, look!" All the kids here today were younger than her and two were younger than Kevin. She was the leader. They had been wet for hours, jumping in and out of the wading pool with its soft inflated sides and bottom printed with seashells. Sometimes she and Kevin pretended they were fish on the bottom of a pond, but today the pool was a deep lagoon, and she was the Pirate Queen and Kevin was a pirate, too, and the other children were going to walk the plank, which was a little stool they had dragged over.

Her mother looked and waved. She looked hot though they were sitting under the trees. If she were by herself Cory would run over and give her a hug, but the ladies were there. Except for Connie, Cory didn't like the ladies. Mildred and Joan were from church. They had older children and nice houses, houses with real built-in pools. Cory loved outdoor pools. The water was the crayon color *cornflower blue* in the morning. In the afternoon it was like turquoise chips in a souvenir bracelet she got once from Connie. At night the blue was like the cobalt-blue glass of some plates in their cupboard. These outdoor pools had white cement sides, rough as sandpaper, and sun rippled over them, making patterns that kept changing.

In outdoor pools Cory and Kevin learned games from the older Clark and Perkins children and their friends: how to shoot from one side to the other underwater like miniature cannon balls; how to play water blind man's bluff, which they called Marco Polo; how to hold one palm straight out and rush the other forward like a pinball lever released, to make a fine splash of water in someone's face. They also learned to be careful: not to hold anyone's legs, not to push anyone down, to remember that people could panic when they got in the water, and people when they panicked could drown.

Cory could only imagine drowning on purpose. The membrane that separated her waters from the waters she swam in indoors and outdoors sometimes seemed permeable, so that there was no separation at all. In water her limbs moved in ways they couldn't know on land. She was all of a piece, connected from the heart, buoyant, weightless. She could float, she could exuberantly propel herself forwards or backwards; she could thrust herself up in a shower of bubbles and feel the water calling her back down. She could catch a wave and be carried high on its back, till suddenly it took a notion to fling her inside its mouth and grind her up with teeth of shells and stones.

What separated her from water was her skin, but the water

made her skin change, made it look pale and greeny and elongated in a tepid swimming pool, made it sparkle brown and gritty as she shot through a wave in the ocean. At times her skin was crusted with the white rime of salt; other times it shriveled like old fruit or it wrinkled dry, a desert blown by winds. The water protected her from the sun, but it also washed the lotion from her back and shoulders. At the beginning of every summer, when water reflected the sun like a mirror and her head grew feverish and heavy, Cory's skin burned badly. But oh, what luxury lying on clean white sheets with a sunburn that weighed down every movement, how fascinating when the skin puffed up in white bubbles and then began to peel, turning to paper you could lift off in patches. Her skin was always scented with water smells, with chlorine and Ivory soap and Coppertone, with sweat and salt.

She never disliked water, even when it got into her nose or throat or eyes. Once someone gave her a snorkel and a face mask, but that was worse than swallowing or snorting. She didn't like anything between her and the underwater world. The rubber pressed against her face if the strap was too tight, but if the strap was loose, then water became trapped inside, gurgling into her nostrils, jostling up to her eyeballs. She preferred to close her eyes—she didn't really care about seeing—and know the water through her body. She scorned children with earplugs and pink nose plugs dangling on umbilical cords around their necks. She laughed at kids who jumped from diving boards with two fingers pinching the bridge of their noses. When she jumped, she was ramrod stiff, arms at sides, toes pointed as instructed "like a ballet dancer." Her orifices she closed up tight, herself.

Cory was good at finding breath; she loved to take in a huge gulp of air and ricochet from one end of a pool to the other and back again. How long could she stay under? She held the air in her lungs till the oxygen was gone and a hard pressure built under her ribcage. She held it till stars and blackness began to descend in front of her face like a spangly velvet curtain. Was this how it would be to have an iron lung? She'd seen a picture of it in a magazine and asked her mother what it was. "It does breathing for children who can't breathe." "But why can't they breathe?" "Because," Polly said, her freckles screwed up the way they did when she couldn't quite explain something. "Their parents don't believe in Truth enough, I guess," she said. "But what if the iron lung stops?" Cory said. Her mother only shook her head.

"Look, Mama," she shouted again. "Joe is walking the plank. The crocodiles are going to eat him!"

Connie, Joe's mother, laughed, but the other ladies looked sober. In Christian Science, Cory remembered, crocodiles didn't eat people.

"I'm worried about the kids," said West, the fall of 1955 when the newspapers had been full for days of the coming push to get all children in the United States immunized against polio. "I think they should get the Salk shots too. I know you've been against it Polly, but now that Cory's in the first grade and they're giving the shots at the schools, don't you think she should get one? At the very least, you don't want her singled out."

"They'll both have to learn to stand up for their beliefs," said Polly.

"But they don't believe anything yet," said West, still trying to be good-humored. "She's six and he's three. Maybe they believe in Santa Claus, that's all."

"Nothing is going to happen to them," said Polly fiercely.

"That's what you said about the DPT immunizations. And then they got whooping cough."

It was a sore spot between them, the memory of their little children coughing last winter until they were blue in the face, until they could hardly breathe.

Polly was stubborn. She could have held out against West's

arguments then, that they needed to see a doctor, that he had to take them to a doctor. She could have held out, but his eyes had suddenly filled and he'd said, "You know, my baby brother died of diphtheria in the orphanage, and I barely survived myself. They're so fragile when they're young."

So she'd let him take the children to the doctor for the whooping cough, because she wouldn't go herself. She'd never been to a doctor in her life, except when she'd had Cory and Kevin, and even then she hadn't gone to a hospital, but had had the babies in a small maternity home with two beds. She let him take Cory and Kevin though and she wouldn't say she wasn't relieved—though of course she wasn't surprised—when he brought them home again saying, "He said they're basically extremely healthy young kids. There's nothing that can be done now. Just give them some cod-liver oil and they'll be fine."

"You see!" said Polly.

Cory remembered the cod-liver oil, a gagging tablespoonful of grease, followed by a handful of candy corn that was meant to take away the taste of the fish oil, but that only got ground up with it like a sweet fishy paste at the back of her throat.

She remembered the hours of lying in bed, the racking coughs passing through her like waves when her whole body seemed to jerk up and down and her lungs were like sandpaper and ached and ached. She remembered her mother sitting between her and Kevin, whose crib had been brought into Cory's room, hour after hour, with her morocco-bound Bible and *Science and Health*, repeating the Scientific Statement of Being: "There is no life, truth, intelligence, nor substance in matter. All is infinite Mind and its infinite manifestation, for God is All-in-all. Spirit is immortal Truth; matter is mortal error. Spirit is the real and eternal; matter is the unreal and temporal. Spirit is God, and man is His image and likeness. Therefore man is not material; he is spiritual."

Polly repeated this over and over until it became a kind of delirious song, mixed with bits of nursery rhymes and poems and lullabies to keep them quiet.

Cory remembered the doctor's office, the gleaming white walls and the steel tables papered over with stiff white sheets, and the nurses floating in the corridors with white caps like wings. There was a peculiar smell, half sweet, half metallic, and very cold. The old doctor wore a white coat over his real clothes and had a shiny round disk hanging off two rubber tubes he put in his ears.

"Nothing to be worried about," he said, putting the cold metal disk over her heart. "It's just like the toy stethoscope in your nurse kit when you play doctor."

"I don't believe in doctors!" Cory said very loudly through her coughs.

And her father had explained, embarrassed, appealing for understanding, "Their mother is a Christian Scientist."

"Oh, I see," was all the doctor said, and after a moment he tickled their chins and pronounced them essentially healthy children who'd be back on their feet in no time.

"Still," he added to their father, "I'm glad you brought them in. Don't hesitate to bring them back if they get worse, or if anything like this should ever happen again. Better to be safe than sorry. No need to mention it to your wife. I've known a number of Christian Scientists. Very fine people."

But out in the corridor Cory heard one of the nurses saying to the other, "They say they don't believe in medicine and doctors, but when something happens, where's the first place they come running?"

And the other nurse said, "Haven't they ever heard that untreated whooping cough can cause blindness?"

That was when Cory was five, in kindergarten. Now that she was six, she had to carry a note to her new first grade teacher, Mrs. Gowan.

"Don't give it to me. Give it to the nurse," said Mrs. Gowan with a pinched mouth. The whole class was being marched in a single-file line through the hall past the school library and office, then outside past the cafeteria to the third and fourth graders' playground to the school nurse's office that was also white and steel with that strangely sweet, metallic smell.

"Please, Mrs. Gowan," Cory said urgently as the line moved up one by one and the children entered the nurse's office. She couldn't see what was going on in there, but every once in a while a child cried and all of them came out with Band-Aids pressed tightly over a bleeding spot on their arms. Cory's heart was pounding in fear. "Please, Mrs. Gowan. I'm not *supposed* to."

"I wash my hands, I wash my hands," said Mrs. Gowan finally, and dragged her out of the line up to the front which was inside the nurse's office. "Give them your note, Cory Winter," and to the school nurse, "She's the little Christian Scientist girl."

"But this is a national epidemic," said the nurse, reading the note and staring hard at Cory in her scuffed Buster Browns and blue corduroy jumper. "Won't you help your little friends by not giving them a terrible, terrible disease? You wouldn't want anyone to become crippled or to die because of you, would you?"

Cory stared at her Buster Browns in shame. Surely she couldn't be the only one who had a note in the whole school. But she was.

"I don't believe," she started to say, "I don't believe . . . " Then she burst into tears.

Mrs. Gowan took her by the hand and led her away. "It's absolutely criminal what these parents do to their children," she said.

"Do you ever wonder how to explain this crazy religion of ours?" Connie said to Polly. It was the beginning of the next summer, 1956, and none of their children had gotten sick from polio, though none of them had had the vaccine. They were at Alamitos Bay in Belmont Shores, where they often brought the kids, driving them in Connie's sandy old Plymouth station wagon. They would prop up the big striped beach umbrella and two cotton backrests and spread out the bright towels. The children played down by the water's edge, perfectly safe with Cory and Joe watching over them. In a minute or two one of the kids would run up, carrying a shell to show, sprinkling water over them, or begging to have a nickel for a Fudgesicle from the concession stand, Woodie's Goodies. But at the moment they were alone, Polly in her new yellow swimsuit and harlequin glasses, Connie, who'd never been able to get rid of the weight she'd gained from little Sal, in her muumuu.

"I don't know if you can explain it," said Polly. "I grew up going to Sunday School and it always made sense. It was my life. It's the same with Cory and Kevin. You just believe it, because you've seen it works. You can't imagine life without it."

"I know," said Connie. "But you'd think that something so powerful would be something everybody would believe."

"Sometimes it takes a Demonstration," said Polly. "My mother used to be a Seventh-day Adventist and so was her best friend, and her friend almost died of tuberculosis until she tried Science. That convinced my mother."

"My mother says it was a friend who brought her into the church, too," said Connie. "But all *my* friends, except for you, think I'm nuts."

Polly laughed.

"Just like your neighbor Sharie. I think she was hoping our kids could get polio just so she could be proved right."

"I hardly see Sharie anymore," Polly murmured. "I think the afternoon with Mildred and Joan was too much for her."

"You know, Sal put his foot down. He says the kids have to get the Salk vaccine. He says he'll divorce me if I don't agree. I told him he can't, because he's a Roman Catholic." Although Connie laughed, Polly knew she was serious. "If they do get the shots, it won't mean that I haven't healed myself and Sal and the kids a dozen times."

"I know," said Polly, and confessed, "I sometimes think, it's not fair that we have to deal with issues that our parents never did. They never used to have vaccines. It was prayer or death."

"So you've thought about it?" Connie asked.

Polly nodded. "And then I think, my mother would kill me."

"She'd never know!"

"I've got to believe," Polly said. "You know that. I can't not believe."

Then the children rushed up and suddenly there were warm peanut butter sandwiches all over fingers and towels and orange Kool-Aid in paper cups overturned in the sand. Polly and Connie slathered them again with Coppertone and sent them back down to the water. "Can't we go to the real ocean?" asked Cory, as she always did.

"You're still too little," said Polly.

"This is the baby beach!"

"Next year," promised Polly. "And anyway, this is a better beach for sandcastles. Will you build me one?"

"Okay!"

"One thing I like about you, Polly," said Connie after they'd been lying there a little while longer, "is that you have a strong faith, but you're not self-righteous. Not like Mildred and Joan and the rest. That new woman who just joined, Dorothy Dragon, is more like us. Though I've heard she smokes."

"*And* drinks beer, Mildred says," Polly laughed.

"Shocking," said Connie absently, and then she said, "I'm going to miss you, Polly."

"Hmm?"

"I haven't wanted to tell you this, but Sal's brother wants us to move to Nevada, outside Las Vegas. He's got a big dry-cleaning plant. Sal would be a partner. It's a great opportunity."

Polly took off her harlequin glasses. The day seemed oddly frozen, in spite of the heat, as if the breath had been knocked out of it. Most of the children were down at the water's edge, where a sandcastle was going up, cup after packed cup, but Cory was out in the water again, bobbing and watching them all. Connie's plump arm lay next to Polly's freckled one, and Polly thought, I never really had a friend before Connie, not like this.

"But Connie, when?" she managed to say, and her voice unfroze the moment, and Connie, who had also stopped breathing for an instant, was full of things to tell her about Boulder City.

"I feel as if I'm starting over," said Connie. "Like when I came to California ten years ago. I'm looking forward to it, I admit. I'll miss *you* terribly, but not most of the rest of them."

"I wish I could go with you," Polly burst out.

Ever since her mother's first visit two years ago Polly had had a sense of the past catching up with her, and of her own fresh start fading.

"But your life is so good here," said Connie. "Your gorgeous garden, West getting his CPA license, two bright, good-looking kids. And everybody loves you in the church."

"My life is good," repeated Polly. As a Christian Scientist she knew life *was* good. Why then this fear, this loneliness that tugged at her heart now, this sudden longing to throw everything up and go somewhere where she knew no one but Connie and where her mother couldn't find her?

"We'll write," said Connie. "And you'll visit. Won't you?"

"Oh yes," said Polly, and tried to smile. "Often, I hope." And she let her hand touch Connie's soft arm, while inside she had a sense of something wordless and bereft tightening in her chest in the bright, warm day.

Out in the calm waters of Alamitos Bay Cory bobbed and watched the shore. She liked this view of things: Connie and her mother on their towels under the umbrella, arms almost touching, talking quietly; the little kids on the shore making a sandcastle. She kept a special eye on Kevin. He couldn't swim as well as she could; she had to make sure he didn't come out far into the water.

She could go out far. She wanted to go out farther. She always asked her mother, "Can we go to the real beach?" but her mother usually said no. The bay was separated from the ocean by a spit of land like an arm. They were meant to play in the curve of that arm, in its soft inner crook, as if held in its soft embrace.

The ocean was big, that's why Cory liked it. She liked the long white beach with the umbrellas anchored against the wind and the fold-up chairs where old people sat reading or playing cards. She liked the length of dark, sucking sand, littered with a million shell fragments and poppable bulbs of bull kelp. When she went into the Pacific she was alone in a way she never was at the Bay. On the shore of the Bay she had to struggle for a little space in the water and some kid always said, You splashed me, I'm telling, even when you hadn't been trying to. The ocean was large enough to hold everyone lying on the beach, large enough to hold the whole city of Long Beach, if everyone should one day get it into their heads to walk away from their schools and jobs and homes and walk right into the water and be swallowed up.

The ocean was green and blue and white, the same colors as swimming pools, lagoons and water from the garden hose. But it was a completely different kind of water! Ocean water was alive— with dolphins and sharks and sea bass and starfish and crabs and snails and sea urchins and sea anemones and kelp and jellyfish and a million other things that she had only seen at an aquarium. Ocean water went on forever, this Pacific that washed up in places as far away as Hawaii, Japan and New Zealand. Ocean water had islands and volcanoes and ice floes and coral reefs. Ocean water was bigger than California or the United States. Ocean water could carry a thousand boats on its back. Ocean water spoke to Cory every time she entered it, every time she stood at its white frothing feet, every time she tried to see how far she could look into it. Ocean water held her up; it lifted her to the sky and plunged her face first into gritty sand; it stormed around her and sucked her in; it tossed her like a juggler's ball; it respected her struggles and deposited her on the sand to try her luck with it again. It stayed where it was when she panted her way back to shore and threw herself on her towel, gasping with the shock of being cold in a blazing hot world.

But for now the ocean was a place she couldn't be. She had to be here, with her mother and brother. She had to take care of her brother. She had to show her mother she was taking care of him. She had to make sure he wouldn't drown. She could see his little cold legs in the water, and his narrow brown shoulders. His head looked too big. She could tell he was getting tired, faithfully following Joe's directions to gather more and more sand for the sandcastle.

She began to float slowly in, letting the little waves carry her. She remembered last year, when her mother read to her from Genesis, about the creation of the world, that she had believed that the waters divided by the firmament were the two waters of Long Beach—Alamitos Bay and the Pacific Ocean. She didn't know the word *firmament* at first, didn't know that it was supposed to be the sky. She thought it was something like cement, like something firm under her feet, like wet sand pressed down and hardened under the sun, like sand she could run on down by the water's edge. She thought that the firmament dividing the waters was the spit of land between Alamitos Bay and the Pacific Ocean, the arm that stretched out from the body of Long Beach.

On one side, in the secure crook of the inner arm, was the safe, sun-warmed water in which she floated and swam alongside the land rather than out, and looked often at the bright beach umbrella and island of terry cloth where her mother was sitting, in her yellow cotton swimsuit and upturned sunglasses, talking with her friend Connie Sabicca. On the other side of the arm was the ocean, the wild water, the hard and exciting and terrifying water with its waves that knocked her down and stood her up again, and sometimes didn't let her see the shore, or her mother, or anything but the water itself.

"Mama, Mama!" she shouted. "See me do a somersault?"

Did her mother see her? She was listening to Connie with a sad look on her face. "Kevin!" Cory shouted then. And when he looked, his face full of interest at the strength and agility of his older sister, Cory started her somersault. The main thing was not to stop once you started. You had to bend and fold like a jumping jack, going round and round, and you had to close your eyes and relax. There was nothing else to do, as you turned over and over again, except hold on and keep breathing.

NUMBERS

FROM THE MOMENT she could make sounds, Cory loved to sing and chant. Songs she learned in kindergarten and Sunday school, chants she made up from words she heard: "BOSCO, BOSCO, CHOCOLATE *MILK*!" she roared. She didn't care if the words rhymed, it was the rhythm that set her marching all around the house, arms swinging, feet held high: "There was a little girl, who had a little curl, right in the middle of her forehead. And when she was good, she was very very good. And when she was bad, she was HORRID!"

She loved Horrid and Forehead. She liked big bold words that filled her mouth with large round sounds: Muffet, Tuffet, Hickory Dickory *Dock*.

Polly read poetry to her from her own childhood books: Kipling, Robert Louis Stevenson, the Brownings, A. A. Milne. Cory memorized the words by swinging her arms and jumping up and down, because poetry was about moving, not sitting still.

> *Whenever I walk in a London street,*
> *I'm ever so careful to watch my feet;*
> *And I keep in the squares,*

And the masses of bears,
Who wait at the corners all ready to eat
The sillies who tread on the lines of the street,
Go back to their lairs
And I say to them, "Bears,
Just look how I'm walking in all of the squares!"

At night there was Sleeping Beauty and Pinocchio, but in the afternoons Polly read to Cory from the Christian Science Lesson of the week. Cory liked the Bible part of the Lesson, with the long passages that she didn't understand, but loved for the cadence and the strange words: *hallowed, harkened, covenant, prophet, pestilence.* She swam in the language of the Old Testament, in the stories of Daniel and the Lion's Den, Moses in the Bulrushes, Joseph and His Coat of Many Colors. The *Science and Health* part of the Lesson was harder. She didn't understand the texts of Mrs. Eddy that were meant to help them understand the real meaning of the Bible. There was a coolness, as of clouds overhead, in sentences like: "Man is never God, but spiritual man, made in God's likeness, reflects God," and in the common phrases of Christian Science: "Divine Mind" and "false sense impressions" and "all-seeing," "all-knowing." These words were neither story nor rhythm; they were soft flannel blankets, just washed, hard to hold on to, but comforting all the same. Cory liked the songs in the hymnal though, soaring and sentimental hymns with odd breaks and contractions like "Brood o'er us with Thy shel'tring wing" that made her think of the purplish pigeons billing and cooing on the pavement at Ken's Hamburgers.

Cory loved to hear words and she liked to tell stories, but she didn't like to read and for a long time she couldn't. In the first grade Cory was put into the Giraffes' Reading Group. The Giraffes were the dumb ones, slower than the Elephants and Tigers. The

Giraffes had to sit in a circle on wooden baby chairs, and hold the heavy readers with their thick pages and silly pictures on their knees, and take turns reading aloud with a special teacher, not Mrs. Gowan, who was with the Elephants or the Tigers, but Mrs. Simmons, whose bronze fingers smelled like Cory's father's pipe tobacco, only not so sweet. When it came to Cory's turn she could hardly say a word. The letters were squashed insects on the page, they were not her friends.

"Cory," said Mrs. Simmons with professional patience, "What's this letter?"

Cory shook her head.

"Now look at it. It's a J. See the fishhook and the surface of the water? And who has a name that starts with J"?

"Jane," she sighed reluctantly. She looked over at the Elephants and Tigers, whose murmuring did not cease as each child— Wendy with the curly hair and soft lower lip, Craig whose father drove the Helms Bakery truck, Denise who had a big Shepherd dog, none of them so very smart—plodded through the endless story of Dick and Jane, Mother and Father and Spot.

Anybody could make up a better story than that! Anybody could make up a family where the children did more than PLAY and SEE, and the parents did more than WORK and COOK. See Spot run. Who cared?

Cory had invented the Feeble Family while she and Kevin washed dishes. Jack and Nancy Feeble were a brother and sister who lived with some invisible parents named Mr. and Mrs.

Everybody thought Jack and Nancy were not very smart— Nancy couldn't read and Jack couldn't count. But they were not stupid, not at all! Nancy was very smart, smarter than Jack, but only because she was three years older.

"Two years and eleven months," said Kevin. That one month out of the year when they were only two years apart was important to him.

The first time the Feebles were sucked down the sink in their saucer boat to the Drain Kingdom was a mistake. They were just washing the dishes, when the next thing they knew—whoa! "Hold on, Jack!" They'd almost slipped into the jaws of the garbage disposal and been chewed up like hamburgers mixed with bits of Keds sneakers and underwear elastic. They'd almost been knocked unconscious by a low pipe and thrown sideways by a sudden bend. Once in the Drain Kingdom problems came up. Could they drink the water there? And wasn't it rude to hold your nose when talking to people?

But after that first mistaken flushing Jack and Nancy chose to visit the Drain Kingdom more often than not, and gradually to explore its mountains and jungles, its borders on the Land of Junk and on the Country of Glass and Fire.

The Feebles were for Cory and Kevin, but Polly heard bits and pieces too, not about the awful nasty scary things that could happen, but about the milder adventures where everything turned out right. She said, "I wish my brother and I had been closer in age, as close as you two. Eight years is a long time—I was like an only child until Steve was added to the family. I took care of him—we didn't really play. And then I went to college and he turned into an only child too. I never knew him. Never felt that close to him."

Cory couldn't imagine life without Kevin. He was her first memory, the day he came home from being born and lay in his crib, bleating softly, hairless, helpless. She didn't remember being one, only two, never alone, always together. Always in relation to, always older, smarter, taller, further. Always responsible, always teaching, translating, always to blame if something happened to him, always pushing, caring, adoring, bullying. Always the older sister.

"Two plus two is . . . ?" she coached him over and over, holding up her fingers. But he only stared at her with big, smoke-blue eyes and said nothing. He stared at her fingers and later on he stared hopelessly at the page of arithmetic problems that his teacher sent home with him. His first-grade report card said, "Reads well for his age, but has difficulty grasping subtraction."

"Reads well for his age!" Polly said.

"Cory never has any problems with math," said West.

Numbers were friendly, Cory knew that and so did her father, who taught her arithmetic before she learned it in school and crowed that she was smarter than half the students in his basic accounting classes.

She didn't know how it happened, but answers leaped into her head. Forty-five; sixty-two; seventeen. She had her special numbers. 5 was best, it was red, with a straight back, pouchy stomach and a flat hat; 7 was dark blue, mysterious with its elegant slant. 6 was silly, reminding her of puppies rolling on the rug, and 8 made her smile, too—it was like a clown with a round face running in circles. 9 was serious, like an older brother, almost getting to be an adult two-digit. 3 she didn't like as much, the way it went deliberately backwards; 4 was like a little girl new to class, bashful with her head down and hands behind her back; 1 and 2 were little baby numbers, almost neutral and very useful. They were best combined with the older, bigger numbers, which gave them stature and wealth.

Numbers obeyed her, especially zeros that lined up in rows. She liked the sound of a million, a billion, a trillion. She liked the language of numbers—carrying and dropping. When she added and carried, she imagined the agile 1 or 2 climbing up to the top of a human pyramid in a circus, and causing a chain reaction that tumbled down through the line to the strongman below. Subtraction was a mirror image of addition; instead of hello, it was good-bye, good-bye. Long division was like swimming; numbers dived off the board into the sea, splashing with the zero fish they found there.

Polly said, "I'm no good with numbers, it was always my hardest subject. I guess Kevin takes after me. Cory takes after you, West."

Cory wanted to be like her mother, but she knew she was like her father. She had been his Peanut since Kevin was born. They had both lost a little of Polly to Kevin, but they had gained each other. That was how a family worked. Nothing ever went missing without turning up somewhere else. With Polly Cory might have become second, but with her father she would always be first.

Cory liked to visit him in his office and he never told her to go away. When she was small she sat on his lap while he showed her how the pale green rounded adding machine, a sort of numerical caterpillar, could hum through complicated additions and subtractions, busily shooting paper streamers from its forehead. In her father's office there was always green paper printed with a hundred tiny slightly darker green squares, and yellow pencils with pink erasers and points sharp as needles. His heavy walnut desk was covered with a green blotter with brown leather triangles at the corners. Like every place he inhabited deeply—the bathroom, the car—his office was permeated with the scent of cherry-scented pipe tobacco. Little flakes of golden leaf found their way into crevices in the car upholstery, into the pages of *U.S. News and World Report,* and in the edges of the desk blotter. The flakes were choking bitter, but the pipe cleaners that came in flat, yellow envelopes were fun to make white bendy animals out of. Smoking gave her father a tickle in his throat and that's why there were always small boxes of Luden's cough drops on the car seat and in his top desk drawer. When she opened the drawer a smell of menthol blew out.

Her father used to have an office downtown at Atlantic and Linden that he shared with Don Feldman. Don and his wife Arlene were once professional ballroom dancers. Arlene liked to show Cory and Kevin photographs of a dapper man in a tux twirling a girl with a skirt like a flower. That was supposed to be Don and Arlene, though Cory politely didn't believe it until Don came in one day and spun her around the room.

When Cory was seven her parents built an addition on to the garage, two rooms with a bath in between. One room was an office for West, and the other was a guest room for Grandma Cooper. When Cory was small Grandma had never come to visit them, but since Grandpa passed on, she had been coming twice a year on the train. At first Grandma stayed in Kevin's room and Kevin slept in Cory's, but then Polly said Grandma needed more room, and maybe now was the time to do what they'd been talking about, build West an office so he could be at home more, and West said, "Fine, as long as there's a door with a lock on it between me and her . . . Oh Polly, you know I'm joking . . . your mother's always welcome here."

When Grandma wasn't visiting, Polly let Cory and Kevin use the guest room for playing. She set up a big table in the middle of the room, plywood on two sawhorses, a table much bigger than the one in the kitchen nook, and bigger too than the redwood picnic table under the apricot tree. The floor was linoleum laid in alternating squares of dark brown and light tan. It had a new, cool smell, and it didn't matter if clay and papier-mâché paste and paints got on the floor. On hot days they often spent whole afternoons there. The room was sheltered by trees that had grown up around the edges of the yard and by a profusion of scented shrubbery they called the bee bushes because the delicate white flowers drew swarms of bees. On those late summer afternoons when the grass was too stiff with dry heat to play on, when they were tired of trying to invent games with the kids on the block, when they were bored to death and ready to scream, Polly would say, Let's go out to the playroom! And she would organize them with strips of newspaper and pots of flour paste, and jelly glasses of water that turned brown and gray even though the watercolor cakes were all the brightest colors. The room would be cool with the sweet breeze of the roses and the bee bushes coming in through the screen door.

Later on Polly would go in to cook dinner and Kevin would go looking for his friend Billy and Cory, hearing her father come home from teaching and into his office, would go through the bathroom between the two rooms into his office. On his desk would be the light green paper with the squares, and up and down in neat columns would be her father's precise small handwriting. It gave her such pleasure to look at those numbers, so tiny and perfect on the page! And she would sit on his lap while he talked to her.

"You could say I'm a self-made man," he told Cory. "I was in the right place at the right time. Never thought I'd teach accounting, though. I was always good in business class, but history was my major. Latin and the classics. *The Decline and Fall of the Roman Empire.* One of the greatest works of all time. Gibbon. I read all six volumes—twice. Still, you take what life gives you. You turn it into something you want, or could learn to want. Fate plays a large part in life, Cory, you'll understand that someday. Things come to you, things you never expected, but other things are taken away. Now look at me." West held up his hand with all the fingers pointing up. With the other hand he began to pull the fingers over, one after the next. "I never knew my mother, she died when I was one. The child she was carrying died too. My father had to put us in an orphanage and my other brother died there of diphtheria. I was spared. Then my father died. Everyone in my family dead before I remembered them. Four people [four fingers, all held down by the other hand, only the thumb sticking up like a stump after a storm], my family, all dead. I was spared. But I was alone."

"What about the Kiesewalters?" Cory asked. They were the older couple with the farm where he'd lived and worked for four or five years. "Why didn't you stay with them?"

"I wasn't a Kiesewalter. I was a Winter. I had an identity. I was an orphan. Nothing could change that. No, you grow up an orphan, you make your own life. Fate makes you, but you make your life. I thought after the war I'd go back to Wisconsin and become a history teacher, but I met your mother here and decided to stay. A job came up teaching accounting at the business and technical division of Long Beach City College. 'Can you take it, West?' they said. 'I certainly can.' Now I love it. There's something about numbers that I find very satisfying. I think you see it too, Peanut. I like the numbers in the squares. I like things to add up. I don't like loose ends, messy columns, mistakes.

"But I never take anything for granted," he said. "Security doesn't exist in life. All this, everything we have—an earthquake, a fire—gone in an instant. All I can hope is that, once again, I'll be spared."

Grandma was coming! Even if her mother hadn't told her, Cory would know. The house was cleaned and scrubbed. She and Kevin got new shoes and haircuts and Polly began to wear dresses and pull her unruly hair back into a bun and read Mrs. Eddy more than usual. But the biggest change was in the guest room. Play was banished and everything to do with play. The sawhorses and plywood—gone! The tablets of construction paper, the newspapers, the pots of paint and glue, the little bags of stars and glitter—gone! The boxes of dress-up clothes and costume jewelry for plays and the circus—gone!

Even before Grandma arrived on the Santa Fe train at the station in Los Angeles the room had become her room. It smelled of freshly waxed floor and old lady's scent. In the closets and drawers of the chest were lavender sachets. There was an easy chair and a small table next to it piled with the latest Christian Science *Monitors, Heralds* and *Sentinels.*

If everything was not perfect in this way Grandma would frown when she came in the door and say, "Well, I suppose I can't expect things to be like home." But if the room *was* perfect, Grandma would smile, and Polly would smile too, and everything would be all right.

♦

Grandma Cooper had a heavy step, so you always heard her coming before you saw her. Thump, ka-thump. Thump, ka-thump. Because of a stiffness in her hip, one foot always hit the floor with a slightly different sound. Her shoes were white with tiny holes like termite borings on top, and soles thick as bricks. Thump, ka-thump. You heard her muffled step on the carpet in the living room, more distinctly on the kitchen linoleum and sharpest of all—cracking-sharp—on the wooden floors in the hall and bedrooms. "What do you mean you're not up yet, Cora Winter! Get out of bed and get your school clothes on right this minute!"

Her nose was big and blobby, contained by two clever green eyes that were set closely on either side like perfectly matched sentries, marching up and down and turning sharply in unison. "I have my eye on you," she often told Cory; eye only, never eyes. And it *was* as if Grandma had only one eye, like the Grey Ladies in *The Tanglewood Tales*, a single eye that was all-seeing, even in the dark. "Is that you out there on the porch?" she would say when Cory stayed out too long in the evening. The big nose could sniff out mischief and the all-seeing sentry eye pin the culprit to the wall with a bayonet look.

No one was immune from this look except perhaps the dog. Grandma liked the dog, liked to have Sallie with her in the room and to take her for walks. "Your mother likes that damn dog better than her grandchildren," said West.

Polly didn't laugh. "She's lonely, West. She misses my father."

"Well, she's got Steve there, hasn't she?"

"Steve is more a trial to her than a comfort."

"She should throw him out. What a thirty-year-old man is doing living with his mother, I don't know."

"It's just till he gets back on his feet. That divorce really threw him."

"That divorce was two or three years ago."

Cory had never met her Uncle Steve. She had only heard about him. How he had been a "little terror." How he had run away from home at seventeen and joined the Army. How he had come back and gone to art school. How he had traveled in Europe. How he had married a beautiful girl called Rachel in Chicago. How she had left him. How he was at loose ends. How in Grandma's eyes he could do no wrong.

West said to Polly, "What the heck does he have to be miserable about? He's good-looking, he's talented, he's free as a bird. I only wish I'd had his luck in life. Two parents to love you, a sister like you, a stable home. Sometimes I think where I could have gone if I'd had people who cared."

"You never had anyone to spoil you," said Polly. "Never had anyone to make excuses for you every time you made a mistake or did something wrong. My brother would probably be better off if he'd been an orphan like you."

"I thought you liked your brother?"

"I feel guilty about him. That's not the same thing as like."

Cory was listening to her parents in her father's office. She had taken, now that she was eight, to eavesdropping. In the house everything was small and everyone knew where you were. But in the addition, secrecy was possible. She could stand in the guest room, now Grandma's room, with the door to the bathroom open and hear how her parents had escaped from the house to have this conversation. She could stand in her father's office with the door to the bathroom open, having come in to borrow a pencil, and hear her mother and Grandma talking. The two rooms were separate, linked only by the bathroom. Her father never walked through into Grandma's room when she was there, and Grandma never disturbed West. Only Polly went back and forth that way, from one to the other. Cory stood quietly in one room or the next, or sometimes outside, next to the bee bushes, in the midst of the buzzing.

Ka-thump, swoosh, ka-thump. Polly and her mother were cleaning the guest room. Grandma was going away again, but "Never let it be said that I left a mess behind me."

They were washing the dark and light squares of linoleum. Cory heard them from her father's office, where she was hiding under the desk to get away from Kevin. She was looking at a *National Geographic*. There was an article about the science of volcanoes. Now that she was older she understood that there were Scientists and scientists, and she could be one but not the other. The teacher she had now, in third grade, Miss Chicoletti, said it was too bad that Cory had to be excused from class every time they got out their science book to study some interesting topic like "Cloud Formations" or "Temperature." She said that with Cory's mathematical abilities she could be a fine scientist. Because of Sputnik the U.S. needed all the scientists it could get. Cory had to set her straight. "I'm going to be an accountant," she said. "Oh, are you?" said Miss Chicoletti and laughed, before sending her off to the library with a pass.

It wasn't so easy with the other kids. "But *why* can't you stay and do the experiments?" asked her friend Trixie Matthews who sat next to her. "They're really fun."

"'Cause we don't believe that stuff," said Cory. She couldn't imagine telling Trixie what her mother said, that science was the study of Matter and Matter was not real. She couldn't imagine telling her about Mrs. Eddy and the false sense impressions.

"You don't believe in *weather*?"

"No."

"You don't believe in *rain*?"

"No."

It was an argument Cory could never win. Her mother said she should never argue, but only demonstrate her faith. Cory said, "It's more about bodies. We don't believe in bodies."

Trixie Matthews looked at her and she looked at Trixie Matthews, two little girls in plaid jumpers and white shirts, with white socks and scabbed knees, straight hair refusing to hold a curl even though their mothers stuck little metal rollers on their heads at night sometimes, their new teeth growing in so much bigger than the old ones, and Trixie said, "You don't believe in *bodies?*"

"No," said Cory hopelessly, and went off to the school library, where the two sweet librarians welcomed her every week and gave her a corner of one of the big maple tables to work on. In the second grade reading had become easier and now she loved words on the page almost as much as she loved numbers. Sometimes she read fairy tales and myths and legends and sometimes she did special projects, like creating the legend of Hercules and the Golden Apples at the end of a shoe box. She made a little garden from juniper twigs and lantana flowers, and then rolled three gold foil candy wrappers into balls and stuck them in the tree. Afterwards she put the lid back on the shoe box and made two holes, one a kind of skylight above the scene and the other at the other end of the shoe box for viewing.

Thump, ka-thump brought Cory back. She thought of the poem about keeping in the squares, and the bears in their lairs and she imagined Grandma as a bear with a single huge eye fixed on Polly, who kept stepping on the lines, unaware of the danger she was in, the silly.

Grandma said, "Polly, you've got this perfectly good guest room now. I don't know why you don't ask your own brother to visit you."

"I have asked him, Mother," Polly said in the meek, guilty way that Grandma inspired. "He's always said he's too busy. And we've just had the guest room a year now."

"Well, I want you to ask him to come for a visit this summer. Take him on your vacation with you. Get his mind off his own miseries."

♦

"I called your Uncle Steve and asked him if he wanted to come visit later this year," Polly told Cory and Kevin at dinner that night. "And he said yes. He's going to come on our vacation with us to Arizona too," she said smiling. "He'll bring his raft for the river."

West said, "It will be great to have some help with the long drive. We'll do some fishing."

And Grandma, who didn't often look pleased, gazed with something like kindness at her son-in-law and daughter. "You wait, Steve will surprise us all. I've said from the very beginning, haven't I, that underneath his wild ways that boy is as talented as they come."

Mr. and Mrs. Feeble had died, or passed on as they said in Christian Science. They had vanished in a flood one day, and been drowned because they couldn't swim, but "Don't worry, Kevin," Cory reassured him, "If they had parents, Jack and Nancy couldn't do the things that are fun to do."

Tonight they were off down the drain on a raft with their Uncle Valiant, who had come to stay with them after their parents died, and who let them eat all the cake they wanted and never take a bath and watch TV all night. He was an orphan, too, and he said it was the best thing in life, because then you were free, you didn't have to worry about anybody else.

Down, down the drain into the Land of Junk they went, and their raft swirled through sewers and got caught on rusted cars and was practically destroyed by a school of broken toaster fish and still they sailed on, eating the hamburgers from the trees, and the flying Twinkies that looked like birds if you didn't know.

Thump, ka-thump. "Are the two of you still doing the dishes? Cora, you're as dreamy as your mother. I don't know what any of you will do after I'm gone!"

◆

That night, before Cory went to bed, she ran out across the patio to kiss her father good night, but stopped outside when she heard her mother's voice, low because Grandma was in the other room.

"*I have* tried to stand up to her. You don't know how I've tried. But she's my *mother*, West. As long as she wants Steve to visit, I can't say no. If you had a mother, you'd feel the same way."

West said something, but Cory couldn't hear what it was.

"She's *not* a bully. It's just that she doesn't see that I have a different life now. To her I'll always be her daughter, and Steve will always be my brother, and I'm responsible for him."

A low laugh from West and something in the joking tone he often used when things got tense. Usually Polly laughed too, but tonight it seemed to be making her mad.

"You! What do you know about being attached to anyone, Mr. Self-Sufficient out here in your office every night. I used to envy you, you know, I thought you were so independent. But sometimes I think you don't see anyone but yourself, don't care about anyone but yourself."

Her mother's voice had risen, but her father's voice was steady. "I care about all of you, Polly. Don't I work hard to make a good home?"

"Work isn't a proof. It's an excuse." There was a pause, and then Polly said, her voice low again, so low Cory could hardly hear it, "It's just that I get lonely sometimes."

Her father should have said something, but he didn't.

Cory flattened herself by the side of the building as her mother slowly came out, clicking the screen door behind her, and across the patio back into the house. She had her hair in a bun, the way Grandma liked it, and from the back it was not so hard to imagine that it was Grandma.

The light from his office spilled out through the high window and through the screen door onto the red-painted surface of the patio. Above the door was another outdoor light, with bugs clustered frantically around it. The back yard was still and dark, except for the crickets; there was an intoxicating scent from the roses and from the bee bushes. Inside the office through the screen door all was calmness and order, from the walls made dark brown by leather-bound volumes stamped in gold on the spine: *Principles of Cost Accounting* and *Tax Digest, 1957*. The light from the green shade on the desk lamp cast a circle over his pale green paper, and the hand she could see before she saw the familiar face scratched out numbers in precise small columns. The hand paused only to fill and tamp and light the pipe.

The tobacco fragrance floated out through the screen door and mingled with the scent of the roses and bee bushes, filling Cory's chest with a like fragrance, unbearably sad and sweet.

"Daddy?" she called out tentatively.

"Hi there, Peanut," he said, and she went in as if she'd never paused an instant and never heard a thing. She sat on his lap while he showed her a tax return he was working on. "I take on extra work in the evenings so that we can have the things we need," he said, a bit loudly. "A teacher's salary isn't so much, you know. And it wasn't so inexpensive building this addition."

In the bathroom they heard Grandma getting ready for bed. She would be combing her thin white hair into a plait and taking out her teeth and putting them in a glass. Then she would kneel by the daybed and pray for all of them. Cory wondered if she ever got scared in the guest room, with the linoleum squares keeping back the bears in their lairs only if you didn't tread on the lines.

But in her father's office everything was safe and sleepy, as he held her on his lap and showed her how he got his results with numbers, numbers cool and clean and friendly, lined up in long tiny columns, protected in their squares of green on green.

A GHOST TOWN

HOW DO YOU trust a memory insubstantial as a dust-clouded ghost town, full of twisted porches and roofs turned back to front, of boardwalks that lead up into the sky or vanish into the hillside, of entire houses turned upside down? A memory like a fantastical town glimpsed through the corner of a dirty back car window on a hot afternoon in July, 1958?

Uncle Steve is driving and he drives fast around the hairpin turns. He passes cars on curves and laughs to see the blanched faces of the drivers he narrowly misses. Something in him likes this and will not listen to reason.

"Steve, Steve," says his sister, Polly, "We're getting carsick, take it slower."

"You want to get there before dark, don't you?" Steve calls back to where Polly sits between Cory and Kevin.

"If we don't get there before dark, we don't," says West, in the front. He reluctantly turned the driving over to his brother-in-law in Prescott and they have been racing ever since.

In the afternoon light the ghost town of Jerome is a brown curlicue of smoke wiggling up and down the red hill. The whole landscape here is red, baked the color of flowerpots. Nine-year-old

Cory stands on her seat and tries to crane her head out the open window. Her mother hauls her back in.

"I want to see the ghost town," she says. "Please! I've never seen a ghost town."

"Want to stop, want to stop," Kevin chants, crowding into Polly's lap.

"Steve?" asks Polly.

"It's two thousand feet to the bottom of the canyon where we're going tonight," says Steve. "That won't be easy in the dark."

Polly takes out the guidebook and reads aloud: "Jerome was one of the largest copper mining towns in Arizona at the turn of the century. At its height Jerome boasted over 15,000 inhabitants. But the mines gradually hollowed out Mingus Hill, on which the town was constructed. Eventually a series of dynamite explosions made parts of the hill collapse and brought down many houses, while shifting others up and down the hill. This disaster, along with a fall in the price of copper, brought mining almost to a standstill, and eventually the town was almost abandoned. It is slowly coming back."

"Well, that was a pretty stupid thing to do," says West, tamping down his pipe. He smokes a cherry-flavored blend that Cory finds reassuring. "Digging tunnels right under where you live. Any kid who's played in a sandbox would tell you what the end result of *that* was going to be."

"Oh stop. Please stop. Please!" Cory's voice rises. Her face is pressed against the back window of the Chevy; it is a Pyrex bowl burning her cheeks. It seems unbearable to her that they should not take the road to this magical sinister town that is falling down and flying up at the same time.

Polly tugs her back down, but she is wavering. Her curly dark hair is sticking to her forehead and there are half-circles of sweat under the arms of her sleeveless yellow dress. She smells of Pond's Cold Cream and Secret Deodorant.

"Steve?" she says to her younger brother. "Couldn't we stop for half an hour. Just a little while?"

"There's nothing there any more," he says. "Who wants to see a lot of old abandoned houses?"

And, pressing on the accelerator, he drives right on by.

The ghost town recedes through the back window, like a dream that Cory can never quite remember, and never quite forget.

Arizona is full of canyons. Earthquakes and eruptions and floods caused them long ago. Some, like the Grand Canyon, are vast as oceans, planets unto themselves. Some were inhabited by cliff dwellers, who built caves and houses into the sides of sandstone—"the first apartment buildings in America," says the guidebook—and then abandoned them for unknown reasons. But Oak Creek Canyon, where the Winters have rented a cabin for a week, is red sandstone and black basalt, growing thick with alder, maple, sycamore and cottonwood trees, with a creek running through it, a strong-running creek stocked with rainbow trout.

West has been thinking about those trout since he read about them in the guidebook back in California. "I haven't fished since I was a boy on the farm," he says. "Have to get some gear and give it the old college try."

Uncle Steve has packed a folded Army surplus raft. Because he used to be in the Army, Cory and Kevin have some idea that Uncle Steve made use of this raft in his tour of duty in Panama. They imagine him slinking past the enemy in his olive-drab raft in the jungles of South America, fighting off the crocodiles that want to get him and the Indians with their blowguns and poison pellets.

There are many things you could imagine Uncle Steve doing. Although they hear West complaining to their mother that Steve really needs to settle down and find a job, Cory and Kevin think of their uncle as far too adventurous to take a teaching job like their father, who goes to work and comes home in a very unexciting, normal way. Sometimes after work West brings them

Necco wafers, sometimes he makes popcorn. He reads aloud to them and rocks them in the rocking chair and watches *Wagon Train* with them on Wednesday nights when Polly goes to church. He isn't much of an athlete, he'd be the first to admit it, he says. In the orphanage and on the farm where he was taken in, there'd been no time for games, only for work. He knows all the college football teams, but he never played football. The only games he knows are Parcheesi and Checkers.

Uncle Steve is restless and dangerous, not like their father and the fathers they see on television on *Father Knows Best* and *The Donna Reed Show*, fathers in cardigans and slippers. Uncle Steve is like the gunslingers and cardsharps on the riverboats and in the saloons, the ones who keep their tempers until the last minute and then fire from the hip and kill two or three men at once. He smokes Winstons and puts the hard case in his rolled-up T-shirt sleeve. He scuba dives and rides horses and drives too fast and even swears, though not when Polly is around. He used to be married and in graduate school, but then everything fell apart and his wife left him and ever since then he's been on edge.

That's what Cory hears Polly telling her father, who says, "When I was his age I didn't have time to be on edge. I had a full-time job, a wife and a baby on the way. He's over thirty years old, Polly!"

But Polly says, "Give him time."

The cabin has two bedrooms because when they planned this vacation they didn't know Uncle Steve was coming along. Polly and West take one and Cory and Kevin the other. Uncle Steve is going to sleep in the roll-away in the living room. Everything in the cabin is made of wood. The chairs and sofa are unstripped saplings that have hardened into curves and circles. The kitchen is primitive but Polly doesn't care. "I'm not cooking much," she announces. "Cereal for breakfast, sandwiches for lunch, and West and Steve will catch all the fish we can eat."

The night they arrive they eat peanut butter sandwiches. West has a beer and Uncle Steve has four. The more he drinks the more stories he tells. All about his trip to Europe and the museums he saw there.

"Rachel was going to support us while I went to art school in Chicago. She really thought I could make it. Well, there's no way I can do it now."

"I went four years to college on a scholarship," says West. "And worked the whole time I was in college."

"You'll have to do some painting while you're here, Steve," says Polly. "Maybe you can teach Cory. I think she's very talented."

"I didn't bring any paints," Uncle Steve says.

"I did, Uncle Steve," Cory says excitedly. "I have watercolors and crayons and everything."

He smiles at her. "Yeah, well, we'll see."

"Tomorrow, fresh trout for dinner!" says Polly.

Early the next morning, West takes Cory and Kevin with him to a general store that smells of salt and wood and where the shelves hold dusty cans of beans and peas along with Fritos and Lay's Potato Chips and Hershey bars and fishing lures and bait. Rods hang from the ceiling and the walls, and the owner of the store takes them down one by one and shows them to West. The man wears a canvas cap and a plaid shirt and when he smiles a few teeth are missing, which gives him a foolish look, as if he doesn't know how to profit from the city slickers who come his way. He demonstrates the different rods to West, whipping them back and forth over his head with a sound like trees in the wind. He pretends to reel in big ones, and laughs about the high price of everything in the store. "Why the heck anybody'd buy anything from me at these prices, I don't know. But they do!"

In the end West buys two rods—one for himself and Uncle

Steve to share, and one for the kids.

The river is light gold at the bottom of the canyon, rushing over the boulders like honey on toast. When Uncle Steve sees the fishing rods and tackle he says, "You can use as much fancy gear as you want, but what it all comes down to is will power."

"How's that?" says West.

"The best fishermen are hypnotists, didn't you know?" says Uncle Steve. "I'll tell you what I do is, I think very hard about the fish I'm going to catch. I imagine it. I get to know it. Then I *will* that fish to come to me, to see my bait and be unable to resist it. I *hook* that fish through sheer will power. And even though that fish knows it's going to be painful, it can't get away. It can never get away from me!"

"Well, that's a very interesting theory," says West. "But the man at the store assured me I'd have no trouble catching dozens of fish in this river. This bait he sold me will have them jumping out of the river."

"Good luck then," says Uncle Steve and strolls off under a cottonwood tree to have a cigarette.

Polly and West confer and West says impatiently, "Of course I'm going to let him fish. Though you'd think the great fisherman would have brought his own gear."

It takes West a long time to get the reels ready for himself and the kids and by that time the sun hangs directly above the canyon walls. Uncle Steve strolls back. "You'll never catch anything in the noonday sun," he advises. "Morning and evening, that's when they bite."

West clenches his jaw. His forehead is sweaty and reddening. He gets sunburned very easily, but has forgotten a hat. "Well, we'll see about that," he says.

Earlier there were a few other men standing by the banks of the river, but now there's only West and Cory and Kevin. Uncle Steve has taken his raft in the car to get it blown up at the general store; he doesn't come back all afternoon.

Polly sits in the shade of a scrub oak by the cabin and reads her Christian Science Lesson for the day. It takes all her concentration, even after years of study, to focus on Mrs. Eddy's words: "Science reveals material man as never the real being. Personality is not the individuality of man. A wicked man may have an attractive personality." She remembers Steve as a little headstrong boy, sliding down the banisters while her mother looked on indulgently. Polly had never been allowed to do things like that. She would have had punishment for a week. But Steve had always been allowed to do what he liked—everybody else had to be responsible for him. Had to take care of him—but even then he wasn't grateful. He wouldn't go to church, said—to his mother's face!—that Christian Science was a crock of shit. He couldn't stick to anything, not school, not work, not marriage. Polly was glad, no that's unkind, but she *was* relieved for Rachel's sake that she left him. She understood what Rachel had seen in him, but men like her brother never make good husbands. Someone like West, steady and sober, even if he wasn't a Christian Scientist, was someone you could rely on.

But what else could Polly say when her mother told her to invite Steve for a visit, but yes. He was family, he needed help. He might have changed. He could not still be the little boy of five she'd once discovered teasing the kitten by holding it upside down in front of the window where the mother cat clawed against the glass.

And, resolutely, Polly shuts her mind against the memory of the piteous mews of the kitten and the frantic powerlessness of the mother cat. She bends over her lesson again and the reassuringly opaque words of Mrs. Eddy well up from the onion-skin page. "Man is incapable of sin, sickness, and death. The real man cannot depart from holiness, nor can God, by whom man is evolved, engender the capacity or freedom to sin."

◆

The afternoon sun seems stuck for a long time in the broad crack of the canyon. The air smells clean and muddy; the light glares down full on the surface of the fast green water. There are fish somewhere underneath, but none of them seem hungry for fish eggs.

At first West says things like, "This is the life"; and "Work seems a million miles away"; and "This is something I've been wanting to do for ages."

He tells Cory and Kevin about a striped bass he caught once when he was eleven, how it weighed ten pounds and was the biggest thing Mr. Kiesewalter, his foster father, had ever seen come out of the lake on the farm.

The lure bobs like a tiny beach ball on the surface of the water and over and over Cory imagines the fish jumping up to the baited hook and how she'll be ready. Kevin loses interest first, and wanders off to play tag with a boy and girl who are just his age. For a long while, out of loyalty, Cory stands with her father who, she knows from experience, will not give up easily, but eventually she carefully sets her rod down on the sandy bank and says she's going to the bathroom.

Then she joins her mother on the bench under the scrub oak.

Although people tell her she can't remember so far back, she knows that once things were different between her and her mother. Their life together was like a big box of crayons that they shared. All the colors were there and the ends were sharp, and you could still read the magical names on the paper wrap: burnt orange, jungle green, mahogany.

But as Cory grew older, she began to hear a faint hum of anxiety in the background all the time, like radio static. Perhaps it started after Grandpa Cooper died. Maybe it got worse after Connie Sabicca and her family moved away two years ago. Maybe it has to do with West working so many evenings out in his office. Or perhaps it's only about how Grandma Cooper calls more often from Michigan, and how she sounds more insistent and lonely and talks longer and listens less. Perhaps it's about Uncle Steve and what to do with him.

"I wonder where he could have gotten off to," says Polly now to Cory. "You didn't see anything but the general store nearby, did you? No . . . restaurants?"

One of the things about this anxiety that Polly carries around with her is that it has to go somewhere, and mostly it goes to Cory. It's like a glass of milk that Polly has filled too full and then handed to her daughter. And Cory has to carry it without spilling a drop.

"I didn't see anything but the store," says Cory, and then begins to worry that she's missed something and can't give her mother the right answer.

"Your Grandma thinks the world of him," Polly says. "When he was born I was eight—a little younger than you. Grandma used to call me 'little mommy.' She thought it was so sweet to have me feed Steve and change him and put him in my buggy and walk him around the neighborhood. 'Some little girls have baby dolls,' she used to tell her friends, 'but Polly has a real live baby!'"

Polly smiles, but not very happily. "He was always a handful. You never knew what to expect. Not like the two of you, Cory. I always know where you are and what you're doing. You never give me a moment's worry. But Stevie—oh, he was something different. He had a wild streak, a contrary mind. Grandpa called him 'a little rascal' and laughed, but Grandma used to pull me aside and say, 'If anything happens to Stephen, Polly, I'll hold you responsible.' I was supposed to protect him, but it wasn't easy. I had my own life to live." She looks almost defiantly at Cory and Cory feels again as if the full glass of milk is being passed to her and she mustn't spill a drop.

"I didn't *want* to know everything Stevie got into."

At the river's edge West continues to fish. He casts and casts; the lures bob up and down, most enticingly. The sun doesn't seem to move for a long time, and then abruptly a shadow falls out of the red and black canyon wall over the stream and through the maples and aspens.

Uncle Steve comes striding with his newly-bulky, olive-drab raft down to the water's edge. Next to red-faced West, Uncle Steve is muscular and tan, dark hair curling forward into his mocking brown eyes, voice a little slurred, teasing:

"Are they biting, pal?"

Cory sees her mother's shoulders soften in relief, and then tighten again when West turns to the younger man. West thrusts the rod at Uncle Steve's chest and walks away without speaking.

The water is a dark green gold as Uncle Steve waves the springy rod easily above his head, and the line drops over a black pool on the far side of the stream where the canyon wall slips into the water. A moment later he begins to reel in a fish.

It's a rainbow trout, glittering like a jeweled pin for an instant in the sun before it lies gasping and ignored at Uncle Steve's feet. Within an hour he catches four more trout, one for each of them for dinner.

Cory has tried to pry out of her mother from time to time what it was that Uncle Steve did as a boy that was so bad.

"Nothing *bad*," Polly said. "I suppose it's just that he had a wild streak."

Was he mean to animals, or to other children? Did he squash bugs or steal candy from the store? Did he lie? Did he refuse to go to church?

Cory knows that she has a wild streak too, that it runs twisting through her life like a river through a canyon, contained by red sandstone walls, but cutting a deep path all the same. She wants to be wilder than she can be, being a girl and wanting to please her mother. Wild means *no*, means *immovable*, means *selfish*, means *yes*. It's in her with no place to go.

She looks at Uncle Steve with interest. What can she learn from him about being wild, being bad, having your own way, doing what you want without worrying about hurting someone? She tries hard to get his attention, to get him to tell her stories of Paris and Italy, to draw pictures with her in the evening, to teach her things she doesn't know. One night, after he's had several beers, he seizes the box of crayons and draws a quick, vicious caricature of a portly man reeling in a stone.

"That's Daddy!" Kevin laughs.

But Polly takes the drawing, crumples it and throws it in the fire before West can see.

West doesn't fish again that week. He takes walks alone or with Cory or Kevin through the canyon, or sits reading a novel by Zane Grey called *The Call of the Canyon*, which is set in this very area of Arizona's Red Rock Country.

He tells stories to Cory of growing up an orphan and life on the farm. "If I'd had a family, I mean, a real family, a father, I would have grown up knowing how to fish," he tells Cory. "There's a limit to what you can teach yourself."

She tries to get him to tell her about the Kiesewalters. She likes the story of the old German couple who lost their sons after World War I in the influenza epidemic and who came to the orphanage in Madison asking about a foster boy to help on the farm. It makes Cory see her father as less lonely in the world to have the Kiesewalters driving him away in their milk wagon.

"They were kind people," he says. "But it wasn't the same as having a real family."

When Cory walks with him he also tells her stories about pioneers and prospectors and Indians. "It's a great shame what happened to the Indians in this country," he said. "More than a shame. A tragedy. Their ways, their quiet ways were not respected."

When the kids in the neighborhood play Cowboys and Indians,

the Indians are always shot down in the end. The Indians are never quiet, which is why Cory always wants to be one—they scream war whoops and hurl tomahawks. Their part in the game is to be as frightening as possible.

"History is told by the victors," West says. "But the victims, the ones who've just barely survived, also have a story to tell. And maybe their story is the more important one."

Late every afternoon Uncle Steve sets off in his olive-drab raft with the fishing rod and comes back an hour later with fish. But they're all getting tired of fish, and Polly has been up to the general store to buy pork and beans and canned peas for dinner. During the day Uncle Steve floats in his raft and swims; sometimes he takes Cory and Kevin with him down the river to a swimming hole, an emerald pool where the trees grow thick and close, and the banks are lined with pebbles. He puts a six-pack of beer in the water to cool and sets his hard pack of Winstons on a high rock so they don't get wet.

He talks to Cory sometimes, about books he's read and sights he's seen.

"Everybody should see Rome once in their lifetime," he says. "The whole city is an art gallery. It's the same with Florence, Venice, Siena. You can't imagine how gorgeous the streets are, and the cafés. The coffee and wine flow and flow, and the food is incredible." When he talks like this, his dark eyes glow, and he drinks his beer as if it's water, but sometimes, at the end of the day, when the beer is gone, everything seems to make him mad.

He wants to go traveling to Europe again, but he has no money. He wants to go back to art school, this time in New York, but that costs money too. Everything that Uncle Steve would like to do seems out of reach with other people standing in the way. "Your grandma's sitting on a few thousand," he says. "She could sell that house, move into an apartment, let me have something."

There are a lot of people who've done him wrong, especially women. "Your mom shouldn't have left home," he tells Cory. "Left me alone with the old biddy." But mostly he talks to Cory about his ex-wife, Rachel. "*She's* the reason I had to leave Chicago," he says. "I couldn't bear running into the bitch. I thought I might kill her."

He shows Kevin how to fish, and Cory how to dive off a big black boulder at the entrance to the emerald pool. The boulder is basalt, hardened lava, Uncle Steve tells her. Polly is happy watching him with the kids; at least when he's with them he can't get into trouble. As the days go by Polly's face relaxes and she rests often in the shade with her books in front of her. She's been so tired lately, she doesn't know why. It's good to have a vacation, even if it wasn't exactly what she'd wanted.

She'd hoped to spend two weeks here and one week with Connie Sabicca in Boulder City. They've been writing for two years now, cheerful letters, even though Polly doesn't always feel cheerful. Last Christmas Connie wrote and said, "I miss you so much! I want to sit for hours and talk the way we used to. I don't have anybody like you here."

Even when West said he couldn't take off three weeks because of summer school, they could still have gone to Nevada to see Connie if Steve hadn't come out to stay with them.

"Next summer," she wrote to Connie. "I won't let anything stop me. Next year."

"Uncle Steve, can I come with you on the river?" Cory asks. He's setting off by himself in his raft, as usual, in the late afternoon. There's a hard, distant look on his face, and in the bottom of the raft the bottles of beer make a clinking sound as they roll together. Earlier Cory heard her mother telling him that he would have to get a job or West wouldn't let him stay with them anymore. "The two of you can go to hell," Uncle Steve said.

"No," Uncle Steve says now, but Cory begs.

The wind is up this afternoon, and the restless feel of the wind is in her blood. Tomorrow they're going home and back to everyday life; she longs for that ordinariness and chafes against it. The wind is hot flowing through the canyon and beats the water with hard little slaps.

"Get in," he says.

For an instant, seeing his face, feeling his anger, Cory hesitates. She looks back up the bank to the little cabin. Under the scrub oak, peaceful as a dream, her parents read, her mother from Mrs. Eddy, her father from Zane Grey. Kevin plays with his Lincoln logs. Her mother looks up and waves, "Have a good time!"

Cory waves back. She jumps in the raft and she and her uncle are carried away by a swift current.

They're going to the secret emerald pool. It's a place no one else knows about, where no one else knows to come and fish. It's invisible from the river, guarded by the big black boulder. When you get to the boulder you have to paddle hard to the right to go by it and into the pool of dappled green darkness.

Uncle Steve puts the raft ashore and Cory immediately begins to build a town from the river pebbles, surrounded by a complicated network of dams and locks.

Her uncle is on the shore too, up to his knees in the shadows of the green water. He lines up his brown bottles of beer in a row. There are more than usual. He doesn't say anything for a long time, only drinks and fishes, and Cory, with her back turned, half forgets about him. The water sloshes at her feet and the wind is hot and dry in her hair. She is opening and closing locks, raising and lowering the water levels, creating droughts and floods.

"Cory," he calls to her in a strange, thick voice, and she turns, startled and expectant. Perhaps he's caught the big trout he claims is hiding in the deepest darkest part of the pool.

But he's standing there, a few feet away from her, his white skin reflected in the dark green water. For a second she doesn't understand how his skin can be so white, when it is usually so brown and tan. Then she sees, she understands, that his bathing trunks are down and he's holding his penis straight and heavy in his hand.

"Come here, Peanut," he says, in that same thick voice, using her father's word for her. "I want to teach you something nice."

The canyon walls are steep and there are no handholds up to safety. The current is too fast to swim away and the pool is guarded by the black boulder. Everything is too loud to hear what to do. Underneath the water's surface the fish are tearing past, screaming with open mouths, Fly, flee. Fly, flee.

But Cory's legs are paralyzed, the world is paralyzed by the sight of her uncle. His eyes have locked on hers, with a look that is partly pleasure and partly the joy of causing pain, and the look is so new and so strong that Cory can't break the spell.

"Come here," he says. "Come here."

She opens her mouth to say no, but no words come out. She tries to take a step back, but he lunges forward and grabs her arm, catching her, forcing her head down.

On the way back to California, no one wants to stop in Jerome. They left the cabin sleepily at six in the morning, and it's still early when they go by the turn-off that reads 15,000, 10,000, 4,000, 1,000, Ghost Town. West is driving and Cory and Kevin sit up front with him. West smokes his pipe and the smell of cherry tobacco is a thin curl of comfort in the cold car.

Polly and Uncle Steve talk in low tones in the back seat.

"Yes, I plan to look for work as soon as we get back," Steve says sincerely.

Polly says, "It's only that Mother *worries* about you so."

"There's nothing to worry about," Steve says.

"You know how mothers are," says Polly, and Cory hears her voice from far away, as if underwater. "They couldn't bear it if anything happened to their children."

"The best thing," says Uncle Steve with a laugh, "is just to keep quiet. That way, mothers don't know enough to worry. They feel better."

Where do memories go when the years blanket them with red dust? Where does a spirit go when a body is abandoned? Where do the people of a cliff dwelling or a ghost town go when their homes become uninhabitable?

Cory looks out at the broken silhouette of the old copper mining town. If she tries she can almost hear the muffled explosions inside the hill that brought the houses crashing down and flung the streets helter-skelter so that it was impossible to walk directly from one place to another anymore. If she tries, she can almost hear the screams of people trapped inside their buried houses. Did anyone ever come to dig them out? How far away the screaming is. No one else can hear it.

West switches on the radio to hear the news and static crackles weakly out. The ghost town is behind them now; it has disappeared in a cloud of dust. Cory leans into her father's solid bulk and closes her eyes.

Memory will flow around that week, that day, that afternoon, like a river around a boulder. Everything else will be transparent as water, rushing by and always changing. But the black boulder, smooth and mute, will never change or move. It will stay there, guarding the pool, a rock dense as grief, as silent as hardened lava.

HIPPO

CORY AND KEVIN were supposed to water, but they always forgot, and now in late July, most of the flowers in the garden had withered into sticks poking out from a dusty mulch of papery brown petals. The roses had not been sprayed or pruned for almost a year, and their leaves were spotted and chewed. Only the apricot tree had continued to thrive and to bear fruit, as if it needed nothing more than sun and the rains that came of their own accord in January and February. In the spring it had flowered and now, midsummer, it spread its wide canopy of heart-shaped leaves over a blanket of split, pulpy fruit, uneaten and uncollected.

West had left Cory strict instructions that Saturday morning before he left for the hospital. She and Kevin were to clean their rooms thoroughly, straighten up the rest of the house, wash the dishes and water the back yard. It should only take them a couple of hours and by eleven, eleven-thirty at the latest, he would be home to take them to Disneyland.

All summer long they'd been waiting to see if they were going to have a vacation, like last year when they went to Arizona. West kept saying, "We'll see, we'll see how strong your mother's feeling."

We'll see and see, and this is what it came down to, a day at

Disneyland, the three of them without Polly, who lay in a bed at the hospital.

Still, it wasn't often they'd been to Disneyland, three times at most. The first time Kevin didn't remember and Cory had only been six. Disneyland had just opened. There were no freeways then; they had to drive long miles on Lincoln Highway, past dairy farms and through thick orange groves. And then suddenly Sleeping Beauty's castle rose up from the uniform groves, and they walked down Main Street and saw Abraham Lincoln speak and there were horseless carriages and ice cream parlors and before you knew it you were in Tomorrowland, where you could see how everyone would live in the future.

As soon as West left the house that morning Kevin and Cory hastily made their beds and picked up the living room. Then they got out the map of the Magic Kingdom from a previous visit and began to plan their day. Just before eleven they'd do the dishes (the watering—tomorrow—they'd do that tomorrow), but for now they needed to spread out the map on the floor of Cory's bedroom so they could see every possibility.

"Spinning teacups! The Matterhorn! Tom Sawyer's Island!" Kevin shouted. The black-framed glasses he had recently been forced to wear sat on his soft, unformed nose like a disguise, serving to hide the startling color of his smoke-blue eyes.

At seven he was still small for his age, but agile and quick, unlike Cory who no longer felt as if her body fit her. She was pudgy and awkward now at ten, and didn't like to run or play softball as much as before. The way he smelled reminded Cory of her own childhood, the way she'd smelled a long time ago, milky and soft, like crayons and fresh dirt ground into an elbow scrape. She wanted him to stay that way. Ever since he'd been born he'd been part of her, belonging more to her than to her parents. His loyalty to her was—it had to be—complete. It was the footstool she stood on to reach where she had to go.

"We'll go to Adventureland first," said Cory. "That's the best."

"It's the best," echoed Kevin, but his fingers touched the sharp peak of the Matterhorn.

Adventureland was the place where the Swiss Family Robinson tree house was and the Jungle Cruise, where you took a flat-bottomed boat with a striped awning down a murky river—it could have been Africa or the Amazon or Thailand—a landscape dense with banana trees and bamboo, where brilliant macaws screeched in the criss-cross lianas and monkeys swung bright-eyed over the depths where tigers lurked. They saw elephants in a wallow, squirting each other and even the boat, and some giraffes at a distance and a horned rhino too. The safari guide told them on no account to put their hands in the water, because of the crocodiles, but secretly Cory did it anyway. There was a bumpy rock in the river, gray and glistening where the river washed over it like silk, a thin transparency of green-brown water parting at the crown of the boulder like hair falling down on either side. Two little beige leaves sprouted on top. She was hardly looking at the boulder, but suddenly it was looking at her. It had small bright enraged eyes under bulging lids, at the waterline, and the leaves were its ears. The rock glared, and then it sank, without a trace, not even a bubble.

The guide had been courageous and stern about their journey, but even he seemed frightened when the head roared back up out of the water in a different place, and the huge mouth opened pink and cruel. "Hippo on the left!" he shouted and everyone cringed and fell back. A rifle popped and the hippopotamus sank back down.

"'Member? Mama was scared of that ride," Kevin said.

But this was forbidden. They never talked about Polly between themselves. It was a secret how thin and distant Polly had become. They called her Mama still, but they'd lost the easy habit of being with her. When she came home from the hospital, the door to her bedroom was usually shut; the whole house had a sign over it that read: Quiet.

"She wasn't scared," Cory said, in spite of herself, the longing to speak her name rising up. "Because she knew that none of it was real. Just like sickness isn't real," she reminded Kevin.

Once Cory wouldn't have even have used the word *sickness*, but that was when her mother still read her the Lesson every day. Now they rarely went to Sunday School even though Mildred Clark offered to drive them. Polly went to church sometimes still; she prayed and read the Bible and the Lesson when she was at home, and sometimes she read it to Cory and Kevin, in a weak voice that never sounded convincing. She would not name her illness because that gave it more power. But everyone around her called it sickness, and sometimes they used the word, in whispers, *cancer*.

Cory used to think that only Spirit was real, and not the body. But now she was confused. Laurie next door explained that cancer was a growth, but it seemed to Cory to be more about loss. For a long time she didn't understand that her mother had lost a breast. No one had said anything about it. They only said *operation*. Cory didn't know that operation meant *removal*. But one morning, early, she had pushed her way sleepily into the bathroom just as Polly stepped out of the shower and reached for a towel. Seeing Cory, Polly immediately clutched the towel to her chest, but not before Cory saw that next to the empty sack of a breast on the right, there was only a pink and white glistening scar that ran from under her armpit up to her collarbone.

Eleven o'clock had come and gone, and so had twelve. West called at twelve-thirty and said he'd be on his way shortly and had they done the dishes? Yes, Cory said.

They went into the kitchen and started washing up. Cory threw some banana skins down the garbage disposal and ran it long and hard. She didn't know why, but for a while now when they washed dishes she'd had the urge to put her arm down the drain, or her brother's arm, or some piece of flesh that she could see get ground up into gristle and blood.

As usual Cory washed and Kevin dried, and she told him a story about the Feeble Family.

Mr. and Mrs. had gone and Jack and Nancy were all alone in the world. Kevin had asked once what happened to their adventurous Uncle Valiant and Cory said harshly, They never had an uncle, he was pretending.

The stories were uglier now, and worse and more scary things happened to Jack and Nancy. The Land of Glass was full of shards and the Land of Fire burned the soles of their feet.

Kevin didn't like some of these new stories as much as he had the old ones, but he listened anyway, drawn in by Cory's telling, and Cory liked seeing how she could frighten him with some of the descriptions. To him Jack and Nancy Feeble were real people and sometimes he was Jack and things that happened to Jack, happened to him. To Cory, Jack and Nancy Feeble were only characters in a story, and she could do whatever she wanted with them.

Today she decided to send them on a mission through rat-infested sewers and weedy pestilent ponds to the source of all filth, the great Volcano of Mud. In the past Jack and Nancy would have figured out a way to plug up the crater before it erupted and would have saved the villagers whose huts and farms lay directly under its path, but now Jack and Nancy had to watch helplessly as the thick, choking mud spurted up out of the mountain top and poured in a hot gooey mass down the slope towards them, burying everything and everybody who had been stupid enough to try to live there.

"Jack and Nancy Feeble ran and ran, but they couldn't run as fast as the boiling volcanic mud, and pretty soon the mud was at their heels. Because Jack was littler and not as fast as Nancy, the mud got him. He was covered with it, it was in his nose and eyes and down his throat, and into his stomach and he couldn't throw it up, it just stayed there and then he died."

Cory paused and let the dish water out. It gurgled away, leaving dirty foam clinging to the sides of the sink.

"But Nancy was spared."

Kevin frowned. "You mean, she got away?"

"Yes, that's what *spared* means."

"It's not fair," said Kevin. "Why does Jack always get hurt?"

"Because he's too little and weak," said Cory. "Too weak to defend himself."

"Am not!"

"Are too!"

They wet their dishcloths and went out into a far corner of the back yard, behind the rose bushes to a mound that had been left when the old sandbox was taken apart and grass grew over the sand. It was a new harsh game that Cory had invented: whipping each other with the wet cloths on the legs and back. They played until Kevin's glasses fell off and he cried. Once Cory would have been punished for touching her younger brother; now no one knew and no one cared.

Then they played Bad Man. Like the whipping, Cory didn't know where this idea came from. It was about running away, running with panic in your throat, back and forth. "He's coming, he's coming!" They had played this at the ocean, running over the dunes, clutching at their throats—"He's coming, he's coming," and then collapsing with relief when they saw the ocean stretching far and wide, the calm lapping waves. In the back yard they worked themselves into a kind of hysteria, running away and away, and then, chastened, they came back into the house and tried to be good again.

They scrubbed the kitchen sink and cleaned the bathtub with Ajax. They vacuumed. When the phone rang they thought it was their father, and rushed to get it, but it was only Grandma.

Grandma had come to stay for a month right after Polly's operation last fall. They had to eat big dinners of meat and potatoes and say Yes Ma'am, No Ma'am. Cory learned to make cake from scratch and to iron sheets, and Kevin had to polish Grandma's white Swiss-cheese shoes. They had to go to bed at eight o'clock and miss *Wagon Train*, and their father wouldn't even stand up for them. "Do what Grandma tells you, kids," he said. "It's easier all around." Grandma's rayon dress went swish, swish, swish, as she thumped from the kitchen to their parents' room with glasses of water and juice for Polly. Wasn't it just like Polly, her every movement said, to have failed at a religion that healed everybody else?

Mildred Clark was the only person allowed to visit because other people were supposed to be too tiring. Mildred and Grandma would sit on either side of Polly's bed in metal fold-up chairs like they had in church, and they would pray with their heads down. And through the half-closed door to her parents' room, Cory heard the endless arguments go on, Grandma in a stern voice, Mildred in her rich, reasonable one, both of them telling Polly she must let go of the false beliefs that made her think she was ill, and at the very least she must not take the pain medication the doctor had given her, the pills in the brown bottles lined up haphazardly on the night stand like soldiers that had never been called on to defend anything before.

But when Polly didn't take the pain medication, she cried, and she and Grandma quarreled, and Polly said, "I don't care! You're not me, you don't know how it feels!" And finally Grandma left again for Michigan, saying it was clear that Uncle Steve needed her more. "Yes," Cory had heard her father saying in a scornful voice. "He needs her to buy him his bottles at the corner store. How she reconciles that with Christian Science is beyond me."

"Cory?" said Grandma's flat high voice on the phone. "Where's your father?"

"He's at the hospital, Grandma."

"Is everything all right? I can't get through to your mother's room there. They say she's not taking calls."

"Everything is fine, Grandma," Cory said . nechanically. "We're going to Disneyland in a little while, we're going to Adventureland to go on the jungle cruise, and a bunch of stuff. Disneyland stays open really late, you know!"

"That's good," said Grandma, not listening. "I'm going to try the hospital again now. When you see your father, tell him to call me."

"Okay. Bye."

"Well, I guess we're not going to get to do everything at Disneyland," said Cory. "So we better decide."

She saw in Kevin's eyes how the afternoon shrank, how the possibilities declined.

"Maybe two lands," she allowed. "You choose one. I'll choose one. I choose Adventureland."

Good-bye to Autopia! Good-bye to the submarine voyage!

"Tomorrowland," said Kevin. "The Matterhorn."

Cory was ruthless. A few hours ago, the whole day stretched before them, and now she'd become parsimonious and calculating. She was no longer living in her imagination but in a mathematical universe where every pleasure could be measured and compared.

"I don't think we *can* go the Matterhorn," she said. "Because we might have to stand in line for half an hour and we would be wasting time. We should go on the rides that aren't so popular, because they'll have the shortest lines. Like Dumbo."

That was how life got reduced to its smallest, most practical elements. Don't try for the impossible, accept what you can get. Dumbo the Flying Elephant was for babies, really, nothing like as thrilling as the Matterhorn, but it was within reach.

"Don't want to go on Dumbo," Kevin muttered.

"Well, you have to. You have to do what I want."

It was three o'clock. They went out and splashed some water quickly around the roses, so the earth would get wet and it would look like they had watered, but the ground was so dry that nothing soaked in. The water pooled strangely in dusty beads and bubbles and slid over the surface like oil. Kevin asked if they could go to the guest room, but Cory didn't like to go there anymore, since last summer when Uncle Steve had stayed there. The guest room had gotten all mixed up with his smells and it made her feel sick to even think about the thin brown rug that covered the brown and tan tiles. Polly had gotten the rug at a yard sale and had had it cleaned, but the cleaning smell had never left it and had gotten combined with Grandma's old lady white talc and Uncle Steve's whiskey and cigarette ashes. Sometimes even, when Cory was in her father's office, she could catch a faint whiff of the rug coming through the bathroom and underneath the hollow core door, and it was like the rug smashed her face and rubbed it up and down. Sometimes even the comforting fragrance of her father's pipe tobacco and leather-bound accounting books and the sun on the redwood siding wasn't enough to keep out the smell of the guest room. It seeped through like a thin creeping poisonous fog that pressed against her face and made her feel like throwing up.

They decided to go into their parents' room instead. But it stank too. It used to smell like Pond's Cold Cream and fresh laundered shirts and furniture wax. Now it smelled of sickness. The air didn't come and go, as in the rest of the house, it just sat there, like morning breath that lasts all day. It smelled like sweet medicine, cloying, and like dust bunnies under the bureau, and of physical odors that couldn't be washed away, urine and vomit and the dark smell of a body turning itself inside out and decomposing.

And yet they had to love the smell because it was their mother's, and all that they had of her.

They jumped on the bed a while and looked in the drawers. They would get in trouble if their father came home and found them there, but he wasn't going to come home, they knew that now.

Nobody cared about them, and how they felt. Adults were

mean and selfish, and their mother was the most selfish of all. She lay there looking like her old self, only paler and thinner, but she acted completely different. Can you get me a glass of water, she said, but when Cory ran to get it, carefully, pulling the ice tray from the freezer, jerking the metal level back, filling the special glass with the daisies around the brim, rushing back with it, all she could say was Thank you and close her eyes.

In the beginning there were always too many people around Polly, but later when there was nobody, Polly didn't seem to want Cory and Kevin either. Cory could have read to her, the old Bible stories or fairy tales or the *Sentinel* stories about illness being just a bad dream that you could wake from if you tried hard enough, if you prayed long enough, if you really truly believed. But Polly didn't want Cory's company, or only for short periods. Mostly all her mother wanted—when Cory could have given so much—was to be alone.

West came home about seven, after Cory had heated up some Swanson's Chicken Pot Pies and they were watching television. Her father was always unimaginably old, thirty when she was born and middle-aged now. They all used to joke about the white hairs in his dark brilliantined hair, but now most of his head was dull gray and even his eyebrows had stiff gray hairs sticking out. They used to joke too about how fat he was getting, but now, without even getting any exercise, he was skinnier. He had deflated somehow, and his skin hung loose as rhino hide and his trousers bunched around his waist. He had folds in his cheeks, too, as if something had fallen down that was holding up his old cheerful expression.

Everyone was always saying what a good father he was. Her fourth-grade teacher Miss Peeper had said it, and Sharie Palmer and Mildred Clark and, once, even Grandma. But he wasn't a good father, he just did what he had to. He shuttled between the hospital, his classes and home, and when he was home he was usually out in his office working on people's taxes for extra money. He did the shopping and the cooking. Mostly they ate scrambled eggs or chicken pot pies or minute steaks that came in stacks of twenty—thin squares of tough, chewy, compressed meat, individually wrapped.

When he first told them their mother was sick last year, he had been angry and scared, but now it was like he was deep in some dark place where they couldn't go, like a prospector in an abandoned mine, chipping and chipping with his pick at a worn-out vein of silver.

At first West said nothing when he arrived. He simply sat in a chair and stared. They were angry and tried to ignore him. He didn't even apologize!

"Your mother," he said finally. "She's not doing too well. All day we were waiting for the tests to come back. They said they'd come back at ten, and then eleven. But the lab was behind, and then it was lunch. The afternoon went by, your mother wouldn't eat a bite. She's so tired of their food, and of the hospital.

"I know I shouldn't be telling you this," said West. "Not like this. But I'm at the end of my rope. Your grandmother kept calling and Polly refused to speak to her. The tests came back—the illness has spread. They want to do another operation. Your mother said no."

There were tears in his blue eyes.

"Dad," said Cory. "Daddy, stop." Kevin shouldn't be hearing this. He was staring at the TV screen, rigid in his little boy jeans and T-shirt.

West was oblivious. A tear ran down his cheek. "I talked to your grandmother because Polly wouldn't. She said, 'Of course Polly shouldn't have another operation. She shouldn't have had one in the first place.' I said, 'Cora, you realize what you're saying? Do you realize what it means?'" He put his head in his hands. "I give up. When you get married, you marry a family. Never forget that, Cory."

"Dad," she interrupted. "We don't care that we couldn't go to Disneyland today. I mean, it's not like it's going anywhere, is it? We can go next weekend, or the weekend after. We have our lives to go to Disneyland. It's not that big a deal, is it, Kev?"

"No," he mumbled, without looking at his father, hunched in his chair, or his sister, standing urgently between them.

"Because the next time we'll have all day," Cory said. The image of her mother, thin and weak in a hospital gown, reading and refusing to eat, rose up in her mind. "Mama can go with us next time. We'll do everything, even the most scary things," she said to her father's crushed shoulders.

"The Matterhorn?" said Kevin, his eyes beginning to shine.

"'Course the Matterhorn. As many times as we want." Cory's voice was strong and confident. She could feel the cold winds rushing at their cheeks and the sickening drop of their stomachs as they fell and fell, only to gather their powers and grind slowly up the incline again. "'Course the Matterhorn!"

Cory went to sleep immediately that night, but when the phone rang she was bolt awake. She heard her father answer it but she couldn't hear the words. Was it the hospital? Was it her mother dying? Was it her grandmother?

Her father put the phone down, and she heard him weeping in the living room. She almost got up but didn't have the courage, and eventually she heard his footsteps go into the bathroom and then into his room.

He would have told her if Mama had died, wouldn't he?

She lay there thinking of Disneyland, of all the rides they could have gone on, and her mind went back to the Jungle Cruise, to the murky green water, to the claustrophobic vines hanging down, to the eyes glinting from the darkness. Her mother had jumped half out of her seat and put her hand to her heart when the hippo surged like a volcano up out of the dirty green water, roaring in fury, its huge mouth gaping like a pink and white scar, the stumpy teeth glistening with greed. But Cory hadn't been afraid of the roaring hippo head; if you could see it you could fight it, you could pop it with a gun and kill it dead. What was frightening was knowing it was there, somewhere under the surface. You might be the only one who knew it was there, the only one who had seen those angry little eyes staring at you right at the waterline. But what was frightening was not the moment you saw the eyes, not even the moment when the rock started to turned into a monster. It was the moment when the hippo sank back under the water's surface, when you wanted to say, "Something was there!" but you didn't, because you knew that no one else had seen it, and no one would ever believe you.

HULA GIRLS

CORY'S MOTHER, POLLY, had never been like other mothers. It wasn't just that she was more religious than anybody else in a religion that wasn't like anybody else's, it was that she didn't like to do things that other mothers did.

Cory's mother didn't like to cook or clean. She didn't know how to sew or knit. Polly had never baked anything besides a Betty Crocker cake, and mostly it was so they could lick the batter off the beaters and sides of the mixing bowl. For dinner they always had hamburgers or fish fingers or cheap steak with Tater-Tots or mashed potatoes from a package, along with a salad of iceberg lettuce and cottage cheese sitting on a pineapple ring. Their only cookbook was *The Joy of Cooking;* it stayed on the shelf, unused. Polly had showed Cory how to wash dishes and how to make a bed and when to put the fruit cocktail in the Jell-O, but other than that, she didn't pass on much that was domestic or useful. No recipes were handed down, no Polly Winter methods of keeping house. The housework that Polly liked and had Cory help her with was mostly for fun: polishing some silverware with paste and a rag; spraying lemony Pledge over the furniture and buffing it to a gloss; hanging up wet clothes on the line to dry in the sun.

Polly had been a kindergarten teacher and she knew a hundred things to make and do, and how to change what was ordinary into what was new and magical. She could turn a milk bottle into a painted vase holding silk flowers; she could make an Easter hat or a Halloween mask from a paper plate; she could transform a shoe box into a boat or a train, a house with windows or even a diorama that you could look at through a hole at one end. She knew how to make her own Play-Doh from cornstarch and papier-mâché from newspaper strips and flour and water. The Winters' house was always littered with construction paper and dried hunks of paste and bits of clay, and every shelf held wobbly play-doh figures and lumpy painted papier-mâché trays and animals.

No other home Cory had ever been in was like this. In most houses there were ironing boards and baskets of laundry, and macaroni and cheese or tuna and potato-chip casseroles, and soap operas on TV with their droning sweet music and wide-eyed heroines getting news of disaster and death. Other mothers vacuumed around their family's feet and cooked meatloaf with oatmeal and made new curtains or went to work or had a hobby like cats or knitting. If these mothers went to church they only went on Sunday mornings all dressed up in hats and dresses. They didn't spend hours reading the Bible and praying. If they had gardens they had simple ones, with snapdragons and pansies and here and there a yucca or an avocado tree.

Polly prayed to excess, and gardened that way too. No other mothers spent so much time watering, weeding, mulching and planting. No other mothers grew the kinds of flowers and plants that Polly did, all riotous and fruity and clashing with reds and oranges. Cory didn't see other mothers from the kitchen window late at night, standing in the rose garden, pressing petals to their faces and wailing out to God in an angry, lonely voice. No other mothers walked up and down the yard when the dew was wet on the grass, crying that they were too young, that they had believed what they had been taught, that it wasn't fair, that they didn't want to die.

From the beginning, right after Polly went into the hospital last fall for her operation and radiation treatment, Cory was thrown upon the goodwill and guilt of other women, other kinds of mothers. Grandma first and then Mildred Clark. But after Grandma went back to Michigan, her father began to put Cory in the hands of neighbors and friends. Her father seemed to feel that he could manage Kevin all right, but that Cory, being a girl, needed something more, needed something mysterious and female.

Yolanda Ray Cory had known all her life. She lived next door to the Winters with her longshoreman husband and three children. Once, when Cory was three, Yolanda had taken care of her for an afternoon. Even at that age Cory was terrified of Yolanda's brisk and unforgiving nature, too terrified that day to ask to go to the bathroom. Yolanda had been pushing her in a stroller; when she yanked Cory out and saw the mess in her pants, she shouted "Filthy pig" at her and dragged her upstairs where she ran a bath and made Cory sit in it, the loose turds floating and crumbling all around her. "You'll never do that again, will you, young lady," she said. "This will teach you."

Yolanda wore wide flowered skirts cinched tight at the waist, and short-sleeved knit sweaters with a strand of false pearls around her neck. Her black hair was tied back from her face with a scarf and her lips and fingernails were red as bougainvillea. She was always screaming—at her daughter, at her husband and sometimes you could hear her on Saturdays, shrieking wildly next door, though Polly said with a smile that she wasn't really being murdered, she was just practicing her solo for Sunday at the Baptist church.

During one of the times that Polly was in the hospital for a long stretch, Cory's father came up with the idea that Cory needed to learn to sew. It might have been because buttons were falling off her clothes and her zippers were breaking—at any rate, he got it into his head that Yolanda Ray would be the perfect person to teach Cory what he called the sewing basics. So every Wednesday evening for a few weeks Cory went next door to the Rays' house.

They started with buttons and simple mending. Yolanda handed Cory a box of buttons of different shapes and sizes, from brass to wood, square and round and diamond. "Tiny stitches! Tiny stitches! Cory!" The living room was dark and cluttered with colonial furniture, pine and maple, slip-covered with a print of horses and carriages. Above the rocking chair, where Yolanda sat sewing, was a perfectly embroidered sampler: "East or West/ Home Is Best." Polly would have let Cory look carefully at the wealth of buttons but Yolanda said, "Your father's not paying me to let you sit around, young lady," and gave her a sharp look, as if she could see right through Cory's square of cloth to the bunches of knots and thread wads that grew like tree fungus under each button.

Bernie Ray sat snoring behind his newspaper. Sometimes the radio was on, but more often it was quiet in the lamplight—not a peaceful silence, but a seething one. Upstairs the three Ray children, all older than Cory, did their homework or talked to their friends on the telephone or played their Elvis records. From time to time Yolanda would scream up at them to turn that damn wailing off, or for Laurie to get her butt down here and finish cleaning up the kitchen. Whenever fifteen-year-old Laurie came downstairs Cory would get a respite, as Yolanda lectured her: "You need to get a haircut. And why can't you straighten up and lose some weight? I'm twice your age and you don't see an ounce of fat on me."

Laurie hung her head so her greasy brown bangs fell in her eyes and Yolanda looked at her in disgust, with a loathing so profound she could hardly speak. "Have you been popping your pimples again?"

Laurie and Cory never spoke now, though they had played together sometimes when they were younger. It was too dangerous in that house. But how could a mother hate her own daughter, Cory wondered. A mother might fall ill, go away, become a stranger, feather-thin and haunted around the eyes, but she would still kiss you when she saw you, would still ask about school and your friends. She might not be able to play with you or help you, but she would still smile when she saw you. She wouldn't try— on purpose—to hurt you.

After buttons and learning to sew a straight seam, Yolanda had Cory make a handkerchief and then a small tablecloth. Yolanda got her started on a sampler, too, a pre-printed one from a package that said "Happiness Is a Hug." At first there was something fun about fitting one wooden hoop into another to make a tight drum of cloth, and the array of bright soft embroidery threads. But very soon it was like everything else that Yolanda gave her to do, only a way of making her feel small and stupid. She felt Yolanda's eyes on her, how Yolanda looked at her with dislike. Yolanda and Polly had never been friends. "Oh, Yolanda thinks I'm a terrible housekeeper," Polly used to laugh, and then, sobering, "I'm so sorry for Laurie sometimes. I know how she must feel."

One evening when Cory had been dreaming and dawdling over her sampler more than usual, Yolanda called up her father and made West come over. Then, over Cory's head, she told West that she'd taught Cory everything she could and that it was hopeless to try anything more, that until Cory could get her head out of the clouds, she would never learn anything. And she wrenched the little hoop and cloth out of Cory's hands and showed it scornfully to West. The motto had been stitched in, though crookedly, but Cory had come to grief on the rosebuds, which required some sort of French knot that she couldn't quite master. The back of the cloth was tangled like an overgrown garden, and there were spots of blood here and there.

Since Polly's operation West had grown less sure of himself and more ready to believe that he was in the wrong. "I never should have paid any attention to that cockamamie religion," he sometimes said. Now he took his daughter home again and said, "Well at least you know how to sew on buttons. I suppose that's something useful anyway."

"Why doesn't Kevin have to learn to sew?" she asked.

"No reason why he couldn't. I sewed on my own buttons when I was in the Army."

"Then why don't you teach us to sew?"

But her father said he was too busy.

After this Sharie Palmer across the street and two doors down came into the picture. She took an interest in Cory's hair, which was universally believed to be difficult. She would take Cory with her to the beauty parlor every two weeks and put her into the hands of Irma with a martyred sigh. "See what you can do with it this time, Irma." And Irma, after quickly setting Sharie's perky bubble hairdo and whisking her under the dryer, would run her fingers gloomily through Cory's hair. "I've never seen hair that grew so fast . . . and it's not like it's particularly *pretty* hair for there to be so much of it. And the cowlicks! I keep thinking that we've got to try the Pixie cut, though I worry. I tell you, I worry. She's got such a round little face, that if I take off too much, she's going to look like a bowling ball."

Sharie Palmer's house was full of breakables, which was strange because she had two sons, younger than Cory, who were very athletic. In fact, it was only Cory who broke things there: the trunk off a glass elephant, the leg off a china ballerina "in the family for three generations."

"You only have to look at something for it to break," Sharie often sighed. But in fact it was Sharie who only had to look at Cory—with that concerned, expectant frown—for Cory to break something.

"I used to tell your mother," Sharie said, "When I saw you tearing up and down the sidewalks on your skates or playing softball with the boys, I used to say to Polly, that girl should be playing with other girls. It's all right for boys to roughhouse, but girls shouldn't be encouraged. If I had a girl I'd dress her up in frills and send her to dancing school, I told Polly. But Polly always laughed—you know how she was . . . is. And now you see the result."

Sharie wasn't cruel like Yolanda, and she never exactly told Cory not to come over. She gave Cory chocolate milk and let her read novels lying on the couch, books about boys who blew up their faces with firecrackers, and then went blind and got really nice guide dogs, that made Cory cry. But after a few too many breakages, Cory began to avoid Sharie's, and when Irma's threatened Pixie took off most of her hair, Cory stopped going to the beauty parlor with Sharie too.

Linda Spritz was Janet Spritz's mother. Years ago Mr. Spritz had died in a car accident and Linda had never remarried but had brought Janet up by herself. The two of them lived in the next block and Janet and Cory were in the same Bluebird troop, but Cory and Janet had never spent much time together. Whenever Cory went over to Janet's, things happened. Dolls lost their hair, parts of puzzles went missing, something that was supposed to be saved for company got eaten, and Cory was always blamed.

But West knew Linda Spritz from the community college where she had taken his basic bookkeeping class after her husband was killed and, after Polly got sick, Janet started inviting Cory over after school sometimes.

Linda Spritz and Janet shared a large bedroom with two identical twin beds covered in pink chenille. There were two identical white-painted French provincial chests and two milk-glass lamps with ruffled pink shades on each chest, and two quilted jewelry boxes, a white one for Linda and a pink one for Janet. They both had curly brown hair and freckles and wore skirts and sweaters that often matched.

Linda said, "We're as close as a mother and daughter can be." She said, "I think of Janet as more a *friend* than a daughter."

Linda did talk to Janet as if they were friends the same age, but underneath the sweetness of the plural was a hidden threat: "Sweetie, wouldn't be a good idea if we put away the toys, *now*?"

Linda talked to Cory in the same confiding yet erasing way. Janet was used to it and knew the messages under the questions, but Cory didn't and would answer as if she were being allowed to give a real opinion. So that when Linda said, "Aren't they expecting you at home soon, Cory?" Cory might answer, "Oh no, not for another hour," and then be surprised when Linda glared at her.

The only thing Cory had heard about femininity was that it had something to do with being a girl. She thought it was connected with hygiene perhaps, she wasn't sure. But femininity was a word that Linda Spritz used all the time; it had to do with the color pink, eau de cologne (Friendship Garden from Avon, light and fruity, girls should never wear perfume) and ways of sitting (knees together) and talking (quietly). Janet had always been feminine, Linda told Cory; it was the main thing a mother could pass on to her daughter.

Once Cory asked Janet what it was like not to have a father.

"I was just little when he died," Janet said. "So I don't really know. Sometimes I remember sitting on his knee, or how he laughed, but mostly he's just in the photos."

She was a deliberate, careful, sad, don't-touch kind of girl, Janet, and now she looked thoughtfully at Cory. "But I think it must be better to lose a father than a mother. Because a mother is a girl like you. And if you don't have a mother, there's nobody to teach you anything."

That August, when Polly couldn't be home anymore but needed to be in the hospital all the time, Kevin was packed off to visit their grandmother in Michigan and Cory was taken to spend two weeks with Dorothy Dragon.

Dorothy was a Christian Scientist, but not a very pure one. The first time Cory met her, Dorothy had been sitting in her back yard wearing pedal-pushers and a chartreuse bathing suit top with sharply outlined cups, and drinking a Budweiser from a can and smoking unfiltered Camels. Cory had rarely seen anyone— much less a woman—drink or smoke before, and she always thought of Dorothy Dragon as wicked and exciting. West got on with Dorothy better than with most Christian Scientists, perhaps because of the drinking and smoking, and maybe that was why he asked her if Cory could spend some time there that summer.

Like most of the women Cory had ever met, Dorothy Dragon had a husband who worked and who read the newspaper and said little. Unlike most women Dorothy didn't have any children. She had two miniature poodles instead, a gray one and a black one, named Rover and Randy. These dogs were very old and had pink rheumy eyes and slept on their fat stomachs in a corner of the living room on two little wicker beds.

Dorothy and her husband lived like adults, not families. The walls of their house were creamy-white, hung with Japanese scrolls of mountains and pines; in the pristine living room the nubby ivory drapes were always drawn. The breakfast nook had wallpaper with a gold and green bamboo design. There were clear glass ashtrays on every surface and a few magazines and the familiar Christian Science publications on the teak coffee tables, though Cory never saw Dorothy reading them. There were also a number of exotic sculptures carved in dark wood of women with naked pointy breasts and elongated heads. A record player console in the hallway played Frank Sinatra and some of the big band numbers that Cory's father liked.

On either side of the front porch Spanish dagger yucca plants dueled with sharp stiff blades. Umbrella palms softened the lines of the square house with their grassy clumps. A small path of stones led up to the house, with miniature metal lanterns on either side, lending everything a mysterious air. Dorothy Dragon did not garden, she landscaped. There were no roses or fruit trees here. Next to Dorothy Dragon's back yard, Polly Winter's garden was as gaudy as a carnival. "Ornamental" was a word that Dorothy often used; it was a different kind of boldness than Cory had known. It was the boldness of sharp edges and unusual plants. Against the back fence giant bamboo canes formed a massive green wall that rustled in the wind. The canes gave off a coolness, as of being underwater. Smaller clumps of Chinese goddess bamboo and dwarf bamboo were planted around a small basin hollowed out from a single flat stone.

Being in the back yard was like being in another country, an empty Asian country, a quiet country with nothing much to do or to look at, not for kids but for grown-ups.

Dorothy Dragon took Cory in hand, but in quite a different way than Yolanda or Sharie had. She didn't try to tell Cory anything or teach her anything. She was mostly concerned that Cory not "hang around the house" and so for the first two days she was always sending Cory off on errands to the nearby grocery store or pharmacy.

Cory liked that. She took her time and looked closely at everything around her, just the way she liked best. Dorothy Dragon seemed bemused by having Cory around; she wasn't friendly or unfriendly, she just didn't have a good idea what to say to Cory. In the mornings when Cory got up, Dorothy was usually out in the back yard, working in her garden. She always put out a box of cereal for Cory and a bowl. In the evenings the three of them watched television without talking much. Dorothy didn't seem to care how late Cory was up reading at night, and so Cory stayed up far past midnight, reading all the Laura Ingalls Wilder books again, and all the fairy tales in Andrew Lang's Fairy Tale Books.

Everything that Dorothy said was what she meant. She never said things that you had to try to figure out. She had a tough look to her, not a feminine softness. She never wore dresses or make-up. Her graying blonde hair was pulled back into a knot and her eyebrows were very thick and straight. She didn't talk to her poodles in baby talk, in fact she didn't say much to them at all, nothing except "sit" and "stay" and "time for a walk."

She talked about as much to Cory. "Time for dinner." "Guess I'll hit the sack." "Anybody want ice cream?" West had told Cory when he dropped her off with her suitcase not to be a bother, because Dorothy wasn't used to kids and didn't know how to act with them. It seemed to Cory that Dorothy did know the best way to act with kids and that way was to leave them alone.

But Dorothy must have worried that she wasn't providing enough distraction for a ten-year-old, so after a couple days of sending her on errands for Coke and toilet paper and dog food, Dorothy suddenly announced that she'd enrolled Cory in the YWCA day camp and that starting tomorrow Cory would be spending four hours an afternoon doing crafts, going swimming, and taking hula dancing.

She said it very matter-of-factly: "hula dancing." As if that were something lots of people did and that Cory would be interested in. Cory wasn't interested. But there was something about Dorothy Dragon you just didn't say no to, and anyway, Cory had accepted for the last year that you just had to go along with things if everything wasn't going to be worse than it already was. And so she obediently followed Dorothy Dragon to the YWCA the next afternoon and let herself be enrolled in the girls' day camp classes.

Crafts weren't bad. Molding and squeezing and cutting and pasting and scraping and pounding and lacing and knotting were all soothing, familiar things. She didn't have to worry that she didn't know anyone around her, because she could throw herself into making something and could forget about everything else and then the teacher would come over and say, approvingly, "Very nice, Cory," and she would feel good for a few moments. Praise wasn't love, but it was as close to love as she could get anymore.

But dancing! Hula dancing!

They had to stand in a room with wooden floors and enormous mirrors, fifteen girls all shapes and sizes. Cory was all wrong. She didn't have breasts or any sort of figure yet, not like some of the girls who had a definite difference between their hips and their waists, a difference they seemed comfortable with and that helped them in their dancing.

"Now for the benefit of you new girls, I'll just tell you briefly that the hula comes from Hawaii and is a traditional dance where each gesture has a meaning," said Miss Carson, their teacher. She showed them a palm tree, a grass shack, a rainbow, the trade winds that carried the one you loved far away. "You don't do a lot with your feet—that's good news for some of you. Small steps right and left. Most the movement is in the hips, in getting a rhythm going with your hips and then forgetting the hips and concentrating on the arms and hands as they tell their story.

"So first we're going to practice with the hips and then we'll concentrate on the story the second half of the lesson."

She turned to the portable phonograph in its pink cardboard box and set a 45 rpm record on.

"Now, ro-tate, girls! Swing those hips around—back, side, front, side, back, front, side. Think of a circle. That's right, a nice big circle. And then some little circles, a little faster now. *Feel* the music, *feel* the ocean breezes, and the waves and the sand and the drumming beating beating beating like your heart. Okay, very good . . ." She looked at Cory doubtfully. "This is your first day, right, Cory? Well, don't worry, you'll get the hang of it."

But after Cory had been going to hula dancing class a few days, she still had not gotten the hang of it. If she thought about the hips, she forgot about the hands. If she thought about the story she was telling—a boy goes off in his boat and a girl wishes him a safe journey—somehow her hips stayed still, though she could sometimes shuffle her feet.

Dancing was about feeling, said Miss Carson. But Cory wasn't good about feeling anymore. Mostly all she tried to do was not to make any mistakes and not to get people mad at her. She was so used to that look people threw around her, the doubtful, exasperated one, that it didn't really hurt her the way it used to. She sometimes tried to remember if her mother ever gave her that look, but she didn't think so. She hadn't seen her mother since she went into the hospital the last time. Cory had told her good-bye and she had hugged Cory gently, but her mother had not looked closely at her. She had seemed far away. If Cory had had a mother like Yolanda, she wouldn't care if her mother didn't seem to see her. But Cory hadn't had a mother like that. She'd had one who loved her.

Every day, Cory's father stopped by between his last class at summer school and the hospital. He didn't stay long. Sometimes he had a beer with Dorothy, but usually just iced tea. They sat in the dining room and smoked. He always asked Cory how she was and she always said fine. She had lost the trick of talking with her father this summer. He looked at her as if he couldn't quite remember who she was. Once she had been his Peanut, his favorite. Now he clapped her on the head coming and going, and spent most of his time talking with Dorothy.

"How is she?" Dorothy would ask, low.

And sometimes, if Cory didn't seem to be close by, West would tell her.

That was how Cory knew everything.

She was supposed to stay two weeks with Dorothy, but it had

begun to stretch out to three. Kevin was still in Michigan with Grandma. Occasionally West brought a letter from her. Grandma never asked about Polly, but said she was praying hard for her. Mostly the letters were full of everything Kevin was doing. He had friends on the block, he was in Little League, he was going canoeing and fishing with Uncle Steve.

Cory got a frozen knot, like a stone, in her stomach when her father read that part, about Uncle Steve and the fishing, and she saw the same feeling on her father's face. It made her feel better that her father didn't like Uncle Steve either.

"Is Kevin going to come back?" she asked once, after her father finished reading her a letter.

"Of course he's coming back," West said, surprised. "Next week."

Weeks are long when you're ten. She had thought—sometimes—that maybe they planned to leave her with Dorothy Dragon forever. But if Kevin came back, she would need to go home to take care of him. He was still only seven. The thought, that he needed her, he had always needed her, made Cory feel more like herself, not so much like a ghost wandering through thickets of bamboo.

All the same, after West left that day, during the gray hour when Dorothy and her husband sat having a silent drink in the living room, Cory went to her room and began to kick the legs of the bed. It wasn't fair that Kevin had made friends at Grandma's, and that he was outdoors all day playing catch and softball and hide and go seek. That he got to go canoeing—she had never been canoeing, only on a stupid raft—and everything. That he was having a vacation and she was stuck here.

No one ever made him act like a girl.

No one ever made him sew or sit quietly or be nice and feminine. No one ever made him take hula dancing.

She stopped kicking the bed and got down on her knees and clasped her hands upwards. They didn't pray like this in Christian

Science, they merely bowed their heads, but Cory had seen photographs in *National Geographic* of Catholics in Italy. Praying looked more serious like this.

"Oh God, don't forget about me," she prayed. "Make Mama get better."

Cory closed her eyes and tried to remember all the words from *Science and Health* that pushed away matter and sickness and sin, but all she could think of were the words she'd heard her father say to Dorothy Dragon over the last two weeks:

"Not eating much."

"Refusing everything but pain medication."

"Doctor says it's hopeless."

"Only a matter of weeks, maybe days now."

It wasn't fair. Nothing was fair. Being here. Being a girl. Being a girl without a mother.

Why didn't Dorothy Dragon pray? Why didn't they go to church? Why couldn't Cory visit her mother? Why didn't her mother love her anymore?

There was a knock at the door, but Dorothy didn't come in. "Time to eat, Cory," she said.

And Cory dropped her hands.

Dorothy Dragon was in her patio sunbathing one afternoon when Cory returned from the Y. She had been reading a novel that she immediately turned over so Cory couldn't see the cover, but Cory caught a glimpse of two ladies in slips anyway. Dorothy was drinking a Budweiser and her ashtray was full of cigarettes. Against the green wall of bamboo her tan arms and shoulders stood out like a particularly hard strong kind of wood.

Cory sat by the little pool of water that had been hollowed out of the flat stone. The bamboo made such a lonely sound in the breeze; it made her want to say to Dorothy Dragon, Can I stay here with you in your house? For all of a sudden, she knew clearly—the sound of the lonely tall bamboo in the wind told her—that her mother wasn't going to get better, and that soon she would have no mother. She would have to go back to her father and brother, and they would not be able to teach her to be the kind of girl she wanted to be.

But as soon as she thought this—all without looking at Dorothy Dragon, at those brown strong arms she wanted to have tight around her—Cory felt a terrible longing for Polly's wild hair and freckled face and the wide smile and the laughter, oh, that long-ago laughter between the two of them, when everything had been safe and happy and unchanging.

"Are you all right?" said Dorothy.

"I don't like hula dancing!"

"I see," said Dorothy. She stubbed out the cigarette she had just lit. "Do you know how the hula was invented?"

Cory shook her head.

"In ancient times, in Hawaii, Pele, the volcano goddess, was tired of all the old songs, all the old tricks. She asked her younger sister, Laka, to entertain her with something different. Laka came up with a dance that would combine music and gestures, a dance that would tell a story without using words."

Dorothy stood up. She was wearing a halter top that made her shoulders look wider than ever. She began to hum and sway her hard little hips a little:

> *Lovely hula hands*
> *Graceful as the birds*
> *In motion.*

"I was stationed in Hawaii during the war," she told Cory. "What beautiful girls they were, what eyes they had." She smiled and pulled Cory up from the stone pool. "I often thought I never should have left the islands. But my sister was sick and then I ended up getting married." She unpinned her knot and her shoulder-length gray-blonde hair slipped down over her broad shoulders. "Too lazy to work, too much of a coward to live the life I wanted." She kept moving and gestured to Cory while singing,

> *I can feel*
> *the soft caresses*
> *of your hula hands*
> *your lovely hula hands.*

Her hair flowed softly over her shoulders. Dorothy was as tall as her father and smelled a little like him, like tobacco and a deodorant for men, not women.

"Come on Cory, dance with me."

Shyly Cory rotated her hips and raised her arms. Long ago she and Polly used to dance together, outside under the apricot tree, funny Mexican hat dances and square dances with do-si-dos and dances where Polly lifted her up and swung her around and around. And Cory had never been shy then, had laughed and couldn't stop, while the green reeled around her and the smell of the roses had blended with the sky.

"That's the girl," said Dorothy Dragon, smiling at her. "Cory, you're a great dancer! And don't ever let anyone tell you different. You just keep dancing." She sang:

> *Fingertips that say*
> *Aloha*
> *Say to me again*
> *I love you.*

Dorothy Dragon crossed her arms in front and looked towards her right shoulder, the gesture that Miss Carson had told them was "I love you."

"Lovely hula hands," sang Cory, and for just a little while, the bamboo sounded like water rather than sadness, and she felt beautiful and beloved, the way she'd felt as a little little girl, like the Hawaiian girls that Dorothy had known back a long time ago in the islands.

The day before Cory was to leave Dorothy Dragon's house and return home, she woke up with a sore throat and a runny nose. She went looking for Dorothy and found her in the garden, pulling weeds. Her hair was in its usual severe knot, but her back was wide-shouldered and brown. She expected Dorothy to bring her back into the house and to sit her down and then to read to her from the Bible and Mrs. Eddy. But instead Dorothy said, "Oh damn," put down her trowel and felt Cory's forehead.

"I think you're coming down with something," she said.

"It's mortal error," Cory said helpfully.

"Yeah, yeah, I know. We'll get you some orange juice and you can go back to bed."

Dorothy straightened up the sheets and tucked Cory back inside. "The best thing for you to do is sleep," she said. "You can skip day camp today." She held out a tall glass of orange juice and a small white pill.

"What's that?"

"It's aspirin," said Dorothy. "It will bring down your fever, make you feel better. Don't tell me you've never had aspirin before."

Cory shook her head. "We don't take pills at our house."

"Suit yourself," said Dorothy. "But you know what they say: The Lord helps those who help themselves. God doesn't mind if we help his healing along a little."

"Yes, He does!" said Cory fiercely. "If you take pills it means you don't believe enough. My mother said!"

"Your mother is a goddamn fool," said Dorothy. "Don't make the mistake of growing up like her." And then she stood up as if she were too angry to speak and closed the door, hard, on Cory in the neatly folded white bed.

Out in the hallway Cory could hear her crying.

Then Dorothy came back and kneeled down at Cory's bedside. She felt Cory's forehead and then Dorothy let her head drop, as if she were praying. But instead of saying the familiar prayers, she began to talk.

"My sister is a Scientist. I always thought it was the most damned-fool thing. But then she came down—thought she came down—with polio. She went to a practitioner and was healed. I don't understand it, but it happened. I know it can happen. I want to believe it."

The room was close and warm, and Dorothy smelled of cigarettes and coffee and the weedy dirt of a garden.

"Who the hell knows anyway?" said Dorothy. "Praying certainly can't hurt. The important thing is that your mother is a damn fine person, one of the finest women I ever met. Someday, when this is all over, not now, you'll understand how much she loved you."

Dorothy Dragon kissed Cory's forehead, and it all ran together—the fever, the longing for the woman who wasn't here, the longing for the woman who was.

After Dorothy had left Cory crossed her arms over her chest and turned her face to the right, to the wall. In hula-talk it meant love, meant longing, meant loss, meant over and over again, I love you.

CROSSING THE DESERT

"WE'RE THIRSTY, DAD!"

He would do something about it if he could, but since the radiator almost boiled over two hours ago, West didn't dare stop the car until they had crossed the desert. It was lucky they'd been close to a roadside pump and store when it happened, when the gauge spun out of control and steam began to drift up from under the hood of the Chevy. It had always been reliable, still there was a limit to what you could ask a car to put up with.

The wooden sign had blistered in the heat: "Buddy's Gas" and underneath, in a more scraggly print "And Trading Post." The small store had thick walls that had once been stuccoed and painted pink; now chunks of the stucco had fallen off, revealing chicken wire underneath. There was a small flyblown sign in the window—*Closed* it said—propped against a faded plastic bucket filled with pyrite, fool's gold, that gave off a dull glitter in the sun. A dented truck was parked by the single rounded pump and off to the side was an equally battered aluminum trailer. The only shade was a couple of inhospitable Joshua trees, branched like coral in every direction.

"Hello, hello?" West called. The car sounded ready to explode.

The kids had already scrambled out, clamoring to get a soda pop. Polly didn't move, she was bent double from the pain. Why had he let her persuade him to make this trip to Nevada to see an old friend "one last time"? Because you couldn't say no to a dying woman, you couldn't say no to anyone's "one last time."

The Mojave shimmered around them, with nothing in any direction.

"Shouldn't oughta be driving in the middle of the afternoon," said a man's voice, coming from the door of the trailer. He was unshaven and half asleep, had probably been taking a nap. He looked at them a moment and then strolled over, a straw hat pulled down over his forehead and a cigarette in his mouth. He walked as if he'd been a cowboy once, or a sailor, rolling on the outside of his feet. With a filth-encrusted rag he wrenched the metal cap off the radiator and jumped back. The blue Chevy boiled like a lobster in a blast of steam.

"It's not going to blow up, is it?" asked West, standing by Polly's door to evacuate her if necessary. Her eyes were closed, lids pale over too-big eyes, and she could not hold her head straight; she seemed unconscious except for the rasp of her breathing.

"Nah," said the man—Buddy—letting water from a hose run over and inside the radiator and engine. "Wife all right?"

West saw that he wasn't as old or as dull as he had first appeared. And he wondered what had led a man, his own age, not yet forty, to live out here in the middle of the Mojave, with no one else in sight. No family, no kids, not even a wife, not even a dog.

West shook his head. "She took a turn for the worse in Boulder City, decided to get back home right away."

Kevin and Cory had their heads in the big aluminum ice chest in front of the store. "There's orange and grape and 7-Up, Dad. And some root beer. You want some root beer?"

If he'd been thinking, he would have bought up the contents of the ice chest, but he was still wondering about the man, envying him in some strange way, how self-sufficient he must be, not to need anyone, not to be responsible for anyone but himself. He watched Buddy put the radiator cap back on and tighten it with a twist of his black-greased fingers, then attach a heavy canvas bag filled with water to the front of the car.

"You should get to Barstow by sundown," he said. "Might want to find a motel there and start early again the morning. Or maybe you just want to keep driving. But I wouldn't stop the car between here and Barstow. You might not get it started again."

"Thank you," said West and paid—exorbitantly, he had miles to realize later—for the gas, the canvas bag and the sodas. Cory had gotten him a root beer, and a 7-Up for Polly.

In fifteen minutes the heavy glass bottles were empty and the afternoon stretched out before them. It was still only two o'clock. There was a terrible silence and a shimmering all around them.

"We're thirsty, Dad," Polly heard from a great distance. She wondered if she were thirsty too. She'd had some 7-Up a while ago, she thought, but perhaps she was thirsty now, and thirst was part of the pain. She tried to separate out the thirst from the rest, but it was impossible. Pain made everything blur together.

She had often had cause in the last year to wonder about pain, what it was and where it came from. Long ago the question would have been immediately answered: It doesn't exist; it comes from bad thoughts.

But that was when she didn't really think, when she had simply parroted the metaphysics of Mrs. Eddy. When her mind was strong and solid and fortified with Science. If Polly had not been a Christian Scientist, if she'd studied physiology or biology in school, maybe she'd have an answer to do with nerves or cells. There would be one of those rational explanations that doctors tried to give her now and that she could never really understand. Their medical vocabulary, even simplified, was like a foreign language to her. She had lived among people who spoke this language of disease and cure all her life, but she had not learned it and it was impossible to do so now.

She had the language of her mother and Mrs. Eddy—many grand words and impenetrable paragraphs about Principle and Truth—but they didn't answer the question: where was the pain? What was it? From what part of her did it come?

Once it had been specific. From the line of stitches that marked where her breast had been. It was a sharp, contained pain, that she could soften a little if she didn't move quickly or in certain ways. But afterwards the pain had gotten much more diffuse and harder to pin down. Part of it was the radiation, how the radiation made her feel. They told her that the big machine was the killing the bad cells, told her that as if she were an idiot child. She didn't believe, even now, that there were bad cells; and she didn't believe in killing them. But what she believed or didn't believe, it was all the same. There was pain, and there was a dry mouth, and there was nausea beyond belief.

Polly had always been taught that her body was not really her, but now she understood it in a different way. Not as a Principle of Science but as a result of too much time in hospitals and doctor's offices. Her body wasn't her, not because it was unreal, but because it was a thing. A thing to be cut open and sewn up, stabbed with needles, pumped with blood and intravenous fluids, rolled over on to stretchers and into beds, wheeled around, prodded and poked a dozen times a day. She was a thing, without the right to privacy or modesty. How could you be modest in a thin gown, and that thin gown constantly pushed up and pulled aside by total strangers?

And yet at the same time, her body was now *more* her own, *more* itself than it had ever been. It belonged to her more now than to anybody else, because pain was the most intimate, the most personal thing there was. It stopped her caring much for anything or anyone she'd cared for before, and focused her attention entirely on herself, her breathing, her drinking and eating, her wastes, her reactions to drugs. Her pain was no one else's and no one could know it as she did.

A body in pain was not a torso and four limbs and a head. It was a field, a universe, that spread out like a burning desert, empty of thought, radiating the present, sometimes erasing memory, sometimes bringing the past so close she could touch it. Pain took away everything that had been important, had seemed all-consuming. Nothing mattered, or perhaps it mattered in a larger, less complicated way. Her mother—all those fruitless years of struggle to get away from her—what did it matter now? Her mother was like a box filled with love, but the box could never be opened, the love could never be taken and given freely, could never spread and flow. Only if Polly squeezed herself up tight and made herself small and crept like an insect inside the box, could she get the love that was there. That was the choice. Polly had been stuck, she saw it now, in the keyhole of the box, half-smothered, half-free.

More than anything she had wanted to let Cory go, to give her freedom, to let her be herself. Perhaps she had given her too much freedom. She had lost track somehow of Cory when things began to happen late last summer after Steve had finally left. She'd felt a lump, and had told Mildred Clark, Mildred told her to wait and pray. Weeks went by, the lump grew bigger. She told West. No time then to waver. Everything had to be done immediately, and it was still, she knew, too late. Afterwards, the months had gone by like a dream she could only wake from periodically. First it was October and she was packing for the hospital, and then it was home for a Thanksgiving dinner she couldn't eat. She blinked again and there was the sound of "Jingle Bells" in the hospital corridor and presents at the foot of her bed; again and there was an Easter basket. And now it was almost fall again, early September.

If she tried she could remember back to last year, to a day at the beach, right after her brother's visit. They'd finally quarreled over his drinking and she'd asked him to leave, and what a feeling of guilt and of joy she'd had. He was out of her life. Her mother might be angry, but her mother was still in Michigan. She'd taken Kevin and Cory to the beach with Mildred and Joan and their kids, a last outing before school started. Joan Perkins wasn't Connie, but she could be lively, and that day she made Mildred and Polly laugh. The three of them had spread lotion on each other's shoulders and joked about getting older. "Oh Polly, your fortieth is coming up. You'll be over the hill like us!" And far off in the ocean, she'd seen Cory, not playing with the other kids, but separate, jumping up high to catch the top of a white curl of wave.

She remembered thinking that day how Cory had clammed up lately, how she'd become more distant at the same time she clung more. "It's the age," said Mildred, who had two teenage girls, girls who were wandering off down the beach at this very minute, flirting with the lifeguards. But Cory was nine, not fourteen. Just recently she'd been having bad dreams too, had started sleeping with a flashlight—now why was that? Polly thought that day she'd have to sit Cory down sometime, talk with her, lovingly, the way her own mother had never talked to her. But that day she only had waved and then tugged at her swimsuit . . . and was that the moment her hand, straightening the bodice of the yellow swimsuit, had brushed against something small and hard and sore?

She had lost track of Cory and now it was too late. She wasn't going to be there for Cory, Cory would have to take care of herself, and she would have to take care of Kevin. She already did, to an amazing degree. Ten years old and so responsible. Yesterday at Lake Mead with Connie and her kids, Cory had watched out for the younger ones and helped them float in their inner tubes, and Connie and said, "You must be so proud of her, your Cory, so grown-up and responsible." But the pain had already been gathering itself then, gathering itself the way it did like an animal in the pit of her stomach and then spreading out, less like an animal than like a weather system, moving in, obliterating everything. And when the pain came there was no room to think of Cory and Kevin.

Connie was still a Christian Scientist in spite of no encouragement from her husband and in spite of hardly going to church. But she took her religion seriously, especially the parts about loving-kindness, about healing through love. She loved Polly in the right way, not a punishing way. She cradled Polly in her arms, took out her Bible and read to Polly, from Deuteronomy, the Lesson that week:

Who led thee through that great and terrible wilderness, wherein were fiery serpents and scorpions, and drought, where there was no water; who brought thee forth water out of the rock of flint; who fed thee in the wilderness with manna, which thy fathers knew not, that he might humble thee, and that he might prove thee, to do thee good at thy latter end.

Polly murmured the verse now, through cracked lips: "fiery serpents and scorpions, and drought, where there was no water . . ."

"Hang on, Polly," said her husband. "It won't be long now."

"We're thirsty, Dad!"

"Well, you'll have to wait, that's all. I'm sorry, but that's the way it is. Don't think about being thirsty and it won't seem so bad."

There was a pause while Kevin and Cory tried not to think about thirst.

"Can we have another cough drop?"

"They're all gone. But have some raisins. They have moisture in them."

Kevin and Cory chewed on raisins. I'm *dying* of thirst, Cory almost said, and stopped. Well, you *could* die of thirst, it *could* happen to them here in the car the way it happened to people on the Oregon Trail going through Utah, wagon wheels breaking, cattle foaming at the mouth, buzzards flying overhead. She pictured herself at the side of the road, tongue hanging out, and someone like Dorothy Dragon bringing a tin cup to her lips. "Drink this, Cory. You're all right now."

She wouldn't be thirsty if she was a cactus plant. She would have sucked in all that water from turquoise-blue Lake Mead yesterday. "Succulents are the misers of the plant kingdom," she had learned last year in the fourth grade when Miss Peeper had helped them build a terrarium. It had a little barrel cactus and a tiny prickly pear and a small saguaro, some sage and tumbleweed and a large flat rock where Ralph the Lizard basked under the florescent sky. Miss Peeper had just been to the desert that spring. "You wouldn't believe how many flowers come out just after it rains. Every plant in the desert really knows how to make the most of every single rain drop, every bit of moisture that comes its way. Do you know how many gallons of water one of those big barrel cacti can hold?"

Cory shifted on the seat; it was scratchy as a cactus against her bare thighs. Her skin was red from the sun yesterday. What a short vacation! She'd been so excited when Polly told her they were going to Nevada for a week to visit her old friend Connie. Cory had thought Polly would never come home from the hospital this time, but she had, and Kevin had come back from Michigan, and Polly had held them close and told them they were going to see Connie. "I didn't write her all this time, I don't know why," Polly said. "And now I know I have to go there." And they had rushed around packing. Maybe her mother wasn't so sick anymore, she thought.

"Maybe God healed her," she whispered to Kevin as they got their swimsuits and their water toys out. She knew that he wanted to believe it as much as she did. For almost a month he'd been in Michigan and every day Grandma had prayed for Polly, he told Cory. Maybe it had worked. Maybe she was going to get better.

Her mother was tired—but they were all tired—when they got to Boulder City two days ago, but yesterday morning she said she was fine. They'd all sat around the breakfast table, Connie and her husband Sal and their four kids, Joe and Danny, Susie and little

Sal. There were corn flakes with fresh peaches, and Mr. Sabicca had said they could rent a boat on Lake Mead and spend the day there.

Oh, yes! The deep turquoise water and the red hills around. Mr. Sabicca steered the flat-bottomed motorboat with its cheerful striped awning to a deserted cove, and the kids all piled out on to the shore with Mr. Sabicca and their father. Mr. Sabicca wasn't a Scientist either, so he and West drank a beer and talked college football. Connie and Polly had stayed on the boat in the shade. From time to time Cory had seen them talking a little, Polly so thin-looking in her sundress, her arms white freckled sticks, her face deep with hollows, Connie so large and merry. After a while they had stopped talking, and it seemed like Polly was resting. She lay in Connie's lap and rested like a baby.

Cory would have liked to have swum out further into the lake, but it was fine to play with the littler kids on the shore, piling up stones and knocking them down again. The pebbles were pretty reds and ochres. Some of the best ones she'd found were on the car dashboard up in front so her mother could see them if she opened her eyes.

Succulents are the misers of the plant kingdom. If only there was something to drink! She shouldn't have drunk up that orange pop so fast, she should have only wet her mouth a bubble at a time, then she would have plenty left. She could have given her mother some. Her mother hadn't said much since they left Connie's this morning.

"I thought we were going to stay a week," Cory had said. But her father had bundled them all up in the car. "We need to get home," he said, and didn't explain.

Water, if only they had some water. In Christian Science she had learned that you had power over mortal mind and that she could pray to see the true nature of things. In the monthly *Sentinels* there were always children's stories of kids who healed their hurt animals, or who prayed to understand something their parents or neighbors did or didn't do. Maybe something would happen now if she prayed for water. She closed her eyes and conjured up Lake Mead, blue as a turquoise stone. Cool and wet under the blazing sun. Let a lake like that appear in front of them! Cory opened her eyes and there it was, in the middle of the highway, between her parents, a shallow, wide body of water, blueish gray, winking in the sunlight.

"Dad!" she cried. "There's a lake."

"Where?" said Kevin, jumping up and spilling his melting crayons everywhere.

Polly opened her eyes and made a low moan.

"It's a mirage," said West, sounding annoyed. "You know what a mirage is, Cory."

Of course she knew, she wasn't stupid! All the same, it had looked like a lake.

She helped Kevin pick up his crayons.

"Want to draw pictures?" he offered.

"No. I hate to draw."

From the front seat her mother's voice floated back, in a croak of protest, "But Cory, you used to."

Cory's legs were stuck to a barrel cactus, her throat ached, she hated them all. "Well, I can't draw, and I'm too old for coloring books!"

"Read us a story," said her father. "From one of your fairy books."

"I don't want to," she almost shrieked. "I'm thirsty!"

"Here!" To her surprise, West thrust two red lake pebbles from the dash back over the seat. "Suck on these."

"They're rocks!"

"When I was little," said West. "We didn't have pop. We had water from the well. My foster father taught me this when we were haying. It makes the saliva flow."

There was nothing to be said to that. There was never any right answer when her father talked about his childhood on the farm in Wisconsin, a childhood in which there was no allowance, no shoes, no chocolate bars and now no soda pop.

Cory and Kevin took the red pebbles and stuck them in their mouths. Kevin returned to his coloring book and Cory stared out the window again. She saw a lone cactus flash by, a tall saguaro with its arms outstretched as if it were praying or calling for help. Under its thick skin it had a heart of water, a heart it kept closed. Cory's tongue ran over and over the smooth stone, trying to keep it wet, trying to create a little moisture.

They didn't appreciate it, but they had it easy. Not like on the farm thirty years ago. It was another life then, simpler: simpler pleasures, simpler problems. He'd always known he didn't belong there, he had his eyes set higher than the Kiesewalters' farm. He was cocky. The arrogance of youth. You thought you understood it all. You didn't understand what it cost to survive.

They passed another roadside station, but West remembered Buddy's warning and didn't dare stop. Who did Buddy talk to, how did he pass the hours when no one stopped? Did he have a radio or TV? He'd get mail, maybe a newspaper, a day or two old. What had brought him there? It couldn't be ambition, rather the reverse. That was the way to live, pared down, no meetings, no deadlines, no tests to grade, no taxes to do, no one to care for and worry about. Just yourself. Once he too had been on his own, a bachelor, never lonely, as an orphan you knew you were alone. It made you resourceful. He might not know a lot about cars, but he knew how to run a vacuum cleaner, make scrambled eggs. And he'd had cause to be glad he knew how to vacuum and cook eggs since Polly got sick.

He glanced over at her next to him. She was motionless except for the slight shaking that the car produced. He thought it was getting a little cooler; in another hour it would be sunset. She was so brave, he didn't know how she bore it sometimes. That religion of hers—however it had let her down, let them both down, for he too had believed, not in Christian Science, but that a person's faith was her own business—still Polly had not abandoned it. With all the evidence to the contrary, somehow it did provide for her, gave her some kind of strength.

Yes, it was definitely cooler now. The kids had said nothing for a good half hour. Cory was reading one of her books and Kevin colored. Every once in a while he heard a slight sucking sound from the stones in their mouths. They were good kids . . . Yes, the heat was less pervasive, less oppressive now. Or maybe he was just getting used to it. You could get used to living in the desert. Your body just adjusted. Like Buddy's had.

Maybe in a few years, when the kids were grown . . . because when you came right down to it, he had always wanted to be alone, had seen himself alone in the world. There were friends, but no close ones, and many acquaintances that he wouldn't care if he never saw again. Once he'd been close to Polly, in the first years after they met, when they were getting married and starting a family. He wasn't sure when that closeness had ended. Had they even noticed when it was over? Marriage and family were about a lot of other things than being close, things you don't even imagine when you're young. How had his father felt when his mother died? He didn't know, he didn't know how people felt about things. No one had ever told him. He had to learn it all himself.

There were lights in the distance. The sun was going down and the heat was lifting. Billboards advertised motels and restaurants only thirty miles away.

"Shall we stop for the night, Polly?" he asked. "Or keep pushing on home?"

Her eyelids lifted and he was shocked at the desert he saw there, a universe of pain that swept him in.

"Home," she whispered through cracked lips. "Home."

The lights of the city were behind them now. And a vast cold dark loneliness spread out on either side of the little car. Her father never asked them what they thought, if they wanted to stay the night in Barstow, in a motel.

It would have been fun, especially if there had been a pool. It would have kept them together longer, postponed the moment of homecoming when, even though they would be together in their house on Wildwood they would separate, perhaps never to be together in the same way again. But her father didn't ask them. He stopped at a gas station. The car had survived the heat and was fine. He stopped at a hamburger stand and they used the bathroom and got some greasy fries and burgers to bring back to the car.

Under the neon sign her mother's face was flushed with a greenish-pink light. She sipped from the paper cup of 7-Up Cory had gotten her. "Thank you, sweetheart," she whispered.

Now they had plenty to drink, extra large cups of too-sweet orange drink sloshing in ice. It was hard to remember the thirst of a few hours ago. The drink was too cold and made her teeth ache and there was too much of it, but she had to drink it all, because she'd asked for an extra large cup and there was no place in the back seat to put it down.

She was tired of being good! She wanted to scream, to shout, to spill the drink down the shirt collar of her father right in front of her, to rip the wheel out of his hands and turn them back to Barstow where there were people and lights. She had heard her father murmur to her mother, "About four or five hours, Polly, that's all." He'd put a flannel blanket around her, the only blanket they had, from the trunk. What about a blanket for them? They would be freezing soon.

Cory hated the dark. She couldn't remember if she had always hated it, but now she did. Hands coming at you, decapitated bodies with hands like lobsters scratching at the windows at night, trying to insert a claw. She lay there in her room at night holding her breath, holding on to the one thing in life she trusted, a heavy metal flashlight that she took out of the utility cupboard every night and tucked into her waist band so no one would see. At night she lay clutching the flashlight as she had clutched her stuffed rabbit. The metal was cold as ice at first but then it grew warm, almost hot. "Cory, Cory look over here," the voice from outside said. She planned how she would shine the light on its face and it would disappear like snail slime on a hot day. Or she would knock it on the shoulders and beat back its clawing fingering from the window.

"Cory, Cory, look over here," it perpetually whined. "Cory, I've got something nice for you. Let me in."

She would never let it in. Sometimes she stood on her bed holding the flashlight like a sword and threatened the window. "I'm gonna feed you to the crocodiles," she threatened. "I'm gonna put you down the garbage disposal and grind you up."

But sometimes she couldn't stand up against the scrabbling, whispering unknown *thing* outside the window, and she buried herself in her blankets and pillows, hugging the flashlight to her chest. Once or twice last year her mother found her with the flashlight in the morning and thought that she'd been reading in bed.

"It's not good for your eyes," said Polly the first time, but smiled. "What book were you reading?" But there was no book and the second time Polly found the flashlight she was as stern as she ever got.

"What do you want this in bed for?"

Cory couldn't answer. She wanted to tell her mother about the headless things with lobster claws but in the light of morning it seemed unreal. That was what she'd learned in Sunday School, that bad things were unreal, simply dreams. And all you needed to do was know the Truth and the bad dreams would vanish. She wanted to tell her mother, but then her mother had gone away. The flashlight helped her.

"Cory," Kevin tugged at her arm. "I'm cold." He spoke in a whisper, as he often did, only to her. When he came back from Michigan she'd been so glad to see him, but she hadn't wanted to hear about his trip. All those stories about Uncle Steve. Didn't Kevin know she didn't want to hear anything about Uncle Steve ever again? Nobody had wanted to hear about Uncle Steve and going canoeing and fishing. After the first day back Kevin had gotten quiet again.

She let him huddle against her in the dark. His little body was icy. He was still wearing shorts, like she was. The frames of his big black glasses had gotten broken at Lake Mead and Connie had taped them together crookedly.

"I know," she whispered back. "I'm cold, too. Do you want me to tell you about when the Feebles went to the Land of Snow, Ice and Stars?"

"Yes."

"One day, Jack and Nancy Feeble were washing the dishes as usual. It was getting dark outside and they knew their mean uncle would be home soon. He always beat them when he was in a bad mood and it was hard for Jack and Nancy to protect themselves. The only place that was safe for them was the drain.

"Tonight, when they heard him coming and they could tell he was in a bad mood they jumped into the sink as fast as they could and pulled out the plug. They hopped into their saucer boat and pinched their noses and closed their eyes tight and the waterspout sucked them down, down and around, around, through the drain into the pipes and to the very bottom, under the ground. This time they came to a place they'd never been before. They were far beyond their friends in the Drain Kingdom. They were on the *opposite* side of the world, in the Land of Snow, Ice and Stars."

"Are you telling a story?" Polly asked. "Can you speak up so I can hear it?"

Cory switched out of her whisper and into a brighter *Sentinel*-story tone. "Everybody wants to know, What is it like in the Land of Snow, Ice and Stars? Because very few mortals have ever been there. Well, I'll tell you. It's not the way you might think. Even though it's as white as white and as icy as icy, it's not really cold there. It's not like Lapland or Narnia where you get frozen to the heart if you don't have a big heavy fur coat. It didn't matter that Jack and Nancy Feeble were only wearing shorts. Because this snow was . . . warm. It *looked* cold all right, but it was warm and thick as peanut butter on toast. If you rolled in it, it was like taking a nice warm bath; if you ate a handful it was like having a cup of hot chocolate.

"So it was a nice place, not cold. But on the other hand it was all snow and ice, and not very many things could actually grow there. It was like the desert, flat and empty under the stars. The only thing that could grow there was the Bumpa-Wumpa tree. This was a tree, kind of like a cactus, that didn't have any branches or leaves. It had a big old trunk that looked like a refrigerator and a little crown of ice-petal flowers on top like an Easter hat. The people who lived in the Land of Snow, Ice and Stars all lived inside the Bumpa-Wumpa trees. They got inside by little doors in front. Everything they needed was inside, ice cream and hot chocolate and peanut butter. There they lived very cozy lives. *Except* for one thing.

"Sometimes the stars in the sky fell down on them. Because the stars in that place weren't fixed up there with Superglue like ours are. The Bumpa-Wumpans only had crummy old library paste to hold the stars up in their sky. And you know how library paste gets after a while; it gets dry and it cracks and that's just what happened. Every now and then, the paste would crack and lose its stick, and one of the stars would fall out of the sky and land on one of the Bumpa-Wumpa houses—boom—and squash it flat."

"Oh," said Kevin.

"This made the Bumpa-Wumpans scared to stay in their houses, but also scared to come out of them. And after Jack and Nancy Feeble understood the problem they were scared, too. They weren't that smart, but they knew that if there was a chance you might get crushed any second, you probably couldn't relax too much. They could tell that the Bumpa-Wumpans were even stupider than they were, though, and that made Jack and Nancy realize that they could help them. They looked like ice cream bars with two little stick legs and two little stick arms. Some had chocolate coating and some were coconut. Their eyes were tiny and so were their mouths. They slept on trays in their refrigerator houses, all stacked up on top of each other.

"'First of all,' said Nancy Feeble. 'We need some stronger glue.' She looked around for something to make it with and didn't see anything. But she remembered that in her back pocket she had a pack of chewing gum from the real world. She got a pot from the Bumpa-Wumpans and Jack had some matches to build a little fire. They put the gum in the pot and boiled it till it was thick and sticky. While they were doing it, a couple of stars fell down near them and crushed a few Bumpa-Wumpans. So they knew there was no time to waste. They got a long, long ladder and propped it up against the sky and then with their pot of strong glue, they climbed up and re-stuck all the stars in the sky, so they would *never* fall down again."

Cory would take good care of him; she would have to take care of him. And West would take care of them both. She would have to trust that, Polly thought. Through the car window Polly saw the familiar stars of the late summer sky coming out; so clear, you never saw them like that in the city. Hercules and the Swan, the Eagle and the Dolphin. And there was Cepheus and Cassiopeia in a reclining W.

She remembered her father teaching her the names of the constellations on those warm mosquito-bitten nights on the lake where they rented a little cabin most summers.

"The mind can make order, can make stories and connections out of very little," he said. "Different cultures of the past linked the stars in different ways. If you wanted, you could draw completely different lines between the stars and make different shapes and figures. You could make up different stories for how the stars got their names."

Her father paused. "What a thought, eh? This same firmament we think we know so well, all criss-crossed with different lines."

"Why do the stars have to connect?" Polly asked him.

"If they didn't connect, the night sky wouldn't be such a friendly place," he said. "Just a lot of random pin-pricks of light up there in the blackness."

He pointed out the brilliant stars that made up the summer triangle, blue-white Vega, bright Deneb and Altair. He told her about the Northern Crown, Corona Borealis, the cluster of bright stars that looked like a crown. It had many stories from many cultures about it. But the one Polly liked best came from the Shawnee Indians and told the story of twelve beautiful maidens who inhabited the stars and would descend every night to Earth and dance in the fields. One of the Maidens fell in love with a human, but like all star people she couldn't remain on earth with the mortals. In the end she had to return to her sisters in the sky.

Sometimes Polly heard her mother berating her father. "If you believe in Science then why aren't you more successful?" For some people, Polly knew, Christian Science was nothing more than a kind of positive thinking that would help them accumulate worldly goods. Mildred and her husband Bob were like that. They wore their belief smugly, like a thick coat that insulated them from every hardship and gave them status. But her father hadn't been like that. For him it was a simple matter: Why would God create a world of sadness and suffering? It was simply impossible. And so if *we* saw sadness, if *we* were suffering, then it was *we* who must change, not God.

He and Polly sat at the end of the dock with the huge warm night sky above them and Polly felt herself lifted up. Everything her father said was simple, and in the most beautiful *right* way.

She remembered feeling the same the night she met West, and trying to tell him that. How *right* it felt. Behind them the lights of the Pike's midway, the arcades of shooting galleries, the swirl and screams of the Cyclone Racer far away like birds calling to each other. And above them the overarching constellations. West had known none of them, even though he knew all the Greek gods and myths from his reading. He had asked if he could put his arm around her, he'd told her he had no family. He reminded her of her father, of someone steady, of someone who would stand by her. But mostly what she felt was the simplicity of things; that she had only to leave Michigan and her mother for her life to begin unfolding in a wonderful pattern that was new but familiar.

Polly looked over at West driving. He had turned out to be steady and reliable, he had not disappointed her. But the warmth had gone from their marriage long before she lost her breast. There was some way in which he had no warmth to give. He'd been angry with her, angry and frightened, that she'd delayed telling him about the lump.

"You told Mildred Clark," he'd shouted, West who never raised his voice. "Two months ago?"

And then afterwards, after the operation and radiation, he'd begun to draw away from her. He did everything he was supposed to, sat by her for hours, took care of the kids, made sure everything got done. At the hospital the nurses all talked about what a *good* man he was. But all the same, he had drawn away, protecting himself. It was as if Fate had pointed a finger at Polly, and West needed to make sure the finger stayed pointed at her, that it did not waver, did not slip in his direction.

Not like Connie, who said on the phone last week, "Polly, why didn't you tell me sooner? Oh my darling Polly, yes you can come and visit." And when she saw Polly, saw how it was, how it really was, she had embraced Polly for a long time, with all the warmth that Polly had been longing for, and that no one, no one for years, had been able to give her.

◆

"All right, honey?" West asked, but she was sleeping, it seemed. The kids were sleeping too, snuggled against each other for warmth in the back seat, like two lost puppies. At least three hours before they got home. Now the drive didn't bother him, now he had fallen into a rhythm. It was like the drives he'd taken by himself, a few Saturdays over the last year when he'd left Polly at the hospital and the kids with a babysitter, when, telling no one, he'd simply gotten in the car and headed north, past Malibu, almost to Santa Barbara on Highway 1, or east to the San Bernadino Mountains. Five, six hours at a stretch he'd drive, smoking his pipe, the radio on. Everyone thought he was working, but he was doing nothing, not even really thinking. It was a way of being free of all of them, of Cory coming out to his office and hanging around, asking if they could have ice cream and could they have some money to buy comics and was he going to take them to get new shoes because the old ones pinched and was it okay if she went on a field trip with her Bluebird troop; of Kevin looking fearfully at him as if he'd done something wrong, god knows he probably had; and of Polly herself, Polly at the hospital and Polly at home, sometimes able to cook and manage the kids and sometimes not. In the early spring, in February, after the scar from the operation had healed and the radiation seemed to have done some good, she'd had a burst of energy, and had gone into the garden every morning and weeded and planted, and he had thought, with just a little hope, that maybe, just maybe the cancer was not going to spread. But by the end of April she was too weak to get out of bed most mornings, and by June, when she went into the hospital, they found she had a new tumor in her lung.

All this could have been prevented, he knew bitterly, if she had gone to the doctor right away. Now she was dying and would leave him, just as everyone else had.

At the orphanage in Madison they were all the same, all marked with the same badge of loss. West was one of the lucky ones: he'd lived there since he was a baby, he knew nothing else, didn't remember his parents or his brother, not at all. Some of the other kids, who had lost their mothers and whose fathers didn't want them or couldn't keep them, or those children whose parents had abandoned them and who'd been claimed by the state, now those kids suffered.

But one of the nurses had told West early on, "Being an orphan can be a blessing. You're not beholden to anyone. You don't have to be what someone else says you have to be. You can make your own way."

When he was fostered out to the Kiesewalters for four years, they always talked about adopting him. It wasn't that he wasn't fond of them, Mrs. Kiesewalter with her double chin and apple dumplings, Mr. Kiesewalter with his kind stern face and enormous hands, who said that if young Wesley would stay they'd leave him the farm. But it wasn't what he wanted, to be Wesley Kiesewalter, owner of a dairy farm in Wisconsin.

He ran away, he went back to the orphanage, and then he was given permission to board with a family who lived across from East Madison High School. He became West then, West Winter, President of the Latin Society, Phi Beta Kappa, Class Valedictorian, a full scholarship to college. He had written on the application, "I want to be a professor of History. Our Classical heritage has many applications for life in the Twentieth Century." There was no one to help him, and yet over and over strangers did help him, impressed that he was an orphan, that he had no family.

It still made him proud that he was an orphan and had made his way alone. Only occasionally he realized what he'd lost—when Cory was born, for instance. She was so small in Polly's arms, and something welled up in his throat. He told Polly it was amazement and pride, but it was something more, some terrible wretchedness to see how small she was, how helpless. Without her mother holding her, how could a child like that survive? If you didn't have a mother, how could you possibly get what you needed?

Around him in the car, all was silence. Outside it was silent, too. The tires on the pavement made a smooth, dry sound. Occasionally a car passed them. He looked across at Polly. He should feel more. She was his wife. He had loved her, he had married her, and soon she would be dead. When she first told him about the lump, he'd felt fear and a terrible anger that she had betrayed him, that all his hopes for this life together had come to nothing. But now he felt nothing, neither dread, nor grief, nor terror.

It was like the night he left the Kiesewalters. He had gotten up and dressed and put on his Sunday shoes. He took nothing except the shoes. The moonlight came into the room where he had lived for four years, the first time he'd ever had a room of his own. He took nothing, not even the photograph Mrs. Kiesewalter had taken of the three of them. He tiptoed through the hall past their room. He didn't want to say good-bye. He heard them breathing in their sleep. They had treated him like a son, like the son who would replace Ernest and Carl who had died in France and whose innocent strong sepia faces still stared out of brass frames on the walnut side table by the horsehair sofa. But he didn't want to be their son. He opened the front door. Their house was in the middle of a field and the moon poured down the road all the way to the main road that led back to Madison. He walked for a long time, and then very early caught a ride with a milk wagon. He should have felt something then, sadness, or guilt, and he did feel those, faintly, like moonlight on a road. But mainly what he felt was nothing, which was the same as feeling free.

Polly tried to open her eyes for a last look at the stars, but she was too tired. All around her, instead of burning heat or icy cold, was a delicious warmth that came from the flannel blanket that West had tucked around her. It was the warmth of Connie's arms around her last night as she lay in bed, unable to sleep. West was on the sofa, and Connie came in to say good night. They had stayed there a long time, close and not talking much. Sometimes Connie said, "Remember that red dress you had?" and "Remember Rose's Bakery?" but mainly she read the Bible to Polly and rocked her in her feather-soft arms. Connie's blonde hair was short now and her eyes seemed smaller in her big face, but the eyes were just the same, they were eyes that saw Polly, had always seen her.

They stayed up half the night, and sometimes Polly whispered, "I'm going to miss my children," and Connie said, "They'll be all right, my dearest," and Polly said, "I didn't want to take the pain medication, but I had to," and Connie said, "God loves you no matter what you do." And Connie kept reading aloud and repeating, "Who fed thee in the wilderness, with manna," she said. She was crying. "Oh Polly," she said. "Oh Polly."

The car was dark and silent and she felt warm. Now Polly felt she was finally falling asleep. She looked at the stars again. She could not open her eyes, but her eyes were open. There it was, yes, high above, the Northern Crown. One of the maidens who came to the Earth to dance with her sisters had fallen in love with a mortal and married him. But it the end it was no use, her sisters called her back, Oh Polly, and she had to return home, to be close and still so far away, so far away in heaven.

The car was dark and silent when Cory woke up for a minute and couldn't remember where she was. In the distance, in front of them, were city lights. They must have come through the desert finally, and through the mountains. They must be on the outskirts of Los Angeles. Her mother was soundlessly asleep and her father was driving. Kevin lay across her legs, with his head in her lap. Cory sighed and fell back into sleep again, reassured. The four of them, her family, were all together in the car, traveling safely in the dark towards home, and everything was just the way it had always been.

PART TWO

RESIST TECHNIQUES

Spring

It was like swimming to lay the delicate blue washes over white paper textured like the rough cement of a pool. It was like swimming back in time to a place where names of colors floated up, old memories: ultramarine, cerulean, indigo.

The instructor said, "Watercolor is a transparent medium. It's not like oil or acrylic, where light reflects off the color itself. The effects of watercolor come from the fact that rays of light penetrate through the transparent paint to the white paper and are reflected back again."

The class sat there, not so much absorbing as reflecting back his eager desire to teach. Their fingers smoothed the Arches paper and touched the points of the soft sable brushes from his recommended supply list. The brushes had cost an arm and a leg and so had the cold-pressed paper. This wasn't like the watercoloring they remembered from their school years, black Prang boxes and newsprint sheets that gave a gray, oatmeal dullness to the brightest colors. This first night it didn't even look like they were going to paint anything. All he had them doing was making value studies, washing on lighter and lighter tints of neutral and blue colors, while he talked of building up layers, of glazing and overglazing color. Some students took notes, some sketched hopefully in pencil, and some, like Cory, were so eager to start that the instructor's words came to them as if in a dream, as if underwater. They had their wash brushes full of watery blue. They were already swimming.

Cory hadn't painted anything for years, but this spring, when she was thirty-five, she'd signed up for a beginning watercolor class at a local arts center in Seattle. She couldn't have said why exactly this class or even why art. She didn't consider herself a creative person, at least, not anymore; in fact she didn't even like the word *creative*, which made her think of wobbly ceramic vases and people finding themselves. But she didn't know what else to call the impulse in her that hadn't forgotten what it felt like to see color spreading out under her fingers on a blank page.

It was an old and wordless feeling. It wasn't like writing. For a while, in her teens, she'd dreamed of being a poet. She'd put down "poetry" on some questionnaire about career interests and the placement advisor had suggested a journalism class. There she'd met her best friend Naomi Stein and the two of them had fallen under the spell of the flamboyant Mr. Hawkins with his black hair sticking straight up like a bushy skyscraper. He'd pushed both Cory and Naomi to major in journalism and as a result she had studied Communications for four years at the University of Washington. She'd been the features editor of the *Daily*. Looking back, Cory realized she hadn't liked the writing so much as the adrenaline surrounding production. She'd loved what hard work it was, and how alive the deadlines made her feel. The writing itself hardly mattered, though she gradually perfected a straight-forward and ironic style that she hoped was convincing.

Once her friend Rae had persuaded her to join her writers' group and to think about fiction. At the time, at least ten years ago, Cory had been part of an alternative newspaper collective, where in addition to hard-hitting articles on nuclear power and recombinant DNA research, she'd written book reviews in which she took a sarcastic view of feminist and particularly lesbian novels.

"Hey, go ahead," urged Rae. "Try a novel yourself. *Anything* you write has got to be better than those novels."

Cory's novel wasn't much better though, and she didn't have the nerve, the confidence, or the simple stupidity to go on writing fiction until she improved. Rejection crushed her, as it had flattened so many of her friends, who also had dreamed of becoming writers and artists. One by one they gave up those dreams. Fell in love, volunteered for important causes, struggled to pay the bills, had children, went back to school, found demanding jobs that left no time for anything else. And if anyone remembered to ask, as the years went by, Are you still writing? Or, Whatever happened to that novel of yours? Cory mumbled something vague, usually about lack of time and too much work.

Everyone understood that, for no one had enough time and everyone had too much work.

That night after her first class Cory went home and used up a block of Arches paper just to feel her brush swimming with blue from one side to the next. It wasn't true she hadn't thought of painting before now. It was only that she remembered it always as something she'd done in childhood, at the redwood table under the apricot tree, a wall of brilliant roses behind her and under her fingers swirls of butter yellow and crimson red. There was a heavy summer smell of ripe fruit and roses, and of her mother bending over her in her yellow dress that smelled of flowers and freckles. Her mother holding up the still-wet paper, admiring everything, putting the pictures up on the refrigerator and the wall. Cory was careful when she thought of her childhood not to remember too much; but making pictures was something she could remember, and with pleasure. Words didn't interrupt the pictures, didn't ask questions she couldn't answer.

She spread the blue-washed pages over the desk, which was piled with tax returns in process. For ten years she'd been living in this building just off Eastlake Avenue. Downstairs was a hair-dressing salon and a used bookstore specializing in children's books. On the first of every month her landlady and the bookstore's owner, Irene, changed the window, displaying Nancy Drews in June, and fairy tales in winter. Up a flight of stairs the whole space was Cory's.

There was a large room and a small one. At first the large one, which overlooked Lake Union, had been Cory's combined living and bedroom. She'd used the small narrow room fronting the street for an office. It was where she'd first, tentatively, put a desk and a file cabinet, where she'd admired the business cards that said, *Cora Winter, Certified Public Accountant.* Later, as her business grew, the small room became her bedroom, and the large one, with a bigger desk, file cabinets and chairs for clients, became her office.

When she first moved here she used to lie on her futon on the floor and watch how the lake changed from hour to hour, from season to season, and how the weather moved across the sky, behind the huge metal structures of Gas Works Park. Tonight the instructor had spoken of high-key palettes and low-key ones. Seattle was mostly low-key, luminous grays, a hundred shades of gray, and dark green and marine blue. Cory liked the muted colors of the Northwest, the clouds and rain and lack of sun. The bright glare of her childhood in Southern California faded and softened, replaced by neutral tints without the force of memory.

At the second session the woman seated next to her—who had possibly been there the first time, Cory couldn't remember—

broke into her spacious state of mind with,

"Oh no! I forgot my paper. I can't believe I did that. It was on the dining room table, the big pad, and then the phone rang and I ran out because I was late. Oh jeez, I'm such a stupid . . . oh, would you mind? Thanks!"

She was round and freckled, with short, dirt-colored curly hair, a little younger than Cory, and wearing belted khaki pants and a cotton shirt that didn't favor her plumpness. She was the kind of woman who, in junior high school, Cory had always avoided, the kind of girl who had always wanted to be her chum: normal, eager, friendly—too friendly. Cory was always sitting next to girls like her in some class, girls who wanted to walk home together or eat lunch together, and talk about idiotic girl things like baby-sitting or which Beatle was cutest. Slightly lonely girls who, though ordinary, felt excluded, and latched on to Cory as someone who also didn't quite fit in, but who seemed easier with it.

"I'm Rosemary," the woman said, smiling largely.

"Cory Winter."

She saw it all, how Rosemary would monopolize her time in class, asking her all sorts of personal questions, and giving Cory in turn all kinds of information about her husband or boyfriend, information Cory couldn't care less about. And she would suggest getting together to paint some Saturday, to do nature studies.

But the instructor began talking about washes and tints again and about negative space and how to create shapes and shadows with just a brush stroke or two. Using only darker and lighter tints of black they were to paint the crumpled white paper bag he set on the table in front of them.

It was surprisingly difficult and when Cory next looked up, class was over.

"That's really good," said Rosemary, a little wistfully. She showed Cory hers. The paper bag looked like a decayed molar. "I bet you've had a lot of experience painting."

"No, not really. When I was a kid I used to draw and paint a lot. But that was years ago."

"Why did you stop?"

"No particular reason. I got interested in other things."

"How old were you?" Rosemary had finished putting away her things and had turned, plump and eager, to Cory, as if this really were an interesting conversation.

"Oh, nine or ten."

"I don't think I was even that old. My father is a chemist and my mother went to nursing school. We got play stethoscopes and doctor's bags for Christmas, and my brothers got science kits. I was never encouraged to be artistic. How about you?"

"I just stopped painting."

"No, I mean, what was your family like? Did they encourage you?" Rosemary's hazel eyes were intent on an answer. Everyone else around them had gone.

Cory didn't answer for a moment. After all these years she still thought there should be some easy phrase for being without one parent, so you didn't have to say *lost* or *died* over and over. You couldn't just say I'm half an orphan, but it would be easier if you could. Easier still if you could just wear the words tattooed on your forehead, so you didn't have to discuss it at all. "My mother died when I was ten."

"Oh." Rosemary's freckled skin was the kind that held a flush like color on white paper. "That must have been hard."

"I survived," Cory said, her usual reply, and her shrug was automatic too. "See you next week."

Sometimes Cory did nothing more than put color on paper. She would start with cadmium yellow and add larger and larger increments of cadmium red or permanent rose, just to see what happened, how she could change colors from warm to cool and back again. She had pages of color schemes, of purples made from crimsons and blues and of greens ranging from the teal of viridian to the citrus of sap green. Other times she didn't even have to paint to see the colors of the world. Some mornings, early, she would walk along the Burke-Gilman trail around the north end of the lake and murmur out the names of grays and blues to herself—tell herself how she would paint the way the silver light struck the indigo water at seven o'clock on a spring morning. It was like learning to see again, like finding her way back to an old sense of her place in the world. When she returned home from these walks she'd make a pot of tea and paint the lake, over and over, until nine when the phone began to ring.

Cory didn't tell anyone about the class she was taking. She didn't want it to be like those days in her twenties when she used to sip her way through a bottle of wine in the evenings, hardly noticing because she was on the phone to Rae or someone else from the group talking about the page or two pages she'd written that day. Long, earnest conversations about the right *voice* and about the difference between fiction and journalism. Sincere discussions about the purpose of art, the literary life, the characters' motivations, the difficulty of constructing a believable plot, the struggle to get the dialog to sound *real*.

It shamed Cory to think of that novel now. The falseness of it and the falseness of her conversations with Rae and others about it. She'd meant it to be the story of her life, except that she would control and disguise everything that she told. Any time anything remotely true about her life emerged, she squashed it down. She'd disdained the idea of writing an autobiographical novel, and so did everyone in her writers' group—most of them gone on now to other jobs, most of them a little embarrassed when they met. Donna, who had wanted to write like Jane Rule, worked at a software company sixty and seventy hours a week; and Jill of the confused but gorgeous prose poems had become the manager of the restaurant where she'd waitressed. Miriam had published a small magazine before going into the trades as an electrician; and Sue was an arts administrator who cited her three publications on her resumé but hadn't touched a pen in years. Only Gretel, now straight and the mother of three, admitted she still planned to write a novel someday. "This time it will be a potboiler for money," she said cheerfully, she who had made them cry with her poignant and always unfinished short stories.

Rae, too, had turned away from fiction, but she wrote poetry now, poetry that was published more and more frequently but didn't pay the bills. As a Poet-in-the-Schools she went from elementary to elementary around the state, returning from Eastern Washington with harrowing stories of being called that "black bulldyke teacher." She was thinking of getting into theater, writing plays—"another lucrative profession," she joked.

As for Cory, everyone said, "Who would have thought you'd be so good at business?" She'd taken over the convoluted bookkeeping at the alternative newspaper, discovered it came easily to her and had gradually begun to work with other non-profits to untangle and reorganize their sad affairs. Now she was a CPA and had her own accounting and consulting business, wore jackets with her jeans and carried a briefcase.

It was one of those situations where you couldn't switch your seat without hurting someone's feelings. She could have done it after the first session, but not after the second, not when everyone had settled in. She had tried being late the third time, but Rosemary had yoo-hooed her. "I've saved you a seat!" Now she was stuck, in the seat and with the realization that Rosemary didn't have a husband or boyfriend, but was looking for a girlfriend instead.

It wasn't that Cory didn't like Rosemary, but Cory was there to paint, not to pick up women, and Rosemary was not her type anyway. Cory liked women more like herself, flip and unsentimental, who could deflect feeling like water sliding over stone.

Rosemary had a tough side, but she would never wear a leather jacket and a mocking grin like Cory's last lover. Rosemary's toughness was inside and came from having grown up in a family of boys, with a father who ran dinners like exams and a mother who should have been a world leader but had had to be content with the Presidency of the St. Paul PTA.

"My mother has heard about human weakness," said Rosemary. "But I don't think she believes it. You can tell her, 'I had a bad case of jet lag,' and she'll say, 'I don't believe in this jet lag everyone talks about. I think it's all psychological. *I've* never had it.'"

Rosemary followed Cory out into the corridor during the break to tell her these stories, and sometimes out into the apple orchard that surrounded the former convent building where the classes were held. It would have been easier if Rosemary had been straight—then she could have had her pick of several nice men in the class, including one who clearly wanted to get to know her—and then Cory could have talked to her without weighing everything she said.

"So what do you do for fun?" Rosemary asked nervously. She had already wormed out of Cory what she did for a living, where she lived, and where she had grown up. She knew how old Cory was and who she had voted for in the last election. She knew that Cory's brother Kevin lived in San Jose and had two children. She knew that Cory had moved to Seattle right after high school to go to the university and had stayed on. She knew that after Cory and Kevin were gone her father married again, a woman named Georgia who'd never made them feel very much at home. She must have known, too, the answer to the question she didn't know how to ask.

It was a rainy spring but often, like tonight, the sky cleared in the evening and the air was full of the spicy scent of apples.

"We should get back," said Cory. During the first half of class the instructor had told them about using resist techniques, and Cory was eager to return to her painting to try it out. He'd held up a bottle of rubber-based art masking fluid. "This is to protect areas of your painting so you can paint over them without disturbing what's underneath. Put this on the place you want to cover, paint over it and then peel it off. You'll have a clean surface underneath that you can leave blank or fill in."

"No, really," said Rosemary. She'd be nice-looking, Cory thought, if she weren't trying so hard to be a dyke. In an old-fashioned rayon dress that showed off her bosom, with dangly earrings, and with her curly hair long so that it fluffed around her face; yes, then she'd look great. Now, in spite of her flannel shirt, she looked like a dowdy suburban housewife.

"What do I do for fun?" Cory repeated. "I don't know. I work a lot. And now I'm painting more and more."

"How about . . . there's a great Irish pub nearby . . . a beer after class?"

The sky was pale cerulean with mackerel clouds in peach and rose. Rosemary's nervousness steamed off her skin like perspiration. It was so hard for her that in spite of herself Cory wanted to make it easy. She would let her down as responsibly as she could, over a quiet drink.

Afterwards Cory knew she'd had too much. It was always that way. She wouldn't drink from one week to the next, wouldn't even think of it, and then someone placed a beer or glass of wine in front of her, and she was off.

The alcohol made everything easier, it always did. It stopped her mind from getting stuck, from sheering away. It let her float over everything that was an obstacle when she was sober.

Rosemary had less to drink, but even a half pint made her more loquacious than usual.

There was no husband, though there had been. They'd married in college and gone into the Peace Corps together, to Tanzania. Afterwards there had been law school, then the move to Seattle because he'd been offered a job. Rosemary finally found a job at a legal clinic specializing in women's issues. They'd been divorced for two years.

She wasn't bad-looking, Cory thought again, especially when she dropped that overly agreeable smile, and showed her true face, which was smart and powerful. She had nice eyes, warm hazel eyes, and all kinds of curves. She was funny, she was obviously interested in Cory. But she was completely wrong, wrong in every single way.

"My family's huge and Catholic," Rosemary said. "Irish Catholic on my dad's side, *Bavarian* Catholic on my mother's. I'm the youngest of four, and we're considered a small family. When the Reardons get together for our annual picnic in St. Paul we have enough to make up two softball teams with replacements and a cheering squad. When the Buchmeisters get together on a holiday, you can't button your pants for days afterwards. Cake city!"

She looked down at her glass. "I told my mother I was a lesbian a year ago. She didn't take it well. I'm the only daughter."

Yes, I know, thought Cory, and now the whole confession will pour out, and she'll want the same from me. But Rosemary surprised her. "She'll get over it," she said, and drained her glass. "Are you seeing anyone?"

"No," said Cory. "But . . . I'm pretty busy."

Rosemary nodded ruefully. "Well at least I can tell my therapist I asked you."

"It's not easy to come out," said Cory. "You'll find somebody."

"Oh, I know," said Rosemary. "But the dating part is hard. I hated it in high school and college, and now it's even worse. I went out with another lawyer last year for a few months and thought I was set. When she broke up with me, I felt even more lost than before. Where do you go to meet people anyway? "

"Dances, bars, political groups. Take a class."

They looked at each other. "Right," said Rosemary and laughed. But as they were leaving the pub, she said wistfully, "The only thing that makes me sad is that I know I have a great capacity for love that's not being used. My parents have a happy marriage, so do my brothers. Why not me?"

◆

They went out again after the next class and the next, and each time Cory drank a little too much and was sorry the next day. On the last night of the class she went home with Rosemary, to her house on Capitol Hill. It was a warm evening and they sat out on the deck in the back yard and had some cognac, and then Rosemary, very forcefully, almost desperately, came over and put her arms around Cory and kissed her.

They ended up in Rosemary's quilt-covered bed, in a rose-painted bedroom with lace curtains and photographs of the Reardons and Buchmeisters. There was a rocking chair and a cat; it was like being in a bed and breakfast, and although Cory tried as hard as she could, she couldn't make it be more than what it was—an awkward meeting of two strange bodies.

She managed to come, but Rosemary didn't and Cory was just about to tell her it didn't matter when Rosemary said, "Where did you go?"

"What do you mean?"

"You weren't . . . I don't know . . . here."

"What do you mean? I *was* here. I was here." But something told her she had been elsewhere, perhaps in some fantasy, perhaps nowhere at all.

"Maybe it's because we've been drinking," Rosemary said. She seemed deflated and unsure. "We shouldn't need to drink to do this."

"I'm not drunk, if that's what you're saying," Cory said, drawing away. And in fact she didn't feel drunk, only headachey and sad.

"I guess I'm just sensitive," said Rosemary. "I still carry around this picture of myself as this hugely overweight teenager. I imagine that people are repulsed by my body."

"What are you talking about?" Cory asked impatiently. She was thinking, Why do I get involved with women who want to analyze everything, with women who have all this weird stuff about their bodies? "You've got a perfectly fine body. It's beautiful. It's not fat . . . a little maybe."

"You are repulsed."

Oh God. What *was* it with women? Why couldn't they just fuck and forget it? Cory got up and started putting on her clothes. "I need to go," she said. "Have a long day tomorrow."

Rosemary didn't try to stop her. She lay there with the covers up around her neck, watching Cory. "It's just that you . . . seemed so distant," she said. "It reminded me of how I was with my husband. Out of my body. Not present."

"I was right here the whole time!" Cory said. "I came. You didn't. What the hell is wrong with you that you want to put it all on me?"

She fled before she could get an answer, thinking, I'll call her in a day or so to apologize, knowing at the same time that she wouldn't.

Summer

Rae telephoned to ask about getting together. Their relationship in college had been brief and friendly, and had left no scars, something that seemed increasingly important as they grew older and counted off a string of affairs that had ended badly. For fifteen years Rae and Cory had stuck with each other through the ups and downs of lesbian life, though if they spent more than two hours together they usually got in an argument about something.

They met for dinner at Julia's 14 Carrot Cafe on Eastlake so that Rae could tell Cory about the women writers' workshop she'd been to last week. For a long time now Cory hadn't invited anyone to her house. She didn't like to cook and besides, it was really an office now, not a home.

Tonight Rae was vibrating in a golden shirt that showed off her coppery brown skin. She was looking good, with earrings and all sorts of rings; looking good now that the stiff little dreads the size of pencil stubs were getting longer. Not many women in Seattle were growing their hair out yet, but Rae had been to Philadelphia earlier in the year to visit her sister and had come back determined to have a full head of beautiful black braids.

"I thought of you the whole time I was there," said Rae. "You're a much better writer than most of them. You just never took yourself seriously. What ever happened to that novel?"

"I recycled it."

"I don't believe that. Where is it?"

"Rae, it doesn't matter where it is. It was two hundred pages of garbage and that's all."

"That's not true, two editors said it had possibilities."

"Oh forget it. I don't have anything to say as a writer. Anyway, I've started painting."

She hadn't meant to say that, hadn't meant to tell anyone, but there it was. She tried to soften it. "I took a class last spring. Maybe I'll keep going with it, who knows?"

"That's great," said Rae, "Now, what about your love life?"

"The same—nothing has happened for months. It's like I'm dead. I did go to bed with someone from my painting class. I don't know when I'll ever learn. First, she's practically just coming out. Second, she was one of those women who want to process."

Usually Rae would be right there with her, would cry, "I hear you," and would be able to contribute a story of her own about some woman who had suggested that Rae move in with her after they'd known each other two weeks, but tonight, Rae just couldn't do it. She was in love, and it wasn't just a passing thing this time, she told Cory, it was for real.

Nicole was from Cincinnati; she was a poet too, and she was going to move to Seattle just as soon as she broke up with her girlfriend, quit her job and got some money together.

"Oh, give me a break," said Cory. "Rae, don't you know you're letting yourself in for a lot of pain? She's probably not even going to *tell* her lover she met you."

"She's already told her, for your information. What about some support on this, girlfriend?"

"Aren't you the one who's always told me not to rush into things?"

"This is different!"

"What about your independence?"

"I'm thirty-six. I'm sick of being independent. I want to have a partner! And you would too if you'd only admit it."

And so once again they quarreled and went away from each other irritated in spite of a kiss on the cheek.

"If only we could be going through the same thing at the same time," Rae sighed.

"But then I'd have to be madly in love, too," Cory said. "No thanks."

That evening Cory got out her old manuscript. It was bound in heavy red cardboard and the pages were dog-eared after eight years and several readers and two submissions. She had typed it on an old manual typewriter and used liquid white-out to make the corrections. What a long time it had taken her to type a clean copy! Far longer than to actually write the wretched thing.

She remembered very well the summer she wrote it, in the mid-seventies, when she was twenty-six. It was just after she'd moved out of her group house and into this place. It was a coming-out story about a woman named Laura who had always wondered about her sexuality and who finally in college found her true love, Maureen. Years afterwards, reading reviews in women's journals that heaped contempt on coming-out novels, Cory was incredibly relieved that hers had never gotten published. It was full of lines like, "She had never felt like this about a man, she realized." And, "The touch of a woman's hands was what she had been longing for."

Who was Maureen, everyone in her writers' group had wanted

to know. There was no Maureen. She was based on a straight woman in Cory's senior English class on whom she'd had a terrible, never-mentioned crush. In fact, Cory had never found her true love, certainly not in college when she'd still been hanging out, toughly, with the mostly male staffers on the *Daily*. There was Rae, of course, but they'd known from the beginning that they were friends more than lovers. It wasn't until she was working on the alternative paper that she had her first true romantic lesbian affair, with Brett, the separatist whose mode of discourse, unfortunately, was not the bill and coo of love, but the drone of reprimand.

"I know we'll be happy together for the rest of our lives," said Laura on the last page. Her writers' group said, admiringly, "It's so great to read a lesbian novel that ends *happily*."

There were still some lines of the novel that Cory thought about though. On the first page she had written, "Laura's mother, Harriet, was not like other mothers." That was the truest line in the book and Cory remembered staring out the window at the lake as she wrote it, longhand, on a college-ruled sheet of notebook paper. It was a bright summer evening, like tonight. Her desk was all arranged, with a dictionary and thesaurus, and a pile of crisp paper just taken out of its Bartell Drugs plastic wrap. She'd opened a bottle of red wine and poured herself a glass, because she'd discovered how much easier writing was, how the thoughts flowed, when she drank.

How exciting it was, to start a novel, to begin. She had a glass of wine and then another. The first sentence sat there, like a train that should have left the station long since. At first it was only slightly delayed, just waiting for the signal, but eventually it became apparent that something was seriously wrong with the engine.

Why was Laura's mother Harriet so different from other mothers? Cory Winter's mother Polly was different because she was a Christian Scientist, but Cory didn't want to write about that. Whenever anybody asked her what religion she'd been brought up in and she said Christian Science, they said, "Oh, isn't that the religion where they don't go to doctors?" And Cory would nod and change the subject. She didn't want anyone to make a connection between not going to doctors and her mother's death. She didn't want to write about her mother. She didn't want to remember her mother. She *didn't* remember her mother.

So Cory had written a second sentence finally that set the book off on a completely different path, one that reflected the feminist spirit of the times. "Laura's mother, Harriet, was not like other mothers. She was an astrophysicist and she had raised her daughter not to be afraid of anything to do with the male universe."

In the box where she kept the old novel were a few other things—five or six photographs of her parents and herself and Kevin as children and a few folders of writing that she'd been meaning to throw out for years. Few of the pieces inside the folder, poetry and sketches, were dated, and none of them were finished. Unlike the novel they had some warmth, but they were sentimental, concerned with childish memories. Descriptions of swimming; fragments of old dreams and nightmares about hands at the windows; Job-like lists of questions that could never be answered. She had cried when writing some of these pieces— alcohol could do that to you. But without alcohol, and she had given it up, along with sex that meant nothing (the episode with Rosemary was not so much a misstep as an important reminder), where was the warmth in life? If she was distant, she was safe; if she didn't put things into words, she was safe. But she was cold, and in danger of getting colder.

Cory put everything back in the box. All that—those words that didn't tell the truth and were sentimental and drunk—was the wrong way. She set the box back in the closet and got out her pad of thick white paper and her tubes of paints. She wouldn't think about anything, about being cold or warm or truthful or forgetful, only how to capture the color of the evening light on the water. Once again she painted the lake, fresh marine blue, with a light sweet glaze of cantaloupe over it.

Fall

She ran into Rosemary Reardon by chance at the Wallingford Center one October day. Rosemary was in the ethnic clothing store where a percentage of every sale was donated to a worthy cause. She was holding an inkat-dyed vest to her chest and looking at herself in the mirror.

"Looks great," said Cory coming up behind her.

Rosemary flushed. "Do you think so?" she said doubtfully. "Shopping brings out all my old stuff. Like going past the pre-teen section to the section for chubbies. That's what they called us. Only I was even bigger than the chubbies after a while. My mother had to make me clothes. I didn't go into a store for about eight years, not till sometime in college."

"It would look great on you," said Cory firmly. "I think you should buy it."

She waited for Rosemary while she made the purchase and designated the money to go to the battered women's shelter. Cory had forgotten why she came into the Center; she only knew that she didn't want to say good-bye yet. "Want a latte?" she asked.

They sat down outside at the bagel place with their lattes, huddling a little into their jackets because the wind was cold and carried a hint of rain.

"So, how've you been?" Rosemary said a little nervously. "Busy probably. It's funny that since I met you I've run into a lot of people who know you, your business and everything. Maybe next year I'll call you up for my taxes. Not that they're that complicated or anything. Actually I thought of calling you once or twice, just to say hi, ask if you were still painting. I'm not, myself. I'm taking tai chi, always looking for some kind of exercise that's not too boring . . ." she trailed off. "You wouldn't believe it," she said. "But

I'm considered very strong in the courtroom, very firm and decisive."

Cory smiled at her. "Oh, I believe it." She was surprised at how glad she was to see Rosemary again. It had been a lonely fall. She and Rae had made up after their fight—Rae was too happy to hold a grudge—but now that Nicole had moved to Seattle and they were living together, Cory didn't see much of her friend. Not that Nicole and Rae didn't invite her over, but there was actually something painful about seeing them together and witnessing their delighted pleasure in each other's company. Nicole was fun and beautiful and she and Rae had already begun to write a play together. Rae said, "The right person always comes into your life at the exact time you need her." She had never said such things before. Of course there was no arguing with her. The right person *had* come into her life. Cory, meanwhile, plodded on, still working too hard, and taking another painting class. She had not been drinking, but she had been noticing that empty part of her that wanted to have a drink, and noticing how, when she resisted, that she filled up the emptiness with work. The observation didn't make her happy.

Now seeing Rosemary, she remembered not their sad night together, but the hopefulness of the spring in the apple orchard. She had not noticed then that Rosemary had such a beautiful mouth, and that her curly hair, now growing out from its regulation dyke cut, was really more golden brown than dirt-colored.

"I've thought of you, too," Cory said. "I wonder if, maybe, you'd like to see a movie sometime?"

They started to go out again, not to bars, and not to bed, but to restaurants and films and for walks.

"Now that we've gotten the sex out of the way," Cory told Rae, "we can be friends."

"Don't be so sure," Rae said. "I've met these midwestern Rosemaries before. They're persistent. And she's the one who did that big domestic violence case for the Northwest Women's Law Center."

But a friend was what Cory needed, not a lover, but a friend like Rae had been before she fell in love. A friend Cory could get to know slowly and depend on, someone she could, gradually, talk a little to, someone who might ask the right sorts of questions. Because Rosemary was someone who could put things into words. She could talk about her insecurities, her anger at her ex-husband, her ambivalence about her mother, her pain at having grown up fat. She worked through things by talking. "Well, I'm a lawyer, after all," she said. "Words put the bread on my table."

"What are you thinking?" she was always asking, and "How do you feel about that?" And even though Cory usually said "Nothing much," and "I don't know," at the same time, the questions made her curious. She went home from their dinners and walks and wondered what she was thinking, and what she did feel.

"I don't want you to take this wrong," said Rosemary in late November, when they were slogging through a wet path in the Arboretum one drizzly Saturday, "but I feel like something more should be happening."

"Like what?"

"Meeting your friends, spending some time at your place or mine, not just restaurants and movie theaters."

"We agreed we'd keep this casual, didn't we? And you did meet Rae."

Rosemary could get a set to that beautiful mouth. "We ran into her and Nicole at the market and talked ten minutes."

"Look, I don't want to go as fast as you, all right? Don't *push* me. You're always *pushing* me."

"I'm *not* pushing you. I'm interested in you, is that a crime? I think we're well-suited, we could get along, maybe even be happy together . . . well, okay, maybe that's pushing . . . maybe I do push you . . . sometimes."

"I don't want to rush into anything. We rushed it before and look what happened that night."

"Because you shut off."

"I didn't shut off," said Cory. "I just didn't like it when, well, when you got on top of me. I don't like anyone lying on top of me."

Rosemary stared at her. "You never said that."

"You could have seen."

"But . . . " Rosemary didn't go on. Finally, she said, muffled in the green REI anorak that made her look like a pup tent, "I should have been paying more attention. I was totally freaking out. I wanted to have a woman lover—you—so badly. It blinded me."

They walked on again in silence, but it wasn't the tense silence it had been. There was, in fact, an ease between them that hadn't been there before. They were learning to talk to each other. The trees rose up very dark and green around them and water seeped and sighed through their branches. Sometimes when Cory wanted her tree branches to be hard-edged she used masking fluid first and then peeled off of the rubbery material. It still amazed her to find that underneath the paint, untouched, the blank surface waited, a fully shaped, negative space, waiting to be touched.

Rosemary said cautiously, after a while, "So you're not ruling it out completely? The possibility that we might . . . we might try again?"

"The right person always comes into your life at the right time," Rae had said. "So maybe Rosemary is the right person for you."

"She can't be," Cory had said. "For one thing, she talks too much."

But now she took the hand poking out of the green anorak and squeezed it gently. The trees dripped all around them and their boots squished wet leaves with every step. It felt like they had been walking a long time together and only now realized how far they'd come.

"No," said Cory. "I wouldn't rule out anything."

WIVES

"WHATEVER YOU KIDS don't take," said West. "I'll toss."

He hadn't yet started to pack, that would come later. Georgia's funeral had been last week. He was moving from this apartment into a retirement community in Seal Beach at the beginning of the month.

"It wasn't a sudden decision," he said. "She'd been sick for some time."

Although he hadn't begun to pack, the apartment looked chaotic. Boxes of books and files spilled out of his old room, which had once been an office-bedroom and then had become entirely an office. It wasn't that he or Georgia, who had helped him, had had so many clients, it was that they'd kept them, so some people's files went back twenty-five or thirty years. Her brother's room had been turned into a storage space for files as well. He and Georgia had slept in Cory's old bedroom.

Photographs were spread out on the dining room table. Cory and Kevin sorted through them. Kevin wouldn't look at any of Polly. "You take them," he said. He was most interested in those that showed him in his early years, with fine thin blond hair and enormous smoke-blue eyes. His hair, like Cory's, had turned brown long ago and now his was receding up a high domed forehead. For a long time the blue eyes had been half-hidden by heavy-framed glasses.

He touched his childhood wonderingly. "Betsy and the kids will want to see these. You can tell them all you want that you were a kid like them, but they never believe you."

There were fewer photos of Kevin as a child than of Cory. Cory had been the first, with a baby book that carefully described every photo: "Cory on her back in the crib." "Cory blowing bubbles." "Cory in the sunlight."

Polly had always meant to put the photographs in a scrapbook but it had gotten put off and put off. Instead many of the black and white snapshots were in little booklets that Kodak had made in the fifties, bound with a metal fastener into yellow covers. Inside were photographs of early childhood. Of Cory and Kevin in the wading pool and at the picnic table. Of birthday parties at the redwood table under the apricot tree. Of Cory drawing and painting, of Kevin making Play-Doh figures. Loose in the box and now on the table were the faded Kodachrome pictures, of the roses in the rose garden, of weekend trips and picnics with friends and neighbors. But there were not many of these. The last photos were from the summer they went to Oak Creek Canyon in Arizona. Cory kept looking through the box for more snapshots, but that was it. Her childhood seemed to have stopped just before her tenth birthday.

There wasn't much of her father's childhood either. A few old photographs of Madison, the orphanage, his teachers. None of the Kiesewalters. There were scarcely more of Polly. A mother or father had written on the backs of these pictures: "Such a lively little girl!" and "Polly with her sweet baby brother."

She'd been a gangly girl, with unruly curls tied back with a ribbon, and freckles that made her look almost homely. Gingham and no shoes half the time; long legs and a huge shy smile. That girl had turned into a quiet-looking college student and then, for two or three photographs anyway, a young woman with big costume jewelry and high heels, usually with a palm tree in the background. There was a black and white snapshot of Polly arm-in-arm with a plump young blonde woman. They weren't posing but were walking. They looked as if the world was going to begin that afternoon, and as if they were on their way to see it.

West was going through a box of books. "You kids might want to have these," he said, handing them a matching set of a morocco-bound Bible and *Science and Health*. Kevin didn't want either, so Cory took them both.

"At least there was no nonsense when Georgia got sick," West said. "She knew something was wrong, she went into the hospital, she was a trooper till the end. 'West,' she said. 'It's been seventeen good years. Thank you.'"

Cory and Kevin looked at each other. Georgia had been a brassy blonde who dominated their father and kept the two of them away. But it was true, she was no-nonsense. And he had lived with her longer than he had with their mother.

"I often think," said West, "How many people I've outlived. Here I am, only sixty-seven, and yet I've buried two parents, two siblings and two wives."

"Not two children," said Cory. "Not yet."

"Some people," West continued, "Feel their best years are ahead of them at this age. I don't feel that. Even though I've been spared so far."

"Oh Dad," said Kevin. "Once you get to this swinging seniors place, you'll get your pep back."

But West looked tired. "If you kids don't mind," he said. "I think I'll take a nap. Why don't the two of you take a walk? Go over to your old schools, take a look."

Cory glanced at her brother and saw he had the same pained smile she felt on her lips. "Okay," she said. "We'll be back in an hour or so, then we'll have dinner, okay?"

West nodded. His hair was crisply white, but underneath his

face was lined with deep vertical folds. He shuffled a little as he got up and went into his bedroom.

Cory and Kevin set off down the outside stairs and through the patio. When they had moved into this apartment building it had just been completed and smelled of new carpets, chlorine and fertilizer. It was angularly modern in the style of 1960, mustard-colored stucco, outlined with fledgling palms and shrubs. There were maybe twenty units built around a patio—the apartment manager always called it a *lanai*—with a small, tear-drop pool. The building looked different now, not just because they themselves were older, or because it was particularly run-down. It wasn't. But like most structures in Southern California that had once been airy and bare, sitting clean in the sunlight, surrounded by freshly seeded lawns with stakes and string and spindly trees and tiny bushes, it now gave the impression of being enveloped in layers of thick, dusty green vegetation. The Northwest was green, but it was the green of tall, lacy-fingered cedar and needle-feathered fir, damp with the woodsy scent of bark and humus. Southern California, in spite of the drought that had been going on for a few years and that had parched the lawns, seemed to have been swallowed by a mass of undifferentiated shrubbery.

"Do you remember how strange it was," said Cory, as they skirted the pool, "to live in an apartment after having grown up in a house with a yard?"

"I remember that in the beginning Dad used to drop me off some Sundays to play softball with the boys on Wildwood, and then one Sunday we didn't go and I asked why, and he said, 'You need to make friends where you live. Not where you used to live.'"

"He said he chose this place because it was in a good school district."

"But then we had to change schools," said Kevin. "Why did we have to leave our house and friends? We didn't have a place to play. They wouldn't even let us swim in the pool here."

Cory and Kevin had been almost the only children in the building. "Now you've got to be quiet," Cory remembered their father telling them. "We don't want to get in trouble."

"He always wanted us to go to the school playground," Kevin said. "Remember? Just like now."

"Oh yes."

They were standing in front of George Washington Elementary. The eucalyptus trees, which were very large now, rustled high and mentholated overhead. After school Kevin and Cory would still be sitting on the lunch benches or walking around the asphalt playground. They didn't think their father knew and they didn't know how to tell him that about an hour after school the recess monitor collected up the dodge balls and tied the rings together so you couldn't swing on them.

He didn't abandon them, not exactly. He rearranged his teaching schedule so he could be home by five every day, and he moved his office into his bedroom so that he could work there evenings and weekends. It was more as if he said to them, That's it. That's it for family life, that's it for childhood.

"When I look at this school," Kevin said, "And then I think about Jessie and Peter being eight and ten now . . . "

"I know," said Cory. "I get that feeling whenever I look at kids. They look so young. And I felt so old."

Rosemary was always trying to get Cory to be more specific about her growing up. "You only talk about your childhood up to when your mom died. After that it's like nothing happened."

"Nothing did happen," said Cory. "That's the point. With my mother's death the sadness was supposed to be over and we weren't supposed to mention it, but just forget and move on. Occasionally, in the beginning, my father would tell us stories of his life and say, I know what it's like to be an orphan, and we'd be confused, because we weren't orphans, we had a father. But that was how he tried to tell us he knew how we felt."

"But what was it *like*?"

"I don't remember that much, just going to school and coming home for a long time, and then going off to college and not coming home."

She did remember certain things. How her room was no longer yellow, but a light green, with a green glass lampshade on a second-hand wooden desk. How she got a bookcase at a garage sale and painted it black. It had started out with Louisa May Alcott and Laura Ingalls Wilder and gradually filled with Steinbeck and Salinger and Hesse. With *The Lord of the Rings*, *Stranger in a Strange Land* and *Totalitarian Man,* and pamphlets about resisting the draft. How on her bulletin board, the day she left for college, was a quote from Kafka and a photograph from *Time* magazine of a napalmed Vietnamese baby.

She remembered in high school going to her friend Naomi Stein's for dinner and spending the night. How fascinated she was by the close, volatile connection between Naomi and her mother, Aline. Aline and her husband David had been trade unionists and were involved in civil rights causes and the beginnings of the anti-war movement. They listened to Odetta and Joan Baez and ate their tuna fish on bagels. Aline had a black friend named Charlene who used to come over occasionally. Charlene and her two little kids were the first black people Cory had ever gotten to know. She didn't dare tell Naomi or Aline that, for fear they would think she was a racist pig, and she didn't tell her father, because he *was* a racist pig. She blamed her father for raising them in a such a white world, but even at the time she suspected that Polly wouldn't have had a friend like Charlene. Polly probably wouldn't have gone on an anti-war march either. Cory had to do her adolescent rebellion against her mother vicariously, through Naomi and Aline's relationship. But it was hard, because Cory idolized Aline and sometimes thought Naomi was an obnoxious brat, just as Aline told her she was.

"Oh Cory," Aline used to say. "Why can't Naomi be more like *you*! If only I'd had a daughter like *you*!"

She and Kevin were walking past Abraham Lincoln High School where Cory and Naomi had first begun their friendship in the office of the school newspaper. They used to walk home down this street after staying late and just as they got to the point where Cory needed to turn off to go home, when Cory would begin to feel miserable and lonely, Naomi would say, "Why don't you come home with me for dinner!"

It was football season and at the high school boys were out in the field running around with shaved heads. After Cory graduated, she went to college in Seattle and rarely came home, but when she did, she always found Kevin with a shaved head. Football, basketball, softball, track. He had something every night and weekend. At the time she'd been embarrassed. "My brother the jock," she told her friends. "My brother who thinks we should bomb the hell out of the Vietnamese."

"I think Peter is going to be a good baseball player," Kevin said. "He's like me, too wiry for football, but fast. I go to see all his Little League games. You know, Dad never did that. He always said he was too busy."

"How are Betsy and the kids?"

"Great. Everybody's great."

Kevin and his family lived in San Jose, where he worked for an electronics company. He had gone to community college and then enlisted in the Army just as the war was ending. Now he lived in a tract house not so different from the one they'd grown up in, in a neighborhood where there were plenty of kids.

He was staring at the young boys practicing flying tackles. It was a warm late afternoon, already some of them were walking away from the field. "Got to get home," one of them called. "My mom said I can't be late for dinner tonight."

"And you?" Kevin asked. "Sounds like business is good."

"Oh yeah. Really good."

He didn't ask about her personal life, though she had told him tentatively about Rosemary. "Hanging out a lot these days with a lawyer." Very off-hand. She still was awkward about a visit she'd made years ago with her girlfriend Brett. It was in the late seventies and separatist Brett had spent the evening significantly silent, lifting her eyebrows whenever two-year-old Peter tried to push away just-born Jessie from Betsy's breast. Afterwards Betsy and Kevin used to ask about Brett, until Cory stopped lying and said she never saw her anymore.

"Dad doesn't seem too depressed," Kevin offered as they started back to the apartment.

"Do you think . . . he loved her?"

"No," said Kevin. "But I think he was used to her. You were gone by then, but he started spending a lot of time with her back when I was a junior. She never seemed to ask for that much. She kind of reminded me of him, you know, a kid from the Depression, kind of hard-bitten. She was used to working hard too. That's sort of how I imagine them, sitting around doing tax returns."

"They used to go on vacations," said Cory. "They went to Hawaii every year."

"Did they ever come to visit you?"

"I don't have the room," Cory said quickly.

"They never came to visit me," said Kevin. "She didn't like us. She didn't like that he'd had a life before her."

"Some life."

"You know what she told me once? She said, 'What your father did before he met me is his own business.' I was trying to tell her something about *me*, about the dog we used to have. She was the same kind of person as him, I'm telling you. She'd been married and divorced twice. Did we ever hear about those husbands?"

"What's past is past," Cory said. She had sudden memory of her father saying that when they were growing up, of him saying it often. "I think we're all a little like that," she said. "But I sometimes wish . . ."

Kevin interrupted her. "Well, you have to be," he said. "If you stayed in the past, where would you be? You've got to move on with your life. If there's one thing I've learned from Dad, that's it. Keep your chin up. Keep going. Don't look back."

Although West had white hair and a shrunken look, and Kevin was tall and balding, for a moment Cory caught a glimpse of her father in her brother. "I don't know which past to put behind me, which childhood," she said. "It's as if we had two. One all together, the four of us, a long time ago, and another one that came later, not even spent together, the three of us."

"I don't remember much about the first childhood," said Kevin.

"Things were richer then. I don't mean money. Afterwards life got pale somehow. Our lives used to have, I don't know, more color."

Kevin shook his head. "Yours did, Cory," he said. "I just listened."

At dinner they talked about computers. West didn't have a computer. "I know I should, but I'm just about to retire. What's the point? I've done taxes with the adding machine for years. What do you use, Cory?"

She told him about Lotus and Excel, and then they talked about the spread of fax machines and modems and cellular phones, all the ways that people could now communicate quickly and effortlessly.

The meal was take-out from the Chinese place down the street, and they had had it many times in the past: chop suey, chow mein and sweet and sour pork. Chen's Kitchen had not moved with the times, for the food was exactly the same, gluey-thick with corn-starch, as it had been twenty-five years ago.

"Now when I was boy on the farm," West said. "We didn't even have a telephone. No indoor plumbing, no electricity, no telephones. If you wanted to speak to someone you had to go to them, either in the buggy or walking." He had pushed away his food, barely touched, and taken out his pipe. He began the ritual of emptying it, cleaning it and filling it. "Later on, of course," he said, and Kevin caught Cory's eye, "we had automobiles."

It was these stories that had always seemed to put their father in another century, that had made him seem part of frontier America instead of Wisconsin in the twenties and thirties. Cory remembered once when she and Kevin were watching *Maverick* on TV with West and six-year-old Kevin had said confidently, "That's like the town where you grew up, Daddy." And West had said, "Just about. Maybe not so many saloons," and he had winked at Cory. It was only then she had realized that Madison probably didn't look like that.

"You should get yourself a little PC, Dad," said Kevin. "Then you wouldn't have to worry about taking all these files with you whenever you move. You'd have them on disk."

"This will probably be my last move," said West. "That's why I'm getting rid of most of this stuff."

After dinner Kevin called Betsy and the kids—a loud, family-style conversation with nothing private about it, not the kind of talk Cory could have with Rosemary in the presence of her father and brother. Then Kevin went out for a while to see an old high-school friend of his, and Cory and her father were left sitting alone among the boxes.

She remembered her first year of high school, when Aline Stein used to drop her off at ten after an evening spent studying with Naomi. Her father would still be up, still working in his office-bedroom. As a child Cory had loved visiting her father in his office, but now the sight of his gray head bent over the green pages, the pipe smoke curling in the lamplight, only irritated her. Fresh from Naomi's, where the talk was of the new art museum in Los

Angeles and Johnson's War on Poverty and Aline's parents visit to Eastern Europe, Cory looked at her father impatiently. Why was he always working? How could he be a Republican? Had he always been so hopelessly stodgy?

In junior high Cory and her father had still talked a lot. He told her stories of his life, over and over the same ones that imparted the same message: You're on your own. You have only yourself to blame. You make your bed and lie in it. God helps those who help themselves. You can't depend on anybody but yourself.

At thirteen Cory had been for Barry Goldwater, too, just like West, in spite of the sneers of her locker-mate Jill, whose father, a sociology professor at Long Beach State, had told Jill that Goldwater was a psychopath and would blow them all to kingdom come. But at fifteen Cory reversed or rejected all her previous opinions, and "Mrs. Stein says" prefaced everything she said. "Mrs. Stein says that you can't expect people to pull themselves up by their bootstraps when we live in such an unjust world!" "Mrs. Stein says that anybody could have seen the Watts Riots coming!" "Mrs. Stein says that we're only getting into Vietnam to protect U.S. interests and not the people of Vietnam."

At first her father argued with her, but by her junior year they just stopped talking about politics. He had met the Steins a few times, dropping Cory off and picking her up, but he'd never lingered to talk, had never tried to get to know them. "That Stein girl," he called Naomi. "And her beatnik parents."

In one of the boxes for Goodwill Cory saw familiar books.

"Are you sure you don't want to save this, Dad?" she asked, picking up volume one of *The Decline and Fall of the Roman Empire*. When she opened it up a scent of pipe smoke and redwood came out, the scent she used to think was the smell of History itself. It was inscribed by the principal of East Madison High as a valedictorian gift.

To West, one of our most promising students ever,
"Those who do not learn from the past
are condemned to repeat it."
—George Santayana

As a child Cory had asked her father what that meant and he'd told her, "You can learn from your mistakes." And then he'd added, "But it's the tragedy of humanity that we often don't learn."

"No," said West now, without looking at the book. "I went through everything already."

Most of the photographs were still in piles on the coffee table. Kevin had taken only a few snapshots, mostly of him. Cory began to flip through them again, to turn them over, looking for messages.

"Which ones should I leave you, Dad?" she said.

She thought he was going to say, None, or I don't care, but instead he said, "I've already taken out the one I wanted. It was taken on a happy day, just after your mother and I met."

"What was she like, Dad?" It was a simple question, but one Cory had never managed to ask before. Right after Polly's death it would have been peculiar, for there was so much evidence of Polly still around, a lingering scent, both of illness and cold cream, of rubber gloves still under the sink, of books with slips of paper continuing to hold the page. Later, after Polly had been boxed up and given to Goodwill, after they had moved into this apartment, Cory was aware that talking about her mother only brought her father pain. She became the unmentionable thing that had happened to all of them.

"Polly," he said. "In the early days, she sparkled. She was loud, in a way I don't think was her real personality, but that she was trying on. It was part of being in California, I guess. And the time after the war, it was a loud time. She wore bright red lipstick, I remember. And rhinestone jewelry. She had a yellow dress with big red poppies on it that she wanted to wear to a faculty club party. I said, Polly, that's a pretty strong statement. And she laughed and laughed, and afterwards she used to say to me, 'I'm thinking of wearing a strong statement, West, what do you think?'"

The photo of Polly and the blonde woman, strolling in their rayon swirly dresses, with their hair up and their rhinestone earrings, was black and white, but for a moment it glowed a little under Cory's fingers. She put it in the box, along with all the others. She would take them all, since no one else wanted them.

"Now Georgia was a real loud woman," West said. "I mean, at the core. There was something big about her. She was more like me—independent—she didn't have a family. Oh, I know she could be prickly. She was set in her ways. She was fifty-five, you know, when we met."

"She was older than you then," Cory said. "I didn't know that."

"Well, she probably wouldn't have told you. But I didn't pay it any mind. She suited me." He looked at Cory. "She didn't have a family, anyone to trouble her. Not like Polly. Polly could never make her mother happy, no matter what she did. Right up until the end, almost, your grandmother let Polly know she was in the wrong."

West looked around at the boxes. "After Polly died," he said. "I felt dead myself for a long time. I just wanted to get away from everything that reminded me of the old life. It wasn't until Georgia came along that I started to live again."

Your dead period was my adolescence, Cory almost said. "You must miss Georgia a lot, Dad," and he nodded.

What a powerful urge she had suddenly, to talk to her father about Rosemary, to tell him things, quite ordinary things.

Rosemary likes to bowl, she would tell him. It's not something I ever expected I'd be doing with my girlfriend, hanging around bowling alleys, wearing those funny shoes, drinking Cokes. She likes Coke. She used to go bowling with her brothers, and she's pretty good at it.

She likes a lot of things like that—ordinary things, miniature golf and card games and watching old musicals on TV. She knows all the words to *The Music Man*—she sang it to me in the car once through Wyoming. She's a gardener too. Her garden is amazing, vegetables and flowers, more kinds of flowers than you could imagine. And she cooks, she loves to eat. There's something about her that's good at being alive. I'm learning from that. She works hard, but not like me, not so . . . relentlessly. She works and then she has time for pleasure. What a concept, huh? Faults, oh yes, she's got faults. She talks too much, for one thing, especially when she's nervous. She's insecure about her weight. I really can't stand it when she goes on and on about it; she's not that fat and even if she were, it wouldn't matter. And then there's her family—they don't live in Seattle, thank God, but there are a lot of them, I mean, really a lot, and sometimes I feel like I can't stand it, all the visiting and phone calls and remembering the birthdays. Her mother in particular is always in our face, she's a very insistent kind of woman. It's not as if they don't include me—that's part of the problem. I don't want sixty new relatives.

Many years ago she had tried to tell her father she was a lesbian. He held up his hand to stop her, just as he had when she tried to argue with him about the Vietnam War. "I always knew you would never get married," he said. "Now we don't need to say anything more about it."

But here Kevin came in and found them sitting just as he must have left them an hour ago, silent and staring at the photos. "I'm only here for a sec," he said. "Baxter's out waiting in the car. We thought I should spend the night at his house because they've got tons of room, and it would give you guys a little more space . . ." and then he was out again with his small bag. "See you tomorrow morning!"

"Just like old times," said West. "I swear, during Kevin's last couple of years here he was over at Baxter's house all the time, practically lived there. Good people, his parents, I met them once or twice."

•

Her father had gone to bed, and Cory was back in her old room. It looked quite different. The walls were rose-pink and hung with framed crewel work, a hobby of Georgia's during her illness. It had been lung cancer, no surprise in someone who had smoked for fifty years. She hadn't lived very long after the diagnosis, had chosen not to have radiation or chemo.

All those years Georgia had lived with her father and Cory had never really gotten to know her. Now all that was left of her was a smell of cigarettes so strong it had permeated the bedspread and carpet of her old room, and the elaborate crewel landscapes on the walls. It was a tired smell, not so much of death, more a slightly burnt odor, as of a sturdy mechanical part that has finally failed, the motor of a blender or mixer in the kitchen that is not worth replacing.

She wasn't sleepy. She got out the photographs again. Here was Polly as a baby, held by a woman that Cory could recognize as Grandma Cooper. Her nose was big even then, but she was much thinner and livelier. How frightened Cory had been of Grandma as a child, always hiding from that heavy step and accusing voice. But in the photograph her grandmother was holding Polly close and beaming. Cory had told Rosemary about her grandmother once, about her harshness, but Rosemary had only said, "It was a different generation. They were so much more rigid then, those Midwestern grandmothers. My mother's mother is the same way, showing her love by always finding fault, just like my mother does with me."

After Polly was gone Grandma Cooper had never come to visit again, and had died a few years later. She left Cory and Kevin each a few thousand dollars, which had helped them with college. Uncle Steve had gotten the house. He sometimes sent a Christmas card, never came to visit. Neither he nor her grandmother had come to the funeral.

Here was Uncle Steve as a young boy, with Polly's arm around him, protective, older-sister-like, as if the photographer had arranged them like that. Steve was eight or nine, in knickers and a wide-collared shirt, a straight shock of brown hair. He seemed to struggle in his sister's embrace, and his eyes held mischief—once it had just been mischief.

She put Polly's photos aside and went back to her own. She was standing on the edge of the wading pool, a plastic doughnut around her waist. Her blonde hair stuck out in little wet cowlicks. She didn't care. She was five and absolutely at home and easy in her body. Behind her Kevin burbled like a tiny whale in the bottom of the wading pool. In photo after photo Cory had that high-spirited ease, at three, at six, at eight. The faded colors of Kodachrome touched the roses, the water, brought out the green of the grass, reddened the flesh of the apricots, caught the memory of the bright yellow mimosa. The redwood picnic table was new and unweathered, the red patio had just been painted, even the flowers, in all their abundance, looked fresh and new.

She came again to the last photos of her childhood, the trip to Oak Creek Canyon with her family and Uncle Steve. It was peculiar looking back that West had never taken any more. There was no record of Polly's illness, not even a snapshot of her during one of the better times. It hadn't all been grim. They'd still had a life together, they'd still gone a few places. They had gone somewhere right at the end, to ... Nevada. Lake Mead with ... what was their name? And they'd come home across the desert, just before ... or had crossing the desert been part of an earlier trip, the trip to Arizona?

Her eyes kept uneasily going back to the four or five photographs of Oak Creek Canyon. There was her father with a fishing rod, and Kevin very small and thin in a bathing suit that hung off his hips. Polly wore a yellow sundress with spaghetti straps, and the harlequin glasses that hid her eyes. There was not a single photo of Cory alone here; she sat with her mother in one picture, and stood by her father as she tried to fish. And in one she was in a raft with Uncle Steve, waving as they set off down the river. He wasn't waving, but had his back to the camera. His straight brown hair flew up, his back was broad and tan.

Brown skin, white skin, green water.

He couldn't have been that old, thirty perhaps. Her father had told her that Polly fought with him that summer over his unemployment, and he left in a huff, back to Michigan. After Grandma died he'd sold her house and ended up in Chicago. He never went back to art school, as far as she knew, nor to Europe. They'd had no contact except for a card now and then, and once, when Cory was in her last year at high school he'd called and in a thick wheedling voice asked for West. By then Cory knew he was an alcoholic. A few years later he was dead. He'd put West down on some hospital form as next of kin. That was how they knew.

The last photo of the group must have been taken by someone else, for all five of them were in it, looking miserable. Why was that? It had been one of the few long vacations they'd ever taken—usually West taught summer school and couldn't get away. In the photo Uncle Steve stood behind Cory in his bathing trunks with his hand on her shoulder. She was in her bathing suit too, with a weak unhappy smile on her face. The bodily ease of the earlier photographs was completely gone.

Brown skin, white skin, green water.

Cory turned the photo over. In her mother's handwriting was written "Our last day at Oak Creek Canyon!"

With an unexplainable feeling of nausea she put the photograph back in the pile.

Cory picked up the morocco-bound Bible. It was inscribed from her grandfather to her mother, and just as West's books had held his smell, so the Bible, when its onion-skin pages fell open, released a thin fragrance of rose and prayer. Tucked inside the Bible were two letters.

The first was a note from Dorothy Dragon. The writing was large and untidy, but the paper was thick and deckled. It must have been sent to Polly in the hospital:

Dear Pol—

Just wanted you to know Cory and I are having a fine old time
here, watching TV, eating ice cream, living the bum's life! I've
got her enrolled at a day camp and she's doing the hula, ooh
la la. Seriously, Pol, you've got a great kid there. We're thinking of you.

Dorothy

Dorothy Dragon. Her quiet house, her quiet husband, her quiet
bamboo garden. And then her strong shoulders, her tough spirit.
Dorothy Dragon. Rosemary had never believed that was her real
name.

"It was only years later," Cory had told Rosemary, "that I figured out what kind of books she was reading."

The second letter was signed Connie and written in a comfort-
ably messy hand.

Dearest Polly,

What joy to have you visit us! I'm so happy I got to see Cory
and Kevin again. Kevin is just a doll, and Cory has that energy
that doesn't stop. . . .

"I'll think about you and this visit for a long time, Polly," the letter ended. "I love you so much."

Connie, yes, that's who the young blonde woman arm-in-arm
with Polly in the early photograph was. Connie—what was her
last name? But no matter. Connie was Polly's first friend in California, the mother of Joe and Danny and Susie and little Sal, the
one they'd always gone to the Bay with, the one who had moved
away.

Cory held up the envelope, and with a start realized it was

postmarked a week after the day her mother had died. Boulder City, Nevada. And now that visit came back too, the day at Lake Mead, the drive across the Mojave. But the woman in Cory's memory wasn't the girl of the photo. She was a big, generous-looking woman in a muumuu, who had surrounded her frail mother and held her close. They'd been sitting under an awning, on a boat rocking in bright blue water.

Holding the two letters, the photos, Cory had a sense, fragmented but clear, of Polly and her life apart from her family. A woman who was not only her mother, but a friend. Who was loved by two women with large scrawly handwriting.

What had happened to all those people from the past, to Dorothy Dragon and Connie? To Mildred Clark with her awful girls, and to Joan Perkins? Were they all still alive somewhere? Were they still Christian Scientists?

Even after they moved from the old neighborhood, Mildred Clark had offered to drive Cory and Kevin to Sunday School every week, but her father had said no, and had not taken them to any church ever again. There were times in high school when Cory went with friends to church, was fascinated by the Catholic Mass, repelled by fervent Baptist preaching, underwhelmed by Unitarian teen hootenannies. The Steins called themselves "nonobservant," which didn't mean they were atheists, exactly, and had nothing to do with being Jewish. No one ever asked Cory about having been a Christian Scientist and she couldn't have explained it if they had. She had rarely met another Christian Scientist in all the years since, and the topic only came up as a curiosity when Cory couldn't join into a group discussion with memories of childhood illnesses or playing doctor.

Rosemary, too, never asked about it, though she herself could go on for hours about growing up Catholic. "You're so lucky not to have had a religious childhood," she said once.

"But I did," said Cory.

"I mean, a real religion."

Cory opened the heavy, thin-paged Bible up at random to the Psalms and read:

> They that go down to the sea in ships,
>   that do business in great waters:
> These see the works of the Lord
>   and his wonders in the deep.
> For he commandeth, and raiseth the stormy wind
>   which lifteth up the waves thereof.
> They mount up to the heaven, they go down again to the depths:
>   their soul is melted because of trouble.
> They reel to and fro, and stagger like a drunken man,
>   and are at their wit's end.
> Then they cry unto the Lord in their trouble,
>   and he bringeth them out of their distresses.
> He maketh the storm a calm,
>   so that the waves thereof are still.
> Then are they glad because they be quiet;
>   so he bringeth them unto their desired haven.

Cory got up off the bed, she couldn't stay here, not in this old room reeking of death, not in this apartment where everything was a reminder of all she hadn't had and all she'd lost. She went through the dark living room with its boxed-up memories ready to be discarded, and out onto the landing. Through the palms the tear-drop swimming pool gleamed among the shrubbery. A few underwater lights made the water look azure at the edges, but in the center it was dark blue. The night was clear and perfumed. Night jasmine? It smelled so sweet, it smelled like the past. Never had anyone swum in that pool. It was too small for laps, too public for socializing, too adult for children.

She didn't have a swimsuit, but she went in anyway, in her underwear. What were they going to do if they found her, the manager or anyone who lived there? Throw her out? She didn't live there anymore. If anyone said anything, she would be loud.

The water was coolish, then warm. You didn't get that in the Northwest, not that sense of being embraced. There were hot tubs, there were cold lakes, there was the freezing foggy ocean, but no pools, no pools carved out of the warm night, enclosed by night jasmine and tropical palms, no pools that held you like your mother's arms.

Outside the pool were all the sad and frightening things that she would have to continue to keep at bay; inside she floated as she always had, at ease with her body, and at home.

RAKU

JANE ABEL CAME into Cory's life as a client, someone who had heard that Cory understood how to do taxes for artists, understood and didn't make them feel bad about having everything, in no particular order, in a shoe box.

"You're an artist, not a bookkeeper," Cory said in the soothing voice she used with these clients who appeared in her office with shame and fear written on their faces. "No reason to worry. That's what I'm here for," she said, as Jane handed over her shoe box.

Jane Abel seemed no different to Cory than most of the others who came to her as sinners to a confessional priest, asking for intercession with the heavenly powers, in this case the IRS. She had hennaed red hair, short and spiky, and wore a cobalt-blue silk bomber jacket over a crisp white shirt. Her glasses and earrings were both *interesting*, and so were her narrow, pointed shoes that looked hand-made. Perhaps Jane had a little more humor and a little less embarrassment than many clients when she told Cory that she had not filed a return in two or three years . . . "though it might be four . . . It's not like I make any money," she added. "You'd think the IRS would have other more important things to worry about, like tracking down Wall Street criminals. And it enrages me to think that the tiny amount that They want to wring out of me is going to go directly to the Pentagon."

All these beleaguered and resentful artistic feelings were familiar to Cory, as was Jane's offer that they do a trade. Jane was a potter and sold her work at Seattle street fairs and around the country.

"I'm sure you do wonderful stuff," Cory said. "But I'm going to need to be paid."

Jane's eyes had gravitated to the framed watercolors on the wall behind Cory. "Those aren't payments?" she asked, with a smile that took the tartness out. "Just gifts from the clients you've rescued in the past?"

"Actually," Cory. "They're mine. I painted them."

"Really," said Jane and got up to look at them more closely. "It's not that often that numbers people are artists, too."

Later that evening Cory would tell the story to Rosemary and mimic Jane Abel. "Numbers people! It consistently amazes me how people think that if you can count past ten you can't hold a paintbrush."

Cory had smiled her professional smile at Jane. "Oh, I don't really think of myself as an artist," she said.

"Why not? What's stopping you? I know people a lot less talented who feel very free to say they're painters or whatever."

"It's just a hobby," Cory said. "I mean, I don't take it seriously. Just something—to relax."

"I see," said Jane, with that amused look, and left it.

Cory had some preliminary figures the next time she talked to Jane. "But I need to know what your income was in 1986."

"Shit," said Jane. She sounded very far away on the phone. "I thought I gave you everything. Well I'll have to look again. I'm just starting a firing, it will have to be later." She paused. "Are you interested?"

Cory paused too. "In what?"

"In seeing how I do raku. Why don't you come over and watch? And then I'll look through my other shoe box."

It had been one of those days when the phone rang too often and too many numbers were missing, when she had a headache and kept looking out the window. She had always liked this view of Lake Union because it made her feel part of life even when she was working, but on this brisk dry afternoon in early autumn, with the sunlight full on the marine blue waves and so many people out in their sparkling white sailboats, it was torture.

"I'm *five* minutes away in Fremont," Jane said.

Jane's rental house had been constructed by its owner of old window frames and salvage lumber; it was low in places and tall in others, with various roofs to fit each addition. The cedar shakes were falling off and the whole place had an overgrown, ramshackle look that Cory liked. Her apartment had that same funky appearance, in the old wooden building on Eastlake with the creaking stairs over the used bookstore. She'd had it for almost fifteen years, and still every summer Irene, the bookstore owner, put the Nancy Drews in the window and every winter the fairy tales. Of course, it was mainly an office now, and a place to retreat to when things with Rosemary were either too intimate or too hard. Rosemary's house was where they spent most nights and almost every weekend. And why not? Two stories, spacious, it had everything that was needed, from a red tile fireplace that Rosemary kept well-stocked with alder logs to a kitchen big enough so they didn't bump into each other. Summers they worked in Rosemary's garden and had barbecues on the deck. Winters they curled up with the cats in front of the wide-screen TV under the quilt in the queen-size bed. In Rosemary's mind, Cory knew, she and Cory were already living together. She thought that Cory just kept her old apartment out of stubbornness.

Jane's place was more like a fairy-tale cottage than a bed and breakfast, with sunflowers and late-blooming dahlias climbing the fence and a small stone courtyard. Jane had turned the large tool shed at the bottom of the courtyard into a potting studio. On the walls were shelves of unfired pots and those that had been bisque-fired. Mostly she did pots and vases, Jane said; she threw them on the wheel.

"I sold almost everything out during the summer at the different fairs," she said. "Now I'm working on pots for the holidays."

In a red sweater under a pair of tie-dyed overalls, baggy on her thin frame, a bright blue kerchief knotted at her neck, Jane was in her element. She'd already packed the kiln that sat next to a metal container full of sawdust and leaves, and a drum of water. Now she turned the heat on in the kiln.

"There's no uniformity with raku," said Jane. "That's what I like about it. Every piece is a little bit of an experiment. It will never turn out exactly the way you predict, even though sometimes it can be close."

By this time the light was going, though it wasn't yet completely dark. Evening was Cory's least favorite part of life; there was something so melancholy to her about the cold blue paleness of the shift from day to night. So it was good to see the pots turning red-hot through the vent. They were an unearthly burning coral color.

"It's a very hot firing," Jane said. "The same temperature as molten lava. In a minute we'll take them out." She had on goggles now, over her deep red hair, and looked like an old-fashioned pilot, very competent and practical, about to cross the Atlantic on a solo flight.

"When they're still hot like that?"

"It only works when they're burning hot," Jane said and laughed. There was a way she had of making everything sound sexual and teasing that went oddly with her matter-of-fact movements. She pulled on a heavy apron and huge fireproof gloves, and with a pair of long-handled tongs, reached inside and firmly grasped a pot and brought it out and set it in the metal box of leaves and sawdust. She took out all six pots which glowed like ingots from a steel mill. The mixture of sawdust and leaves was already smoking and after another few seconds a fire broke out and charred the already red-hot clay. It hadn't rained in August and instead of the usual damp humus smell of the earth, the air was crisp and smelled of leaves and apples; it combined now with the slightly acrid burning smell to make something like excitement.

Then Jane carefully pulled a pot out of the little fire, as if it were an archeological discovery, blackened with time, half-carbonized from some historical moment when the barbarians swept down unexpectedly upon the village. Jane plunged the pot in the drum of cold water, where it sizzled—the way, as a child, Cory had imagined the sun sizzled when it sank into the sea. To Cory's surprise, when the soot was washed off, the pot shimmered with a metallic rainbow of copper, rose and turquoise.

"I'm doing lurid at the moment," Jane said. "Personally, I like a simpler look, just cracked white and smoky black, with maybe a glint of silver or gold, but people seem to go for the brighter things."

She held the tongs out to Cory. "Here's your opportunity. Want to take a chance?"

"It's late," Cory said. "I should go."

But Jane said, "How about dinner? I was just going to heat up some soup and I have some good rye bread. Stay a while longer."

"I can't," said Cory. "My . . . lover is waiting for me."

"Oh," said Jane. "Have you been together long?"

"About three years."

"But you don't live together?"

" . . . No."

"Well, we'll have dinner another time," Jane said. "As friends."

♦

They began to meet occasionally for coffee, even after Cory had finished Jane's taxes. Sometimes they went to the art museum or to galleries. It was a slower period for Cory; she was mainly working on helping a small woman-owned business set up an accounting program on their new computer. She got into the habit of stopping over at Jane Abel's when she knew Jane was firing, at the transition between day and evening. In the end Jane had never paid her for preparing her tax return, but she had given her a lovely lurid pot and had offered to let her use her studio anytime and to give her lessons on the wheel.

"We should have her over sometime," Rosemary said. "She sounds interesting." But Rosemary had an intense court case on the boil—she was defending a woman who'd been stalked for two years by her ex-husband and who'd ended up shooting him so he became paralyzed—and often had to stay late in her office and work weekends. "It's great you've got a friend to do something with while I'm so busy," Rosemary said. "Are you going to start doing raku yourself?"

"I'm thinking about it," said Cory. "Maybe it's time to try something new."

It was late at night and they were in Rosemary's bedroom. It had been another long day for Rosemary. She came in around nine, absently ate the Thai take-out that Cory had brought over, talked about the case a while, took a shower, watched a TV program with Cory and was now almost asleep in her flannel nightgown. They hugged each other close, and then Cory heard Rosemary sighing into sleep. Instead of snuggling into her warm, broad back as she usually did, Cory turned on her side, thinking unwillingly of Jane.

"Why did you choose watercolor?" Jane had asked.

"Color," said Cory, after a moment. "I like to look at colors."

"It's so visual," said Jane. "So restrained. You and your tiny paintbrush. I like to get my hands dirty."

"Yes, it's visual," Cory said, "but I feel it."

"But it can't be a very passionate sensation, can it?" Jane said, in her challenging way just this side of a hard kiss. "Not like squeezing wet clay through your fingers."

Rosemary was snoring softly. She was so tired these days. Whose fault was it that they never made love anymore?

It had begun when Cory returned from visiting her father the previous fall. She'd returned with photographs that she was reluctant to show Rosemary, as if they were some secret shame or evidence of a crime. She was both afraid that to Rosemary they would be ordinary—not special at all—but also that they would provoke questions to which she couldn't give the answers. What happened, and what went wrong?

"But what a cute kid you were!" exclaimed Rosemary. "Look at that grin. I never suspected what a clown you were."

Instead of making Cory happy, these comments stabbed. What happened? What went wrong?

Rosemary passed over the Oak Creek Canyon photos—"Oh, family vacations, I remember those!"—and settled on one of Cory and her mother. "You should get this enlarged and frame it. We could put it in the bedroom."

"No," said Cory, snatching it away. "I don't want . . ." But what was it she didn't want? Not to have anyone see what Polly looked like? Not to have anyone see that Cory had ever had a mother? Not to have the photo up in what Rosemary thought of as their bedroom, but wasn't?

Their sexuality together had rarely been effortless. Cory sometimes had the feeling Rosemary expected more from lesbian lovemaking than she got. Cory suspected that while Rosemary complained that in her marriage everything was structured around her husband's pleasure, at least it had a structure that Rosemary recognized. As for Cory, when she stopped drinking, she realized that she'd never had sex without alcohol before. From her college days, when she'd gone home with various flirtations from the newspaper staff after long evenings of beer drinking at some Pizza Hut, to her first encounters with those sexy dyke pool players at the Silver Slipper, Cory had been used to drink as the preliminary to passion. The absence of alcohol meant that there was nothing between her and her partner, nothing that could carry her along so she didn't have to think about what she was doing.

Cory and Rosemary had had spells like this before, and Cory always told herself that wild sex wasn't the reason she'd gotten involved with Rosemary in the first place. She'd had wild sex before; this time she wanted something deeper and more meaningful. Yes, they'd had weeks and a couple of months once like this before, so at first it didn't seem unusual. By that time it was December and for the second year in a row they went to St. Paul to spend Christmas with Rosemary's family.

The first time it had been nerve-wracking but strangely exhilarating and even fun. By that time they'd been together over a year, and Cory had already met Rosemary's parents on their annual trip out to Seattle. But Christmas brought all the relatives together and they went from party to party for over a week, in one roomy old house to the next, all of them blazing with lights and decorations, while outside the snow was piled high and the air was so cold your breath crackled. At every house Cory was carefully, respectfully introduced as Rosemary's "friend" and while some of the older people pretended not to know what that meant, others said, "Welcome to the family, Cory! I hope you know what you're letting yourself in for."

Phil, Rosemary's father, was impressed that she had her own business, and talked to her for hours about tax shelters to show he wasn't prejudiced against homosexuals. Anne, her mother, got teary-eyed at the end as they stood at the airport gate, and said, "I feel as if I have another daughter now."

The second time the snow had been patchier, not pretty at all, blown about by harsh Arctic winds. Rosemary's grandmother had just died, suddenly, from a stroke, a few weeks before, and Anne was depressed, sharper and more inclined to make pronouncements and find fault. She pointed out several times the first day that Rosemary had put on weight and wondered if she might want to skip dessert, a dessert which of course was some incredible Bavarian recipe with butter and cream and hazelnuts and chocolate ("Have another slice, Cory. My mother, bless her heart, gave me this recipe!") handed down through generations of German Catholic pastry chefs.

Day by day Rosemary lost all sense of herself as an independent adult and became the youngest girl again in a family of boys. She was no longer a progressive lawyer, a role model for her ten nieces and nephews, but a divorcée, a lapsed Catholic, a shameless, hugely fat unattractive lesbian. Of course she couldn't make love when she felt this way about herself, no matter how many times Cory tried to tell her she was beautiful.

Back in Seattle, January passed in a gloomy fog, and February, the most depressing month of the year, when everyone in the Northwest began to say that they absolutely could not take it, could not take *another* day of this incessant rain, these lowering skies, this darkness, was worse.

It had been in February that Cory woke up from a dream one night, as if she'd been underwater and was shooting to the surface. There was Uncle Steve standing in a green pool flickering with light, and he was holding his penis, and smiling.

That was all. Cory got out of bed, and her stomach heaved. It wasn't the penis so much as the smile. She stood by the window, staring out at the black sky streaming with rain. *It must be a dream. How could it be real? It was a bad dream.*

She wanted to tell Rosemary, but had trouble finding the right time, or the words. Everything sounded so melodramatic, so intense. In the shower, driving, she experimented:

Cory: "You know my uncle?"

Rosemary: "What uncle?"

Cory: "My Uncle Steve."

Rosemary: "You've never mentioned any Uncle Steve."

Cory: "My *mother's* brother."

When it finally came out, burst out of her, it was in the middle of trying to make love, when Cory suddenly began to shake uncontrollably.

And of course Rosemary didn't say, "What Uncle Steve?" Very tenderly she held Cory and said, "Oh my God, Cory. Tell me what you remember."

She was clinging to a boulder in the middle of the river, a river that was rushing fast, trying to pull her with it.

She was drowning in a milky white river; every time she tried to come up for air something forced her down and made her swallow.

She was staring at a brown rug, very close to her face. The air was very cold against her skin and the brown and tan tiles were like a naked body where you see the lines the sun has made against the bathing suit.

Where was Kevin?

Where was her mother?

Where was her father? Was he in the next room? Did she cry out? Did he hear her? Did anybody hear her?

Where was her mother?

Every night Cory woke from nightmares of pale hands trying to drown her and claws scraping at the windows, and every day she was afraid in the pit of her stomach. Rosemary said she should go to a therapist or to an incest survivors' group, but Cory said that wasn't her way. She didn't remember enough to talk about what had happened, and she didn't want to remember any more. Talking to a therapist might make everything worse. Her uncle was dead, and she couldn't do anything about it now. And maybe—

maybe—she was making it up anyway. She would have told her mother if something like that had happened, wouldn't she? Why hadn't she told her mother right away?

In March she'd gone unsuspiciously to the doctor for her routine pap smear and the doctor had suggested beginning a yearly mammogram because of her age and her history.

"Now I don't want you to be worried," the doctor had said a few days later. "It's not a lump. It's more sort of a shadow on the mammogram. Just to be safe, we'll do an ultrasound."

She hadn't told Rosemary about the mammogram, but she told her about the results of the ultrasound. It too had picked up something, nothing so definite as lump, yet still nothing that could be dismissed.

"Why didn't you tell me right away?" said Rosemary.

"Because it would make it seem more real."

"It is real," Rosemary said.

"I'm going to die," Cory said. "I'm exactly my mother's age, thirty-nine. That's when she found her lump."

"Yes, but you don't even have a lump. And your mother's case, from what you've told me, was pretty well advanced by the time they . . . because she . . . "

"Because she was a religious fanatic, right? Go ahead and say it, 'She was an idiot.'"

"That's your opinion," said Rosemary. "I never knew her. I doubt though," she added softly, "that she was an idiot."

The biopsy had shown nothing. There was nothing to show.

Rosemary took her out to dinner. "I *knew* there wouldn't be anything," she said.

"There's always next year's mammogram," said Cory.

"We'll tackle that next year," said Rosemary cheerfully.

But now Cory lay in bed and thought, I know there won't be a next year. She felt already half-dead, and as if it didn't matter much what she did. The nightmares had stopped, replaced by something worse, long empty nights by Rosemary's side. While

Rosemary slept exhaustedly and dreamed of defending her client from her horrible ex-husband, Cory lay there stiff and sleepless, imagining her own death in grisly detail.

"What's that?" said Jane Abel after they had made love in the candlelight of her low-ceilinged, pine-paneled bedroom.

"What?"

"That scar, on your breast, underneath. It's not that old."

"I had a biopsy in the spring," Cory said. "You know these mammogram fanatics. And then they see something, not even a lump—a shadow—and they've got their knives out."

"But you're young to have a mammogram," said Jane. "I thought they didn't start with them till you were in your forties. Unless you have a family history."

"I have a family history."

"Your mother?"

"Yeah."

"Died?"

"Yeah."

"Well," said Jane. "Me too."

Afterwards, trying to explain to herself not why she got into bed with Jane, but why she stayed for such a long time, it was this conversation Cory thought about. Always she dreaded the moment when someone asked about her mother, and she had to say her mother was dead and the other person said, I'm sorry.

But with Jane that was unnecessary.

"I had this girlfriend," said Jane. "Who was always trying to get me and her mom together. 'Let's go shopping with my mom,' she'd say. 'Afterwards we'll go out to a restaurant and gossip.' I *hated* being with the two of them. It was so incredibly boring. I said to Beth, 'I hate to shop,' and she said, 'But buying things isn't the point, the point is to do it together, to talk girl talk and just ... be girls together. I thought you'd like that, since you didn't have it when you were growing up.'"

Cory and Jane looked at each other and shuddered. "Girl talk!"

Jane said, "I finally had to look Beth in the eye and say, 'I don't know how to do girl things and I don't want to learn!' And then we broke up."

"And now that their mothers are getting older," Cory said, "And getting sick sometimes, they go on and on about what they're going to do when something happens to them. A friend of mine, thirty-six years old, says to me—to me!—'I know I'll feel totally devastated when my mother dies.' Like I should feel sorry for her." It was Rosemary who'd said that, but Cory didn't tell Jane.

"Nobody ever assumes that you might not want to hear about their fucking mothers year after year," Jane said. "I was at a brunch a few months ago, with a group of women I didn't know, and they start trading stories, you know, the usual: My mother says and My mother does and My mother is always, and the refrain after every story was 'Well, you know how mothers are,' at which they all sighed and nodded their heads in that fucking way they *do*, and I wanted to shout, 'No, I don't know how mothers are, you insensitive bitches.' And I couldn't believe, at the age of thirty-five, twenty years later, that it could still hurt so much to say I *didn't* have a mother, I *don't* have a mother."

Sex with Jane was hot and uncomplicated, with an edge that was new but also familiar to Cory. It reminded her of her early days as a lesbian, when drinking and stigma went along with the excitement of a woman's rough jean-clad thigh pressed against her on the dance floor, a leather belt that rubbed against her stomach, a sweaty band of skin where her T-shirt lifted up in back, a head thrown back, a neck exposed. It was never exciting to wake up with these women in the sour, sweat-dried mornings, to feel puffy-eyed and cranky, to see the room filled with the shabby detritus of the seventies' group house—political posters on the walls, *Rubyfruit Jungle* by the side of the bed, Meg Christian on the stereo, over and over that gym teacher song—but even on those mornings, walking home hung-over past housewives weeding their gardens, it was possible to enjoy the dissolute pleasures of secret perversity.

The excitement was in the forbidden, and Jane was forbidden. But it was more than that. Jane wasn't a kind and good person in the way that Rosemary was and that Cory had been trying to be. Jane was flip, cynical, even mean-spirited, and somehow that was refreshing. Rosemary was always certain who was good (the battered wife) and who was bad (the abusive husband); she worked herself to the bone for good causes, believed in the innocence of those she defended, the righteousness of the law, the theories of justice behind the flawed legal system. She'd grown up protected, thinking she could change the world.

She believed in fairness, and goodness, because nothing bad had ever happened to her, Cory thought. She might defend people who had gone out of control, but Rosemary herself would never go out of control. She had no idea what it felt like. No idea what it could feel like to *want* to go out of control.

Besides that, sex with Jane proved that Cory wasn't the one with the problem. Because Jane didn't seem to have any hang-ups about her body, and that meant Cory didn't have to think much about Jane. Jane could take care of herself. She liked sex fast and rough; she had little time for tenderness and after she'd had an orgasm, always very intense, the fire burned out of her eyes and she was bored. The excitement was all in the build-up, and afterwards she was cool, not so much hard as off-hand. She could talk about what she liked, she knew what she liked; it almost seemed a matter of indifference to her though.

That was fine with Cory. She could let herself go, she could come without thinking about Jane or anybody or anything else. She didn't have to think about her uncle when she was with Jane, she didn't have to think about her mother, or her own approaching death; she didn't have to think about Rosemary, she didn't even have to drink to get to a red-hot flame that burned everything in its path.

Cory had begun to work with clay. Watercolor was color and light, evanescent, delicate. It wasn't so much what she painted—usually the same places, Lake Union, the houseboats, the drawbridges, ferries on the Sound—but the state of mind that painting put her in. Clay was not meditative, she found. It was something she could pummel and tear, smash and rip, something she could grapple with. Clay was also something she could hold tenderly, a bowl the size of her cupped hands, a body that stood upright, a face that could look back at her.

She let her fingers form small figures, four and six inches high. The first one came as a surprise. It had a broad torso and a wide head that sat directly on its shoulders. The legs were thick and short with heavy feet that anchored the figure and made it feel firmly connected to the ground. The arms folded over the belly in a gesture of protection. She decided it was a girl or a woman and gave her snub breasts, but no genitals, no holes down there. So she could breathe, Cory gave her a tiny mouth, and two round-punched little eyes. The face looked young, a little alarmed. Where the hands met over the belly was a frightened feeling.

Rosemary would have said, "Who is this? Is this you? How old are you here?" But Jane only picked it up with interest and re-marked, "If it's solid, it will crack when it's fired. You need to hollow it out."

"I don't want a bunch of holes in it."

"No, no," said Jane. "We'll just leave some ventilation through the soles of the feet. Where no one will notice."

Cory didn't want a rainbow effect, so she brushed the figure with a glaze that would turn brown and light copper and put it in the kiln. When it was the temperature of molten lava she

reached inside and took it out, then buried it in sawdust and cedar chips. Brushing the soot off afterwards she was strangely
moved. The figure stared up at her with wide-open eyes, asking
not to be hurt because it could not hide itself.

It was when she worked the clay that the rage came. It came flood-
ing through her like a river and made her twist and pummel the
damp elastic clay. She made shapes only she knew the meaning of
and squashed them flat. Her grandmother's face, her mother's
breast, her uncle's dick.

"I hate you," she told the clay as she molded it. "Why did you
always push my mother around? She wasn't like you and me, she
wasn't tough underneath. All she did was try to please you and
you found fault with her. You never saw her spirit. All those stories about your courageous wild girlhood, where did it go, why
didn't you save some of that for my mother?"

She threw her grandmother across the table and squeezed her
mother until words she'd never said before burst out, in fury now,
not sadness:

"Why didn't you stand up to Grandma? Why didn't you go to
the doctor the moment you felt that lump? How could you believe
in all that Christian Science garbage about truth and healing? If
you had to belong to that church why couldn't you have taken the
whole thing less seriously? Why couldn't you have been like everybody else? I needed a mother, if I'd had a mother I wouldn't
be as fucked up as I am. You let your brother molest me. Where
were you that day on the river, and the two other times he attacked me in the guest room? If you hadn't gotten sick you could
have done something. But you didn't do anything. You just died
and left me to deal with everything on my own."

But her greatest rage she reserved for her uncle. She felt his
alcoholic breath bubbling out of the clay as she bent it and
stretched it and dropped it on the floor and walked on it. She felt

his voice, still potent, with its dangerous contempt, oozing from the clay when she picked it up again. All her figures of her uncle were monster-like and they shaped themselves over and over again from innocuous material. "I hate you, I hate you, I hate you," she could tell the clay that was her uncle, "Do you think that just because you were drinking, it didn't matter what you did?" But as long as she touched it, it told her what to do and made her obey.

She finally turned away from him and made more of the small, child-like figures. They began to change, to become less vulnerable; less hurt and wide-eyed, not so weak at the shoulders and so feeble at the knees. One afternoon she made a new and larger model, one that was taller, fiercer. Her legs were sturdy, wide-apart, and her feet were like rocks, immovable. Her arms hung slightly bent at her sides, ready to punch, to lunge, to grab him by the scruff of the neck, to spit in his face and to grind him into the dirt. The head was held high and the gaze was steady and hard. She made more like this one, and each one was stronger. Cory began to glaze these figures with stripes, to give them breastplates and armored legs and arms, to make their faces glow with right-eousness and anger. When she pulled them out of the fire with her tongs and set them in the straw they burst into flame with their fury and grew harder and more resistant, shimmering underneath their blackened coating. A few of them broke, but the rest stayed whole, taken from the ashes, raised up again.

As long as Rosemary didn't ask, Cory didn't have to tell her. But one day the court case was over. Rosemary had won again, but the whole thing had been a strain. She was ready to relax, and spend more time with Cory. By that time Cory and Jane had been in-volved for almost a month.

"But we agreed," said Rosemary, dumbfounded. "We agreed we'd tell each other before anything happened."

They were in Rosemary's bedroom. It was early morning, a

terrible time to argue. Rosemary was standing at the foot of the bed in her slightly stained flannel nightgown, her curly hair half-brushed. She was just starting her period and she looked large and disheveled—undone—by the news. All she had asked, casually, was, "What about an early dinner and a movie tonight?" as Cory was slipping out the door.

"Can't," said Cory awkwardly. "I . . . have a date with Jane."

"You see her all the time," said Rosemary. "I hope you're not thinking of having an affair." Her tone was light, then she saw Cory's guilty expression.

"But we *agreed*," Rosemary wailed again. Her hair on one side was wild and tangled, on the other calmly ringleted, as if the news had gone in one ear and had not yet penetrated to the other side.

"It doesn't work like that, Rosemary," said Cory. "Things can just happen."

"But why didn't you tell me earlier?"

"You were busy."

"Not too busy to hear you were leaving me for someone else!"

"I'm not leaving you," Cory said uncertainly.

"No, you're not, because I'm throwing you out. I've had it with you. Do you hear? The whole year—everything we've been through—and I waited—I supported . . ." She was sobbing now, and Cory stood paralyzed.

She wanted to put her arms around Rosemary and she also wanted desperately to leave.

"Oh, get out," said Rosemary, throwing her hairbrush at her. "Don't even think about staying. Don't you know you've hurt me? Do you have any feelings at all?"

Cory stumbled out of the room and ran downstairs. She did have feelings, but she didn't know what they were. She only knew that she didn't want Rosemary's feelings. She couldn't bear to think, even, what those feelings were.

♦

Cory moved her things out of Rosemary's but she didn't move them into Jane's funky little house. Now, more than ever, she needed her own place, where she could go, not so much to some-place orderly, but to someplace familiar. It stayed very much her own, too, because Jane didn't like to set foot there.

"It's like being in an office building, like my father's office building," she said. Jane despised her father. He had married her stepmother less than a year after Jane's mother died. "What an absolute cunt," said Jane. "She was an *interior decorator*. I couldn't wait to get out of the house. The last two years of high school were torture. I spent most of my time smoking dope and at friends' houses. That's when I discovered art. How if you completely ab-sorbed yourself in making something, you wouldn't feel anything else."

"I've found it to be different," said Cory. "At least with the clay. It's when I'm making art that I feel something. At least, something moves through me, and afterwards, it's better."

"That probably means you're doing therapy, rather than art," Jane said, with her usual smile that held something provocative and perhaps even cruel in it.

If Rosemary had said something like that, Cory would have argued with her or let it go. But in Jane's mocking tone words were darts, and things she said left sharp deep holes that festered into abscesses.

Being with Jane reminded Cory of how she used to be with earlier lovers. How she would open up and show something she shouldn't and then get hurt. How the whole relationship or affair, after the first glorious sharing, would be one long retreat, until by the end they had no words left that weren't tainted with the mean-ing of how they had been used before.

Cory noticed these days how often Jane used words like *cunt* and *bitch*. Men were stupid, or pals, or sweet guys. But women were sluts and whores and assholes and deserved to be machine-gunned or locked in a basement for the rest of their lives. "I can't help it," Jane said. "Women are a mystery to me. I'm drawn to them but they drive me nuts. Women say to me, Are you butch? Are you femme? And I say, How the hell do I know?" She laughed the seductive laugh that had needles in it. "I'm not a girl. I somehow missed out on the major lesson of how to enjoy being feminine. But on the other hand, I'm not sure I like girls that much either."

At first Cory had experienced a frisson of rebelliousness when Jane talked like this, when Jane said, "I can't be PC, I just can't. Women can be as bad as men, *worse* than men." She'd sometimes joined Jane in making fun of women and their emotions. Jane called them *feelinks*.

"Oh, I'm having a feelink," she said. "Let's share it!"

They had talked, often, about how they felt confused by what women wanted.

"I grew up around two guys," said Cory. "Around them I felt emotional if I said *Hello, how are you?* It's been hard to know how to be around women. I feel panicky when they start crying. It just makes me want to run away."

Jane had tried to pull out of Cory how things had gone with Rosemary that morning, to fan some jealousy perhaps, or set the triangle in motion again. "I'm drawn to couples," she admitted with a laugh. "I know it's fucked up, but it's an old pattern. Trying to get my dad away from the old bag."

She wanted Cory to make fun of Rosemary and her *feelinks*. Their affair depended on such sneering. But after the scene in Rosemary's bedroom, Cory had found it more difficult. Would it have been better if Rosemary had just shrugged her shoulders and said, "See you around"? Only once since that meeting had they talked on the phone—about when Rosemary would be gone so Cory could pick up some clothes. Rosemary had been in her office, legal and distant. She'd said, "I don't see any point in getting together right now to talk. I feel like you're behind a glass wall. You can see me but nothing I say could possibly sink in."

Cory didn't tell Jane about that phone conversation. Jane preferred to think of Rosemary rampaging around in PMS fury, acting like a betrayed woman. "She'll be calling soon to beg you to come back to her," Jane predicted.

But Rosemary didn't call. Two weeks passed, three. Cory kept having conversations with Rosemary in her mind, in which she'd explain and Rosemary would understand. She wanted to show Rosemary her raku figurines and have Rosemary say, "Now I see what you've been going through."

She had a sense, though, that she might never hear Rosemary say that. Not now.

The last time Cory saw Jane was a cold day in November. She had known for a while that Jane was getting involved with someone else, but she pretended not to mind. She went over to use the potting shed and that was when Jane told her it might be better if she didn't come by anymore.

"Things with Sarah are heating up," she said. "She's decided to leave her girlfriend and is going to need a place to stay for a week or so. It would be awkward trying to explain you at the moment. It's a big step she's taking, she might get cold feet."

Jane added, "Don't look at me that way. I know, I know, I'm fucked up. But what can I do? I can't go to therapy, I don't have any money."

"Oh really?" said Cory, but she had never been as good as Jane with sarcasm. Perhaps Jane was just better at ignoring it.

"I hope we can keep in touch, Cory. I'll definitely be calling you next March about my taxes. That is, if I decide to keep paying them! Are you going to leave me any examples of your work, or do you want to take them all?"

Cory thought of smashing one of the figures that sat on the shelf at Jane's feet, or saying something cutting, like, "Why would you want them? It's not like they're art or anything."

But when she picked up the earliest figure, with its open mouth and eyes and timid, don't-hurt-me look, a wave of tenderness overwhelmed her. She packed up all her work in a box while Jane, who had to make an urgent phone call, went inside, and left Jane a note, written in soot on a pale bisque-fired bowl, that said, "Get some help."

Then she took the bowl with her.

Cory went over to see Rosemary the next day, which was a Saturday. She found Rosemary in the back yard, raking yellow horse chestnut leaves into a pile, with her curly hair tied back in a utilitarian ponytail, in a stained sweatshirt and dirty jeans. There had been a storm a few days ago and most of the last leaves on the trees had come down. What was left was a curious reversal. As if the world had turned upside down. All the crinkled, soggy leaves were on the ground and the branches were bare as tree roots against the milk gravy sky.

Cory started helping Rosemary, stuffing leaves in bags. After they'd been working without speaking for a while, Rosemary said, "It's almost been a year since we went to St. Paul. My mother's been calling asking if we're coming for Christmas. I just told her no. It's harder than I thought to tell them about us breaking up. It's one thing to fail as a heterosexual. They could always say I got divorced because I wasn't 'quite . . . you know.' But now I seem to have failed in my lesbian partnership, too."

"That's something I don't have to worry about," said Cory. "I don't mean to sound flip," she added, seeing Rosemary's face. "It makes me incredibly sad, in fact, to think there's no one in my family who would notice, much less care, if you and I stay together or not." She began to cry, something she almost never did.

Rosemary just looked at her; she didn't come over to enfold her in those soft, comforting arms. "I don't understand," she said finally. "I thought we *were* broken up."

What a dull gray day it was, how heartless and cold. "I've stopped seeing Jane," Cory said.

"Ah."

The Rosemary she knew was one who rushed into the bare spots of the conversation and filled them up, who was uncomfortable with silence, who was all questions and explanations, who said what most drove her crazy about her ex-husband was how he just said, 'Ah,' as if that were the end of it.

"I miss you," said Cory, standing with her rake in hand. "I love you."

"Ah." Rosemary stood there too, though not as if she were happy to hear it. "I don't know why I should, but I still care—love you, too." she said finally. "But if we started up again, it would have to be different."

"How different?"

"Very different."

"Ah." Now it was Cory's turn.

"I don't always want to be reacting to you. I refuse to be a sap ever again."

"Well, I know that I . . . "

"I'd want to go to couples therapy," Rosemary interrupted her, "and to make some clear agreements about what we expect and don't expect in this relationship. You can't lie to me."

"I won't lie," Cory said. "It was just that . . . "

Rosemary shook her head. "Don't try to explain it now. I really can't take it at the moment." Her voice grew softer, but was still stern. "I also think that you should go to therapy on your own, to deal with your incest memories."

Cory wanted to say no, not yet, but it came out, ". . . I know I have to do something" instead.

"I'll stand by you. I'll keeping trying to be patient. But you have to promise to deal with it, not run away like you have been doing."

It was getting to sound too much like every single thing was

Cory's fault. "Well, I'm not going to your family's for Christmas. I'm sick of your family."

"All right," said Rosemary, and she almost looked as if she were enjoying this. The tough greedy look was on her freckled face and Cory was amazed she'd ever told Jane that Rosemary suffered from terminal niceness. The woman was a trial lawyer, for God's sake. "What else?"

"You work too much."

"So do you. I'll cut back if you will."

"I'm keeping my apartment."

"Good. I want you to have someplace to go when I'm fed up with you."

"And it can't be some New Age therapist with crystals that we go to."

"Oh darn!"

"And stop worrying so much about your weight. Your body is beautiful, there's nothing wrong with it."

"There's nothing wrong with yours either," snapped Rosemary.

But this was almost too near the bone, because deep inside, each of them did feel damaged, hurt and scared.

They twisted the tops of the green plastic bags full of leaves up tight and lugged them around the side of the house to be picked up Tuesday morning. They went back to start preparing Rosemary's garden for winter, planting iris bulbs and mulching over the beds.

Next spring the irises would come up, lavender and yellow by the score, and waving on their tall stems. Their outer petals would fold back, ruffled and striped and bold, their inner petals would stand upright, curling slightly in, half protecting, half revealing the soft secret heart of the iris. You had to count on that, when you planted the hard papery bulbs in the dreariest and drabbest time of year, that by spring everything would bloom again, everything would again rise up in flower.

STILL LIFE

NO PART OF a city, if you've lived in it long enough, has only one history. The past is not replaced; instead, new layers of memory build up. In watercolor, this layering is called glazing. A thin wash of cobalt over crimson and over that another wash of crimson makes a different violet on the page than if the colors are mixed first on the palette and then painted on. Already, a year after the affair with Jane Abel, Fremont was not—or not just—the neighborhood where Jane's potting studio had been, but the part of town where Cory's therapist, Roberta Lu, lived. Before Jane, Fremont had been where her travel agent used to have her office, and before that, where the anti-nuclear group had its meetings. After Roberta, it might be anything. If there ever was an after-Roberta.

Cory had had a standing appointment with Roberta Lu for over six months now, every Thursday at three in the afternoon. She took off early from work then; it was her way of making time to think about her life. Sometimes Cory walked to Fremont, both ways, right around the north end of Lake Union, past Ivar's Salmon House and Gas Works Park, to the old-fashioned brick blocks of the small business district.

On the way there, Cory walked quickly, composing in her head all the things she wanted to tell Roberta, all the things that had happened to her that week, all the things she'd thought about. But on the way home, Cory walked slowly and thought about what she'd really said, which always surprised her and was nothing like what she'd planned.

She was walking home now. Earlier it had rained and it would again. The air was wet, sharp, solitary. Now, in November, it would be dark by five. The lake was a deep gray-green, with a scudding of silver waves reflecting the late afternoon sky.

They'd been talking today about memory, about loss, about sex. The usual things. Cory felt she wasn't moving forward, and sometimes persuaded herself that, in fact, she was moving backwards. It used to be, when she didn't remember, that her suffering was silent and contained, something that could be pushed to the back of the refrigerator and forgotten. These days she was raw. Trying to find the words, to have the emotions that went with the words, Cory felt like she had in the old days when she couldn't read, when she'd been given a heavy book full of black insects and been told to sound them out, to turn them into words.

It had been the same—only worse—with the couples counselor she and Rosemary went to earlier this year for a few months. That therapist, Lois Larkin, was fluent in jargon and believed that everyone else should be, too. In her mouth "incest survivor" sounded like a normal thing, like being a car mechanic or a nurse. "How do you, Cory, as an incest survivor, feel about that?" she would say. Lois had short black hair and button black eyes. She usually wore loose cotton trousers and a striped Guatemalan shirt over a turtleneck. She was active in progressive circles, and Cory had first met her in the seventies at an anti-racism workshop. "As a former Catholic, raised-middle-class lesbian . . . " Lois used to begin her self-examinations.

Lois and Rosemary bonded about their Catholic girlhoods and about being "partners of incest survivors," who needed to be supportive but also "to take care of ourselves around this." Sometimes Lois spoke of her girlfriend, without using her name, and told them of a book the girlfriend had read that had been helpful, or how the two of them had resolved some issue. Cory knew who the girlfriend was—she was Donna Laura—who was a cashier at the Ravenna PCC. Sometimes when Cory put her vegetables on the counter, she looked at Donna Laura, a slight, brown-haired, ordinary-looking woman in jeans and a canvas apron, and wondered about her and Lois's sex life. Lois always spoke about sex as if it were a matter of making a nice, healthy vegetarian soup. Get the recipe book out, assemble the ingredients, chop a little, blend a little, cook it up and serve it—Delicious! Something that was tasty *and* good for you, too. Sex, the sex-manual kind, was unabashedly good, positive, warm and loving. It was not mysterious, demonic and wild. It was not harsh and strange and overwhelming, with a core of numbness that let you forget what was going on even as it happened. It was not subject to rare, unexpected moments of grace, when there was a connection, a melting between you and your lover, between you and your universe.

"Everything that has been learned can be unlearned and relearned," said Lois. And, quoting from a well-known lesbian sex counselor: "All you need is a willingness."

Going through the PCC check-out line ("Got your co-op card?" asked Donna Laura with a cheerful smile), Cory imagined Lois, bouncy and solicitous in her half of the queen-sized bed, saying "Darling, how 'bout it? Do you have a willingness tonight?" And Donna, slight, shy, saying, "Well, as an incest survivor I don't really have desire, in fact I have fear—perhaps even revulsion—but I do feel a slight willingness. Let's go with that."

But Cory never had a willingness nowadays, forget the desire. All she seemed to have was a resistance as heavy as a boulder blocking a spring.

Talking with Roberta wasn't easy, but it was better than trying to talk with Lois. Roberta was about fifty, Chinese-American, with wild, crackly gray hair and jewelry that she said she made her-self—twisted copper wire and chunks of topaz and tourmaline. She laughed quite a lot—inappropriately, Cory thought at first—was a therapist supposed to be quite so casual and lively? Roberta shrugged off Cory asking how other women dealt with memories of sexual abuse. "How are *you* going to deal with them?" Roberta didn't use jargon, and even if she said, "You must have felt abandoned by your mother even before she died," it sounded like a normal person expressing sympathy, not like the calculated probe of a trained therapist.

Lois's office had rag dolls and Teddy bears sitting on the windowsills and pastel boxes of Kleenex, which Cory never used, on every table. Roberta's had a tatami mat, two rattan chairs and a few Tibetan prayer flags on a line by the window. The room was upstairs and caught the western light if there was any. For the past two months there had been some kind of construction project going on nearby, with jackhammering.

Roberta had Cory tell her stories.

"They're not stories," Cory had protested at first. "It's just—flashes, pictures. Skin, water. A rock. Over and over, the same thing, the same sick helpless feeling. My uncle's eyes, his weird smile. The pictures just flash up; I can't get rid of them."

"The images will always have a disruptive force until they're integrated into some kind of narrative," said Roberta. "That's their power—to force their way into your consciousness. You can't get rid of them, but you can give them a context."

"I don't remember enough," Cory always began, and then she talked for an hour and Roberta had to pry her out of the chair. Afterwards she had more than the sound of a rushing river in her mind, more than a sense of choking, and of breaking. She had an alcoholic uncle who had wanted to be a painter. A grandmother who had been whipped every week of her life. A mother who wore harlequin sunglasses and couldn't see what was going on.

This afternoon, just before the session was ending, they'd

gotten back to sex. A jackhammer pounded in the background with the fury of slow progress on tough asphalt.

"Rosemary doesn't ask me about it now," said Cory. "But I know she's wondering if it will ever happen again between us. What if it's years? I know she must be thinking that."

"What if it is?" asked Roberta. "How would you feel?"

"Guilty," said Cory. "I mean, especially now that we're planning to live together."

"But hasn't Rosemary been the one to push for you to live together?"

"Yes."

"Yes?" Roberta smiled. Why was she always smiling? She looked as if she hadn't a care in the world, as if she were just hanging around in her rattan chair for the hell of it. The only thing Cory knew about her was that she was a Buddhist. "It gives a certain perspective," Roberta said once, but Cory wasn't totally sure what that perspective was.

"Rosemary says she can take care of herself," Cory said.

"How is she taking care of herself?" Roberta asked, simply curious.

". . . I haven't really asked her."

"But you don't believe her?"

Cory sulked. It was all very well for someone who believed in reincarnation to give advice. But what if you didn't? The jackhammer stopped and started; the wind crept through a crack in the window frame and set the prayer flags to rustling. Another session over in a minute and still no progress.

Roberta was patient. "But you *do* think everything is going to be harder when you start living together?"

"Of course it will be," snapped Cory. "I'll have it in my face every minute. My failure. It will be my fault Rosemary's not happy."

"And why wouldn't she be happy?"

"Because it's not really a relationship if you don't have sex,"

Cory practically shouted. Did you have to tell her everything?

Roberta was silent. She did that on purpose, Cory knew, to make a little echo in the room. Then Roberta said, "How would you feel never to have sex again?" She held up her hand, which as covered with copper and topaz. "No, not how Rosemary would feel. Not how Lois would feel. Not how every other normal person on the planet would feel."

"Relieved, I guess," said Cory finally. "Not to have to think about it any more."

"Not to be seen as a sexual person?" Roberta suggested, looking sympathetic while also glancing at the clock.

Cory nodded. Something huge, a boulder, was sitting on her chest. She couldn't breathe for an instant. The rain of tears that happened every session but that she never predicted and never prepared for with a handkerchief, poured down her face. She wanted to say how guilty and ashamed she was, how fearful she was of losing that connection with Rosemary, and with herself, but instead, the words choked out, as Roberta handed her a box of Kleenex, "I want my childhood back."

The rain was beginning again, a drizzle that swept over her face as she crossed over University Bridge and walked quickly up Eastlake, the way she had a thousand times before. As she came up to the building where she lived, she remembered that she'd meant to tell Irene that she was leaving at the end of this month. Not *leaving*-leaving, but going finally to live with Rosemary and turning her apartment totally into an office.

Cory stood on the sidewalk in front of the wooden building. The sign in Irene's side-street entrance read *Closed*, but Cory could see her inside, white-haired now and stooped with arthritis, back by the cash register. When Cory had first moved in, Irene had still been in her vigorous late fifties, just retired from an elementary school library and newly widowed. She'd used her husband's life insurance to buy the building and open the small used bookstore she'd always dreamed of.

There were a few people on the sidewalk of Eastlake and the side street, getting off the bus, going into the café down the block, into the tavern on the corner. It was raining harder now, but still Cory stood there, rooted, and didn't knock on the bookstore's door. She was caught in the memory of a dream she'd had off and on for years. In the dream she was always standing on this patch of sidewalk, looking up at the windows of her apartment on the second floor. It was always dusk, in autumn or winter, that moment just before the streetlights went on, before people came home from work and turned on their lamps.

Nothing much ever happened in the dream. She stood on the sidewalk and looked up at her apartment as the evening darkened, and suddenly a lamp in her apartment was switched on, and another. One in the kitchen, one in the living room. And someone came over and pulled the curtains closed against the dark night. It was always a shadow figure; she could never see who it was, a man or a woman, a friend or a stranger. All she knew is that there was someone else now living in her apartment.

With the bitter certainty of recurrent dreams, Cory knew that there had been a terrible mistake. That *she* had made a terrible mistake. She had moved out, she had left the city or the country and now she had returned but was homeless. She stood on the sidewalk and watched someone else move around in her old apartment. She was homeless, and someone else was living in her home.

Never, in the dream, did Cory dare go upstairs to find out who was there. Never did she try to talk with them directly. No, she always went into Irene's shop or across the street to a pay phone to call Irene.

And their conversation was always the same. Cory begged to be allowed to live there again, and Irene said kindly but firmly, "No, Cory, you had your chance, and you left. Someone else lives there now. I'm so very sorry, dear. I would have liked to keep you as a tenant forever."

I must not leave this place, Cory thought desperately. I have to ask Irene how I can buy the building when she dies so I never have to leave it.

Someone passing by bumped into her and apologized. Cory didn't know how long she'd been standing there. The streetlights were on and the rain poured down, hard now; her hair was soaked. She ducked into the doorway of Irene's shop and banged on the glass door.

"Oh, it's you," Irene said, coming out of her back office, and opening the door reluctantly. "You gave me a start."

In the dreams Irene was a wise, kind woman, but in real life she was suspicious and often disagreeable. She never called Cory *dear*. Cory always forgot this until she was in Irene's presence and the familiar complaining voice began to churn the air around her. It was customers who wanted bargains they couldn't have ("Man came around, thought I was an old fool, offered me ten bucks for that early Nancy Drew. Good heavens, *I* paid fifty for it, I knew what it was worth. I strung him along awhile, then I told him where to get off."), kids who wanted change for the bus, or who— Heaven forbid—actually wanted to look at, to *pick up* the old children's books that Irene had in her display windows. But mostly what she talked about if she got the chance was her married daughter Joan. Joan was Irene's only daughter (Irene had a son, too, but he was a good boy, always traveling for his company, sent her a lovely basket of fruit on her birthday), the ungrateful, selfish daughter who lived in Olympia, which was only an hour and a half away, but who hardly ever came to see her, and couldn't care less if she lived or died. Cory, who'd seen Joan drive up practically every Sunday morning for the last fifteen years to take Irene out to church and then back to Olympia to have dinner with her husband and children, always nodded neutrally. It was better to keep the conversation in the old familiar paths; otherwise Irene might turn on her with those suddenly penetrating, pale blue eyes and say, "I saw a whole troop of little black children hanging around here yesterday. I thought they were going to come in the store and I'd have to deal with them."

The "troop" had been composed of Rae and Nicole's two girls and their friend Samantha, who'd come over for a special brunch one day with their mothers. Once Cory would have tried to set Irene straight, resentfully or furiously, but now she knew that Irene said things like that out of pure malice, just to see Cory's reaction.

But she hadn't raised the rent in almost ten years, and every Christmas she gave Cory a tin of home-baked cookies.

How could such a mean-spirited woman specialize in children's books? Cory wondered for the millionth time. How could Irene keep books that children loved behind the window and in locked glass cases? Cory let her fingers run over the books on the front table. They had heavy cloth covers with gilt-stamped titles or thick boards with an illustration pressed on. Just touching the covers brought her back to some safe place where she could rest a little. She picked up a shabby old volume of Robert Louis Stevenson's *A Child's Garden of Verses*, with illustrations by Jessie Wilcox Smith. The cover illustration showed a golden brown path leading into the distance, hedged in by tall dark green trees, closed off by an intricate wrought-iron gate. Inside, on the thick rag paper, were more color illustrations, of pensive, dreamy, English-looking children in short frocks and trousers, and singsong verses in large type:

> *I should like to rise and go*
> *Where the golden apples grow*

"It's not in very good shape," said Irene suddenly. "Except for the illustrations. Some people would cut out the illustrations. Why don't you take it? I know you wouldn't cut them out."

It was this sort of generosity from Irene that always caught Cory off guard, that kept her dreaming about Irene, wanting something from her.

She blurted out, "You know Rosemary?"

Irene nodded. Her pale blue eyes sharpened, expecting the worst. "Of course. She bought that nice set of *The Little House on the Prairie* books for her niece. She knew a bargain. Though I'm sure I gave her too good a deal. What happened to her?"

"Well, I'm thinking of moving into her house in December. I wouldn't give up the apartment," Cory added quickly. "I'll just use it for an office. It's practically only an office now."

"Well," said Irene coolly, moving away, fussing with the books on the table. "I guess people move on. Times change." She frowned at the Robert Louis Stevenson book in Cory's hands, probably regretting she'd offered it.

"I'll still be upstairs almost every day," Cory protested. "I don't want to move on. It's really important for me to stay here. I love this building, I love the view."

"When I die, they'll tear the whole thing down, put up condominiums," Irene predicted savagely. "This is valuable property; Joan will make the most of it."

"Maybe I . . . "

"It's worth at least a million dollars. Oh, she'll have a ball, after I'm gone. But maybe I'll surprise her . . . " Irene was starting to go into one of her tiresome rants when she suddenly stopped. "You're soaking wet, Cory, go on upstairs. You look like a homeless dog. I'm not going to throw you out, for Pete's sake!" She turned away in irritation, but not before Cory caught something in her eyes, something she'd seen before and not understood. Love, with no means to express itself except anger. "Haven't you paid me rent every month right on time for I don't know how long? I guess I should raise it, now that it's going to be just a business. Yes, I should have raised your rent a long time ago. Heaven knows, your office has been here all along, you're probably making a fortune up there. I'm soft, far too soft."

But as Cory was backing out of the store, Irene barked, "It's not a big secret, you know, you and Rosemary. She's a nice girl. Knows a bargain when she sees one. Show her that book I gave you. And don't cut the illustrations out!"

Upstairs, the rain battered the windows facing the lake. Cory turned on all the lights. She would be moving in three weeks, and had promised herself that she'd start going through her things tonight, beginning with her paintings. She'd been stuffing them in boxes for years; now it was time to sort them out, to throw them out. She put on Pablo Casals playing Bach's cello suites, and set to work.

The early watercolors were spheres and cylinders and ovoids. Red apples with blue shadows; green apples with reddish shadows. Lemons on purple plates, grapefruits in blue bowls, bananas that looked like boats and boats that looked like bananas. Studies in cool and warm colors, with attention to core shadows and cast shadows.

That was her unself-conscious period, during the first joyful months of painting, encouraged by her first teacher. But then had come Intermediate Watercolor and Madelyn the photo realist, who could make water in a glass, sun on a wall, dew on a petal, rust on metal look like the real thing. Cory flipped through her paintings from Madelyn's class. One box alone was full of still lifes of glass and liquids. Most were moderately successful studies; some of the best had the evocative stopped-time feel of Madelyn's own paintings. Here was one, a memory preserved from the past, intact. Two jars of fruit, pears and apricots, sitting on a rough pine counter in front of a window. Raindrops beaded against the small panes of glass; in the background was a blur of wet green trees. The sliced pears were a translucent jonquil in a syrup of champagne; the apricots were whole, big as peaches, poppy-bright. The labels, hand-scrawled, read August, 1986. Rosemary had written them. It was the summer they'd gone to Eastern Washington for two weeks, their first summer together. A hot summer, with long afternoon naps, lovemaking, bushels of fruits at the roadside stands for eating and canning. In the mornings Cory had taken her sketchpad out on walks; in the evenings they read to each other from the books they found in the cabin, dog-eared natural history books by Sally Carrighar and Aldo Leopold. In the afternoon sometimes there were brief storms, like the one Cory had caught in this painting.

A still life, caught forever, gone forever.

She put it down and picked up a study for a portrait of Nicole, pregnant with Ayisha, their first child. After Madelyn Cory had taken a class with Joe, whose specialty was people standing around Seattle streets under umbrellas. He had a stall at the Market and made a good living off the tourists, who thought the umbrellas were cute and *so* Seattle. Cory painted urban streets then too, and portraits. Nicole, round and dark and pleased, Rae, burstingly proud, with Ayisha, and then Aja. Portraits of Rosemary, too, with her hair getting longer, and her body getting more comfortable to her, that Rosemary nevertheless claimed made her look too fat. There was even a self-portrait. Cory hadn't thought it looked like her; a few years later, she liked it better. The gray had already started coming in; the green eyes looked wary, but still hopeful of getting everything right.

Next was a box of skies. That had been the period of weekend-workshops with Justine, who said, "Anything goes here. Let your color sense guide you. What's your inner palette telling you to paint? What are the colors that speak to you? No, don't tell me. *Show* me. Paint me anything," said Justine and then paused a beat. "Just not one of those dull gray Seattle marine-scapes." Cory had laughed self-consciously with the rest, wondering if they too had sketchbooks brimming with masts and sails and sea gulls appearing out of the mist.

All through her intermittent painting career, through the fruits and vegetables, through the glass panes and glass jars, through the portraits and urban scenes, Cory had kept painting Lake Union, her lake of tugs and drawbridges, houseboats and kayaks. Her urban lake she saw every day and never tired of seeing. But even the lake, her marine views, looked different according to which teacher she'd had and which technique she'd been practicing at the time. Madelyn the photo realist used a strict, slow glazing technique. She drew a pencil outline, sometimes in a grid pattern, carefully on the page, then began working in small areas, laying on thin washes of transparent pigment, sometime letting them dry naturally, sometimes using a hair dryer. Madelyn worked with a controlled system of wetting and drying the paper; she built up layers, a dozen or three dozen washes of color that did not seem to thicken, but to grow more and more translucent. Her colors were never muddy, and rarely ran together. Justine taught painting in a completely opposite way. She soaked her paper, both sides, with clear water and splashed on color, held the paper up to make the color run, sponged and dabbed and smeared. Not for her the patience of the slow glaze; not for her the cordoning off of small sections kept separate from each other.

Justine painted wet on wet. Tentacles of indigo reached into swirls of rose and made an atmospheric cloud of violet; a stroke of Windsor blue webbed through lemon yellow to become green, the spring green of new-leafed trees, Justine said, and quickly sketched in a few decisive lines for a trunk and branches. Justine's students were rarely as successful as Justine herself—painting wet on wet needed as much control as dry brush or glazing—and their work tended to be blurred and splotchy, with water marks from uneven drying. "It's a sunset," they told Justine hopefully. "Love your energy," she always smiled. Some of Cory's best—and worst—paintings came from this time. "Catch the spirit of what you see," Justine said. "Don't try to pin it down. Let us see the movement of the universe." Where Madelyn's glassy still lifes had a melancholy clarity, Justine's skies and forests moved and kept on moving.

After an hour Cory had thrown away no pictures; she was painting a new one. She wasn't working from a photograph or a still-life set-up, and certainly not from any view, for the night was howlingly wet and dark outside her windows. It was *A Child's Garden of Verses* that had inspired her, and yet she wasn't copying the cover. She wanted to paint something from memory, memory touched with imagination. She wanted to paint a pebbled path leading to a garden, but not one hedged in by dark English oaks. She wanted to paint bougainvillea and roses, jacaranda and mimosa trees, an apricot hung with golden globes of fruit. "I should like to rise and go, Where the golden apples grow," she hummed, taking out her tubes of paint. "Find your palette," Justine had always told them. "Find what colors speak to you." And Cory had chosen viridian and Prussian blue and indigo for her own. She had watercolor pads full of radiantly deep Northwestern skies and waters. But now she squeezed out all her yellows on the plastic palette, her reds, her brighter blues. Now she painted, not what she saw before her, or what she had ever really seen, but what she knew was there. A garden, with a gate that could be closed against the outside world, where she could walk at will, perfectly safe, in the midst of the flowers that flowed magically from her brush.

"I saw your lights," said Rosemary at the door. "Your apartment was all lit up. I just got out of the office and was on my way home. I thought I'd see if you wanted to go out to eat, or get some takeout. Unless you've eaten already."

Rosemary knew that Thursday was therapy day, and that sometimes Cory sat and cried all evening, that sometimes she needed to talk, that sometimes she needed to be bodily taken out of her apartment and made to eat something. She seemed astonished to find Cory painting with the music turned up. Now it was Mozart's Clarinet Concerto.

"It's a garden," said Cory. "I got the idea from a book Irene gave me. But I haven't put the gate on yet."

An Indian yellow path led smoothly under a rosy arbor, magenta bougainvillea on one side, peacock blue jacaranda and yellow mimosa on the other. She didn't really remember what mimosa or jacaranda flowers looked like, so she had had to improvise, in the way of Justine, splashing on color instead of worrying about detail. In the foreground there were the beginnings of an apricot tree, with heart-shaped leaves and golden fruit.

"Wow," said Rosemary, "This jumps off the page."

"It's not finished," said Cory. "There's the apricot tree, the gate . . . " She stood back, unsure. The gate would be a problem, now she'd put the apricot tree in the foreground. She'd meant to paint the gate French blue with a small dry brush, copying Jessie Wilcox Smith's intricate design with fleurs-de-lis. Maybe not closed, maybe half open. She needed the gate, as Justine would say, to give the painting definition—"and so you can reassure people that you can paint something that looks like something." But how could she put the gate in front of the apricot tree, and if the gate was behind it, then the apricot tree would be outside the garden.

Cory put her brush down, caught up in one of the logistical problems that seemed always to come with spontaneous paintings. Which was more important, the apricot tree or the gate? She could feel her energy suddenly running out. It was almost eight o'clock and she was starving.

"Oh, don't put in a gate," said Rosemary. "Don't touch it. It's beautiful. Really, it's like an illustration in a children's book. Someplace you'd love to wander in and explore."

I did explore it once, Cory almost said. It was my world. But that wasn't quite true. For the last two hours she'd been inside this painting. It was still her world.

"You should frame some more of these," said Rosemary, turning to the paintings spread out over the desk. "I have lots of wall space." She picked up the watercolor of the pears and apricots. "1986," she read from the label. "August. That was such a hot summer," she said, and blushed. She tried so carefully not to make comments that could sound suggestive.

How did she take care of herself, Cory thought. And what did it cost her? What did she do with her desire to touch and be touched, with her hunger to be loved not just for her "good personality," but for her body? Did she have to shut off everything, like Cory did, because it was too painful to feel? The guilt flashed up, but more than that, sorrow. Sorrow for both of them, once children in their free and easy bodies, now adults who had to be careful and patient with each other. It hadn't always been that way with them. Sometimes the gate had been open. She had a flash of memory, not white skin in green water this time, with its weight of nausea, but something bright and fleeting: creamy, freckled skin, golden brown hair, the round heft of belly and thigh, hot wetness between their two skins. The way the warm rain of that summer storm had poured down the windows of the cabin, with the sun right behind.

A still life was always a picture of inanimate objects. In the painting the pale gold of the sliced pears, the rich velvet of the orange apricots pulsed through the translucent jars. Madelyn had taught Cory to keep the color values rich and concentrated, contained by transparency, almost within reach, almost real in a stopped-time memory. But Justine would say, Break the glass, let the color out. Cory imagined the two jars smashing, the pears and apricots spreading across the page, soaking and staining the paper to the very edge.

She wanted her hunger back. Where had it gone? Hunger, not just desire, hunger for the whole of life, for a whole life. For a long time, color had been bottled up in a still life; the river had been surging through a space too narrow for it and echoing against the sheer canyon walls. She heard the roaring in her ears and willed it to become something else, not the river but the ocean. A wave coming that she could master, that would not drown her but would embrace her, would fling her up to the top of the frothing crest and, for an instant, hold her there, let her *be* there.

Rosemary was still bent over the boxes of paintings. She was wearing a warm brown sweater with a boat neck. Her neck and shoulders were bare, creamy, honey-freckled, as she bent over the paintings, pushing back her brown curls with one hand. A sliver of black lace curled sleepily in the corner of the sweater's opening.

It would be so simple to put her hand on that shoulder and turn Rosemary around. All she needed was the willingness to think *wave* not river, *hunger* not sex, *love* not anything else. Now, she told herself. Now. Turning Rosemary around, turning the hazel eyes towards her, pressing the soft mouth on hers, breaking the glass, painting wet on wet to the edges.

IN CELEBRATION AND

REMEMBRANCE

ROSEMARY HAD TWO dishes. One, for cold weather gatherings, was a sweet potato and cranberry quiche from the *Vegetarian Epicure, Book Two*, and the other, for summer, was something called Spinach Roll-ups with Lime Chutney.

Rosemary not only made these dishes, she was known for them. No one else, exclaiming how fabulous and unexpected the tastes were and how they'd have to try them sometime, would ever dare bring either dish to a potluck. They were Rosemary's signature dishes. Her mother, Anne, had impressed upon her that every woman needed one or two signature dishes. In Minnesota that usually meant either a casserole or something bright green with marshmallows, but this was Seattle.

And these were Rosemary's culinary specialties, very delicious, and very time-consuming.

"We need to leave soon," said Cory, who had made a fruit salad long ago. She always made fruit salad because, although it involved a lot of chopping, she didn't have to think about it much, and certainly not in advance.

She and Rosemary were standing in what had been Rosemary's kitchen and was now Cory and Rosemary's kitchen. It was the same place, of course, and nothing had changed since Cory had moved in a year ago. The withered garlic chain still hung on the wall and the string of chili peppers, rather dusty now. There was a large framed photograph of Rosemary's family's reunion picnic last summer, in honor of her father's seventieth birthday, with Cory looking overwhelmed among the hundred and twenty-three Reardons and relatives.

Rosemary pulled the quiche out, inserted the knife and pronounced it still runny. "But not too much longer," she said hopefully. She never believed things took as long as they really did, Cory thought but resisted the urge to point this out. She tugged Rosemary's sleeve away from the soft custard top of the pie. Rosemary was all dressed up in a shirt her mother had sent her, something that vaguely recalled the Renaissance, with belled sleeves. Since Rosemary had insisted on wearing the shirt while she cooked, the bells had narrowly escaped staining numerous times. In fact, one of them *did* have a smear of yellow egg on it, Cory saw with irritated satisfaction.

"I can't believe we're going to another brunch," said Cory. "Every Saturday and Sunday this month it's been something. And it's *January* now, not December."

"You don't have to go," said Rosemary serenely. She must have been rereading one of the self-help books that Lois Larkin had suggested.

"How can I not go?"

The invitation read *In Celebration and Remembrance.* It was Amy's annual birthday party and it had once been Rob's too. But Rob had died three months ago from AIDS.

Cory gave her fruit salad a stir. In spite of the lemon juice she'd added, the apples were already beginning to brown. All she wanted was to go back upstairs, get under the covers and read the *New York Times.* She wasn't heartless, but she was sick of these occasions, these celebrations and memorial services.

"We just went to his funeral," Cory said, "that was hard

enough. Now everybody is going to be crying all over again. And there was Christmas too," she added in a voice she was aware was whiny. "I hate Christmas."

"It's ready," said Rosemary, not ignoring her exactly, but moving things along. "Now, let's see, where are my keys, my coat, my . . ."

Cory had everything by the door, ready to go. "It's not that I don't care," she felt she had to explain as they walked towards the car. "I just like ordinary life. For things to go on as usual."

"I know, I know," said Rosemary, carefully stowing her quiche in a cardboard box. "Wouldn't it be nice if nothing ever changed—except for the good of course."

Amy and her partner Trisha met them at the door. Amy's eyes were red-rimmed, and Trisha was solemn behind her usually delighted smile.

"Happy fortieth!" Rosemary said, extending her glass pie plate.

"Oh, your wonderful sweet potato and cranberry quiche!" said Amy. "And another fruit salad, great."

Cory placed her fruit salad along with eight others on the long table in the dining room. She said a warm hello to Rae and Nicole, whose two children were running up and down the stairs with Amy and Trisha's seven year old, Natalie. Nat was Rob's daughter, too.

She filled a plate and milled vaguely. Rosemary was already deep in conversation with another lawyer about the anti-gay initiatives the fundamentalists were trying to get on the ballot; they were practically shaking their fists, though that didn't stop either of them, both food lovers, from standing by the buffet and eating right off the platters and out of the bowls. The belled sleeves swung dangerously near the onion dip and Cory averted her eyes. That was Rosemary's mother—still sending her daughter ill-fitting and ridiculous clothes after all these years.

They hadn't gone to St. Paul for the holidays this year. Cory had put her foot down; once a year was enough. Instead they had stayed in town and gone to Rae's annual Kwanzaa feast, two Hanukkah parties, one winter solstice celebration, three Christmas brunches, a concert by the Seattle Men's Chorus and the Seattle Symphony's *Messiah*. Rosemary decorated a tree and put a cedar wreath on the door, and spent a fortune on overnight UPS since she only wrapped her packages two days in advance, and all over the mantelpiece and furniture were the winged greeting cards from her millions of relatives. Cory got a card two days after Christmas from her father, and a polyester scarf printed with butterflies from her brother and his family, with a photograph of the four of them in front of their fireplace.

"Next year," she'd told Rosemary. "I want to go to Maui."

Over at the drinks table, Rob's partner of many years, Arthur, was pouring punch for everyone. He was painfully thin and almost bald now, with a lesion half visible on his neck above his ascot. Rob used to joke about Arthur's ascots and fedoras and beautiful shoes. Arthur claimed to have inherited them from his great uncle, an actor or a British lord or a con man, Cory was never sure which, and she suspected Arthur had never been sure either. He looked drunk already and determinedly cheerful.

"No thanks," said Cory and turned away.

It used to be, when she drank, that parties were easier. She remembered conga lines and music that had the police at the door, intense encounters in the kitchen with people she either never saw again or woke up with the next morning. Now she had two possibilities: she could either hang about on the edges of groups of friends, smiling and joining in high-pitched conversations, or she could find a seat and be very sure that someone she didn't know would latch on to her and tell her their incredibly bizarre life story.

It wasn't that she didn't have friends here that she was glad to see, but after she'd congratulated Rae on her recent grant from the Seattle Arts Commission, and heard the story of how their old writing friend Gretel had turned into G. P. McDonald, author of a best-selling mystery series, and after Nicole and Trisha had bent her ear a while about guns in the public schools and if she had children she'd be worried too, and after Lois Larkin had introduced her to her new girlfriend—rumor had it that Donna Laura had run off suddenly to Japan to enter a Zen monastery—Cory drifted away.

She kept milling, though, because the alternative was to cling, couple-like, to Rosemary, who had some barbecue sauce at the corner of her mouth—or was that red froth from anger at the right-wing fundamentalists?

"It's really true," Cory could hear her saying, "You can't rest an instant, much as you'd like to. You have to be ready for them, because they're ready for you. And if they aren't after you this second, then they're after someone else and you'll be next."

"That's why we need to come together like this," said the other lawyer, and for a minute Cory almost went up to them, wanting hard to agree, that you had to fight back and you couldn't fight alone, you needed community, and community thrived on symbols and rituals.

Then she turned away. Ordinary life, ordinary life. That's what she wanted. No deaths, no protests, no celebrations either. Only the luxury of being neither victimized nor victorious.

"Here's the brilliant woman who does my taxes," said Barbara Holleran, pulling Cory over. "Every year I throw everything at her, in total despair and say, 'Help me, help me, Cory!' And she somehow manages to produce a beautiful clean-looking tax return that satisfies the IRS."

"Do you have a card?" two women in the group said at once.

After about an hour, Amy cut the traditional raspberry-filled chocolate birthday cake and made a short speech. The crowd seemed to be smaller than in years past, with fewer men and more children. The kids ran about in a large pack, inefficiently reprimanded and batted at by their busily-talking mothers and sometimes by their fathers. Occasionally you could hear Natalie screeching commandingly at them, "Don't touch that!" She was a skinny kid, in a pink training suit, with frizzy brown hair pulled tightly back. She had Amy's weak chin and Rob's unfortunate ears.

"I thought about skipping the party this year," Amy said, her voice a little unsteady, with a note in her hand that she didn't look at, "How can we give a party without Mr. Party himself, I thought. This annual celebration was always Rob's baby. It was his idea in the first place when he found out we were born the same year, the same day. 'Hey a double party means we can invite more people,' he said. 'And you know what that means—more presents!' Every year, sometime in December when we were up to our ears with Hanukkah and Christmas, he'd want to meet to plan it and I'd say, 'Oh Rob, let's forget it this year. It's so much *work*.' And he'd say, 'Oh honey, it's not work, it's *fun*, and it's not going to be a big extravaganza this year, I promise you, just a tiny tiny gathering of a few, a very few, select close friends."

Amy paused and everyone laughed. "Well, I'm sure many of you remember some of those tiny tiny gatherings over the past ten years. The one with the drag queens doing their act up and down the stairs—our daughter Nat called them the dragon queens—the one where we were all supposed to come as our parents; the one when it snowed and he had us all outside making gay snow people.

"Once, I think maybe after the snow people bash, I thanked Rob for giving me the kind of party I never had as a kid. And he looked at me and said, 'Amy darling, the whole *point* of being an adult is to have the kind of childhood we never had as children.'

"I know that it's for that reason Rob would have wanted us to continue this tradition. I don't say this just because I want to keep getting presents! But because Rob taught me and I think all of us something about the importance of celebrating ourselves. As he used to say, 'Who's going to celebrate for us, Amy? Who is going to celebrate our wonderful sad and joyful queer lives if we don't?'

"And I guess I would add to that, 'Who will remember us if we don't remember ourselves? Who will mourn us if we don't mourn each other? Who will care, if we don't?'" She raised her glass of mineral water. "The best way we can remember Rob today is to have a wonderful time."

Cory felt like she was the only person who wasn't sniffling. She had used up her tears when her mother died thirty years ago and didn't have any left for anybody else. She hadn't even cried at her own mother's funeral, only before, when her father told her, 'She's gone, Peanut.' She looked up to the top of the stairs where Nat stood, dispassionately watching the adults down below, wiping their eyes.

Cory went upstairs. "Where are the other kids?"

"They're outside," said Nat, kicking at a spot on the banister where the paint was missing. "I don't want to play tag. I told them that. It's too cold. They should do what I want. It's my house."

"You want to do something with me?"

"Like what?"

"I could tell you a story."

"Nah." She was probably suspicious it would be morally up-lifting.

"What about a game?"

"What kind of game?"

"Uh, checkers? Cards? Monopoly?"

Nat shook her frizzy ponytail and kept kicking the banister. Finally she said, "We could play Nintendo."

"Let's draw," said Cory. "Do you have crayons and paper?"

Without much enthusiasm—her pink back saying, This is probably going to be so stupid—Nat led the way back to the bedroom of a child raised by progressive lesbian parents. Not a doll in sight, only play carpentry sets and Legos.

Nat got out the crayons and paper and they sat down in front of a small table.

"What are you going to draw?" asked Nat. "People? I can't draw people. I can only draw houses and sailboats and cats, stuff like that."

"It's not that hard," Cory said. She made a series of ovals. "This is what they teach you in basic figure drawing. That's right. That's good."

They drew ovular figures for a while and then some big-headed astronauts going to the planets and some deep sea divers, then they each turned to their own complicated pictures.

"Tell me a story," Nat demanded suddenly.

Cory had been lost, speechless, in the pleasure of coloring. She'd been working on a crayon picture of Lake Union on a cold, starry winter's night. Now that she was living with Rosemary, Cory didn't see that view often, and she missed it. She'd colored in the background with all the brightest colors and then, with small hard strokes, she'd pressed black wax thickly over the paper so that none of the underlying color was visible. Now she was etching, with the tip of a paper clip, the line where earth and sky separated and, and picking out the shapes of lighted boats. In December every year the cruise boats and sailboats strung lights along their masts and lines. Some went too far—decorating the boats with gigantic Santas and reindeer teams, blaring out Christmas tunes from speakers. The best boats were like confectionery icing with sparkles on a smooth sheet of violet-tinted dark chocolate.

"A story? What about?" Cory said absently, noticing how the little curls of crayon were like soap flakes, only black.

"You're supposed to tell me!"

It had been a long time since she'd told a story. "There was this family once," she said. "They were called The Feebles."

"What does that mean?"

"Mean? Nothing. That was just their name. Jack and Nancy

Feeble. And they had two parents, called Mr. and Mrs."

"I have two Mommies," said Nat disapprovingly. "They're called Ms. I had Rob too, and Rob's husband, Arthur. Arthur is downstairs."

"Well this story takes place in the long ago," said Cory, a little desperately. "In olden times."

"Like when Amy and Trisha were little girls?"

"Exactly. So Nancy and Jack Feeble had to do the dishes every night . . ."

"In the dishwasher?"

"No, at the sink."

"We have a dishwasher."

"You have to use your imagination," said Cory. "Imagine a time long ago when things were different. There were TVs but no VCRs, telephones but no computers, and people had to do their dishes in the sink." Nat's silence—was it amazement?—encouraged her to go on. "Well, Jack and Nancy hated to do dishes and as often as possible they escaped by going down the drain on their saucer boat to the Drain Kingdom.

"The way into the Drain Kingdom was down a huge waterfall that spilled over a cliff as high as a twenty-story building. It made a roar like nothing you've ever heard—it emptied out your whole head with that roar, and took away your breath and turned you into nothing but a leaf or a stick.

"When you were over the falls you found yourself on a pleasant river that wandered into little lagoons and between hummocks of moss. This is where the small Drain people lived."

Cory went on for a while about the Drain people. She remembered that in the stories she'd told Kevin that there was always an element of danger and excitement. Terrible things, bloody and scary and violent things. But now Cory felt unable to tell these things to Nat. She was so young, and she had enough to be worried about, drugs and rapists and guns in the schools, besides just having witnessed her father sicken and die from AIDS. At the end

Rob had lain at Group Health hospital in a bed, hooked up to a dozen tubes and bottles. He'd tried to joke, but he couldn't; his brown eyes were far away with pain. It had wrenched Cory to see him like this; what must it have been like for Nat?

But the longer Cory went on with the little Drain people and the crops they grew and the festivities they engaged in at harvest time, the more she sensed Nat's restlessness. "Help me, Nat," she said finally. "What comes next?"

Without hesitation Nat launched into, "Nancy and Jack suddenly got a phone call from their mother who said they had to come back home right away because something terrible had happened to their father. So Nancy and Jack got back into their saucer boat and started to try to get back up the river. Well, the little river that seemed so nice and calm had turned into a boiling mess by the time they got back to the waterfall. It was like going into a hurricane, the waves were so tall, and there was a waterspout they got caught in, and Jack fell out and drowned, and Nancy barely made it to the shore and then a big lizard came up and was going to eat her but she escaped and was trying to climb up the side of the waterfall, but a rock she was holding on to fell off and she fell back in the river, and there was Jack, he hadn't really drowned, he was just whirling around in the waterspout. Nancy got him out and they crawled to the side of the river. They knew they would never get back up the waterfall now, they would never get home in time, and their father was sick and they wouldn't be able to see him before he died and they would have to spend the rest of their lives in the Drain Kingdom, but at least they were alive, at least they were . . . " she searched for the word.

"Spared?" said Cory.

"What does that mean?"

"They survived. But are you sure they never got back home? Maybe their mother came down the waterfall and got them," Cory suggested. "Maybe she threw them down a lifeline they could climb up again."

"I don't think so," said Nat with satisfaction. "I think they never saw their father or their mother again."

"Whew," said Cory, shaken. "That was quite a story."

Nat nodded. "It's better up here," she said. "It's too noisy downstairs."

"I know," said Cory. "I don't like parties that much, do you?"

Nat considered. "Some parties. The one with the snowballs, that was really fun. And with the men dancing like women. Rob was funny. He got dressed up too, but he wasn't like a real dragon queen. You could tell! He had hairy legs. *And* a beard."

"I remember that," said Cory.

"He was fun," said Nat. "He used to take me to the zoo, him and Arthur. Arthur didn't like monkeys. He wouldn't go in the monkey house. He said they made a racket like his mother and her sisters. We had cotton candy."

She put down her crayon. "Last night," she said. "I dreamed Rob was still here. Can you do that, when a person is dead?"

"Oh yes. It happens all the time."

"Like they're still alive?"

"Yes. Exactly like that. It's a kind of gift, I guess. Still to be able to see and feel them, even though they're gone."

"'Cause it makes them seem like they're still alive."

"Yeah."

"I'm going to draw a picture of Rob dancing that time. With his hairy legs."

"It's a good way to remember," said Cory. "Making pictures of people."

"Yes, because then you always have the picture." Nat drew a man with a dark beard and a yarmulke, and two very wild legs. "He was really funny that time. I'm going to give this to Amy."

"We could make one for Arthur, too."

"Yeah! Because you know Rob was his husband. And I bet he feels sad too. I'll make him a picture of me and Rob and him in the monkey house. I like to draw monkeys."

When Cory and Nat went downstairs again with their drawings, the crowd had thinned out a bit. Groups sat rather than stood and much of the food was gone.

"Arthur! Arthur!" said Nat. "Here's a picture for you."

He had probably been drinking steadily. His eyes were unfocused, and he was hanging on the arm of a much younger, attractive man, and talking loudly. His ascot was askew, and the lesion large as a silver dollar.

"Oh thanks," he said, without looking.

Cory shook his arm, unreasonably irritated. "Arthur! Natalie drew you a picture of the three of you in the monkey house at the zoo."

"You and me and Rob!" crowed Nat. She saw the other kids in the kitchen making something on top of the stove, and dashed away.

Arthur was looking at the picture upside down. Cory turned it for him. The monkeys looked like astronauts with big heads and large hands. "I hate monkeys," he said a little unsteadily. "Even as a small child, I hated monkeys."

"That was a wonderful speech Amy gave," said Rosemary, as they left the party. She carried her empty pie plate in her hands. "I still can't believe Rob is gone. He's still so vivid in my mind. I saw you talking with Arthur towards the end. How is he taking it?"

"I don't think he knows what to do except drink."

"He's really at sea without Rob. Rob kind of steadied him."

Cory thought that if it had been Arthur who died there wouldn't have been half so many people at the party, either celebrating or remembering.

She thought that if someday she had to hold a memorial service for Rosemary, that hundreds of people would come, because

Rosemary believed that she'd been put down here on earth to be helpful and do good works. But who would come to Cory's funeral? Some of her clients. Probably none of her ex-lovers. Maybe her brother and his family. Her father, if he were still alive. Maybe. A few friends, five friends? Rosemary's friends. Because the ironic thing was that if Cory died, Rosemary would be capable of organizing a beautiful, meaningful ceremony, one that people would come to not so much because of Cory, but in order to show how much they loved Rosemary and mourned with her.

And if Rosemary died? Would Cory be able to put something like this together? Would she be like her father and never go back to the cemetery again? Would she be like Arthur and fall immediately into alcoholism? Wouldn't she be likely to get on a plane to some foreign country just as fast as she could, and try to put it all behind her and forget as soon as possible?

"I lost track of you at the party," Rosemary said. "Where were you?"

"I was upstairs, drawing pictures with Nat. We told each other stories."

"You're so good with kids," Rosemary said. "I'm always surprised when you say you never thought about having any."

Cory shook her head. Once, a very long time ago in college, she thought she'd gotten pregnant after an unprotected evening of drinking and sex with the sports editor at the *Daily*. She hadn't told him, and finally her period came, three weeks late. She sometimes thought of it. How, if she really had been pregnant, if she hadn't had an abortion, though she surely would have, how her life would have been different. Her child would have been twenty-one now; she would have lived to see him or her grow up. But at the time she never thought she would live that long, had never thought she'd manage to survive to forty.

"My brother had the kids. Maybe he had the right idea. But anyway, I'm an aunt."

They got in the car.

Rosemary said, "You always seem to have such a different experience than I do at parties. All I do is gossip and talk shop, and you come away with something important. Either someone tells you their incredible life story or you make a connection, like you did with Nat."

"Rosemary," Cory said. "I want you to promise me something."

"What?" She looked alarmed.

"That you'll keep forcing me to go to these things. Don't let me stay home complaining on my own."

"I never force you, Cory," she said. "In case you hadn't noticed. You complain, but you always make the choice to participate. In your own way of course."

They arrived at their house, *their* house, Cory had to keep reminding herself.

"All right then," said Cory. "But promise me something else."

They got out of the car, Cory carrying her untouched bowl of fruit salad in front of her.

"What's that?"

"Don't let me do the easy thing, the thing I don't care about, the thing that no one else wants either. Teach me how to make a dish that people want to eat."

"I know just the one," said Rosemary.

IF YOU HAD A FAMILY

HOW MANY TIMES as an adult had Cory dreamed of the old neighborhood? The horseshoe sweep of the streets so perfect for softball (their house right at the curve, behind home base), the way you could see up and down two streets at a glance. No one came down Wildwood Avenue, which changed in the middle of the horseshoe to Faust Avenue, unless they lived there. In Cory's dreams she lived there still, still found herself walking the same streets where she knew each lawn and stretch of sidewalk, each avocado tree and palm, each porch and style of drapes in the window.

It had been a young neighborhood once, and now it was middle-aged. When it was built, in the late forties, it had been an ordinary tract housing development in Southern California, with nothing to the east but bean fields and dairy farms. In the early days the houses had all looked alike—rectangular and flat-roofed, stuccoed and painted pastel colors, with no fences between the houses, so that it was possible to run unimpeded across the lawns and driveways. In those days the occupants had been young too, ex-G.I.s with loans from the V.A., a dozen or more children on the block. Forty years later there were fences or high hedges everywhere. Some of the houses had second stories or additions and enlarged driveways; others looked shabbier merely because they had stayed the same. There were no children's bikes or toys on the sidewalk this Sunday morning, though several houses had basketball hoops over the garage doors. There was still the same dream-like sense of peace that came from the horseshoe curve and lack of traffic.

Their own old house didn't have a second story, but the driveway was much wider, and three cars, junkers, and a pickup truck were parked there. When they first knocked, no one was at home. When her father, West, first knocked, that is. Cory hung back a little, staring at the smallness of the house, the meagerness of the vegetation. In her memory the lawn had been huge and flowers had overhung the porch, glossy orange hibiscus, whose trumpet flowers they had sucked on. A big bottlebrush, scarlet as lipstick—hadn't that been right in front of the house? There was no bougainvillea now, no oleanders, and without the flowers to soften the house, it looked shabby and poor. When she and Kevin moved with their father to the apartment building they'd spent hours talking about the big house and yard they'd left behind until it had grown enormous, palatial in their minds.

Her brother Kevin sat in his car, not getting out, smoking.

"No one's home," announced West. "We'll go over to Sharie Palmer's house, see if she's there."

West had stopped in at Bob Palmer's retirement party ten years ago, he said. Kevin had driven by once about fifteen years ago to show his new wife Betsy where he'd grown up. Cory hadn't been back for over thirty years, she had only dreamed about it; she wondered if she was the only one of them who did.

"At the party Bob Palmer was on an oxygen mask," said West. "I'd be surprised if he was still alive."

Cory straggled after her father, while Kevin continued to sit moodily in his car, staring at the lamppost in front of their old house. Many years ago he had taken his softball bat to that iron lamppost, pounding it so that it rang like church bells, until the glass in the lamp above shattered and fell like rain all about him.

"West, West!" screamed Sharie Palmer most satisfactorily. "And this is Cory. Cory!"

"Kevin's in the car," Cory said, as Kevin got out and came over. He seemed to become younger and smaller as he approached.

"Little Kevin!" shouted Sharie Palmer. "Little Kevie! I can't believe it."

And then they went in. Sharie Palmer's living room was small, upholstered all in white and crowded with the shelves of knick-knacks Cory remembered trying to avoid knocking over as a child. Sharie Palmer looked surprisingly young and full of fun in her jeans and sport shirt, with white hair to be sure, but the same bubbling laugh and bright, slightly malicious eyes.

The Winter family sat there, clumsily pleased, while Sharie chattered. "Little Kevie, so tall now, are you married? Two kids? I can't *believe* it. You, Cory, no? West, how's Georgia? Oh, I'm sorry. Yes, Bob died years ago. Have you been over to the house, seen the Hoovers? I'm sure they'll let you in for a minute. They're not home? They're probably out in back and didn't hear your knock. The Curtises moved away a few years back, and so did Yolanda after Bernie died. She's living with her daughter Laurie—remember Laurie, that heavy girl with the acne? Well, she finally found a husband. And Linda Spritz—she's still down the block. Her daughter Janet has been married three times; it's not like the old days when you stuck with who you got. One of my boys is the same way, only he won't even get married, just has girlfriends. Bob Jr. is the steady one, has a lovely wife and three children. You say *you* have two children, Kevin. Wonderful. And Cory, your hair was so blonde, now it's almost all gray, still keep it short, I see, *never* married, Cory? But you're sure the Hoovers weren't home? Let me try them on the phone. Oh Sally! Hi, it's Sharie! The Winter family, you know, the original owners of your house, they're all here for a visit and they would just love it so much if they could come over and look around, I know you think it's a mess, but just for a minute . . . Oh great! Well, West, kids, it was so wonderful to see you, it really made my afternoon, I'm so sorry you have to leave. Let me hug you and please come by again sometime!"

They walked back down the street.

"She's certainly well-preserved," West said. "Talkative though."

"I remember Jeff and Bobby," said Kevin. "They taught me how to play softball."

"I remember her knickknacks," said Cory. "I'm glad I didn't break anything."

"So Bob died," said West. "And Bernie, too. That Yolanda could drive a man to an early grave, I guess." His steps were slower now, as if he remembered that he'd just come out of the hospital.

Mrs. Hoover was waiting at the door. She was a large woman in her sixties, wearing a tightly buttoned cardigan and a resigned expression.

"The house is such a mess, I really hate for you to see it."

"Oh no, no, no," they said, pushing past her eagerly with many thanks and apologies for this unannounced visit. But still they were all shocked and Mrs. Hoover couldn't help noticing it.

"We've lived here since you left," she apologized. "We've done some remodeling. My husband—he's something of a collector. . . ."

From outside the house had looked almost exactly the same but from the inside it was nothing like the house they had left so precipitously that day thirty-two years ago. Walls had been knocked down, doors and windows had been shifted; the living room now extended a good fifty feet out into the back yard, and it had been paneled in a dark wood that gave it a curiously somber atmosphere. The living room was packed with all sorts of unfamiliar things: a player piano, several rocking horses, tin trays printed with Coca-Cola advertisements, a massive wide-screen TV and several smaller televisions, as well as an abundance of couches, chairs, and end tables stacked with Christmas ornaments, magazines, junk.

There was a washing machine rumbling in the hallway and clothes hung up to dry in the doorways. To get to the bedrooms they stumbled over months-worth of bundled newspapers and plastic bags of aluminum cans. A small dark, curtained room off the hallway was jam-packed with cardboard boxes, as if it were a large closet. With a start Cory realized that it was her old bedroom, the sunny yellow room with the pineapple-posted maple bed and the yellow-and-brown ruffled curtains. The sun had come in every morning on her yellow-and-white quilt and she remembered how the birds had sung in the maple tree out in front.

Back in the cluttered living room she glanced at Kevin who was staring at the wall as if trying to remember where the big glass window had looked out on to the back yard. The yellow mimosa tree had filled the view between the drapes, a buttery Bonnard cloud of flowers squared by the window panes, and set off by the dark green shrubs and weathered redwood fence behind it.

West tried for a hearty tone. "What we'd really like to see is the back yard!" Mrs. Hoover looked even more nervous, but led them through the remodeled kitchen (where was the booth around the linoleum table, the swinging doors that they used to pretend were part of a Western saloon?) to the back door.

Once Cory had burst through that door every morning and met a wall of magenta, a cascade of bougainvillea. Across the patio she'd run, into the still-wet grass, to press her face into the velvet and pearl petals of the full-blown roses. The apricot tree flamed with white wings or spread green leaves and ripe-scented fruit over the redwood table. Whole days were spent at that table painting and making clay and papier-mâché figures. When it was hot they ate hamburgers from the barbecue at that soft splintery table, and when it rained you could hide under the table draped with an old bedspread and play house. If you wanted to run or play catch or croquet, you had space to do it if you circled the mimosa and let the jacaranda be color in the sky and not an obstacle on earth.

Mrs. Hoover said again, "My husband is a real junk hound."

This was how it looked now: Nearly a third of the lawn was gone, destroyed by the remodeling of the house. Another third was paved over and full of car parts and tools. And the final third was scraggly grass with a plant or two here and there. One diseased rose bush stuck up from a parched bit of earth. Where once there had been color and fragrance, verdant shade, luxurious growth, there was now only the faintly unpleasant odor of machine oil and dirt under the smoggy sky.

The apricot tree was gone, so were the mimosa and the jacaranda.

"We tried to keep the apricot," said Mrs. Hoover. "But it wasn't giving fruit anymore." She pointed to a stack of gray branches. "My husband took it out last year finally. We've been waiting for a day cold enough to have a fire."

West finally said, "You still using the addition?"

"Now those two rooms I really can't let you see," said Mrs. Hoover with a strained laugh. "The one in front that used to be your office, I believe, it's full up to the ceiling with old thises and thats. And the back room—well for quite a while we used it as a rec room for the kids, and they really pretty much destroyed it. My husband removed those old linoleum tiles and he wants to do it up for our youngest son when he visits with his family, but he hasn't gotten around to it yet."

A flash of memory, of a tan and brown tiled floor and a brown rug, thin as vomit on glass, and Cory felt a familiar nausea, pale and manageable. She had thought so often about telling her father and Kevin and dismissed the idea. What words to use? Uncle Steve touched me. Uncle Steve molested me. Uncle Steve abused me. She couldn't get the words out and the memories weren't clear—they came and went like moths in an attic. A rock in a river, white skin reflecting sun on water, something hard in her mouth, and later, brown and tan tiles, a checkerboard in front of her eyes. Roberta Lu had said, "That may be all you'll ever remember," and Cory had said, "I hope so."

But the tiles were all mixed up with the roses in the back yard now, and the sweet smell of the bee bushes (for one remained) brought back pain was well as longing. The addition remained what it had been when they left the house: in one room a museum of a life not lived fully; in the other a play area that had been destroyed.

Mr. Hoover and one of his grown sons, Chris, came out of the garage and began to talk, man to man, with West and Kevin. Male talk was something West didn't do very well and he kept staring at the disassembled car parts with something closer to despair than disapproval. Since the surgery his jowls had fallen further and his eyes were yellow around the blue. The doctor said his health problems weren't serious in themselves, only serious because of his age and sedentary life. "You need to get out and walk, need an interest or a hobby," West had repeated to Cory. "My work was my life, my interest, my hobby." He had started doing tax returns for other seniors at the home, but only the simpler ones.

Cory turned to Mrs. Hoover and thanked her. "I wonder if you'd mind," she said, pointing to the pile of apricot branches, "if I took one of those?"

"If I had my way," said Mrs. Hoover with a hopeless look at her husband, "You could drive up here with a garbage truck and take anything you wanted."

On the way out, through the gate this time, where the acacia had once flowered feathery yellow and green, Kevin said to Cory, as if accusing her, "Chris grew up in this house. He got to spend his whole life here. He had my bedroom."

And West said, as they got back in Kevin's car, "You should never go back to anyplace you ever lived. It's just too hard."

This visit to Wildwood Avenue had been Cory's idea and she could tell, on the drive back to West's retirement home in Seal

Beach, that her father and brother blamed her for it, blamed her, but weren't going to mention it. Instead, smoking together in the front seat, her father his pipe, her brother his Marlboros, they began a desultory conversation about politics. At some point during the last five or six years the two of them had begun to resemble each other, and to congratulate each other on that resemblance. West looked far older than his years, with white hair and soft, sagging jowls, and Kevin's hair was still brown, though receding, but they both wore glasses, had rather thick necks, and smoked.

"I don't think Bush has been much of a president," said West, "but I don't know how anybody could seriously consider that Bill Clinton."

"Slick Willie," said Kevin. "He'll never win. Bush's foreign policy record will keep him in."

Cory sat in the backseat, feeling very young, holding her branch. This morning she had suggested going to Polly's cemetery and they had both vehemently said no. She had finally persuaded them to visit Long Beach; this idiotic hope of hers that they could be a family, that they could be like other people, never seemed to leave her.

"My family has an aversion to the past," she'd told Rosemary.

"My family has an aversion to the present," Rosemary had said. She and her brothers were trying to get their parents to move to a smaller, single-story house or apartment. Phil's arthritis had worsened and he was barely able to make it up the stairs. But Anne said, "You children grew up in this house. There are so many memories here. We could never leave this house."

Cory's fingers touched the keys in her pocket by chance. In another day she'd be home again, to the new house that she and Rosemary had bought earlier in the year.

"I can see," Rosemary had said a year ago, "that no matter what we do here, it's always going to be my house. You haven't put a single thing up on the walls or touched the garden in the two years you've been here."

"I'm just not that into homemaking," said Cory. "You saw my old apartment—Early American File Cabinet. I'm completely indifferent to my surroundings."

But she'd never had a home of her own either, and it surprised her when they found the roomy old house in Mount Baker just how much of an obsessive do-it-yourselfer she could be. As soon as they moved in she was stripping wallpaper and painting, was turning the attic into a studio, was reading books on home repair and remodeling. In six months she had a room upstairs, that was vehemently *not* an office, but that could be a guest room when Jessie and Peter, her niece and nephew, made a visit. It was this room, low-ceilinged under the eaves, with its view of Lake Washington, where Cory had set up a table for painting, a bookshelf and easy chair, and where she had begun to hang framed photographs of herself as a child and of her family and friends.

The room looked like her, just as the downstairs looked like both of them, not just Rosemary. In the old house, Rosemary had always said, "Just say the word if you want me to take down those big weavings."

"Oh no, I love them," Cory had always answered.

But now by tacit consent, only one of the African weavings went up. Only some of the Guatemalan baskets were placed around the living room, only a few of the painted bowls from Mexico. Now the living room also held Cory's watercolors and her raku figurines, and they had bought a painting they liked together, and some new furniture. It was the same with the garden. In addition to vegetables they'd planted borders of daffodils, irises and tulips. Rosemary had planted the azaleas she liked so much, but Cory had planted a small rose garden, four bushes so far, one a climbing bush that she planned to train over a trellis she wanted to build from instructions in a book.

She'd tried to tell West and Kevin about the house. She said, "I wish the two of you could come and see it."

"It's hard to get away," said Kevin.

"We'll see," said West. "Wouldn't want to be in the way."

"You wouldn't be in the way," said Cory. "Rosemary's family is always visiting. We can't keep them out of the way."

But he had never come to visit her, not once. First she'd been too unsettled in her life, then there'd been Georgia who didn't like to travel, now West considered everything too much trouble.

"It's two against one in this family, Cory," West said from the front seat.

Could he really be saying that?

"Two Republicans. One Democrat, he means," added her brother.

It was just as they were saying good-bye that the house on Wild-wood came up again.

"I never should have sold that house on Wildwood," West said. "Of course I didn't have a choice, with the medical bills. But we could have managed somehow. A man should have a house to grow old in."

"I don't know why the Hoovers didn't leave the house the way it was," said Kevin. "Of course, I don't blame them. They had three kids and all."

"No," said West. "I never blame anyone either. I've always been the sort of person to live and let live. The past is the past. I have my opinions, other people have theirs. I can get along with almost anybody."

Kevin nodded sagely. "So that's where I get it from. I think that's why I'm such a good supervisor. Taken as a whole, I don't like people. But I understand them."

"I've never had good friends," said West. "Acquaintances, yes, I've always been a sociable person. But true friends, no."

"I'm the same," said Kevin. "I don't seem to need a lot of people in my life. Just my family."

"I have a lot of friends," said Cory. "Friends get more and more important to me. Many of them I think of as my family."

"When I look back on my life," said West, ignoring her, "I think I've had more to bear than the average person."

Kevin nodded solemnly, but Cory thought, What about us? It was our mother.

"But I haven't given up. I still live one day at a time."

Kevin continued to nod.

It was dark by the time Cory and Kevin left West and got back on the freeway. Kevin was going to drop Cory off in Pasadena where she was staying with her old friend Naomi Stein. Then he'd start back up the coast to San Jose.

"Could you believe that back yard?" Kevin said.

"I guess they save on the water bills."

The drought years in California had made Naomi remove her grass lawns and replace them with native plants and an irrigation system that delivered water right to the roots.

"I took out all those plants that never should have been here in the first place," said Naomi. "The hibiscus, the begonias and azaleas, even the roses, though I love roses. But they're the gas-guzzling El Dorados of the flower kingdom at a time when we need efficient little Toyotas and Hondas."

Naomi's low stucco house now sat in a sea of silvery violets and gray-greens that smelled of lavender and sage. There was ceanothus, a scrub bush with lilac-colored flowers, and many kinds of succulents, from a bold sculptured blue agave to a prickly pear with lemon flowers sitting like canaries on the oval segments. Only those lemon flowers and a carroty scattering of California poppies were reminders of the riotous colors of the past.

It was the third time she'd stayed with Naomi in the last two years. She'd been meaning to get in touch for a long time, ever since that visit when she and Kevin had helped West move to the retirement community. She'd thought it wouldn't be all that difficult to find her high-school friend. Naomi had stayed in Southern California after UCLA, she'd heard, had married and had a couple of kids, worked on a magazine somewhere. Cory had thought she could just call up Aline and get Naomi's phone number. But when she'd finally decided to do it, two years ago, there was no longer any listing for an Aline and David Stein in Long Beach, and it took hunting up friends of friends before Cory got her on the phone.

After the first shock, Naomi was pleased.

"I've always wondered what happened to you," she said. "It felt like once you got out of high school, you never looked back. I heard you ended up in Seattle. Still there?"

"Yes, years now . . . Listen, how's your mom?"

There was a pause. "She died a few months ago. My dad died in 1985."

They talked of other things then. Naomi was divorced. It wasn't easy raising two kids, but they were teenagers now, practically in college, and they all gave each other room. Naomi was the managing editor of a magazine for women. And Cory: Was she married, what kind of career had she ended up in?

"I've been with the same woman for about five years. We're happy together. I have my own business as a CPA, doing consulting and taxes."

If there was the fraction of a pause, Naomi didn't let it linger. "That's *great*, Cory. I'm glad for you. But I can't believe you're an accountant. Who would have thought—our friend Brenda Starr from Lincoln High."

Cory laughed and they agreed that when Cory was in Southern California next they'd meet. But when Cory hung up, all she could think about was Aline, how she should have called her three years ago, two years ago, six months ago. You shouldn't put things like that off. Not when you're forty yourself. Once on a visit to Long Beach she'd found herself driving by the old Christian Science

Church where she'd gone to Sunday School, and had stopped in. "Mildred Clark," said the elderly woman at the office inside. "Oh, she retired to Florida many years ago, and then passed away."

"Did you ever know a Connie, a Connie Somebody—it was Italian?"

The woman thought so long Cory was certain she would say yes and tell her Connie's last name.

"No," she said finally.

"What about Polly Winter?" Cory asked, realizing with a slight shock that this old woman was about the age her mother would have been.

"Doesn't ring a bell. You're sure she went to this church?"

"Remember how my mother and I used to scream at each other in high school?" Naomi asked, the first time Cory stayed with her and they were reliving old times.

"She used to say she wished she had a nice quiet girl like me for a daughter."

"Did she?" Naomi laughed. "We got on so well after I got out of college and married. The year before she died we were so close, incredibly close. It was like losing a piece of myself when she died." She stopped. "Sorry, Cory, I guess you know all about that."

It was too easy to make people feel guilty, and pointless and ungenerous. She said, "I miss my mother the way a child does. She never was a friend to me. I never saw her get old. When I think of her she's younger than I am now and full of life. I miss what we might have had together. But I suppose there can't ever be a good time to lose your mother."

"No," said Naomi. "I'm just grateful for what I had."

Oh, it was *hard* not to feel deprived, hard not to be jealous. And it wasn't only her mother she missed, it was Aline. She would have liked so much to sit down with her and Naomi and talk about the days when they sat around addressing envelopes for

Aline's anti-war group, with Odetta and Joan Baez on the record player. She would have liked Aline to see her as an adult, to see that she had learned from Aline, had taken her convictions to heart.

"She's buried not far from here," said Naomi. "The kids and I drive over sometimes. We could go, if you want."

Cory nodded.

"Where's your mother buried, Cory?"

"I don't know."

"You don't know? Didn't your dad ever take you there?"

"No."

"But you should ask him before he . . . Is he going to be buried next to her?"

"Next to Georgia, I think. They bought plots together."

"You never went there."

It had all been so confused, the funeral service, the cortege to the cemetery. They'd driven a long way, and there was a hill, and a wind was blowing and people were crying, and off in the distance was the blue Pacific.

"Palos Verdes," said West when she asked him, but she didn't ask him why they'd never gone.

Cory always stayed with Naomi now when she was in Southern California. Their friendship had slipped back into its old groove; they called each other Winter and Stein, and bored Naomi's children by telling them stories of high school and their passionately flamboyant journalism teacher, Mr. Hawkins. It was better than a new friendship, because it linked them with their pasts, and showed them how they had and hadn't changed.

And now they were able to talk about all the things they never could back then, about Uncle Steve, and Naomi screwing her boyfriend and feeling like she had to keep it a secret from Cory because Cory and Aline were so close.

"So, did you like girls in high school?" Naomi asked. "Did you like me?"

"I don't know. I don't think so. I just don't remember being that interested in anything but the newspaper and ending racism and the war in as short a time as possible. I know I didn't think about you that way then, if *that's* what you're worried about."

"Too bad!"

They talked about Aline and they talked about Polly, and it wasn't that Naomi was closer to Cory than Rosemary was, but that Naomi was closer to the past. She remembered things Cory had forgotten.

"I thought how sad and romantic it was that you didn't have a mother. And I envied you. How I envied you. Your dad seemed so indifferent to everything—how you looked, what time you came home. You never took real advantage of that, you know."

"I'm not so sure I saw it as an advantage," Cory said. "I wanted everything you had."

"A mother who criticized everything you did?"

"Oh yes," said Cory, smiling with the hopeless irony of it. "A mother who watched me like a hawk."

Cory and Kevin sat in his car outside Naomi's. The sage and lavender gave a scent of the Mediterranean, the street lights caught the silver of the native plants.

"Do you think it's true," asked Cory, "that the reason we ended up leaving Wildwood and moving to the apartment building was because of medical bills? I thought it all had to do with putting the past behind us."

"You don't tell kids everything," said Kevin. "Especially money problems. When I was laid off my job that time, I didn't tell my kids at first. I was too ashamed I couldn't provide for them."

They talked about their old house then and things they remembered about growing up there. They talked about Sharie Palmer and how well she looked. And about the fates of their neighborhood playmates, all married or divorced now.

"I saw you looking at that lamppost today," Cory said.

"I didn't know what I was doing. There was a hollow sound, like the whole world was shaking. And then there was glass falling all around me. I can't believe I didn't get cut."

"You were always lucky," Cory said. "I guess we both are."

"We survived," he said.

Cory wanted to take his hand but didn't dare. He'd been such a little boy when everything had happened; it was unimaginable how little he had been. She wanted to tell him she was sorry she used to scare him with the Feeble stories, that she used to hit him and bully him.

"You never said why you were hitting the lamppost," she said instead.

Kevin paused, "I guess it was the day, you know, when Mama, . . . the funeral." His profile was stiff as wood.

"It's not a crime to feel sad, Kevin, or to mourn someone who's dead. It's work we need to do."

"You can't make me do it, Cory," he said, "Sometimes it's like you're trying to make me go through something I don't feel."

"You won't let yourself feel. It's too frightening. But feelings that aren't expressed don't go away."

"That's your opinion."

"Kevin, we talk around and around her. We never say her name. We never tell each other about the good times, or how it felt to lose her and grow up without a mother."

"I was too young. I don't remember."

"That's not true."

"What are you going to do with that branch?" he changed the subject.

"In one version of *Cinderella*, Cinderella asks her father to bring her a tree branch from town, and she plants it at her mother's grave. When the tree grows, it speaks to Cinderella in her mother's voice."

Kevin said nothing.

"Why don't you stay overnight, Kevin?" Cory said. "Naomi has room. In the morning we'll go to the cemetery."

"If you want to do this, fine. But you can't make me. I've got a lot of things on my mind. I'm a father, not a kid. I've got two children and a wife to support. You see things differently when you have a family. You see yourself as an adult, not a child. You don't have time for all this remembering and feeling stuff. If you had a family, you'd know."

His voice dropped; he stared at the street lamp outside. Cory looked at the house where Naomi was waiting up for her. Naomi had been her friend at fifteen and was her friend now at forty-two. When she told Naomi that she and Rosemary had bought a house together, Naomi had hugged her hard and said, "Cory, this is a big step for you. Mazel tov!"

"I do have a family," she said to her brother. The light came through the window of the car and fell on both of them. She took his hand, very tentatively. "I do have a family," she repeated. "And you're part of it."

THE SOUND STONES MAKE

IN WATER

"Do you know why they do it?" Cory asked. "I don't know why they do it."

"What?" Rosemary asked, yawning.

"That rock throwing."

"Oh," said Rosemary, understanding now. "Boys. I don't know why either. They all do it. My nephews do it constantly. They get to a certain age. Then the rocks come out whenever they get near water."

"Cory! Aunt Cory! Rosemary!" Fourteen-year-old Peter called up to them where they sat on a bluff overlooking the small island bay. It was late afternoon on a cloudy July day. "Did you see that one? I skipped it five times. Watch me!"

The two women watched. The next two stones plopped sullenly into the pewter blue water, leaving a single ring each.

"What they *want*," said Cory with impatience, "is for you to goddamn watch them every minute. Just in case. And to be ready to praise them. You don't see Jessie clamoring for attention every second. Where is Jessie, anyway?"

Jessie, newly twelve, stood still as a heron in the shallows of the bay. She might have been noticing the way a water bug sailed along the surface of the water, or she might have been contemplating the reflection of her perfect skin. While her brother struggled with acne, Jessie's face was still baby smooth.

Kevin had had acne too, that last summer she'd spent with him and West in their small apartment. He'd gone from being a runty little kid with glasses to a boy five foot ten with a deep voice and bad skin. So much growing that summer had left him with little energy for anything else. He lay tiredly on the sofa and ate cookies, while Cory came in and out with her excitement over getting ready to go to college in another state.

Peter's voice had changed since she'd seen him last. His hair was limp blond, and hung over his muddy blue eyes, which had a worried, driven look. Like his father he wore glasses, and a large black waterproof watch that encircled his thin wrist like the identifying band on a bird's leg. Doggedly, he kept trying to skip stones. Although the others watched, each one, whether perfectly flat or "almost perfect" went straight down, as if weighted with lead.

"He's practically removing the entire beach," said Cory. She and Peter had not been getting on well this visit. She remembered him shorter and happier, much more agreeable.

"He's homesick," Rosemary offered.

"He begged to come and get away from home. Now all he does is look at his watch and ask me what we're going to do *next*."

Rosemary laughed. "You can't tell what he's thinking, really. Years later he'll say, My aunt took me kayaking once. And that's the reason I'm a marine biologist today."

"Hah!"

Easy for Rosemary to laugh. She'd be going back on the ferry to Seattle in two hours, while Cory had another day with the kids. They'd spent two nights already at the old-fashioned clapboard hotel in the village behind them. Yesterday they'd taken a hike into the woods and up to the top of the island's mountain, from which you could see the whole chain of islands and even snow-topped Mount Baker on the mainland. Yesterday had been one of those perfect sunny days the Northwest could produce from time to time—they'd even gone swimming—but today it was back to gray and green. This morning Cory had made everyone get up at six for the kayak trip. After it was over, she'd persuaded them to walk fast around the lake to warm up. Peter looked at his huge black watch the entire time and wanted to know how long it took to get around this lake, what time was lunch, when was Rosemary's ferry, why did they have to stay another night?

Only for a couple of hours, while they'd been paddling around the coves of the island, had Peter been quiet and absorbed. He'd been in the front seat of her kayak and was the first to spot the large bald eagle soaring by with a whole salmon in its beak. In the other kayak Rosemary was doing all the work. Jessie sat with the binoculars, staring open-mouthed at the eagle, which landed with a cry on a snag of fir poking out through the mist like a mast.

Cory and Peter had pulled steadily together, falling into rhythm. His head in front of her was blond and wet, his shoulders thin and strong under the fat orange life-jacket. She'd taken up kayaking when she turned forty and it was something she could never get enough of, this unanchored yet somehow grounded sense of floating through the water. You were so low you couldn't tilt over; the boat was an extension of your legs, like a mermaid's tail. It was the nearest thing she'd ever felt to swimming. Often now, she took the single kayak she'd bought—and stowed, for extra, of course, in the cellar of Irene's building—and spent a hour or two on Lake Union. She'd been talking it up to Peter, telling him how he would love it. He had loved it, but then it was over.

"Cory! Jessie! Rosemary!" Peter shouted.

"We're looking," they all replied, three women trained to look.

"They never skip when anyone's looking," he complained, as the stones dropped, glub, glub, glub.

"Okay, we're not looking," Cory said.

"Well, how will you see if I do skip one then?"

"We'll have to take your word."

Rosemary closed her eyes again. Was she thinking of the hour they'd snatched in the woods yesterday, without the kids, or about the work that would await her as soon she as got back into the office tomorrow morning? "You may be right," she sighed. "Now I'm worrying about the effect of boys on the beach. Can we rely on the tide to carry back into shore all the stones that they're throwing out into the water? There must be something ecologically unsound about it."

Jessie had come over to join her brother. It always shocked Cory to see how pretty she was, small, well-shaped, with long honey-colored hair that was sometimes in a braid, sometimes in a ponytail, sometimes flowing. She wore earrings and a clean white T-shirt that said Banana Republic and she had a quiet, self-possessed air. If she were rebellious at all, that rebellion ran only to changing the ending on her name as frequently as possible. If Cory sent her a birthday gift addressed to Jessie Winter, the thank-you card came back signed Jessy or Jesse or Jessi. In a few years she might be Jessica. She would probably never be a Jess.

"I was so ugly when I was her age," Cory said. "I was the ugliest person on the planet. Jessie is a girl I would have worshipped in the seventh grade. How is it possible we belong to the same family?"

"She's so graceful," said Rosemary. "She moves like her body belongs to her."

They both sighed, but the sound was more meditative than envious.

"Jessie, Jessie! Watch!" said Peter. The stone skipped twice. "Did you see that?"

"That's good, Peter," Jessie said. She picked up a stone and skipped it four times. Peter said nothing.

"It starts so young. I can't stand it," said Rosemary. "Great job, Jessie!" she called down to the beach.

Jessie looked mildly pleased, but after a moment she went off down the beach, her honey hair swinging, her agile feet finding a way easily over the boulders. Peter continued relentlessly tossing stones. Sometimes he threw a handful and they made a sound like heavy rain, a pleasing syncopated shower.

Cory felt like a failure. How could you counteract a lifetime of TV and Nintendo in a ten-day visit? She had taken them to the art museum, she had taken them to a play, she had taken them to the Pacific Science Center. She had let them roam around the Market, she had given them money to take the waterfront streetcar to the International District. She had talked to them about homophobia, she had introduced them to other kids she knew, the sons and daughters of lesbian and gay friends. But it had been useless: Peter wanted to stay home and watch the Mariners on television; Jessie spent hours doing things to her hair in the bathroom. Peter told Republican jokes he'd heard from Kevin; Jessie read teen slasher novels where cheerleaders were decapitated and run through with knives by other jealous cheerleaders.

Rosemary's young relatives weren't like this. They were in the chorus and played the clarinet and won prizes with their science experiments and read Barbara Kingsolver and Amy Tan in high school and were worried about recycling and gang violence and what they could do to change the world.

"Cory," said Peter, looking at his watch. "What are we going to do *now?*"

They all waved Rosemary off at the ferry, and then it sailed like a giant white cake into the pale blue mist that was settling over the water. The dock smelled of creosote and salt; the sea gulls wheeled above with their lonely cry. Already Cory missed her. It had been something she'd been slow to notice or afraid to notice: how she actually felt better when Rosemary was around. When she mentioned it to Rae, that she had missed Rosemary recently when Rosemary went alone to St. Paul to see her parents, Rae said,

"Cory Winter, sometimes I wonder about you. After almost eight years, I would think you might, you just *might* miss being around Rosemary. I know that when Nicole is away visiting her mom I just can't sleep the same."

For Cory it had been a discovery. It went against her earlier notions of keeping herself independent. She had summed up their relationship often for people by first saying, "Rosemary and I were friends first. We never fell madly in love. So maybe that's why we've stayed together. We live our own lives. We never merged the way lots of couples do."

But Rae and Nicole had fallen madly in love and were still together, still crazy about each other, even after two children and the two plays they'd written and produced together. What was the difference? "What's important is not how you start, but how you continue," said Rae. "How you treat each other year after year, not just during the first six weeks. You've got to keep up the romance. I take Nicole out to dinner once a month, bring her flowers, get all dressed up. Then we come home and—it's hot!"

Cory had seen them when she baby-sat. How Rae in her evening jacket and boots, Nicole in her crepe dress and heels, left the house, and how they came home, holding tightly on to each other.

"We're not that romantic, me and Rosemary," Cory said. But where once she might have felt inadequate, now she accepted it. The mystery of their connection was *their* mystery, no one else's.

"I'm closer to you than I've ever been to anyone," Rosemary said yesterday on their walk in the woods. They'd left Jessie and Peter by the lake, Peter skipping stones, Jessie swimming slowly and methodically within the rectangle marked by buoys and lines.

"Yes," said Cory. "The thought used to scare me—being close to anyone. Now it feels normal. Necessary. It's not being close—losing you—that scares me."

"You never could have said that before. That you were afraid of losing anything or anybody."

"I used to feel I'd be just fine on my own," Cory. "I still would be—fine, I mean. Just not so happy."

They were sitting on either end of red cedar log; the heart of it, between them, soft with age, crumbling more than splintering. The colors in the small open space in the trees were those found in German Expressionist paintings, like Ludwig Kirchner; they were like rubies and raspberries against green fire and cool lime.

Around them there was very little old growth. Most of the Western red cedar and Douglas fir had been logged off, was broken, burnt and fallen. Western Hemlock had sprung up instead, with a dense undergrowth of vine maple, red alder, salal and salmonberry. There were layers and layers of shed needles, crumbled bark and moss. It was a mixed forest and they didn't know half of what lived there, half of what the names were.

They knew some things about the forests of the Northwest. They burned and regenerated, were logged and replanted or reseeded themselves. Over the black charred bark of trees struck by lightening, moss grew protective and thick and vines wrapped their arms around themselves. The ground cover laid green hands over everything burnt and fallen and broken. Saplings didn't wait, but sprang up, wanting to live. The saplings wouldn't grow into the trees that stood here before, not into the old growth that stood for centuries, majestic and confident. But hemlock would grow and red alder, and eventually some cedar and fir, if the forest were left alone. There was still cedar standing.

Cory took Rosemary's hand and held it. It was when they had dropped their expectations that sex had improved, when they learned to talk about it without the old words, when they stopped being deep down afraid and let their bodies open. Cory felt the life of her lover coursing through her palm. If you didn't call it sexual, what she felt, what would you call it? Only staying present. Not giving it a name, at least not the old names. Only love, second growth, sapling, rubies and raspberries, green like fire, green like new, red cedar breaking open like a heart.

Over dinner, Jessie and Peter seemed anxious and eager to be gone. Cory had wanted to take them to Victoria but had dropped the idea, as over the course of the week she had dropped other plans. Tomorrow morning they'd head back to Seattle, and early Tuesday morning they'd go to the airport. They told her about what they'd do when they got back to San Jose, as if they had never been eager to leave. Peter planned to make a lot of money mowing lawns, and he would swim every day at the neighborhood pool and go back to playing ball with his friends in the park. Jessie said she'd be baby-sitting mostly, and getting ready for the seventh grade.

Cory should have spent more time with them when they were younger, she thought, when they still had the freshness of early childhood about them, when they were still *alive*. But there had never seemed a good reason to visit Kevin and Betsy, to stay in the cramped little house in San Jose, more than once every year or two. She remembered Peter at two and Jessie, pink and screaming, newly born; then Jessie was suddenly four and Peter was six, just starting first grade. He'd loved to read picture books then, wouldn't let her out of his sight without showing her how he could read *Goodnight Moon* all by himself. And that time Jessie had climbed in her lap and stared at her. "You're Daddy's sister," she said. "His *sister*." Stroking Cory's face with fingers like grimy rose petals.

Whenever Cory visited she always brought crayons and paper as presents, and sat down with them and drew. Flowers and trees and water and boats. Cory had never lost her taste for crayoning. Once Betsy said, "Kevin told me that when he see the three of you making pictures, it reminds him of the two of you and your mother." But Kevin never sat and drew with them, and by ten years old, Peter didn't like to either. He looked on with superior unhappy longing as Jessie and Cory made houses and gardens, and then he tried to draw a racecar. But he tore it up in disgust. "I can't get it to look real."

When he was little he curled up in Cory's lap and let her read him *Little House in the Big Woods*. But that was a long time ago. Now he said he expected to work in computers like his father, not as a technician but as a programmer. Jessie had stopped drawing too. She said she'd work in a clothes store like her mother had before she got married, because then she could get her clothes at a discount.

They had looked at her with baby-blue eyes; they had smelled like milk and dirt. Now they were talking about this trip in the past tense. Peter said, "I've seen Seattle in a bunch of movies. Now I know what it really looks like. The Pacific Science Center was really cool."

"I liked the ferries best," said Jessie. "I like to watch the birds with the binoculars. I've seen a lot of birds I never saw at home. Like the cormorants and the bald eagle."

"Yeah," said Peter. "That bald eagle, with the salmon! Incredible. I never felt anything like how it was to be in the kayak. Like you're in the water, but you're not. You're floating, but you don't feel like you'll tip over."

"It's a great feeling," said Cory, remembering how they'd pulled together. If you took away the pressure to make a meaningful connection, you were left with a rhythm that didn't need to be explained. Two bodies in the mist, half visible, knowing each other's stroke. *That* was the memory she would try to hold onto.

"It's been really fun, Aunt Cory," Jessie told her. "Thank you."

But afterwards, Peter wanted to know, "What are we going to do now?" and there was nothing really to do. The small village closed down at five and they had already seen the one movie at the tiny theater on Friday night.

They went down to the beach again and in the cold evening light Peter threw stones in the bay and Jessie wrapped herself up in a blanket and watched him.

Plop, plop, plop.

It was uncanny the way Peter resembled Kevin when he'd been fourteen, that time when he had changed from being her little brother into a boy who said little and had a separate destiny. Once he had said to her, "It wasn't easy, after you left, just me and Dad living there on our own for three years. I missed you."

But she hadn't missed him. She'd hardly thought of him. She was thrilled to be leading her own adult life, away from the two of them, away from the memory of what they'd gone through, away from the smell of them, the sight of them, the awkwardness of keeping her privacy as a girl around them. She was glad not to share a bathroom with shaving cream and Mennen's Deodorant, not to see soiled boxer shorts in the wash, not to be expected to cook and clean for them. Not that she ever really had; they'd all fended for themselves or got take-out or eaten increasingly with friends, but sometimes Cory felt a wounded expectation that she didn't manage to take care of them in some way. That she didn't turn into a mother or even a responsible older sister.

When she came home from college that first year or two, she stayed as short a time as possible. She fought with her father about the draft and the Black Panthers and the need for armed struggle in liberation movements. She never spent time with Kevin alone, or tried to talk with him about anything. She mocked him for his interest in sports, and said she wasn't surprised when he decided to join the Army. He'd never fought in Vietnam; he'd gone to Germany instead. He'd met Betsy, gotten married, moved to San Jose, had two children, was a supervisor, liked sports on TV, drank too much beer and smoked Marlboros. He loved Betsy and his kids, was a silent majority-type of Republican and was getting more conservative. He never went to church and had brought Jessie and Peter up without even a basic knowledge of religion. "We don't go to church because our dad had to go too much," Jessie had told Cory once.

Peter came running up, wanting his sweatshirt. His thin limbs were shivering. "Did you see that last one, Cory?" he said. "Five skips."

"I saw it," she lied. "I think you're really improving."

When it got too cold they went inside and played cards for a while in Jessie and Peter's room. They were downstairs and along a corridor in a different wing from where Cory and Rosemary had been staying. It hadn't been possible to get anything closer. She'd thought they would enjoy it, staying in an old-fashioned hotel like this—she would have at their age—but Peter had immediately complained. "There's no TV here," he said, "There's no swimming pool. There's no place to play."

When she left them, it was after ten and all of them were exhausted. In her room, Cory packed her clothes for tomorrow when they'd be leaving early. She was sorry to put her watercolors away without having used them. She had wanted to catch the ruby and emerald look of the forest yesterday, of the red cedar and green moss, of Rosemary's hand touching the crumbling center of the tree. She made a quick sketch, then got in bed and began to read. When she next woke up, her light was still on, her head had fallen against the open pages, and there was a smell of something cooking.

But it couldn't be cooking. Not at this time of night. She roused herself, more as if she were waking into a dream than out of one, and went out of her room and into the corridor. The same smell was there, only more pronounced, a little smoky without there being any smoke to see. There was no one else around, no one else who had come out of their rooms to look. She thought, I'm imagining this, and opened the door of the bathroom across the hall.

Just then the fire alarm went off.

It shrieked like a voice out of control, and she rushed back inside her room, grabbed her wallet and her keys and tore down the stairs in bare feet and her long T-shirt to the corridor where

Jessie and Peter's room was. The smell was very strong here and there was smoke pouring up from under a door across from theirs, a door marked Storage. She pounded on their door, "Jessie, Peter! Fire! Fire!"

There was no answer. She pounded and screamed as loud as she could. No one else seemed to be in this corridor and she remembered it was Sunday night, and most people had left the hotel earlier that day. She rushed downstairs to the office, but it was empty. The fire alarm continued to shriek, and more people were emerging from their rooms, in robes and slippers. They were running to the reception too, looking for someone to call the fire station; they were running outside.

"My niece and nephew are inside one of the rooms. It's locked and I can't get them to open it," she shouted, but no one paid any attention.

Then a man ran down the corridor towards Jessie and Peter's room and she followed him. But he was going to the door marked Storage. He opened it and smoke billowed out in a noxious cloud. "I know what this is," he said, and vanished into the cloud.

"Jessie! Peter!" Cory screamed at the top of her lungs, and beat the door and kicked it with her bare feet. She saw them inside, overcome by smoke and fumes, lying on their beds, dead already.

She saw her brother's grief, the grief he didn't deserve, the grief he was unprepared for, the grief he would never forgive her for.

"Oh God, oh God," she screamed. "Help me, someone."

But no one came. No one had ever come.

She wouldn't leave them, she'd die here too. She couldn't face her brother having survived the fire. She didn't want to survive if Jessie and Peter died. She thought her hand would break, she had to get an ax. The man from the storage room hadn't come back; he was probably dead too. She was sobbing in her fear, the moment was stopped and couldn't go back or forward, just stayed and stayed, with the horror of it.

Then Peter cautiously opened the door, with Jessie right behind him.

"Get out of there, get out right now, don't take anything." She grabbed his arm and Jessie's and pulled them, running, down the corridor to an exit. "Didn't you hear me screaming and pounding? What's wrong with you?"

"We were asleep," said Jessie.

"We thought some people were having a party and just banging on our door."

The man who'd gone into the storage room came out to the street where they stood with the other guests, shivering in front of the hotel. "I stayed here once before when this happened," he said, as if it were no big deal. "Someone forgot to turn the big industrial drier off, and the sheets caught fire and now the drier is on fire."

"This is incredible," said the guests. "Where's the manager?"

There was no manager, or any employees, nor any fire truck either. Someone walking by in the street had called the volunteer fire station though and eventually two trucks pulled up.

Cory put Jessie and Peter in the back seat of her car with a blanket she'd found in the trunk.

"You should have seen your face, Aunt Cory," Peter said with a nervous laugh. "You looked like a crazy person."

"I thought you were dead!" But they had no idea of what she meant, of how it could feel to survive when someone you loved was no longer there, how it could make you look and act crazy with fear and wretchedness.

"We were just sleeping," Jessie explained again, yawning.

"I know," said Cory. "It's all right. Everything is all right now."

She got out of the car. She didn't have her shoes and the wind blew through her hair. Everyone around her was coming to life in the way that people did in disasters. They each told their stories of getting out of the rooms, of the second when they had first realized something was wrong, and then they told other stories, of other fires, of other disasters. They were all gradually realizing that they had escaped something, and so they clung together, talking and staring at the hotel, wondering about the things they'd left inside, and where that damn manager was.

The firefighters were inside with chemical sprays to douse the fire. The hotel wasn't going to burn up, but none of them could sleep there tonight. The manager arrived looking very put out. There was a motel down the block; he would make sure everybody had a room. He did not apologize.

A half hour later he returned with keys and showed them where the motel was. Some of the guests were sputtering and angry; others simply took the keys and set off. Cory drove her car up to the motel and got Jessie and Peter, half asleep, inside. There were two queen-size beds and they slipped into one, on either side.

She couldn't sleep though, and finally went outside to the pay phone booth that stood lighted at a corner of the motel. First she called Rosemary.

"That's outrageous, not having anyone at the desk. And the way the manager refused to take responsibility, especially when it had happened before. I think there are grounds for legal action against them. At the very least, you definitely shouldn't pay your bill."

"Rosemary, I thought they were dead. I thought they were *dead.*" She burst into tears.

"Oh Cory, I'm sorry. You must have been terrified."

"I was," she cried. "I was so scared. And the worst thing was, it was like I had been waiting for this to happen, like I had been waiting my whole life, and wasn't even surprised."

"Have you called your brother yet?"

"No. I mean, we're all fine now." Cory grew quiet. "I wouldn't want to worry him."

But once Rosemary had planted the idea in her head, she had to call Kevin. All she could think of, when she got him on the phone, was that the Feebles had been in a fire once, and that Jack Feeble had been almost burned to a crisp before Nancy saved him.

"Our hotel caught on fire," she found herself whispering. "I mean, there was a little fire, more just a lot of smoke really, we're fine, but I thought you should know."

He'd been asleep, but now his voice had the wary tone she remembered from the last time she'd called him unexpectedly, to tell him West had gone into the hospital.

"Where are the kids? Can I talk to them?"

"They're sleeping now. We're at a different motel. I probably shouldn't have called you, but I just wanted to let you know— we're all right."

"Well, thanks," he said, with an edge of irritation. "Now I'll just go back to sleep like nothing has happened."

"I'm sorry. I hope you and Betsy won't worry."

"She didn't wake up. She never wakes up in the night like I do when there's a phone call."

"Me too," said Cory. "I always wake up, think something has happened."

There was a pause, then Kevin said in a more normal voice, "Well, I'm glad you called. Is everything going okay with them otherwise?"

"Oh yes. Jessie changes her hairstyle six times a day, but she seems to have gotten interested in bird watching. And Peter has been trying to skip stones ever since we arrived."

"Skipping stones," said Kevin. "I used to do that."

He had, too. She had a sudden memory of being with him at Lake Mead, their very last vacation together as a family, and of Kevin standing on the stony shore with Connie's kids, Joe and Danny and little Sal and Susie, tossing red pebbles in the deep azure water. Out on the boat, Connie and Polly sat close together, the one so big, the other so frail, folded into each other.

"What was their last name, those people we went to Lake Mead with that summer?"

"Sabicca," he said after a moment's thought, knowing exactly who she meant.

"Connie Sabicca," she said, "Sabicca, that was it." And then before she could stop herself, she was telling him.

"Do you remember that game of Bad Man we used to play? It wasn't made up from nothing. It was about Uncle Steve. Uncle Steve abused me, sexually, that summer he was visiting. At the river, and then in the guest room."

She was shaking, standing in the exposed bright phone booth on an island in a dark night, and the words hung there, lonely and exposed as the Douglas firs by the edge of the water. But at last the words had been said.

"Dad know?" he said finally. Which was not, "Oh my God, the disgusting bastard, or how horrible for you," but was at least an acknowledgment that it had happened. Kevin didn't not believe her.

"No," she said. The receiver felt hard and strange in her hand, her stomach traveled in waves to her throat and her legs were thin and wobbly as vines. She heard her mother saying, as the two of them rushed up to her, crying, "It doesn't matter who started it, Cory, you're the one responsible for stopping it. You're the older sister." Polly had been the older sister, too, but she had not stopped it.

Then Kevin said, "I'm sorry, Cory. It must have been terrible."

And through the sadness and anger, her heart in joy leaped up, so that she almost felt like laughing.

"I'm glad you told me," he said.

She didn't laugh, but she smiled, though she was crying. Some enormous weight was gone. "Yes," she said. "I needed to tell you. And now I have."

Cory went back to the motel room and let herself in quietly. Jessie's honey hair fanned over the pillow and her limbs stretched in every direction as if she were swimming. Peter lay straight at the edge of the bed, his tanned arms thin above the covers, his wristwatch still on, the numbers glowing in the dark. She couldn't see his face—it was under a pillow—but she heard him snoring.

The room smelled like children, like love and fear, like the hopelessness of protecting them.

How like her grandmother she had sounded when she shouted angrily at them, "Didn't you hear me screaming and pounding? What's wrong with you?" Her grandmother who had burned the barn down and saved the cows, who had told Polly as a baby, "You will be healed," who had lived in fear of losing her children and who had lost them, over and over.

In the forest, earlier today, she'd had some vision of growth and decay, of life never ending, but transforming itself always into something else. In the forest it was possible to take the long view, to see that fire could regenerate as well as destroy, to see that from destruction would come a second growth. But the long view wasn't so easy in front of a locked hotel door with children, your family, on the other side and smoke pouring into the corridor. It wasn't possible not to fear loss and not to be devastated and changed by it. That's what it was to be human, and to feel.

Cory got into her own bed, hearing again the gentle slosh of the water at their feet earlier this evening, how the water pulled through the stones and pebbles with a thousand separate trickles. She had looked up and seen the constellations appearing faintly: the dippers, Hercules, the Northern Crown.

Tomorrow she would not use her grandmother's voice with Peter and Jessie. She would join them in throwing a few last stones into the water before the ferry took them away from the island. Lying in bed, slipping into sleep, she could already feel the weight of the stone tugging at her arm in a gesture she remembered from her childhood—yes, she'd thrown them too—and could hear the sound the stone made as it skipped three times and then sank, a sound of something opening, and something letting go.

AVEBURY

I.

She approached it from the south, turning off the motorway when she saw the sign to Avebury Village. It was the middle of the week, a cold afternoon in February, and there was almost no one else in the car park. Snow had fallen in the last few days; the Wiltshire countryside was lightly frosted, as if a threadbare white coverlet had been thrown over the rolling green chalk downs.

Avebury was not what Cory had expected. Yesterday she'd been to Stonehenge, had paid to stand outside the barbed wire fence and to look at what remained of the stone circle. It wasn't particularly inspiring, not after all the radiant, mystical photographs she'd seen of the standing stones at dawn and dusk, equinox and solstice. A harsh wind mixed with sleet and hail blew over Salisbury Plain. The few tourists trudged around and around the circle, not like ancient Druids, but like people compelled to get their money's worth.

Avebury had a spacious, unfenced, monumental feel. The huge standing stones were rough-cut and weathered gray. Once there had been two inner circles inside a huge outer one, and two serpentine processional avenues leading up to them. Most of the huge stones were gone now; they'd been burned, buried and broken up for building materials. Inside what remained of the large stone circle was a village built from the stones, with a pub, she was glad to see. Cory got out of her rented car and went in to get warm and have some lunch. She was feeling all the bleakness of the season, and the burden of being a tourist alone. She regretted miserably now this decision to come to Europe six weeks earlier than she and Rosemary had planned, to come in the off-season, and to come without Rosemary.

I don't want to be here, she found herself writing on a postcard of two megalithic stones with a dramatic sky behind them. And then tore it up. She was not going to give into fear and sadness, she was going to have a good time—or at least a *meaningful* time—traveling by herself. Otherwise there would have been no point to running away. She might as well have stayed in Seattle and kept her clients instead of sending them off to other accountants. Some of them she'd had for years. She didn't care. None of her father's clients had come to his funeral.

The tea warmed her, but she couldn't eat her ploughman's lunch. The brown roll stuck in her throat and the Stilton was like brine. "I guess I have jet lag," she told the waitress, and finished her tea and paid up.

She was still unsteady, she decided, from stopping off on the way here at the West Kennet Long Barrow, "one of the finest examples in Britain of a Neolithic burial site."

The site had been quite empty, forlorn in the way of important but unvisited places, and the ground was muddy, not as if the snow had melted, but as if there were an underground spring or seepage. A thin cold draft came out of the opening to the barrow as she approached. She knew from the illustration in one guidebook that there was a central passage formed of upright stones, with chambers leading off it and at the end one round larger chamber. Archeologists had found grave goods there, all the things that the dead tried to take with them: clay pots now broken into fragments, flint tools, bone and shell beads. The barrow was shaped like a woman's body, said the more feminist guidebook. The vagina of death, the uterus of death, the Lady of the Tombs, the Mother of the Dead. She felt the cold wind on her face and her feet wouldn't move to take her inside the barrow, though she told herself, This is silly. You've come all this way.

But even to look into the shadowy portals of the stone barrow was to look into the opaque dark eye of death itself; an eye that could see into her, but into which she could never see further than the surface.

At her father's funeral the minister had read from Isaiah: *Thy sun shall no more go down; neither shall thy moon withdraw itself; for the Lord shall be thine everlasting light, and the days of thy mourning shall be ended.*

Soothing words for a grief hardly begun. Soothing words that meant nothing in front of the cold black eye of death.

Cory left the little warmth of the pub and started walking around the top of the henge. The guidebook told her that the outer circle had once been formed of ninety-eight huge boulders called Saracens, some up to eighteen feet tall, which enclosed almost thirty acres. Outside the circle was a vast ditch and a high bank. In many places the stones were missing, for though the site had remained in use for a thousand years and intact for two thousand more, during the Middle Ages the church had caused the standing stones to be destroyed. Not until the 1930s had archeologists laboriously begun to dig up the stones and to set them back in place. Once there had been about 600 stones at Avebury, now there were about seventy. They looked like broken teeth.

The light was hard and grainy, and in a short while it would be dark. She'd return to her bed and breakfast in Marlborough, where Mrs. Hodges had looked at her with such tactful sympathy this morning over bacon and eggs ("On your own then, are you, dear?"), and make a phone call to Rosemary. She'd tell Rosemary that she loved and missed her, would tell her that perhaps the trip wasn't such a good idea after all, and could she come home now? Or could Rosemary please drop everything and come and rescue her?

But of course Cory wouldn't. She'd pretend that it was all very interesting, and even if she did whine, just a little, Rosemary would reassure her and remind her, "But you've always wanted to go to Europe and see the museums. A change of scene is bound to do you good."

The stones were so hard and cold. She shouldn't stop, her feet got too cold. She should have finished her lunch; she was feeling weak and empty. It was just jet lag, it would get better. But the stones frightened her; they seemed to exude some enormous, incoherent power, neither beneficent nor malevolent, simply there. Behind the circle, the trees were bare.

He died so quickly, not at all the way she'd thought it would happen. Simply a phone call that woke her early one morning from the resident doctor at the retirement community. "Is this Cora Winter? Your father West passed away in his sleep last night. It was a heart attack."

She'd flown to Seal Beach and so had Kevin. They packed things up and arranged for the funeral. Only a handful of people came; her father had lost touch with many earlier acquaintances and others had died. A few women from the retirement community came, one in a wheelchair. Sharie Palmer sent flowers.

That's what it came down to when you were born and died an orphan, when you were the survivor who had outlived almost everybody else, your parents, your two brothers, your two wives. Meeting Kevin's eyes over the freshly dug grave, Cory saw the same truth that she felt in her heart—now nothing stood between them and their own deaths.

She put her cheek against one of the rough-faced Saracens, just to feel some connection to something real in the world. Ever since the funeral in December she'd been clinging to anything that would ground her, that would make her feel that she was part of life. It used to be that she could forget everything through drinking or sex or work, especially work, but this year, when she sat down with clients at her desk piled with forms, and they handed her their pathetic manila folders filled with painstaking accounts, or wild estimates, or outright lies, Cory felt like weeping. Other people had nervous breakdowns when their parents died, she had 1040 forms, and they were no longer good enough.

She thought, not for the first time since December, not for the first time in her life, that what she wanted was not to die, but to simply cease to exist. Living was too much effort but suicide was out of the question. If she could just stand here and freeze, though, let her heart become an icy stone in a rock-hard body, then she would.

Rosemary might be sad for a while, but then Rosemary had sent her off to Europe, Rosemary had gotten maps and guidebooks and had helped her plan this trip. Rosemary wanted to get rid of her.

If she froze here, then she wouldn't have to remember anything.

Then she wouldn't have to feel anything.

"Hello," said a voice close to her. "You want to move your feet a bit, keep the blood moving."

Cory jerked her head around. But there was no one there, only a woman in a heavy dark coat and a head scarf walking a large sort of sheep dog on the top of the henge a hundred feet away.

She'd imagined it.

All the same Cory started walking again, and the blood returned to her face, feet and hands. She breathed deeply, oxygen rushed to her brain and her vision cleared. She could see the stone circles, the barren trees, the village, all black on white, an acid etching. She walked across the road, to the beginning of the West Kennet Avenue, a long row of stones on either side, called bridestones. Once young girls had walked up this avenue to the larger circle to meet the boys coming up their own processional way on the other side.

All the way down the avenue of paired stones she walked, and when she came to the end a blue cold twilight had crept up around the edges of the world, putting slanted shadows on the snow.

Did she miss her father because of who he was, who he had been to her, or because his death reminded her so much of losing her mother?

It had been almost unbearable to pack up the remains of his orphan life that day with Kevin. It reminded them of when they'd left Wildwood Avenue and West had made them leave behind stuffed animals and toys, all the papier-mâché and Play-Doh objects and all the hundreds of Cory's paintings that Polly had kept. "We're going to a smaller place," he kept reminding them. "We won't have a playroom. We won't have so many closets." He even got rid of Sallie, the dog. They'd kept asking him, "Where will Sallie live in the apartment?" and he put them off and put them off, until moving day, when they got in the car and came to the new apartment and Sallie wasn't there. They never asked what happened to her, and West never told them.

"I'm moving to a smaller place," he'd told them again when he moved out of the Long Beach apartment and gave away almost everything to Goodwill. Now they stood among his few boxes and divided up the few personal things he'd left behind. Kevin took West's heavy, gold-plated watch, and Cory, for some reason, one of her father's old pipes. By the end of West's life there hadn't been many public places where you could smoke a pipe. "I hardly smoke anyway," West said. "Just fill it, tamp it, take a puff or two, and empty it."

Kevin took the photo of young Wesley in the orphanage, and

Cory took the one of her father and mother at the Pike soon after they met. There were no photos of Cory or Kevin. The last time either of them had talked to him he'd said he was fine, just fine.

Two women had stuck their heads in the door. "We didn't know him well. He kept to himself. But he seemed at peace. We thought you'd want to know that."

When Polly had died all the neighbors from Wildwood and Faust were there—Bernie the longshoreman and Yolanda Ray dressed up in a tight-fitting black suit with a pink carnation on her lapel, and Sharie Palmer with a big bouffant under a thin black veil, and the Curtis boys, with whom Cory used to play softball when boys still let her, and Janet and Linda Spritz, dressed in identical dark navy-blue sleeveless dresses with white knit cardigans slung over their shoulders. Mildred Clark with her big bosom had been there, and dozens of people from the church, one of whom told Cory to be brave and to lean on the *sustaining infinite,* for Polly was among them still. Dorothy Dragon was there, smelling of beer, embracing Cory quick and hard with tears in her eyes. Teachers from Polly's old elementary school came, and so did people from the city college where West taught, as well some of his clients and his former accounting partner Don Feldman.

Cory had forgotten this funeral until her father's brought it back. How many people there had been to mourn her mother, how strong the flowers smelled, how weepy the music was, how many handkerchiefs there were. How her father had sobbed and clung to Cory and Kevin and said, "I know what it's like to lose a mother."

But a month later they had moved, changed schools and stopped going to church. Everything was gone. West turned his back on it.

The avenue of frozen stones stretched out in front of her, back to the village, back to the car, but she didn't think she could make it. It was like her life stretching into the distance, her life as empty and uninhabited as the white fields on either side, as the row of stones, as the road with only death at the end.

She didn't think these kinds of thoughts with Rosemary, but it didn't matter. Rosemary was in Seattle and Cory was here. And who could know whether her life with Rosemary would last? They'd get tired of each other, or one of them would die. Cory, of course, of breast cancer. "Stop being so morbid!" Rosemary would say, but what did she know? Nobody in her immediate family had died except her grandmother. Phil was older than West and had arthritis but still managed to volunteer for the Elks and work in the yard, and as for Anne, that woman was indefatigable, baby-sitting her grandchildren, knitting, sewing, baking cookies and sending them to Rosemary along with Lo-Fat recipes she clipped out of the newspaper.

"Sometimes I think you won't be satisfied until *my* parents have actually kicked the bucket," Rosemary said once to Cory. But that was before West had died, when Cory's grief had been old and obedient.

The woman with the sheep dog was there again, not nearby, but in the distance, through the bare trees, like a ghost in her heavy gray coat. And again Cory thought she spoke, in a voice that was so strangely like Polly's, even though she didn't remember Polly's voice, "Cory, dear," she said. "Cory, dear."

It made Cory want to run after her, but she knew better, knew she was just making it up, the way she had always, except for ten years of her life, made it all up. And still her legs began to move, still her feet began to bite the snow, and her arms swung and her heart beat, and tears ran hot then cold down her face, as she ran back down the double row of stones, as fast as if she really were running towards her mother. As fast as if, when she reached the end, her mother would be there, just once, once again, be there.

◆

II.

April in Amsterdam. A cold gray rain attacked the narrow streets and canals and Cory had to hold on hard to her umbrella. It was her third this trip; one she'd left on a train in Germany and another had blown inside out in Paris. But she didn't care. Tomorrow she'd be on her way back to England and two days after that Rosemary would arrive at Heathrow.

Today, because she'd already seen the Stedelijk and the Van Gogh she was going to the Rijksmuseum, not because she cared much for Dutch art, but because it was something to do. After six weeks she was an expert at filling up her days, and often she had filled them well. Her heart no longer hurt her like a bruised knee throbbing in her chest; she had begun to speak to people she met on trains, and in hotels. She was painting again, and though the rain had followed her from Northern Italy through Munich and Paris, she'd decided that traveling alone in the pouring rain was preferable to traveling alone on beautiful sunny days as she had in Spain.

After some of the places she'd been, and the isolation she'd felt there (that nightmare pension in Madrid, where a woman sobbed loudly all night next door; that sad, slow afternoon in Avignon when she looked at restaurant after restaurant and couldn't force herself to go inside, she was so intimidated by the thought of a waiter who would ask, sneeringly, "*Seule?*" and put her at a bad table and then ignore her; that frightening late-night arrival in the train station in Munich, where the very sound of the language made her feel like she was being punished), Amsterdam was easy. English was sufficient and the cafes seemed to be full of women alone, all reading newspapers or writing in journals. Her loneliness didn't stick out here. And soon she wouldn't be lonely at all. No longer would she talk to Rosemary from a pay phone on some foreign street, using her Sprint card, awake when Rosemary was asleep, half-asleep when Rosemary was awake, the two of them shouting how-are-you's and I-miss-you's.

On this rainy day it was pleasant to be inside the old, dark museum with its wooden floors, and rooms of seventeenth and eighteenth century genre paintings. She had been looking at art almost every day for over a month and it seemed normal to her now. When she first began, with the National Gallery in London, her heart used to pound with the significance of it. And she would remember her uncle talking about the museums of Europe, how it was no use looking at reproductions, that there was nothing to replace the thrill of seeing the actual paintings, seeing the actual strokes made by the painter. The Prado, the Louvre and the Gare d'Orsay, the Uffizi and the Pitti Palace—from medieval altar pieces to the Expressionists to art installations consisting of two logs, a stone and a long printed explanation—she had seen it all. Now it was as nothing to stroll past brothel and gambling scenes, to glance at still lifes and portraits, at gray-green landscapes and gray-blue seascapes. She was hardly paying attention then, when her eye was stopped by a small painting.

It was a seventeenth-century interior by Pieter de Hoog with a perspective that led the eye from a room in the foreground to a smaller room where a square of light fell on the floor from a door, the top half of which opened into a fully sunny garden. The main room, with its wood-panelled walls and terra cotta-tiled floor, was full of homely things: a wicker basket, a brass bed warmer, and a heavy fabric overhanging the bed cupboard. The painting was richly colored, not opulent, but brown and golden, quiet, timeless. Timeless—that was too hackneyed, and incorrect. It was more that time had stopped, and it was this quality of stopped time, of present tense, that struck Cory and made her stand there, unable to move on and leave the painting behind.

She remembered her talks with Roberta Lu, her old therapist, about time and memory. How Roberta kept telling her that the memory of a traumatic event is not a real memory, that memory can only be coherent if it is part of a larger narrative, that memory *is* the narrative, not the image. Otherwise the event remains outside the story of one's life, an image that repeats unvaryingly. Cory had come to believe this too, because it echoed her own experience: she only began to heal from her losses when the stopped-time, fragmented, frozen pictures began to move, and to shape themselves and to be shaped into a story. When she saw her uncle as spoiled, jobless and divorced, when she saw her mother as a too-obedient daughter, when she saw her father as an orphan and her grandmother as a wild child forcibly tamed.

But now Cory saw that it wasn't true that memory to be memory needed to move forward, needed always to be assimilated into a narrative. It wasn't only a choice between a basalt rock and a rushing river. There were moments that stayed as they were, neither frozen nor moving, moments that lived in the eternal present.

In this painting a little girl knelt on the floor, burying her head in her mother's lap. You saw only the girl's back, her terrible, if transitory sorrow. Above her, sitting on a low chair, her dark-haired mother, in a red, fur-trimmed tunic, bent with infinite tenderness over the girl, touching the girl's head, comforting her.

She had her face in her mother's lap and she was crying and telling her all about it, how it hurt and was scary, how Uncle Steve had said no one would believe her that day at the river, they would think she was lying, that she was dirty, and it was the same in the playroom, he held her down and made her suck his thing until she gagged; he lay on top of her until she was crushed into the carpet and the tile and almost disappeared. But now she was telling her mother everything and her mother leaned over her and listened hard and knew what she was saying. She was angry at Uncle Steve and said he was bad, but Cory wasn't bad. And love poured from her mother's soft hands into her head. She felt it! The warmth of her mother's touch, her understanding, her rage on Cory's behalf.

But perhaps that wasn't it at all—Cory stepped closer—

perhaps she only saw the comfort in the painting, because she wanted it so much. Perhaps the mother was only arranging the hair of the little girl leaning into her lap. The mother's face was sympathetic, but she was smiling slightly. Perhaps she was only— could it be?—picking lice out of her daughter's hair.

The room spoke of order, peace, changelessness. For as long as Cory looked at the painting she was there, with her face buried in her mother's lap. Time stood still; that moment would never change. The past had occurred, but it could be repaired, and nothing further would happen. There was the horror of Uncle Steve, but not her mother's death, not that, not in this rich, arrested moment.

The *sustaining infinite*—the phrase came back to her, that well-worn foggy phrase from the first line of *Science and Health*. She heard again the wet whisper of the elderly lady who had bent over her, musty with cologne and damp handkerchiefs, at the mortuary, and again felt herself jerk away, as if a dry finger had reached out to touch her cheek.

"To those leaning on the sustaining infinite, to-day is big with blessings," Mrs. Eddy, that stern-eyed old metaphyscian, had written. Who knows what she really meant by it? But Cory felt one possible meaning now. This stopped-time moment *was* the sustaining infinite. Life was made up an infinity of moments that sustained.

She didn't notice the dog at first, the ordinary dog on the other side of the painting, the ordinary black dog who sat with its back to the viewer, who was perfectly indifferent to the mother and daughter nearby, who gazed instead into the interior of the painting, into the next room where the square of light fell in a slant from the garden. You couldn't see the dog's face, but the dog sniffed the air and imagined the garden on the other side of the closed bottom door.

The little dog was set apart and lonely. It reminded Cory of her father, attached to the pair nearby, but with another life outside, a life in the open air, out in the world. The dog reminded her of herself, too.

Last year Rosemary had met West for the first time. "I never knew your mother, of course," she said, "so I don't know how much you resemble her, but it's amazing to me how like your father you are."

"Oh, that's ridiculous," Cory had said.

They'd had lunch together, and West was alternately silent and rambling. He answered Rosemary's polite questions with words he'd used a thousand times before, as if he only had to open his mythical biography to pull them out. "I studied Latin and the Classics. With that background you can do anything. History, medicine, law. Have you studied Latin, Rosemary?"

"No," she had to admit.

"They don't teach it any more. It's an unfortunate thing. Without Latin you can't really understand Western History. We're in danger of forgetting our heritage."

"I am *not* like my father," Cory repeated. "What in me could possibly be like him? Only that I'm a CPA, too, and that's just chance. The opportunity came up and I took it. I never meant to become a CPA, I was going to be a journalist."

"It's more that look you get," Rosemary said, "that solitary look. When you're thinking your own thoughts and forget that anybody else is around."

Cory was the little girl with her head in her mother's lap, she was the mother who bent to comfort and console, but she was also, at this fixed moment, her father's daughter, the dog with her nose to the wind, and her eye on the open door.

When Cory came out of the Rijksmuseum it was still raining, but more peaceably and with more warmth. She walked along the Prinsengracht and through the flower market at Singel, where the air smelled of damp earth and tulips. She bought a pair of bright yellow socks at a shop she passed. She bought a book at Vrolijk, the gay bookstore. She felt secure and cheerful enough to eat by herself at an Indonesian restaurant. Afterwards she walked back to her hotel in the early evening over bridges outlined with lights.

She remembered the sense of isolation she'd felt after Polly died, and how it had gradually turned from pure despair into something more complicated, something that occasionally felt like pleasure. Once, when she was eleven, she'd gone to Debbie Warnikow's house after school and stayed for dinner. Her father had said she must never come home by herself after dark; she must always call him or get someone's parents to take her. She could have called home, she could have told Debbie that her mother had to take her home, but instead, she just slipped out.

Debbie lived past the elementary school, maybe a half mile away from the apartment; it was much further away than Cory remembered it being. She should have been scared, and she was scared, just a little. But mostly Cory recalled a wild exhilaration that almost made her teeth chatter. She was no longer Cory Winter, she was Nancy Feeble, Underworld Explorer. She had no parents, only Jack her brother. She had to rely on her wits to protect both of them out here in the dark where bad things lurked but where there was also the scent of jasmine and the glow of the street lights. Other eleven-year-old girls were at home, doing their schoolwork, putting their hair in rollers, learning to make choco- late chip cookies. But Cory was out in the world, listening to the night, taking deep draughts of perfumed air, watching people through their yellow windows live their evening lives. She was an orphan and she was free to make her life what she wanted it to be. No one could stop her.

"I'm an explorer," she told herself that night when her feet got tired, when she wondered why it seemed farther than during the day. "I'm out alone in the wide world, exploring the night."

Cory stopped on a bridge over the Keizersgracht and looked down into the dark water that reflected the street lamps. "I'm really an orphan now," she said aloud, but it still wasn't true. It would never be true. Her parents were with her, always. They were with her this very moment, even when she felt most alone, most free and alive, out on her own in the wide world, exploring the night.

III.

It was amazing how much pink there was in nature. How these stones, these *greywethers*, so ancient and forbidding the last time she'd seen them, now seemed such a soft pinkish gray. To capture them on the page she mixed Alizarin Crimson and Ultramarine with a little Burnt Umber and washed the color in. In the background, in the heady huge sky above there was also pink, blueish pink, low on the horizon, behind the Hooker's Green stand of trees. Hooker's Green was a fugitive color, like mauve and chrome yellow and Van Dyke Brown. "You should avoid the use of unstable, impermanent colors," her teacher Madelyn the photo-realist used to say, "because at some point they'll change or fade away. Fugitive colors are unpredictable in their departures."

Cory was at Avebury again, this time with Rosemary, but it was a Sunday in April, sunny and somehow perfectly ordinary. Rosemary had been dazed by the casual monumentality of it all, but, then, she would be dazed. Cory had picked her up at Heathrow this morning and driven directly to Wiltshire. They were to stay two nights in Bath and then drive to Dartmoor and Cornwall for their vacation. Rosemary wasn't only jet lagged, she was exhausted from all the work she'd tried to cram in before she left. Now she napped while Cory painted, on a bank above the ditch that separated them from the stone circles.

Rosemary was in her picture, a rounded shape of Cerulean Blue on a checkered cloth, between two of the rough stones. Cory looked hard and lovingly at Rosemary as she sketched her familiar body in. There had been a second at the gate when Cory almost hadn't recognized Rosemary. When her eyes had not connected with her memory, when she'd been looking perhaps for someone else, not this beautiful big woman with the mass of curly golden-brown hair and the delighted smile.

"Oh, my God, it's been forever," Rosemary had said, enfolding her. "Let's not ever do *this* again." And her voice, so warm and well-remembered, brought everything together again. Now it was as if they'd never been parted.

Cory had been back in England for several days. This time she had not pressured herself to be the diligent tourist, and yesterday she'd decided to go the big Saturday outdoor market at Camden Lock. It was mid-April and the first sunny weekend day in some time. The crowds were out and the air was shot through with reckless joy. She felt it, too, as if some burden were lifting. Or maybe it was just that, after six weeks of travel, her bags getting heavier in each country, she had arranged with the hotel to store most of her stuff in their luggage room.

It was a marvelous thing to walk freely, without straps criss-crossing your chest, without the weight of a dozen heavy gifts for friends and family pulling your shoulders and your arms down. At Camden Lock, in the sunshine, Cory swung her arms and lifted her head to breathe in spring and the hundred scents around her, from patchouli to old clothes to vingerary fish and chips. Her passport was inside her clothes, her coin purse in her pocket. Her hands were free. She could move.

For two hours she tried on hats, she put rings on her fingers, she tasted Jamaican chicken and Cornish pasties, she walked down aisles of stalls selling herbal remedies and beeswax candles and imports from around the world. She looked and tasted but wasn't tempted by anything until, lost in a maze of tiny shops, she saw the dark-stained wooden box. The shop was Indian, crowded with brass and silver, carpets and embroideries. The box sat on a shelf, not drawing attention to itself, neither new nor antique, simply a useful object. It was about eight inches square, substantial, not flimsy, with a sliding lid and two compartments inside.

"Used for tea," the man at the counter said, when she asked. "Now you use it for your jewelry." But she didn't think she wanted it for that. Maybe she would still use it for tea. Maybe something else. He wrapped it up it in brown paper with a string for her to hold on to.

It wasn't very heavy, this wooden box, but it hung a little on her arm, a reminder of all those peculiar things she'd picked up as she'd traveled, and that had made her stagger through train stations and along busy streets. She had a cup of tea and decided it was time to go. The afternoon was still glorious though, and one thing after another called to her. She almost bought a cane-backed chair, and an old woven basket; she looked into books, she tried on more hats, she did buy a small ring for her niece Jessie. Finally she was at the edge of the market again, but still she lingered. She overheard a woman saying to her friend, in mocking tones, "Eew, I really can't stand these little floral sachet bags, can you? My mum had them in all the drawers when I was growing up. I smelled like an old lady when I was seven years old."

It was a tiny stall selling home-dried potpourris of roses and English lavender. "I grow them all myself," said the vendor, a young woman with a baby in a little sling on her back. Cory picked up one of the cloth bags and inhaled. Dried roses. The smell of their back yard in late autumn, she and Polly picking up the petals and putting them in a shoe box.

"It's not an old lady smell," said the woman, just a girl really, with some anxiety, looking after the pair who were now giggling over some topical buttons across the way. "They're from my garden, from last summer."

"I know," said Cory. "Roses smell like summer. Like the end of summer." And to comfort the girl she bought a sachet with a pound coin, and stuck it in her pocket.

Now she was tired. The sun, the music, the snacks, the crowds that kept increasing, all made her feel that she'd better get back to the hotel for a rest. She left the market and headed for the tube station in Camden Town, still walking slowly. On the way she passed a tobacco shop. In the old-fashioned bow window were pipes of all sorts, carved meerschaums with long stems and Irish briarwoods with rough and smoothly polished bowls. There was no reason to go in and yet she did.

The shop was dark, ancient, permeated with smoke.

"I'm looking for a tobacco . . . I don't know its name . . . it smelled a little of cherry."

The portly man in a waistcoat and spectacles shook his head. "No Madame, no flavored tobaccos here," he said. "May I offer you something else . . . er, for yourself?"

"Not exactly." In embarrassment Cory bought a tin of something golden and flaky, and fought an urge to put a leaf on her tongue when she got outside.

On the tube, returning to the hotel in Tavistock Square, Cory hugged her two parcels, the wooden box and the tin of tobacco to her chest. Along with the sachet—these were all odd things to have bought. What did she plan to do with them? Would she store them, as she was storing the copper colander from Paris, the ceramic cups from Granada, the mirror from Florence, in the basement of the hotel?

She yawned and closed her eyes briefly—a few more useless things, not even gifts—what did it matter? And then, for some reason, she thought of a day a few weeks ago, in a middle-sized town in Germany. A sleety awful day . . . she couldn't even recall the town's name, only that she had gone there to see the art museum and that museum was closed. The tourist information woman had directed her elsewhere, to a small ethnographic museum, and to pass the time until the next train out, she'd gone to take a look. It was in an old stone house with dark, creaky wooden floors, and every room held glass cases of butterflies and coins, pottery shards, Roman perfume bottles, mosaics and the spoils of dozens of nineteenth-century expeditions by the founder of the museum and the collectors, amateur naturalists and travelers who had since added to the museum's holdings. In more recent years it appeared that the curators had tried to minimize the random pillage aspect and to work on presenting exhibits that explored different cultures and different rituals.

Looked at all at once it was overwhelming and rather depressing, but as Cory wandered through the exhibits she found herself more interested than she'd imagined. All the descriptions were in German, but in some rooms there were also printed explanations in English, French and Spanish. On the top floor was a display of masks and ritual objects connected, apparently, with funerals and death. In the middle of the room was a closely-woven small grass hut.

She had walked around the hut several times without seeing a sign to explain it and when she did find the description on the wall, it was of course in German. She asked a guard standing nearby what the hut signified, but he just looked worried and said, "No English, sorry."

An older woman with her even older mother was in the room too. She came over and, speaking English with an old-fashioned and precise British accent, asked Cory what she needed.

"I want to know," said Cory. "What this hut is."

The woman took out her glasses and scrutinized the card on the wall. Then she said, "The tribe built this sort of hut for the spirit of the dead person. It wasn't where the dead person was buried, mind you. It was purely ceremonial, meant to house the spirit between the actual death and the ceremony commemorating the death. The tribespeople believed that if the spirit didn't have a place to go it would wreak havoc on the living."

"Havoc?" asked Cory.

"Havoc," said the woman firmly, removed her glasses and returned to her mother's side.

The train pulled into Russell Square and Cory got out with her parcels, still thinking about the unknown tribe and their hut to house the spirits of the dead.

That evening, when the shadows had closed in, Cory lit a candle in her hotel room and unwrapped the things she'd bought at Camden Lock. She looked at them for a long time. If anyone were to come in now, she would feel a fool, forty-four years old and crying like a baby over her parents. She opened up the cloth bag of rose petals and emptied it into one side of the old wooden box. In the other compartment she scattered loose flakes of golden tobacco. She carried the box to the window, where the glow from a street lamp in the square outside fell softly, like moonlight in an old black and white photograph, over it.

Cory breathed in the scent of roses and saw Polly standing in her rose garden, watering in the after-dinner dusk of a late summer's day. She wore a yellow sundress, her feet were bare in the dirt. The water poured out lavishly from the hose, an oasis of sound in the lingering heat; the roses lapped it up and their fragrance mingled with the warm shadows of the evening. From West's office across the yard came the electric clicking of the adding machine, and through the screen door, the smell of cherry tobacco flowed out. It flowed until it met the scent of the roses under the apricot tree.

> Thy sun shall no more go down; neither shall thy moon withdraw itself; for the Lord shall be thine everlasting light, and the days of thy mourning shall be ended.

Cory waited until she couldn't separate the two fragrances anymore and then she closed the box. There. Her parents' spirits were captured. They would cause no more havoc.

They were at rest.

The only fugitive colors Cory used were Hooker's Green and occasionally Chrome Yellow, which was highly impermanent—or so she'd heard. Sometimes she took out old paintings to see if the yellow had gone; so far it was still there. Mostly, her palette was blues and greens, but almost always now she used yellow. Sometimes it was underpainting, to give a warm tone; sometimes it was just an accent. Cory searched around the Avebury site now for something yellow to put in her painting, but there was nothing, unless you counted the flash of bright yellow from her sock when she stretched out her leg. They were the socks she'd bought in Amsterdam—was it only a few days ago?

She hadn't planned to put herself in the painting, but you couldn't have a sock just lying around a sacred site. A sock needed a foot, which needed a leg and a body. So here she was, her foot, her leg, her body, next to Rosemary in the grass, the formal beauty of the scene, as usual in her paintings, shot to hell because she had let something loose at the end.

Often, when Cory was painting, she thought of her mother. Not that she *thought* of Polly so much as that she was simply aware of the self that she'd been as a child in her mother's presence. *Making pictures* was still how she described her watercolors; she knew she would stay decidedly an amateur, if being an amateur was never to get it perfect, but always to love the result anyway.

She was painting in the stones now with a darker tint, the hard unyielding stones that had survived burial and burning, that were upright again, at least for a while. On her last visit the stones had been so dark and cold, etched against the snow and icy blue twilight. She might have used masking fluid then if she had painted them to get the sharp edge, a resist technique that would have kept the stones distinct from the world around them. Today the spring air was soft and the mid-afternoon light blurred the edges of the stones and made them dark pink-gray. She let the watercolored sky and stones mingle with each other, wet on wet. There was the tiny thin edge that separated them, but mostly what you saw was how the colors were alike. It was more pleasing than it was dramatic, merely an ordinary sky, a normal day.

In the car leaving the airport, driving along the motorway and trying to describe her trip, which now seemed enormous and meaningful, Cory told Rosemary, "When you've lived such a long time trying to forget, it hurts when you start to remember. And then you get used to that hurt and it becomes more real, more familiar than anything. If you were to stop feeling the hurt for an instant, you'd be disloyal. And yet there's a way that, after a while, you find yourself neither forgetting nor remembering, but just living. Living and wanting to live."

And the days of thy mourning shall be ended, Cory thought again now, sitting on top of the green bank in the spring sun with Rosemary beside her, sleeping. It was a moment that was the close of a narrative, or the beginning of a narrative, but it was also a moment of stopped time, a moment in and of itself, captured in the picture she was making, a painting of the fugitive present, with Cory and her bright yellow sock in the picture.

ACKNOWLEDGMENTS

To these friends, readers and innocent bystanders who were there at the right time, great thanks are due: Judith Barrington, Chas Hanson, Roseann Lloyd, Regula Noetzli, Wendy Smith, Carla Tomaso, Leslie Winegrad and Louise Wisechild. Special thanks to Faith Conlon, always an insightful and supportive editor, to my family, especially my brother Bruce, and to Tere Carranza, who listened and read at all stages, and always with an open heart.

Elizabeth Mangelsdorf

Barbara Wilson is the author of a collection of short stories and seven novels, including the popular and critically acclaimed mysteries featuring Pam Nilsen and globetrotting translator Cassandra Reilly. She has translated several works from Norwegian and received the Columbian Translation Prize for her work on Norwegian author Cora Sandel. She was co-founder of Seal Press and is currently publisher of Women in Translation, a small non-profit press. *Blue Windows*, her memoir about growing up Christian Scientist, is forthcoming in 1997 from Picador USA. She lives in Seattle.

Selected Fiction from Seal Press

NOWLE'S PASSING by Edith Forbes. $21.95, 1-878067-72-9. A beautifully crafted story, rooted in the austerity and understated beauty of northern New England, about a woman who faces her exacting family legacy to discover her own life.

AN OPEN WEAVE by devorah major. $20.95, 1-878067-66-4, cloth. Melodic and vibrant, this outstanding debut novel braids together three generations of an extended African-American family.

SWEAT: *Stories and a Novella* by Lucy Jane Bledsoe. $10.95, 1-878067-64-8. The elusive sanctity of sport. The exquisite rewards of risk. The adventure that is contemporary lesbian life. *Sweat* will tempt you from your comfort zone.

DISAPPEARING MOON CAFE by SKY Lee. $12.95, 1-878067-12-5. A spellbinding first novel that portrays four generations of the Wong family in Vancouver's Chinatown.

THE DYKE AND THE DYBBUK by Ellen Galford. $10.95, 1-878067-51-6. A fun, feisty, feminist romp through Jewish folklore as an ancient spirit returns to haunt a modern-day London lesbian.

NERVOUS CONDITIONS by Tsitsi Dangarembga. $12.00, 1-878067-77-X. A moving story of a Rhodesian girl's coming of age and of the devastating human loss involved in the colonization of one culture by another.

EGALIA'S DAUGHTERS by Gerd Brantenberg. $11.95, 1-878067-58-3. A hilarious satire on sex roles in which the wim rule and the menwim stay at home by Norway's leading feminist author.

ALMA ROSE by Edith Forbes. $10.95, 1-878067-33-8. This first novel by a gifted lesbian writer is filled with unforgettable characters and the vibrant spirit of the West. *Alma Rose* is a warm, funny and endearing tale of life and love off the beaten track.

Seal Press publishes books by women writers, ranging in topic from popular culture and lesbian studies to parenting, health and domestic violence, and outdoor adventure. To receive a free catalog or to order directly, write to us at 3131 Western Avenue, Suite 410, Seattle, Washington 98121/email: sealprss@scn.org, or call us toll free at 1-800-754-0271 (orders only). Please add 16.5% of the book total for shipping and handling. You can visit our website at http://www.seanet.com/~sealpress/